SO THOUGHTFUL

First Officer Seymour came back onto the bridge. "The antenna's gone, Skipper."

"Gone?"

"Clean gone. Like it was sawed off, or maybe blasted off with a couple of turns of prima-cord. Gone, anyway."

"Blasted off?" Greiner said. "Sabotage?"

"Looks like it to me," Seymour said.

"If the computer's really out, what happens?" Kevin asked.

"We don't get to Ceres," Greiner said. His voice was grim. "We've got just enough fuel aboard to set us down on Ceres. Nothing to spare for mistakes. Without the ship's computer we could never do it—"

"Can we get back to Earth without the computer?" Kevin asked.

"No. But that's not the problem. It's only the power supply. If we have to we can build another. We can build another antenna, too—ah." He stopped as Felipe Carnel came back into the bridge compartment. "The power system?"

"Blown to hell," Carnel said. "Somebody messed it up good."

"And the spare is gone?" Greiner said quietly.

"Might as well be. Been taken apart into little bits."

"How long to rebuild?" Greiner demanded. His tone indicated that he already knew the answer.

"Days," Carne _____ y."

"By which tim _____ eaded out to nowhere, _____ lot of thought into thi _____

BAEN BOOKS
by JERRY POURNELLE

Janissaries
Exile—and Glory
Fires of Freedom

Oath of Fealty (with Larry Niven)
Fallen Angels (with Larry Niven and Michael Flynn)
The Prince (with S.M. Stirling)

EXILE—AND GLORY

JERRY POURNELLE

BAEN

EXILE—AND GLORY

High Justice copyright © 1974 by Jerry Pournelle; *Exiles to Glory* copyright © 1977 by Jerry Pournelle.

A Baen Books Original

Baen Publishing Enterprises
P.O. Box 1403
Riverdale, NY 10471
www.baen.com

ISBN 13: 978-1-4391-3293-7

Cover art by Clyde Caldwell

First Baen paperback printing, September 2009

Distributed by Simon & Schuster
1230 Avenue of the Americas
New York, NY 10020

Library of Congress Cataloging-in-Publication Data:
2008027064

Printed in the United States of America

10 9 8 7 6 5 4 3 2 1

CONTENTS

ACKNOWLEDGMENTS

HIGH JUSTICE

A Matter of Sovereignty

"We're almost there, Mr. Adams."

Bill Adams woke to the thrum of propellers and the smell of fresh coffee. He stirred lazily and looked up at blue eyes and a heart-shaped face framed in long blonde hair. The girl's soprano voice had a trace of an English accent. She wore a white blouse and a conservative plaid miniskirt that showed off her tanned legs perfectly. It was, Adams decided, one of the better ways to wake up.

"We're almost there, sir," she repeated. "I've brought coffee."

"Thanks, Courtney." Adams stretched elaborately. The aircraft cabin was small. It had a desk and couch and overstuffed chairs, and except for the panel of lights and buttons above Adams's seat it might have been the study at Santa Barbara. Far down below the Pacific

3

flashed blue and calm as it had when he dozed off. Now, though, it was dotted with tiny white rings of surf crashing endlessly on coral reefs.

"Sit with me and tell me what I'm looking at," Adams said.

"All right." Courtney balanced the tray clumsily with one hand as she reached to fold the table down from the cabin wall. Adams hurriedly came fully awake to help her. She sat next to him on the couch and smiled uncertainly.

Courtney wasn't sure who Bill Adams was. She'd seen his name on the Nuclear General Company organization chart, but his title merely said "Assistant to the Chairman," and that might mean anything. Her own title was "Assistant to the Director" of Ta'avu Station, and that didn't mean much at all. She was more than a secretary, but she hadn't much influence over Station operations.

Adams, though, was in charge of the largest airplane in the world, and anyone who could commandeer *Cerebrus* for personal transportation had real power. Courtney suspected that Adams was one of Mr. Lewis's special assistants, the troubleshooters who were said to have no emotions and computers for hearts, but his easy smile made that hard to believe. He was very likable as well as handsome.

Adams sipped coffee and looked out the thick rectangular window. There was more land in sight ahead. They were approaching a series of coral atolls stretched out like jumbled beads on the blue water below. Each was ringed with white, then lighter blues fading quickly into the deeper tones of the Pacific. There was no way to estimate the size of the islands. They might be tiny coral reefs or the tops of the large mountains. One thing was certain. There wasn't much land you could live on down there.

"That's good coffee, Courtney. Thanks."

"You're welcome. I should be thanking you. It would have been three weeks before I could get home if you hadn't given me a lift." The view below was lovely, but Courtney had seen it many times. She was still interested in the airplane. They were the only passengers in the lounge—this smaller one and the big lounge beyond. She knew that Adams had brought others, but they had stayed on the lower decks and she hadn't met them. His own assistant, Mike King, was forward with the pilots.

Aft of the lounges were other offices, laboratories, and several staterooms. Below them was an enormous cargo space. *Cerebrus* was enormous, larger than any other plane in the world, and she shared its luxury accommodations with one man. It was quite an experience. Courtney made good money at Ta'avu, but she wasn't accustomed to posh standards of living.

Adams peered forward to get a better look at the oncoming land, and Courtney remembered why he'd asked her to sit with him. "The first group of atolls is undeveloped so far," she said. "You can just see Ta'avu Station beyond. We'll be over it in a second."

Adams nodded and pushed back sandy hair with an impatient gesture. Except for the short nap, he'd worked at something the entire time he'd been on the plane. He was always impatient, although he didn't always show it. Courtney wondered what he did for relaxation. She noted that he wore no rings. "Before we get there—I've wanted to ask about this plane. How could even Mr. Lewis afford it?"

"He couldn't," Adams answered. "Some African government went broke having it built. Largest flying boat ever constructed. We'd already put in the nuclear engines so we were the principal creditors come foreclosure. Seemed cheaper to finish it for ourselves than scrap it."

"But why propellers?" Courtney asked.

Adams shrugged. He was no engineer. "Something about efficiency. Worked out well. They say it's the props that let *Cerebrus* stay up for weeks at a clip. She's come in handy at that. We can use her to look for ice floes and get our crews aboard first. Competition for good Antarctic ice is stiff, and *Cerebrus* gives us a big edge."

"I'd only seen it once before," Courtney said. "When we were bringing in the whales."

Adams nodded. "Yeah, we'd never have been able to herd the beasts without the plane." He grinned. "Ferrying pretty young managerial assistants home is just a side-line. Is that the Station there?"

"Yes." She leaned across to see better and felt him very close to her. He was handsome and unmarried, in his thirties by his looks, but maybe a bit more. She liked older men. He had grey eyes, and it was hard to tell what he thought because half the time he looked as if something secretly amused him. He would be a very easy man to like. Her last romance had gone badly, and there was certainly no one at the Station—in fact, there was never anyone at the Station. She wondered how long Adams would be there. He hadn't told her why he was flying thousands of miles to the Tonga Islands, and Dr. MacRae would be worried.

"The big atoll in the center of that group of three," she said. "The lagoon is about fifteen miles across, and the Station is on the island at the fringe, the one shaped like a shark. The reactors are just about at the jaw."

"Yeah." Now that she'd given him some idea of the scale the rest of the picture was clear. Ta'avu consisted of seven atolls, but only three were in use at the moment. Nuclear General leased the whole chain from the King of Tonga, paying off with electric power, fresh water, fish, fertilizer, and expert advice on how to support too many Tongans on too few islands. The land area of Ta'avu was insignificant, but it wasn't land they needed.

Now he could make out the big microwave dishes which beamed power from the Station to the inhabited parts of the Tonga Islands. That was an inefficient way to transmit power, but there was plenty to spare at the Station. The plane circled lower, and Adams could see dams and locks, enormous sea walls closing off the lagoons from the oceans. He winced, remembering how much they had cost, and then there were the smaller dams and net booms dividing the lagoon into pens.

A chime sounded and Adams picked up the phone. Mike King, his assistant, said, "We're almost there, sir. Shall we take her in?"

"No. Have the pilots circle the Station. I want a better picture before I land."

"Yes, sir. Want me back there?"

."No, I think Miss Graves can tell me what I need to know. Unless you'd care to join us?"

King laughed nervously, betraying his youth. "Thanks, but I'd rather not . . . Uh, the pilots are giving me a pretty good briefing, sir."

"Fine." Adams hung up the phone and chuckled softly. There was no question about it, Mrs. Leslie King had great influence over her husband. Fancy being afraid to be around Courtney. . . . Of course she was pretty and Leslie would be joining Mike if Adams decided to leave

Mike at the Station. Maybe Michael was right to stay away from temptation. The plane dropped lower, down to five hundred feet. Bill Adams turned to Courtney.

"Where are the whales?"

"In the big lagoon—there, look carefully, you can usually see them. Yes!" She pointed excitedly. "Over there, on the other side from the reactors."

Adams looked for a moment, then gasped. There were three dark shapes visible under the water, and they were *big*. One seemed to grow, larger, larger, impossibly huge, then broke the surface and rolled lazily, great flukes splashing. A hundred feet long, the largest thing that ever lived on the earth.

"That's Susie," Courtney said happily. "She's almost tame. You can get close to her in a boat."

"My God, that's a big animal!" Bill said. "What are the small things around her? Baby whales?"

Courtney laughed. "Those are *dolphins*, Mr. Adams. We don't have any baby blue whales, nobody does. We hope Susie's pregnant, but how can you tell? The dolphins patrol the lagoon for us. You know how we used them to get Susie and her friends here in the first place?"

Adams shook his head. "Not really. I was busy on something else." He made a wry face. "This whale business is strange. Only thing the Company ever did that doesn't at least *threaten* a profit. Mr. Lewis insists on it, but you can't imagine how much it has cost."

"Oh." She looked at him sternly and let a note of disapproval into her voice. "It was worth it, Mr. Adams. Look at those whales! How could you let something so magnificent be exterminated? I guess it was costly, though," she added hastily. Shouldn't get him angry with me. . . . "Never gave it a thought, but—well, training the dolphins to herd whales took a long time. Then finding the whales—there aren't more than a dozen left in the whole world. And even with the dolphins it took a long time to drive four whales to the Station. They kept getting away and the dolphins had to go find them again."

"I know something about how long it took," Adams observed dryly. "While *Cerebrus* was on that project, Southern California Edison grabbed two icebergs from us. Big ones, three hundred billion gallons at least. *Poseidon* and *Aquarius* were left out in the Antarctic with nothing to do for months—it's too expensive to bring the tugs home and send them out again. So I know the costs."

Courtney turned away, not so much disgusted as sad. It was true, then; he was one of Lewis's hard-eyed troops with an account book for a heart.

Adams grinned suddenly. "But it brought us luck. Or something did. A couple of months later we found a nine hundred billion gallon iceberg. A real monster, and we've got it under tow."

And it's still under tow, he thought. The tugs were bringing the monster iceberg up the Humboldt Current. The fresh water was worth at least three hundred million dollars if they could get it to Los Angeles. The trouble was that Ecuador claimed sovereignty out to two hundred miles from the coast, and the passage fees could eat up half the value of the ice. Ecuador wanted cash. . . .

And now *Persephone,* with all that plutonium, was held by the Fijians, and Nuclear General was in real trouble. There were a lot of assets tied up in those two projects, and Mr. Lewis was stretched thin with risky investments. The big bergs made a lot of profit, but exploration and towing weren't cheap, competition was stiff, and the taxes kept going up all the time. If they couldn't get that plutonium back . . .

"The other lagoons have smaller fish," Courtney said, breaking in on his reverie. She wondered why he'd lost his grin, but it came back when she pointed and said, "Rainbow trout in that one."

"You're putting me on."

"No, really, they adapt to salt water very easily. In fact, they do it naturally—haven't you ever fished for steelhead? And hatching them is easy, that's been done for decades."

"Yeah, I guess it figures," Bill answered absently. Come to think of it he had known that. He used to fish for steelhead when he was younger. Hard to think of anything but the plan. It had to work. It had sounded good back in Santa Barbara, but neither he nor Mr. Lewis had ever met the Tongans and it all depended on them.

"You can see the different color waters," she continued. "We pump cold water from six thousand feet down. It's rich in phosphates and nitrates, so the plankton and krill grow fast. Dr. Martinez is experimenting to see what works best. But if we can feed Susie, think how many fish we can grow in the other lagoons!"

Bill nodded. He'd seen the figures. There was a good profit in protein, but production was low at Tonga Station, and there'd be no profit at all if the farms had to pay their own way. He tried to explain that to the girl, but she wasn't much interested. Blast it, he thought, she should know such elementary things about the Company. Without funds and profits you couldn't do anything.

"Profits. I see." Her voice was acid. "I guess you have to worry about that, Mr. Adams, but out here at the Station we're proud of what we're doing. We can feed a million people some day, more even, and prevent kwashiorkor. . . . Do you know how much misery is due to simple protein deficiency?"

"No. But I know we couldn't have built the plants if that were all we were doing out here, Courtney. Breeding plutonium on a grand scale makes power, and as far as the Station's concerned that power is free. But plutonium, not protein, is the reason for the Station."

"Why out here, then? You've got breeder reactors in the States. Dr. Martinez is Director of one."

Adams nodded wearily. "We didn't put new breeders in the States because we can't find locations for them. Everywhere we turn there's protest. They even complain about our sea farms because we introduce new species. As if Kansas wheat were native. . . . Anyway, Tonga's got cold water for the reactors and no regulations about our plutonium sales. In the States the government makes us sell over half the product at their own prices." Taxes were nonexistent at the Station, too, Adams thought. Even though there was no market for the electric power the breeders could produce, it was still worth coming out here. And the protein sales would eventually pull their own weight, even pay back some of the investment Ta'avu represented. It had been a good gamble, but too big, too big; now the crunch was coming. A shortage of cash, and the creditors coming around like wolves . . .

A chime sounded and above the entrance to the flight control deck the NO SMOKING, FASTEN SEAT BELTS signs came on. The chime sounded again and Adams lifted the telephone. He heard Mike King.

"We're bringing her down now, sir. Some nasty weather expected later. The pilots want to get *Cerebrus* inside the lagoon while it's calm. If that's all right with you, sir."

"Fine. Take her in," Adams told him. The big plane banked sharply, leveled, and skimmed lower and lower across the water, touched into the swells outside the lagoon. They bucked four-foot whitecapped waves as the plane taxied to the atoll. Big lock gates opened ahead of them and the plane moved inside cautiously. Adams watched a floating object appear around the hull; it resembled the plastic baths yachts were kept in back in the States, or the floating tanks used to catch fresh water from icebergs. He turned to Courtney with a puzzled expression.

"Biological trap," she said. "They can purge the whole lock area if they have to, but it's easier this way. They'll sluice out the bath with cold water from the deeps and slide the plane off into the lagoon."

He nodded and was about to say something when the pilot came out with Mike King. "That's it, sir," Mike said. "Boat's alongside to take you to the Station."

"Fine," Adams said, but he didn't feel fine. His senses were dulled by the time differential from Santa Barbara; the mild chop taxiing in had upset his stomach, and ahead of him were problems enough to wreck the Company. The turmoil of thoughts contrasted sharply with the peaceful scene of the lagoon and the girl beside him, and he chuckled slightly, but when Courtney smiled quickly he didn't see her.

She turned away hurt, wondering what he was thinking about. Profits, she thought contemptuously. How could any man look at that out there, blue water and sparkling sun, the dolphins dancing around the open companionway hoping for attention—they got enough to eat—and the big Tonga boatmen grinning from their long narrow outrigger; how could a *man* look at all that and think about money? It never failed. The unmarried ones had something wrong with them, and of course that would be true—if they didn't, why weren't they married?

The outrigger flashed across the lagoon, skimming almost silently in the strong trade wind and calm water. Samual and Toruga, the boatmen, handled her almost effortlessly. They weren't really boatmen, of course. They'd call themselves fishermen, or just sea people; back in the States they'd be technicians, and damned skilled ones at that. They and fifty like them tended the sea farms under the direction of Ta'avu's ecologist on loan, Dr. Arturo Martinez, who'd no doubt be anxious to get back to his home in San Juan Capistrano.

There were motorboats at the Station, but the silently skimming outrigger seemed more natural and was certainly almost as fast. Besides, it disturbed fewer sea creatures. After a while Adams was able to lean back and enjoy himself as Courtney chattered with the Tongans in musical Polynesian.

Around the edge of the lagoon was a series of pens and baffles and large fiberglass tank complexes, each served with a network of pipes for delivering both cold nutrient water from over a mile down outside the atoll and heated water from the reactors. Courtney tried to tell Bill Adams what each pen was, but there were too many. After a while Toruga took over at the tiller and Samual came forward to join Adams. Like all Tongans he spoke English. It was the Kingdom's second language, a principal factor in locating the Station at Ta'avu.

"We have all kinds of fish, sir," the boatman said. "Some we catch around the reefs, some Dr. Martinez sends for. From all over the world."

"Which ones grow best?" Adams asked.

The Tongan laughed heartily. "We won't know that for years. Look at what we can do, temperatures, plankton mixes, dry fertilizers—one thing we try is different cleaners."

"Cleaners?"

"Yes, sir. What lubbers call trash fish. Little ones that clean up parasites. And shrimps. Big fish need 'em to live. There's a lot even the sea people don't know."

Adams looked at him sharply and nodded. No wonder Dr. Martinez was pleased with his technicians. They'd know more about the reefs and the water than anyone else, and with their excellent basic school system it shouldn't take long to train them in systematic observation.

"Another thing, maybe you can see down there," Samual said. He pointed down into the clear water. "Different shapes for reefs. We make them out of fiberglass in the shops. Makes a lot of difference what kind of fish live in them."

They passed a series of rafts, each supporting long lines dangling into the lagoon. Samual pointed to them and said, "Oyster farms. That's the hatchery, when the rafts are full we move 'em. Take some outside the lagoon, keep some here."

"What do you do about predators?" Bill asked.

"Look," Courtney told him. One of the dolphins swam near the boat, a starfish clutched in its bill. "Our technicians catch them, but the dolphins do a better job," she said. "It's amazing what you can train them to do. Some are just like dogs, they want to please you."

"Hard to operate here without dolphins," Samual agreed. "That's something we learned from you. But

there's a lot the sea people know that didn't come
from books."

"I'm sure," Adams agreed. "You like working here?"

"Who wouldn't?" Samual asked. "Why would anybody
do something else?"

"We're just learning about sea farming, I mean really
learning," Courtney said. "When I think of the nonsense
I was taught in schools—and there are so many variables.
As Samual said, there's temperatures, reef shapes, species mixtures—and some of the parasites are necessary,
some of them have to be eliminated. All we can do is try
things, there aren't any good theories."

"Yeah." What was it Helmholtz said, Adams thought.
The most practical thing in the world is a good theory. . . .
Well, that was all very well, but this wasn't just a research
station. It was supposed to be a producing farm, and
they'd better start getting something to sell out of those
lagoons if they expected any more internal research and
development funding.

It was nearly dark when they reached the Station, and
there is no twilight in the tropics. The sun fell into the
sea and was gone. The lagoon became dark and mysterious, then suddenly flashed with whites and blues and
greens, phosphorescent streaks, all about them, an endlessly changing light show. Two enormous shapes glided
past the boat, turned, and charged for it again. Adams
eyed them nervously.

Courtney grinned, her teeth barely visible in the pale
moonlight. "I wouldn't worry about them, those are the
dolphins again," she said. Then she giggled softly. "They
like to swim with the boats, and the phosphorescence
makes them look bigger than they are. I pity any sharks
that do manage to get inside the lagoon."

"Some do?"

"Yes. We can't keep a perfectly closed system in the open lagoons the way we can in the pens."

"You know a lot about the operations here," Adams said quietly.

She smiled. "I've been here four years." She sighed. "I like it here but it's time to move on. I've asked for a transfer to Company headquarters."

"Why?"

"Well, I'm not really a biologist, and there's not a lot of management work here at the Station. Dr. MacRae leaves most of that up to Santa Barbara."

I've noticed, Adams thought. He looked at the girl, wondering if she could learn the important points about Nuclear General operations. She did all right with the technical stuff, and Mike King would have to stay here at the Station. She might be good company.

They glided expertly to the landing. The reactor domes were invisible a thousand yards away, and the Station was a low series of concrete rectangles along the reef, much of it extending down into the lagoon itself. There was almost no land, and everything had to be attached to the reefs, anchored deep with aluminum pilings to protect it from tsunamis and typhoons. A natural fortress, Adams thought.

Living quarters were made of fiberglass, constructed like the thatch and frond houses of Polynesia but using artificial fibers. They could be taken below into the concrete blockhouses if a real storm threatened, and they were much more pleasant to live in.

Adams took his supper alone, served by Mike King in his rooms. He'd met no one, not even Art Martinez, and he wanted it that way. When he put down his fork, he realized he didn't even know what he'd eaten, and it was probably a special meal. Well, there'd be time enough for the social amenities later. Now he was as ready as he'd ever be.

"Who all's there?" he asked.

Mike King blushed slightly. Staff men assigned to Bill Adams never lasted long—when Adams wanted to know something, you'd better be ready with an answer or know how to find it. And you could never tell what he'd want to know because Adams himself didn't know what would be significant. Mike had spent as much time as he could talking to anyone he could find, but as sure as anything it wouldn't be enough. Working with Adams was good experience, but Mike would be glad when the trouble-shooter moved on.

"Dr. MacRae, Dr. Martinez, that I know of," Mike said. "And Courtney Graves. Dr. MacRae said if you were going to have an assistant at the conference then by the white Christ—that's what he said, sir—he'd have one there too."

Adams exploded in laughter. "And what about the Tonganese?"

"Prince Toki Ukamea, the Prime Minister, is at the Station, sir. With a couple of members of the Privy Council. But he's out looking at the reactors so you can have a word with the others alone as you wanted."

"Good." Adams's tone was so noncommittal that Mike King looked at his superior closely, but he couldn't tell what the man was thinking. The hidden amusement was gone from the grey eyes, and King didn't envy the people who'd got Mr. Adams so upset.

The conference room was underwater, concrete walls paneled in rich woods framed with sea shells, an enormous rainbow trout stuffed and mounted on one wall. Another wall was completely glassed to show the dark waters of the lagoon outside. Several large fish and one of the inevitable dolphins swam dartingly just outside the conference room.

Dr. David MacRae was a tall, elderly man who spoke with a thick, broad Scots accent mixed with something unrecognizable, and he sucked endlessly on a meerschaum pipe carved into the shape of a dolphin. Adams shook hands with the Director, and let his mental filing system bring up the important facts. MacRae, licensed reactor operator, Master of Arts in marine biology from Wellington University, New Zealand, honorary Ph.D., Edinburgh. Reactor physics courses at Nuclear General's own schools. With the Company over fifteen years, mostly in overseas posts. Apprentice power operator somewhere in his native highlands; that was a long time ago.

Bill turned with pleasure to Arturo Martinez and shook his hand warmly. "Glad to see you, Art. How's Dianne and the kids?"

"Everyone is fine at home, Bill," Martinez said. "I was supposed to go back last week, but now . . . I don't know if I can help, but I thought I would stay until this is settled."

Adams nodded soberly and took a seat at the thick wooden conference table. "All right, Dr. MacRae, how did it happen?"

MacRae lit his pipe slowly, letting the flame play over the entire bowl and taking several experimental puffs before he answered. "We had a storm hit the channel," he said carefully. "*Persephone* was in shallow waters with large waves breaking around her. There were reports of a bigger storm comin' and Captain Anderson thinking of the cargo decided to take her into harbor to be safe. . . . Aye, and I agreed when he called the Station. I had nae thought o' trouble."

"And the Fijians boarded her and took over," Adams finished. "Any change in her status?"

MacRae shook his head. Like all his movements it was slow, almost majestic, as if he controlled time and could slow it to suit himself. "They say 'twould nae be safe to allow the ship to leave harbor wi' that cargo, and their 'experts' will examine her for damage from the storm. 'Tis blackmail simple, Mr. Adams. They've nae experts to begin wi' and there's nae the matter wi' *Persephone*. But you would nae let me report the ship stolen."

"Time enough for that," Adams said grimly. "For the moment it's better we don't have an open break. They don't actually claim the ship or cargo then?"

"Nae." MacRae shook his great head. "But 'tis only a matter o' time in my thought. Then they will 'discover' storm damage that only they can repair and confiscate the cargo for the safety o' the human race."

Adams nodded. "The earth safety boys are likely to support them. Are you sure the cargo's still aboard?"

"Aye. There's no man in Fiji fool enough to go in there, they'll need friends from the mainland for that. The containers are sealed, encased in glassite. In case o' sinking, you know. So the plutonium will nae foul the oceans if the ship is lost."

"Yeah." Adams nodded thoughtfully. "Now tell me about the troubles the Tongans are having with Fiji."

MacRae nodded slowly again. "You know about the politics?" he asked. When Adams didn't answer, he continued, "Both Tonga and Fiji have been under British protection, but now the Royal Navy's gone from the Pacific and both countries are independent."

Adams said quietly, "Tonga always was, of course."

MacRae looked surprised and noticed that Martinez was smiling. "Aye. But Britain managed defense and foreign relations. Now that's gone too. And since the British left, the Fijians hae claimed sovereignty over waters almost to the Tonga Islands, hae seized more than a dozen Tongan fishing boats. Now they've had *Persephone* for three days."

"Did the seizures of Tongan boats come before they took *Persephone?*"

"Aye. I see what you're thinking, mon, but how would we know they'd take a ship flying the U.S. flag?" MacRae demanded. "That they'd take boats from the Tongans does nae imply they'd defy the U.S. flag! Mon, you sit here talking to us when you've only to report piracy and have the U.S. Navy get our ship back!"

Adams laughed bitterly. "Do you think we haven't tried? The State Department says the matter is very delicate . . . and the Fijians have good advice from somewhere. They've unofficially let it be known they'll fight before they give up our ship. The U.S. won't bully a small power to support Nuclear General Company."

"I see," MacRae said. "Then 'tis more serious than we thought."

"But I don't understand," Courtney protested. "Nuclear General has a stranglehold on dozens of little countries. You've got a reactor in Fiji, that's where they get their power . . . and the influence the Company must have, food supplies, everything, surely you can pressure them to give us our ship?"

Adams grinned, but there was no humor in it. "You've misunderstood a couple of things. The mainstay of our power is plutonium, and at the moment we haven't much to bargain with. The Fijians do. They've got a couple of hundred million dollars worth of it aboard *Persephone*. With what they can trade that for, they can laugh at any threats we make."

MacRae puffed at his pipe and relighted it. "Then we're in trouble. But we've the Station, we can breed more."

Adams said nothing. Mr. Lewis's creditors would be on him in seconds if they heard about the loss of *Persephone*. If the iceberg could be got to Los Angeles before the news broke, there might be enough cash to bail the Company out, but the Fijians wouldn't sit on it that long, and the rumors were already out. "Tell me about Tonga, Dr. MacRae. How much of your report about our relationship with the government can I believe?"

"All of it," MacRae snapped. He brooded heavily, then nodded. "Aye. It may sound too good to be true, but it is so. We've nae problems at all wi' the king and government. They're happy to have us here, for their people hae no talent for technology. Or if they do they've no interest."

"They work well with the Project," Martinez added. He nodded confirmation to MacRae's statements. "You've heard me say they're natural ecologists, they'll have no trouble operating when I'm gone. A real talent for sea farming. But David's right, they have no interest in the reactors at all."

"OK. That's the king. What about the people?"

"Same thing," MacRae said. "They respect the king. He gives them good government, and don't forget they're almost the only islands which were never colonized by Europeans, held their independence right along under the same royal family. There's nae opposition to speak of. The king gives every boy a bit of land when he turns seventeen, or something worth the same since there's little land to be had. And they allow no foreigners to own or lease land here. We're an exception, but the land here's worthless without our improvements. With our help they've reclaimed other atolls closer to the main islands, and we've shown them how to build sea farms for their own. . . . No, Mr. Adams, strangely enough this is as close to Paradise on earth as you'll ever find."

"They're good Christians, too," Courtney added. Martinez gave her a wry look and she said, "Well, Methodists then, Dr. Martinez!"

Adams sat quietly for a moment, nodding to himself. "OK. So the basic situation makes it possible for us to survive here. Now tell me about the Station itself."

"What do you want to know?" Martinez asked. "The reactors are fine. And we've got the world's largest sea farms, we're only getting started. *Por Dios,* Bill, it's an ecologist's dream."

"And an accountant's nightmare," Adams answered. "The reactors pay their way in plutonium and the power's free—nearly so, the turbines were expensive, but we had to generate power to pay the Tongans for their atolls. But the real construction—reefs, pumps, pipelines, Art—it's been two years and there's damn little return on investment. The equivalent amount invested in nuclear-powered food processing ships and trawlers would be earning us money right now!"

"Mon, mon, do you nae understand?" MacRae protested. His open palm struck the table with a flat crack. "Trawlers! No matter how modern you make those beasties they're ten thousand years out of date! Civilized men are nae hunters, laddie. We cultivate, we grow what we need, and how can we do that in open water? The investment here will pay for itself, never you fear, and I'm willin' to gamble you'll be putting in more farms with what we learn."

"He's right," Martinez said. "Our open farms in the States are profitable, you'll agree?" Adams nodded, and Martinez continued, "But we have poachers since we can't get title to the sea beds. Out here we own the waters, and nothing at home has the potential of these reefs, Bill. We can grow anything in enormous quantities. The Project's already starting to produce. Give us a year. I've got five square miles under intensive cultivation. We'll clear over a thousand salable tons to the square mile. At fifty cents a pound—and you know we'll get more than that, Bill—we'll take in five million dollars."

"About two percent of the cost of those dams," Adams reminded him. Before Martinez could protest Bill interrupted. "Yeah, I know. You've got a lot more square miles you'll bring in next year. I've seen the projections. But the Company's got cash problems, and this place had better plan on paying its own way." He pushed back his chair, turned to the windows of the lagoon.

"Don't—don't you ever do anything just because it's worth doing?" Courtney asked. Her voice was not quite under control, as if she were holding back anger.

Adams shrugged. "When you're talking about as much money as this Project costs, you get into the altruism game precisely once. OK, if you'll ask His Highness to come in, I'd like to meet him. And I give all of you warning, be careful what you say when he's here."

"Would you rather we left?" Courtney asked.

"No. I may need all of my advisors. But keep your little round mouth closed unless I ask for something, will you? All right, Mike."

His Highness, Toki Ukamea, Prime Minister and Crown Prince, was a giant for a Tongan. He stood six feet two, with broad shoulders and hips. Adams noted the massive hands and legs, and that the full middle had no sag at all. The two councilors were normal-sized Tongans, short and rather slender but well-muscled, and both wore open, flowered shirts. His Highness was wearing a dark suit and regimental striped tie which Adams noted thoughtfully. Cambridge or Oxford, couldn't remember which, or which college . . .

There were few formalities. After the introductions they sat at the big conference table and Adams nodded to Mike King, who began by telling the Prince about *Persephone.*

He was interrupted by a full, hearty laugh. "I already know about your ship, Mr. Adams," the prince said. His voice was deep and rich, with an almost perfect Oxbridge accent. "You must remember that Fiji and Tonga have been close neighbors for centuries, and we have many friends there. My people sail to Fiji whenever they like."

"I thought you would know, Your Highness," Adams said. The amused glint was back in his grey eyes. "But I wonder if you know the consequences of that?"

"Damned awkward for your company, I think," the Prince said. His voice lost the amused tone, and became stern. "For us too, perhaps." Adams nodded and turned to Mike King.

"Yes, sir," Mike said. "Overseas Foods wants the Station. They've got enough of our bonds and preferred debentures to get it. We might be able to keep the reactors, and then again we might not, but they definitely want the rest of the Project. Except for the whales, which they consider an unnecessary expense. They'll butcher them."

"Susie!" Courtney exclaimed. "But you can't let them do that, we're just beginning to—we might even be able to have them bear young, save the species. . . ."

"Aye. And before they can be killed I'll turn them out myself," Dr. MacRae added. "Nae matter what Mr. Lewis says, but I think he'll no forbid it. I hae never met the chief but I'm told he loves the whales."

Prince Toki nodded agreement. "I think even if you did not, Dr. MacRae, the sea people would release the whales. By the way, I'm surprised you've never met Mr. Lewis. But then I haven't either." The simple statement was a demand for explanations.

"Never come to Tonga," one of the councilors said slowly. "Must be a very stupid man."

"No, sir," Adams told them. "Mr. Lewis is crippled. He never leaves his headquarters in Santa Barbara."

"I see," Toki said. "I had heard something of the sort but . . . well, sir. We are agreed that we have common interests. Now what is it you want?"

Adams looked surprised, as if the prince's bluntness was unexpected. "Let's be sure we do agree," he said slowly. "The Project is going well?"

Martinez answered quickly. "Very well. I am astonished at how quickly the Tongan fishermen have learned the techniques of scientific record-keeping. They'll have no trouble operating the farm projects so that the Station can be manned with few non-Tongans, as agreed in the sale."

"A gentleman's agreement only," the prince said. "Quite unenforceable, but I am happy that you have voluntarily kept to it."

MacRae was muttering to himself. " 'Twill be a pity to see the Station go to people like Overseas Foods; they've no sense for the future. And 'tis a bonny project."

"There's no hope, then?" the prince asked carefully. "Nuclear General is in that much financial difficulty?"

"Without the plutonium aboard *Persephone* we are," Adams answered.

"Of course you wouldn't be talking to me if your government were willing to help get it back," the prince said. "All right, Mr. Adams, you've an idea. What is it?"

Martinez laughed and everyone looked at him. "I don't know what he has in mind," Martinez explained quickly, "but one thing I've learned, never count Mr. Lewis out until he's not only dead but embalmed. Not even then. *El Patron* has won tougher fights than this." He gestured significantly at Bill Adams. "And we know he is concerned, to send his prime minister."

Adams gave Martinez and the prince a twisted grin. "He's worried all right." He took a large chart from his briefcase and spread it on the table. "*Persephone's* here?" he asked the prince.

"Yes."

"Aye," MacRae answered. "In that harbor, protected by the entire Fiji Navy, all seven gunboats and a destroyer."

"Radar scanners, I suppose?"

MacRae nodded.

"We can't do much," Adams said. "But you've said that the Tongans sail to Fiji, Your Highness. Even in bad weather. In open boats, small outriggers. Is that true?"

The prince grinned carefully. "It's true enough, Mr. Adams. We have sailed those straits for hundreds of years. I've done it myself often enough. I suppose you've thought of underwater approaches?"

Adams found it was his turn to laugh. "Yes, sir. My company police say the harbor's too treacherous for frogmen. We might train the dolphins, but there's not enough time. On the other hand, our people say the chances of a small outrigger being picked up at night during a storm are just about nil. Of course, no westerner would be able to navigate an outrigger into that harbor under such conditions. . . ."

"What will you tell the Republic of Fiji if this succeeds?"

"Why, that we found our ship adrift and unmanned in international waters," Adams said. The grin was back now, Martinez thought his friend looked quite himself. "We'll even offer to pay a reasonable fee for 'caring' for *Persephone*."

The prince's laughter rumbled through the room. "All right, Mr. Adams. We'll help you get your ship back. I've heard of Overseas Foods and I don't want them for neighbors . . . but none of us could sail her, I think. I'm sure there are no Tongans who can operate a nuclear reactor aboard ship. Or probably anywhere else."

"I will take care of the reactor," Art Martinez said. "I may be an ecologist but I am Director of San Juan Capistrano Station. I know how."

Adams nodded. "And I can sail the ship if you get us to her, Your Highness. I also have a couple of sailing

officers from Company headquarters in *Cerebrus* staterooms. If you hadn't been willing to help, we'd have had
a crack at it alone, but by God, welcome aboard!"

Cerebrus landed in the lee of an uninhabited atoll
seventy miles from Fiji. Her clamshell cargo doors
opened to discharge men and a slender war canoe.

"Now we'll see how it floats," Prince Toki said. "I
wonder that you made your own."

Adams shrugged, then quickly grasped the handrail by
the cargo door as the plane lurched to a heavy sea.

"Fiberglass is a bit tougher than your woods," he said.
"But this outrigger is an exact duplicate of the one in
our harbor. And remember we won't be bringing it back
with us. This one can't be traced."

Toki laughed softly into the gathering dark. "You hope
it won't be coming back." They climbed gingerly down
from the enormous plane to the pitching boat. It was
only three feet wide, but nearly fifty feet long. All metal
tools and weapons were laid in the bottom of the boat
so they would be below the waterline and out of radar
reflection.

"As soon as you're ready," the pilot called softly. "That
blow's coming up fast and it's getting darker. I'd like to
get the old dog upstairs."

Adams waved. The props spun, and *Cerebrus* drifted
away, turned, and gunned into the wind. Spray flew from
her bows and pontoons, then she was aloft, winging just
above the tops of the waves. They'd come in at the
same altitude.

The boat wallowed heavily in the rising seas. Prince
Toki stood in the stern and spoke quietly to the sea people.
Except for a half dozen technicians and company police,

Adams, King, and Martinez were the only westerners. Adams hadn't objected to the prince coming himself; he understood why. It would not have been in a warrior aristocrat's character to send men on something like this and not go himself, even if the Tongan royal families hadn't led men in battle for a hundred years. . . .

The prince's teeth flashed white as Toki spoke carefully in musical tones, his voice carrying easily over rising wind and crashing waves. When he sat again, they cheered.

"What did you tell them?" Adams asked, but the prince had gone forward to see to the sails. The outrigger gathered way under sail, flashing across steadily rising seas. When they left the lee of the island, breakers crashed around them, but no water came aboard. Adams estimated their speed at twenty knots.

Toki came back finally after inspecting sails and rigging. "I told them of their ancestors and mine," he said. "I was named for one, Toki Ukamea means 'iron axe.' We once sailed these waters in revenge against raiders. I could have told them in English but—it sounded better in Tongan!" There was amusement in the clipped accents. "If my professors at Magdalene College should see me now!"

The boat was pitching wildly, and the Americans found it hard to pay attention to anything. The storm rose, wind howling until the Tongans reefed, reefed again until the sail was a tiny patch in the night, but the boat tore on at high speed, leaving a great creamy wake behind, actually outrunning the seas, carried along by the screaming wind.

"Quite a blow," Michael King said. His voice was strained, artificially calm.

"Not really," Toki answered. "You will know it when the storm really hits. There will be rain then. I warned you. . . ."

"Yeah." Adams grimly held the bulwarks. He looked behind, saw an enormous wave building up astern, flinched, but they ran away from it so that it broke harmlessly aft of them. Another monster sea came up, with the same result, but it was unnerving to watch them. He tried to close his eyes, but his stomach heaved and he quickly opened them again, grimly took a deep breath, and held it.

"At night, with this storm, there shouldn't be anyone very alert," Adams told the prince. "I hope."

Toki shrugged. "Fijians might, but I do not believe their Asian masters will let them out in boats." Mike King looked up in surprise, and Prince Toki grimaced. "Malays, Indians, Chinese—they outnumbered the Fijians as far back as the late fifties. We would have gone the same way if we ever let the Europeans control us. The Indians came to Fiji as workers, so did the Chinese. Soon there was no room for the sea people. Our King George Tupuo I kept Tonga for the Tongans. A wise policy, I think."

Adams looked at the enigmatic face and wondered if there were a message addressed to him. His wits weren't sharp, not in this wild sea and screaming wind.

Prince Toki read the expression and smiled thinly. "No, I don't mean your Company, Mr. Adams. I was worried at first, but you have kept your agreement, brought in only enough westerners to run the Station, kept them on short-term contracts. If you had encouraged your people to settle permanently . . . but do you know why I agreed to help you tonight?"

Adams shook his head warily.

"The whales. The sea people have always respected the whales, Mr. Adams. It will be a sad world for us when they're gone. But there's nothing we can do to keep the powers from killing them all off. Your Company is at least trying."

"Be damned," Adams muttered to himself. Had Mr. Lewis seen that coming, or did he really just want to save the beasts for sentimental reasons? No matter, the books balanced nicely now.

"Understand me," the prince was saying. "We can help each other, and the reefs you occupy would never have been much use to us. You can keep them. But I hope you have no other plans for Tonga."

"We don't," Adams said. At least none I'll talk about now, he added to himself. A thick cloud had moved over the already feeble moon, and it was dark and threatening in the open boat. Phosphorescent seas crashed around them. Ominous black clouds astern added an atmosphere of menace. Bill settled his windbreaker around himself and stared miserably at the water.

In four hours they were at the harbor entrance. A driving rain obscured everything, and Adams was amazed at the skill of the Tongan helmsmen who seemed to know exactly where they were. They had sailed to Fiji many times across hundreds of miles of open water, and they had phenomenal memories, but there was no clue to what they steered by in this wet darkness. A tiny reef to port, swirls and breakers in the water, the boat raced on past the harbor bars in silence, and they were in calmer water.

Then, quite suddenly, a white shape loomed up off the starboard bow. *Persephone* riding at anchor, tossing

violently in the big swell that swept in from the Pacific.
Even close up the ship was almost hidden in the driving rain.

The boat moved quietly to the anchor chain and Prince
Toki, followed by three Tongans swarmed up it.
Moments later a dozen followed. Adams heard a scuffling
sound, a noise as loud to him as *Cerebrus*'s engines had
been, then silence. A few moments later grinning bronze
faces peered over the bulwarks.

"They'll have headaches in the morning. What do we
do with them?"

"Set the lot of them adrift in the canoe. Only anchor
it so they won't get lost," Adams said. Despite his sea-
sickness there was a wave of triumph swelling over him.

Toki nodded. "Ready to be cut loose?"

"I think so. Give us a couple of minutes, eh?" Martinez
was already below in the engine rooms with technicians.
It would be an hour before he could safely start the
reactors but the ship's emergency batteries would take
them out of harbor. Adams and a company sailing officer
went to the bridge.

"Everything looks good sir," the mate said. "Plenty of
juice. I think we can put out."

"Do it." As *Persephone* moved silently out of the harbor and into the storm Adams grinned despite the violent
motion. He was miserable, and when it was safe he'd
lose his dinner, but he had the ship. And that's half the
problem, he thought.

The fiberglass lanai set on top of the Station blockhouse seemed like home after the wild ride. *Persephone*
had met *Cerebrus* after the storm blew itself out and a
regular crew took over. Bill and the Tongans returned

to Ta'avu Station while the big white ship raced out to open water escorted by the plane. She wouldn't be tal en again.

Adams carefully squared the stack of papers on the table and placed them in the briefcase. He fussed with their order, being sure that he knew where each was so that he could get what he wanted without hunting and without opening the case wide. As he finished, Courtney came in.

"The prince and his councilors are in the conference room," she said. "They're ready."

"Thanks."

"That was—well, congratulations," she said. She wanted to say more, but he had that preoccupied look again. She wished he would notice her, but now she understood. There was something else, and after that there would be another problem. There would always be another problem for a man like Bill Adams.

"What's that you're carrying?" Bill asked.

"Oh—one of Mike King's books. He loaned it to me." She held out Bernstein's classic *Transportation Economics*. "I thought I ought to study something besides Station ecology."

"Yeah. Keep reading things like that and . . . Look, after this is over we'll see about that transfer you requested. Do you like to travel?"

"Yes. . . ."

"I'm leaving Mike here when I go back to Santa Barbara. Can you type?"

"Damn you!" she shouted.

Adams shrugged. "I can. Bit hard to communicate with the computers if you can't. Can you type?"

"Yes, but I'm not a secretary!"

"Don't need another one. They already gave me four," Adams said. "If you can get over being touchy about being able to type, maybe we can work something out. Just now I've got a conference."

They went toward the meeting room. One of the Tongans came up and shouted to Courtney. She answered in Tongan, then excused herself and ran off.

Prince Toki and his two councilors were seated at the conference table. They stayed there as Bill came in, and he remembered that to stand in the presence of nobility without being asked was considered disrespectful. Evidently he'd been promoted. He shook hands around and took his seat. Everyone grinned openly.

"Perhaps not a feat to compare with the early kings," Prince Toki said, "but wait until the palace musicians are through. You have no idea how strange 'Bill Adams' and 'Arturo Martinez' sound in a Tongan heroic ballad!"

"I'm afraid to guess," Adams said.

"Where is Dr. Martinez?" the Prince asked.

"Some kind of problem in the fish farms," Bill answered. "I'm sure it's not serious. Well. Gentlemen, that turned out well enough. Now let's talk about the next problem. The Fijians are stealing your fishing boats, Your waters too. I expect you want to do something about that."

Toki nodded. "But I wish you would stop saying 'Fijians.' It isn't the sea people, it's the mainlanders who are pirates."

"I'll try to remember, but what do I call them? Anyway, let's do something about your boats. What Tonga needs is a real navy, something to protect your waters."

Toki shook his head slowly. "Frankly, Mr. Adams, the cost of a navy would be greater than all the fishing boats we'd ever lose. Besides, no matter what you saw last night, our people don't enjoy fighting. The real Fijians are more warlike than we are."

"Not true," the older councilor said. "In older times we fight. No one ever conquer Tonga Islands, we have always had our own king."

Toki shrugged. "Still, we're not about to convert to a war economy. And war with Fiji would take time, kill a lot of sea people. No."

"Oh, I wasn't talking about Fiji," Adams said. He flashed a crooked grin. "Now that we have *Persephone* back we can put a stop to *that* nonsense though economic pressures. It shouldn't take long to settle Fiji."

"Then why do we need a navy?"

"Funny thing about this world," Adams said carefully. "Legally, a sovereign government can protect its interests pretty well as long as it doesn't start open war and involve the big powers. Certainly a sovereign government can arm merchant ships and protect them against harassment by international gangsters. But there are a lot of sovereigns in name who haven't the means to protect themselves and have to rely on someone else. . . ."

"You mean Tonga," the prince said. He frowned, then shrugged. "But I must agree. We wish the British were still protecting us. But they're not, and we see no one else we'd like to have as partners."

Adams nodded. "Now also in this world are big companies—like, say, Nuclear General—who have more than enough power to protect their interests but have no legal right to do it because they aren't sovereign. The United States is supposed to look after our interests, but we don't see them doing much of it. Delicate state of relations, world opinion—" Adams broke off, his jaw set.

"Mostly lack of ability, of course. With welfare payments where they are the U.S. can't even do proper research, much less—well. If Tonga were to nationalize some of Nuclear General's ships, you'd have the right to arm them, declare them protected by your sovereignty . . . "

"You're asking us to expropriate your property?" Toki asked.

"Well, we'd expect to be paid for it."

"But we don't have the money to pay you. . . . This is silly."

"You'd have enough money if you leased the ships to us. We'd pay very well for their use. At least as much, say, as we'd have to ask for if you nationalized them."

A slow grin spread across Toki's bronze face. "Let me understand something. Does your offer to help with Fiji depend on this deal?"

Adams shrugged. "There could be even more to it than that, Your Highness. For instance, Tongans go overseas to university. I suppose some of your people have overseas property. But you have no resident ministers or consuls abroad. . . . Now Nuclear General has people all over the world. No reason why they can't be given diplomatic credentials by the Royal government of Tonga, is there? Of course that means we'd have to look out for your interests everywhere."

"I will be—" Toki broke off and said something in Tongan. The ministers laughed and replied. Finally Toki turned back to Bill Adams. "It seems to me that we could use this arrangement to capture and protect more whales, stop foreigners fishing in our waters . . . would you agree to that?"

"Of course."

"Just what is it you want, Mr. Adams?"

"Nuclear General has an ice floe in the Humboldt Current," Adams said. He looked intently at the prince. "It's being towed up to Los Angeles, where we can sell it for quite a lot. But a couple of South American governments think they can charge us enormous fees for passage through what they call their waters. Now if we arm those ships and bring the kind of economic pressures that we can swing, we can talk them out of their designs. But our State Department won't let us do that, and the U.S. Navy won't act to protect our property. But if we register those ships under the Tongan flag . . . "

"I see." Toki was thoughtful for a long moment. "But this might mean war, Mr. Adams."

"Not over the ice floes. As to something else, how safe can you ever be? If Nuclear General was really in trouble, we'd have to pack up the reactors and go. Or lose them to someone else. That's not a threat, Your Highness. I know better than that. I'm trying to point out that Ta'avu Station is valuable and one of these days we may have to fight for it. The decision to try to take it from us will be harder to make if the fight won't be easy. But *we* can't arm the Station, we're not sovereign. You can't because you haven't the weapons. Together. . . ."

"How would you arm Ta'avu?"

"Coastal batteries. We've got some. Also we've got a couple of warships we bought from bankrupt governments. We can keep them around here under your flag if you'll commission our officers. But there's something else. . . . It's widely known that Nuclear General has the knowledge and fissionables to make atomic weapons. If we're acting for you, whether we have them or not I don't think small powers will want to find out—and the big ones won't bully Tonga, while they'd be happy to push a U.S. private company around."

"Why us?" Toki asked quietly.

"Because you're not ambitious. We've no worries that you'd try to use the Company as a lever to conquer your neighbors. And the whole world will believe that, there's strength in being thought small and nonaggressive in this day and age. Especially if you've suddenly joined the nuclear club . . ."

Toki pursed his lips carefully. "I'll have to speak to His Majesty, but—the idea is appealing. Tonga needs powerful friends, and I think your interests are close to ours. We'd thought of alliances with other countries but we . . . I suppose you have a detailed agreement with you?"

Adams nodded happily. "It's rather complete, actually. With some long-term taxation agreements which will infuriate the U.S. Internal Revenue Service, but ought to make you happy . . . now, we expect you'd rather collect most of those taxes in services, here's a schedule of what we can provide. . . ."

He was interrupted by Courtney and Samual bursting into the meeting. Adams frowned as the Tongan technician squatted respectfully before his prince. They chattered in Tongan while Adams looked on puzzled and Courtney tried to look casual, although she was obviously bursting.

Toki's grin was reassuring. "Dr. Martinez sends a message which won't wait, Mr. Adams. You are to congratulate Mr. Lewis and tell him he is the father of a three-ton baby girl. . . ."

Power to the People

Terrazo scratched in the sterile sand, muttering curses to the older gods before quickly thinking better of that and crossing himself. The Umfundis had warned him about that, and now that his body was lost to this awful place, he must be even more careful of his soul. He dug out furrows and planted seeds, muttering again. Nothing would grow here in the Namib Desert! Even Father George, who was a saint, could not pray up enough rain, and the land was barren, the white men must know that. . . .

It had been bad enough in Walvis Bay, where Father George had his last mission. But now to be sent here, hundreds of miles from any town, where there were no people, only a corrugated iron and fiberglass church and rows of prefabricated barracks with no one in them—it was more than he could bear. When he had first been given the job as sexton to Father George, he had been proud. It was a good position, there would always be enough to eat. But the Umfundis had been sane then. Now he was quite obviously mad, to bring Terrazo into this desert where there was no water and never would be. . . .

He finished the vegetable garden Father had told him to plant behind the church. "There will be water, Terrazo," Father had told him. Terrazo shook his head and went inside the church building. Dry baked heat tore at his lungs. Even Christ Himself must suffer in this! He genuflected to the altar, decided to let the dust stay in the pews until night although usually he polished everything at least once a day. The Lord would understand.

Outside again he looked across at the sea, waves pounding ceaselessly against the sandy beach. A cooler breeze sprang up and Terrazo stood gratefully in the shade of the church. A glint from the sea caught his eye and he looked out toward the horizon. . . . Something seemed to be out there, something bright and much too big. He shook his head. The heat could do that to a man. Deliberately he looked away, squinted across barren sands toward the mountains fifty miles inland. There was iron there, and lead, Father George had said, and men would mine it and send it here to the shore to be smelted and worked. And there would be farms here, and houses, a whole city. Terrazo shook his head again, the whites were mad, no one could ever live in the Namib, and who would want to if they could? But he was sexton to Father George, and he would show he was worthy of his post. Perhaps someday he could persuade Father to go back to Walvis Bay, where there were people to come to his church.

The glitter caught his eye again. It was closer now. Terrazo stared unbelievingly, crossed himself, and ran to the tiny parsonage fifty yards from the church, ran in terror, screaming, "Father, Father, come quickly, Father, there is a mountain coming across the sea!"

Captain Rollo Anderson was paying careful attention to his charts. *Hrelsvelgor IV* was nearing her final anchorage and had to be placed just right. He glanced at the speed indicators, nodded, and turned to the mate. "Signal 'Finished with Engines'," he commanded. "And tell the reactor boys they better secure for earthquake. She'll come to ground in an hour."

"Aye aye, skipper. I'll signal the tug, shall I?"

"Right, although I expect they know. But I want them standing by just in case the current's different from what I thought. We'll want to place the old girl just right."

Anderson stood in a heated bridge compartment at the forward edge of an iceberg moving at nearly three knots. It had taken six months to bring the berg from the Antarctic to the African coast, and most of the crew was sick of it; now the voyage was over. She'd gouge out a hell of a hole when she went aground, big enough to form a harbor for ships coming to the Namib, or at least that's what the Company engineers had calculated. Nobody had ever tried making a harbor this way before, although Antarctic icebergs were standard sources of fresh water. Anderson had commanded three previous *Hrelsvelgors*, two to Los Angeles and one to Florida.

"Beacon bearing 20°," a cadet called from his post on top of the berg.

Anderson nodded. "Standby anchors," he ordered. He turned to his charts. Looked like good holding bottom here, and the depth sounder showed they were entering the hundred fathom line. Tricky business, the anchors would be needed to hold the melting berg offshore after she grounded. He could drop them now, or let the tugs take them out later. . . . "Drop stern one and two," he said softly.

The iceberg moved onward. Anderson decided she was drifting off course and had the tug push against her port side to hold her against the current. With the reactor shut down and secured against the coming jolt, he had no power.

The depth finder pinged alarm. It was shoaling rapidly now. "Let go numbers four, five, and seven anchors! Tug clear away!" Anderson ordered. There was a long wait, one minute, two, then the first shudder, another, grinding fury as the iceberg slid inexorably across the bottom toward the shore. Steam boiled up from the ocean, steam and bubbles and mud as the four-mile-long mass ground to a halt.

"Not so bad," the mate said. "No worse shock than I thought."

"Reactor secure. All's safe," the bridge speaker announced.

"Anchors secure and holding fast."

"All motion stopped."

Anderson nodded in satisfaction. Just about where the Company wanted her, anyway. He began to unscrew the brass nameplate above the wheel. "Hoist the black ball, Mister," he told the mate. "And decommission the ship. She's not ours anymore."

The executive jet whistled over the South Atlantic, dropping from its cruising altitude to a few hundred feet.

It was almost to the African coast when Bill Adams looked up to see Courtney Graves's heart-shaped face and long blond hair. She smiled, then blushed slightly. Adams had chosen her as his executive assistant a year before, and so far that's all she'd been, but she could hope . . . only the man was married to his job! She wished he had time for something else, not that it had been all work these past months. Bill Adams knew about entertainment, and in their travels he took her to the most exotic shows in places no one had ever heard of. Sometimes he bought her presents . . . but that's all he did, and yet she knew he didn't have another girl, and his wife and daughter had left him ten years ago. His wife said she wanted a husband, not a visiting father.

Adams stretched and ran long fingers through sandy hair that kept falling over his pale blue eyes. Time for a haircut. "Got me some coffee, Courtney?"

"Yes, sir." She went forward to get it while Bill looked at the desolate African coast. The Namib Desert, said to be one of the bleakest places on earth. Sure is, he thought. He looked ahead for the Station.

The iceberg was the first thing he could see. Partly melted now, it was still huge, three miles of ice angling out from the shore. One end of the berg was aground, the other held offshore by anchors, creating a quiet, protected deep water harbor gouged out by the berg's fury when it crashed ashore. Quite a concept, Adams thought. Too bad we can't patent it.

Courtney brought him the coffee and sat opposite to face him. Nice kid, he thought. Too nice for casual affairs. Besides, she reminded him of his daughter and was the best assistant he'd ever had on the technical stuff, didn't pay enough attention to important matters like finance, but she was learning. Give her a couple of years, she'd be ready to take on a job as an independent troubleshooter for Nuclear General. Then, when she wasn't working directly for him, maybe . . . only then he'd probably never see her.

"Looks like they're coming along nicely," she said. "Of course, we saw it all from the satellite pictures, but . . . "

"Yeah. The real thing's always a little realer, if you know what I mean. Tell me what I'm seeing."

"Yes, sir." She shook her head slightly, rippling long blonde curls. Bill Adams was undoubtedly the most brilliant man she'd ever met, but he acted as if he didn't know much. Sometimes he didn't, either. You could never tell when he was fishing for information and when he had made a thorough study. . . . "The big square color patches are the solar salt works. Brines from the desalinization plants go in one of them, sea water in the others. It took a lot of plastic film to line the bottoms . . . the large buildings along one row of solar ponds are purification plants. Potassium, magnesium, phosphorus, Portland cement, the things we can get from sea water. I. G. Farbenwerke runs that part of the Station."

"Hmm." Adams sipped his coffee. "Heard from von Alten yet?"

"Yes, sir. He's already at the Station. So are most of the others."

"Good. Give 'em time to look things over. OK, what's the rest of this gubbage?"

Courtney eyed him carefully. Just how much was he putting her on? As far as she knew he had never been a professor, he hardly had time for it since he wasn't yet forty, but sometimes he reminded her of one, asking questions to see if his staff had done their homework . . . but then he really might not know. He mostly studied financial reports; his favorite saying was "Leave engineering to the engineers."

"The things that look like railroad roundhouses are our reactors and sea-water flash evaporators, the round ponds next to them are treatment pools where they precipitate out solids with the KOH-HCL process."

"What's that big complex near the runway?" Adams asked.

She nodded. "That's the Allis-Chalmers electrolysis cells. Ammonia synthesis next to it. And just beyond that, the pink concrete building, is the GE experimental steam-hydrogen process fertilizer plant. It's supposed to be a lot more efficient than Allis-Chalmers, but there're bugs."

The plane circled low over the desert as the pilots got landing instructions. Adams pointed as they banked steeply. "I see the railroad's working." With the electric ore train to bring the scale into focus he examined the rest of the Station. He knew from the reports that the industrial complex stretched along nearly four kilometers of seacoast and three inland, and beyond the industrial buildings were three-hundred-thousand acres of land either under cultivation or being made ready for it. The irrigation grid was plainly visible, and bright red tractors moved between the pipelines. There were another fifty-thousand acres of solar salt lakes and bitterns ponds. . . . Otjiwar was *big*, but for a billion dollars it *ought* to be big. "What's the crop now?" he asked, pointing to the tractors.

She took a sheaf of papers from her briefcase. "The crop phasing's pretty delicate," she told him. "Right now they're in the high export value pattern. Harvesting dry beans and cotton, planting winter wheat and potatoes behind the harvesters. This pattern uses the least water, but the government wants them to switch to a high-calorie system for exports to Rondidi."

"Yeah, I know," Adams said. His voice was harsh. "They call it foreign aid. I call it Danegeld. That's why we're here."

Adams climbed down from the executive jet and mopped his brow immediately. Heat shimmers rose from the cement runway. "My God, it's hot here!" he said to the man waiting below the ramp. "Excuse me, Father. . . ."

Father George Percy grinned. "If you want to tell the Almighty something that must be quite obvious to Him, that's your affair." Father Percy was a short, heavy man with no trace of fat but broad shoulders and thick arms. He wore white trousers and shirt with clerical collar, a small gold cross on a chain around his neck, and his accent was the heavy modified British of South Africa. "Have a good flight?"

"Good enough." Adams mopped his brow again. The handkerchief was soaked.

"It's best we get inside," the priest told him. "Aren't your people coming?" He led the way to a waiting Jeep and held the door for Adams.

"There's just the one, and she wants to look at the phosphorus plant," Adams said. "I let Courtney run around these places on her own. She might find out something. Let's go, I want to see Jeff."

"He's in his office. Lot of work for the Station Chief. I told him I'd meet your plane." The priest studied Adams closely. He'd only met this sandy-haired American once before. It wouldn't do to get Mr. Franklin in more trouble than he was in, Jefferson was a good man.

"Quit worrying," Adams said, reading his thoughts. "There are standing orders all through the Company that station chiefs aren't to meet my plane. You're not very familiar with Nuclear General, are you, Father?"

"No. When the Mission Society put me here as their representative I tried to get out. I'm only a missionary, Mr. Adams. I don't belong on something as technical as this."

They were driving across the shimmering runway toward a group of concrete and fiberglass buildings at its edge. The big domes of the nuclear reactors towered over the administration buildings, and beyond them were barracks for the four thousand natives and five hundred foreign technicians living at Otjiwar Station. Next year there would be more than forty thousand people here—if the Station survived, Adams added to himself. It seemed problematical.

Even through dark glasses and white pith helmet his eyeballs and head felt baked. Wouldn't they ever get to the air-conditioned buildings? The Station was *big*, they'd been driving for several minutes now. "How do you like it here, Father?"

"I've been in worse places. We even have air conditioning in the church and some of the houses. But I fear it's a waste of power, and I really shouldn't use mine."

"Trivial waste, Father," Adams said. "Giving the farm workers air conditioning increases production, cuts down on their water consumption. Besides, we pipe the heat from the air conditioning units into the solar evaporators, so we don't lose much." Except to envy, he added to himself. And that might be the biggest loss of all. . . .

The Jeep pulled up at the glaring white Administration building. The native driver leaped from his seat to open the doors for Adams and the priest, another uniformed guard examined their identification before waving them to the elevators.

They went to the top of the four-story building, past a miniskirted European secretary to Jefferson Franklin's office. The Station Chief was in shirtsleeves, his collar open. Franklin stood at a draftsman's table across the room from his desk. His black skin glistened with sweat, and his face contorted with emotion as he shouted at a white man. "I don't care what the Prime Minister says! I can't switch crops. It takes almost 200 gallons of water a day to grow food for one man with *this* crop pattern, and I can't afford the water for the high-calorie system. So stop bothering me about it, Mr. Bloomfort!"

"The desalinization equipment works splendidly, I've seen it," Bloomfort replied. He was a short, dumpy man with beads of sweat standing out above his small brown mustache. Both men looked as if they were out in the plant area, not in an air-conditioned office. "The foreman says you won't give him enough power to operate at full capacity."

"Damn right I won't. I can't, I have the phosphate production to keep up! The fresh water plant runs at full capacity when the sun's up. We never intended to run it full time at peak." He glanced up. "Hi, Bill. Mr. Bloomfort, this is Bill Adams, Special Assistant to the Chairman of Nuclear General. Bill, Anton Bloomfort, Undersecretary of the Interior."

As Adams and the politician shook hands, Franklin continued, "Maybe you can talk some sense into him, Bill. I can't. He wants us to change to ten-crop or high-calorie so they'll have something to give Ifnoka."

"We must give him food," Bloomfort said. "He has an army and threatens to invade. Their sabotage has cost us much already."

Adams nodded grimly. "That's why I'm here. Tell me about this Ifnoka."

"He is Chairman of the African People's Union," Bloomfort replied. "Although Premier Tsandi does not care for him, Ifnoka controls the army in Rondidi, and his party is strong in Botswana. He has followers in the Republic of South Africa, and some here."

"And what's he want?" Adams prompted.

"He says food for Rondidi. Ultimately . . . " The politician's half smile melted to a grim mask.

"Ultimately, he wants Otjiwar!" Jeff Franklin said.

"I've heard." Adams nodded and turned to Bloomfort and the priest. "I've only just arrived, give me a few hours, will you?" Humph, he thought. Only a half hour and I'm already picking up that clipped British speech pattern. "Father, can you take Mr. Bloomfort wherever he wants to go?"

Father Percy smiled. "What you're saying is can we get out of the way so you can talk to your Station Chief in private. Of course. I'll see you later, Mr. Adams. Dinner with the Bishop and me perhaps?"

"Thank you, yes. . . ." Adams waited until the others had left the room. "OK, Jeff, give it to me straight."

"It's simple enough," Franklin told him. He ran stubby black fingers through close-cropped tangled hair. "I can't handle it. I thought I could, Bill, I really did, but I can't. OK, so you wanted a black man as Station Chief here. Looked like a good idea at the time. But that's what you're here for, isn't it? To yank me?"

"Crap." Franklin looked up, surprised. "You think we put you in here because you're black? If I'd had a better white man I'd have put him here. MacRae's on Tonga, Martinez is a sea farmer, Horton's—the hell with it, I'm not running through the list. Mr. Lewis put you here because I thought you were the best man for the job, so stop feeling sorry for yourself and tell me what you can't handle."

"Yes, sir." Franklin looked at Adams quizzically. Adams grinned.

"I'll also fire you the instant I think you can't handle it."

"Yeah." Franklin turned to the draftsman's table. "Technically we're pretty good despite the sabotage. Only minor stuff anyway, tractors, some pumps and water lines, nothing we can't fix. They don't want to hurt the Station, they want it intact." He pointed to the blueprints. "Farms are laid out, getting a crop from eighty thousand acres. Not as good yields as we'll get later, it takes time to condition soil as poor as this, and the workers are only learning how it's done—Bill, they don't know anything! If it wasn't for the Mission schools, we'd be in *real* trouble. Our schools are set up to take people at a little higher level than we've got."

Adams nodded. "I'll tell Courtney we need some of those Sesame Street-type TV tapes. Got TV in all the family quarters yet? Make sure you do."

Franklin made a note on a scratch pad. "Computer's got the usual bugs," he said. "Had to plug some problems through Santa Barbara—our communications satellite came in handy. Weather's held good, hotter than we expected so we get plenty of evaporation. Portland cement and magnesium production are up twenty percent over predicted. . . ."

"How'd the harbor work? Captain Anderson was worried."

"Rollo always worries that he's put one of those bergs a millimeter off. No sweat, and she's melting fine in this sun. If I had four more I wouldn't have a water shortage. Bill, if it wasn't for the sabotage and government pressure I'd be fine."

Adams shook his head. "Finances are close, Jeff. Which puts Meissner and some of the other backers in a mood to cut their losses. The riots in Nigeria aren't helping them decide to sink more money in Africa either. They may bail on us, Jeff."

Franklin whistled. "What happens then?"

Adams shook his head again. "Bad. The Old Man can't finance this deal alone, it's too big. We'll come out all right if we get the plutonium production up, but the whole integrated agro-industrial concept is on trial here. You know what happens if you're on your own better than I do. . . ."

They were interrupted by a knock. Courtney Graves came into the room, her long blonde hair in a tangled swirl, her white blouse soaked. "It's *hot* out there. Hello, Mr. Franklin."

"Hi, Courtney. . . . Look, Bill, if Farbenwerke and Krupp bail on us, we're *dead.* It takes about a grand an acre to develop the farms, and sure, some of that's fixed cost we've already hacked, but it's still about $750 an acre from here to the end."

"A hundred and sixty million dollars," Courtney said quickly before Adams could take out his calculator. He never could do figures in his head. "But that's not the real problem, is it, Mr. Franklin?"

Jefferson Franklin shook his head. "No. The chemical works, fertilizer production, electrolyzers—everything was built modular, and we're just about to capacity with what we've got. We need the new units the backers were sending in. I'm not even sure Nuclear General can recover the investment if we can't finish the project. . . . It all depended on the integration, power and heat and water and everything phased in just right, and it takes a damn big scale for it to be economical. . . ."

"Instant industrialization," Courtney finished. "The only industry in this country. It's just *got* to work! These people have *nothing* without us. . . ."

"This is not a venture in altruism," Adams reminded her.

"It is for the World Mission Society," she retorted.

"We're trying," Franklin said. "When the World Court made South Africa turn Namibia loose, the SAs were pretty generous by their lights. Gave Namibia twenty-four million bucks, that's about forty dollars a head, just about the annual income. Loaned them another ten million on a long-term low-interest deal. And that's *all* these people have got. They sunk every penny in Otjiwar, no wonder they worry about Ifnoka. And look, even in the fertile parts of this country it takes fifty, a hundred, sometimes two hundred acres to feed a man."

"How're you doing here?" Adams asked.

"Current production, we can feed ten people an acre. That's using two thousand gallons of water per acre a day. We've also got enough power to make the fertilizers, and some chemicals and cement for construction and export. I can feed the whole population of Namibia and still have surplus cash crops to sell Israel . . . I could before this mess started, anyway."

Adams found the coffee pot behind the drafting table's console. "Tell me about this refugee situation."

"Over a hundred thousand have come in. Ifnoka encourages them, tells them they'll get jobs, the good life, money—and we can't give it to them. They stream into the cities and make trouble for the government. Even though they get more here than where they came from, it's not enough. . . ."

"Yeah." Adams was grim. "That's when people usually riot, when they're getting more but not as much as they expected." He poured coffee.

"Where do they come from?" Courtney asked.

"God knows," Jeff told her. "The Republic. Botswana. Rondidi. All over Africa, I think. Jesus, Bill. I don't know what to do, and Father Percy's no help. He says feed them, never mind the cost."

"You can't solve famine by feeding people," Adams intoned. "First principle of ecology. If you can't make people self-sufficient, your relief does more harm than good. OK, that's about ten thousand acres, another ten million bucks investment to expand—can you do it?"

Franklin went to his desk and moved a lever. A console pivoted up from the desk top, and he punched at its buttons for a moment. "Won't take ten million," he said. "I can expand another ten thousand acres for about seven. Costs us up to three percent of our chemical export capacity, though, and there'll be no reserve power left at *all*. And what good is it, Bill? There'll just be more of 'em. Ifnoka makes it sound like this is paradise."

"Leave that to me," Adams said. "OK, I want to look at the figures and digest your reports. Loan me an office, I need a console and a phone—Oh. Invite Ifnoka and what's his name, Premier Tsandi of Rondidi, to the conference."

"They won't come," Franklin said.

"They'll come. Ifnoka *asked* to come. I got the message relayed from Santa Barbara. Tsandi's scared to let Ifnoka make deals without him. They'll be here."

The conference room was crowded. In addition to a dozen men at the long table, more sat in chairs or stood at the end of the paneled room. Bill Adams took his place at the head of the table and nodded to the group.

It was quite an assembly. Harrison of Allis-Chalmers, Feldstein from General Foods, Meissner of the Bayer Kartel, von Alten of I. G. Farbenwerke . . . Over in one corner Father Percy sat with a small greying man in black clerical clothing. The Bishop of Exeter, representing the World Mission Society. The orthodox church sponsors included both the Romans and Anglicans, as well as Coptics and Byzantines, and among them they'd raised two hundred million dollars, making their investment second only to Nuclear General's.

Ifnoka sat at the other end of the table. He was a tall man, brown rather than black, and wore green robes trimmed with gold. The garb made Courtney smile, but carefully. Ifnoka had been born Henry Carter of Canton, Ohio, educated in the U.S.A., took advantage of the Emigrant Act of '92. Two thousand dollars and a one-way ticket anywhere you wanted, just renounce your U.S. citizenship and residency rights forever. . . . Handsome enough man, she thought. Tall, slim . . . but cold, staring at Bill Adams with hatred. The man next to Ifnoka was dressed in western business clothes. Francis Tsandi, Premier of Rondidi. His Freedom Party ruled that country. But Ifnoka's African People's Union controlled the army and most of the weapons. China wanted a foothold in

Rondidi, but so far Tsandi had resisted them as thoroughly as he'd resisted the western bloc. Couldn't possibly last long, Courtney thought. But she noted that Adams greeted Tsandi warmly although he had only a perfunctory handshake for Ifnoka. Now just what did the boss have in mind?

Adams cleared his throat. "Let's skip formalities and start at the beginning. When this consortium first planned the agro-industrial complex, we'd intended to put it on either the west coast of Australia or the Rann of Kutch. It looked like maximum profits in those areas."

"And I still say we should have gone to Australia," an Oxford-accented voice said from the left side of the table. "There wouldn't have been any political problems. British Overseas Investments—"

"Argued very well for a Commonwealth site, Sir James," Adams finished for him. "But the limiting factor was money, and the price of money is up to fourteen percent. When Southwest Africa and the Mission Society made their offers, you all agreed."

"*Ja, ja*, we agreed, it is not time for what might have been," von Alten said. He didn't look at all like a Prussian aristocrat, in fact reminded Courtney of a sausage shopkeeper. The appearance was deceiving; von Alten held nearly the same position with Farbenwerke as Adams did with Nuclear General, and spoke for most of the Common Market investors. "While we are discussing trivia, you will please tell us why we must hold this meeting in Otjiwar? You have brought us here for what that we cannot do in Geneva?"

"I think it's well to see the stations, Herr von Alten," Adams said smoothly. "Gives the investors a chance to see what our people are faced with firsthand."

"What your people are faced with I do not know," the German said. "But we are faced with losing a lot of money. We have contracts to deliver phosphates and potassium, and if we do not get them here we must buy on the world market."

Adams nodded.

"And I do not understand why it is that when only a small percent of the power of this station is diverted to agriculture my chemicals production falls by thirty-five percent!"

"If you're hearing complaints, General Foods is getting shorted on cereal deliveries," Feldstein said quickly. "And we have contracts with Israel . . . Do you know the problems involved in trying to arrange transport through U.S. ports? We have the wheat, but the dockworkers—"

"Greed." The single word cut through a rising babble. Ifnoka stood, walked to the window overlooking the harbor. "Greed. You talk of money, and out there are three ships loading with food and chemicals, bound for foreign ports and carrying with them the lifeblood of Africa! For what? To satisfy your greed!"

"Now just one moment, we . . . " von Alten began.

"Let him finish," Adams said.

Ifnoka sat again, resumed his dignified stare. "I can wait. Proceed."

As if it were *his* meeting, Courtney thought. But Adams was letting him get away with it. . . .

"Courtney, if you please," Adams said.

She took her place at the chartboard behind Adams, lifted the pointer, and stood for a moment to gather her thoughts. He's always letting me make presentations. Says it surprises people to find out how much I know, that they pay more attention to me than him, most of them being men . . .

"As most of you know," she began (Damn. Mr. Adams says *never* begin with that phrase), "the key to successful operations of this type is size. For a light water reactor producing five hundred megawatts electrical the best internal return on investment is about six percent, overseas exports to the world market about half that. By increasing the size of power source to four thousand MWe we can get as high as thirty-five percent internal return, and over nineteen percent on the world market, but it requires an enormous capital investment."

"Actually, we don't need that much, do we?" Sir James Fortnum of British Overseas asked carefully. "Namibia operates on internal return, and the Church can stagger along a couple of years with no return at all. Correct, your lordship?" he asked the Bishop.

"Correct for a few years, Sir James. But to raise this enormous sum we had to convince the donors that this is seed money to be recovered for other development work."

"Thank you, my lord," Courtney said. "I was just coming to that. But first, to answer Herr von Alten, the reason chemical production falls so sharply with small unscheduled increases in agricultural production is that this project is very carefully integrated. We can't process the brines without power which is being used for water. The chemicals are concentrated, Herr von Alten, but they are still in the bitterns."

"So my chemical is only delayed?" von Alten asked.

Jeff Franklin answered. "Correct, sir, but the delay is long, because even if we have full power available it's already budgeted. It takes a while to catch up, and with more refugees pouring in demanding food and power—"

"Power to the people!" Ifnoka said quietly. Everyone stared at him but he didn't say anything else.

"I take it there's a point to this?" They turned toward the beefy man at the end of the table. Joe Bentley of Bethlehem Steel. "You're warning us that this can happen to us all, is that right, Bill? We don't expect steel production for a year, but we've got contracts. . . ."

"It could happen," Adams said.

"Then I'm authorized to tell you the Station had better be prepared for delays in equipment deliveries," Bentley said carefully. "We can't afford to invest this heavily in a project that's already telling us it can't meet deadlines. Sorry, Bill, but that's the way it is."

"Und ve think hard about more investments anywhere in Afrika," Meissner, the Bayer Kartel man, said heavily. "Next time, by God, ve go to some *civilized* place to put our monies in, *ja?*"

There was a chorus of muttered agreement around the table, then silence. Courtney began her technical briefing, but she could see it was no use. They'd made up their minds.

The paneled room seemed nearly empty, but there were still plenty of people in it, Adams, Franklin, Father Percy and the Bishop, von Alten for the Common Market, Joe Bentley for the U.S. companies. They waited after the others went to lunch. Courtney brought coffee and took her place at Bill Adams's left.

"Didn't mean to throw it at you like that, Bill," Joe Bentley said. "But it's true. The Board's never been enthusiastic about this goddam African venture to start with, even if there is good iron ore back in the hills and labor at reasonable costs. . . . Political situation's always seemed too damned unstable. Now you've proved it."

"*Ja, ja,* so what we didn't like has come to pass. What now? That's the question," von Alten said. He rubbed his fat hands together. "And I have seen Bill Adams too often pull the rabbits out of the empty hat before. What have you in mind?"

"First, I need an agreement," Bill said. "I've invited Ifnoka and Premier Tsandi to meet us informally without the others. Oh, Bloomfort will be here for Namibia too. Now, I'm going to talk tough, and I need your backing. No wavering, gentlemen, none at all."

"How tough?" Father Percy asked. "Do you intend to threaten them? With force, weapons?"

Adams nodded. "Threaten them and mean it." It's not going to work, Courtney thought. The priests won't . . .

"The Church can't accept that," Father Percy said.

"It can't?" Adams addressed the Bishop. "Tell me, my lord, what will the failure of Otjiwar do to your Mission plans?"

"Destroy them, of course," the Bishop said. "We'd hoped this station would be a model for the world. And once we'd recovered the investment here, we planned to build more stations like this in other parts of the undeveloped world. India, east Africa . . ."

"And instead you're willing to let a two-bit American hoodlum steal your investment and blow all those plans?" Jeff Franklin asked. "Make no mistake, Your Reverence, if Ifnoka gets his hands on Otjiwar, he'll bring the Chinese in. Just what do you think they'll do for the people of Namibia? Or anywhere else in Africa?"

"It had occurred to me," the Bishop said dryly. "Yet—the picture of the Church threatening people with weapons is hardly in keeping with our ideals."

"If you're willing to give up, I can't save a thing," Adams told them. "And you'll have condemned all these people to primitive conditions. What good are your schools without some place for the graduates to work? Damn it, these agro-industrial complexes are the first serious attempt to do something lasting in black Africa, and if this one fails it'll be a long time before anyone else—"

"When I think of the money wasted in gifts here," Father Percy said. "Now, when there is something that might actually change their lives, we must make a profit on it or it won't happen. I find that as distressing as Ifnoka does."

"Don't let your heart bleed over Henry Carter," Jeff Franklin told them. "That bloody crook is only interested in power for himself, not the people."

"Haven't you missed the point?" Adams asked quietly. "The reason Nuclear General is exporting technology is simple: the political situation in the United States is abominable. Between the 'ecologists' and the anti-capitalists we don't dare build a complex like this in Florida. We've all come to Africa in the hopes of making money, not to industrialize people."

Cruel, Courtney thought. But true enough. The World Mission Society could only raise a sum like eight hundred million once. The big companies supporting the project put most of their risk capital here. If it were lost, no one would ever come back. And these people needed help.

"Well, gentlemen?" Adams asked. "Can I count on you? For silence, at least?" There was no answer from the clergymen. Finally Adams turned to Courtney. "Bring 'em in."

It was Ifnoka's turn. The project had been explained, the clergy had pledged Mission Society investments in Rondidi if they could recover their money from Otjiwar.

Bloomfort promised police support for the Station, and Franklin showed that Namibia could handle the refugee population it already had, but not more. Now Ifnoka spoke.

As before, he went to the window. But he had noticed Premier Tsandi's interest in a station like Otjiwar for Rondidi, the man's obvious fear the whites would pull out and leave Otjiwar unfinished, abandon Africa. A weak man, Tsandi. He would have to be replaced soon. The African People's Union was almost strong enough, there were only the Rondidi police to resist a coup. Tsandi had kept the army small, and though it was controlled by Ifnoka it would not be enough if the police resisted. But Tsandi was here in Namibia, not at home. If he could be kept here and Ifnoka get word to Rondidi . . .

Meanwhile, talk. Henry Carter of Ohio was dead. There was only Ifnoka, the voice of his people. He pointed to the harbor. "The blood of Africa sails on those ships. Phosphates, grains, nitrates, fertilizers, cement, the things we must have. And you take them away for money! What Rondidi could do with them! And the food! But you dare tell us we must bleed our land to support your greed! It will not be. The food is here, the land is here, and the people will come here for what is theirs by right. Power to the people!"

He turned to Bloomfort. "Your Premier keeps you and the other whites, to belittle our people. You must go." Then to Jeff Franklin. "And you, traitor, you might have been a great leader of our people, but you are an American now, not African. They have made you an honorary white man, are you not proud?".

"What do you want?" Father Percy asked.

"Power to the people!"

"I see," Courtney said quietly. Everyone looked at her. "You mean one man, one vote, _once._"

Ifnoka's lip curled in contempt. "Woman!" he sneered. He had nothing else to say to her.

"In other words you intend to bring enough of your Union people into Namibia to overthrow the government here," Adams said carefully.

Ifnoka shrugged. "We might win an election. . . ."

"And you'd nationalize the Station." Adams shook a Camel from a battered pack. "Suppose we gave you the keys this afternoon and pulled out? What would you do? You can't finish Otjiwar, or even operate it."

"We have friends," Ifnoka said. "Good friends."

"The Chinese. I doubt they could finish this place, or would. But suppose they do, what does that do for 'the people'? Besides put them under your thumb. Your 'guided democracy' does a lot of guiding."

"And yours does not? You hold up America as a model for the world?"

Adams shrugged. "I'm holding up nothing. Your point, now it's my turn. First, that lifeblood you see out there. Where did it come from? This Station is in the most desolate spot on earth. Sure, there'll be iron production in a few years, but for now all we use is sunlight, sea water, and power from our reactors. There's not a blasted thing of African origin on those ships and you know it."

Ifnoka shrugged. Courtney stared at Bill Adams. This wasn't like him, he never argued with people. But she saw that Premier Tsandi looked interested. If the whites could make all that wealth from nothing, what might they do with the resources of Rondidi? But he wavered, looked at Adams, then back to Ifnoka, shook his head as if to say that promises were nothing. And Otjiwar was here, here for the taking. . . .

"Let us get to the point," Ifnoka said. "That is the purpose of this conference, to halt the strikes and infiltration, is it not? Well, I can do that for you. My price is a share in the management of the Station. My officers to take control of security here. African People's Union trainees in all supervisory positions. And foodstuffs for disposal as I see fit. In return, you will be permitted to complete this plant and take out enough goods to pay for your investment. But no profits! Nothing for greed!"

Adams smiled thinly. When he spoke it was directly to Ifnoka, but he kept a wary eye on Premier Tsandi. I see, Courtney thought . . . but could he do it?

"Let me make you a solemn promise," Adams said. "Before anyone—anyone at all—takes control of this Station away from us, there's going to be a regrettable nuclear accident. The only thing left of Otjiwar will be a pile of radioactive slag even less useful than the Namib was before we got here."

"*Ja.*" Von Alten nodded vigorously. "So, Mr. Prime Minister Tsandi, you think on that for a while. With no Station, you got all those people came here, others coming through your country to get here, and they got nothing to eat, *ja?* You think maybe they come looking for you with blood in their eye for sending them here?"

"Whereas, if you'll close your borders and stop this infiltration, Rondidi can benefit quite a lot," Adams finished smoothly. "You've got iron ore in your hills, more than here in Namibia. It'll take a while to develop, but we can get a railroad in there to bring it here."

"Why would you do that?" Tsandi asked. He saw Ifnoka's scowl and winced, but continued to look expectantly at Adams and von Alten.

"For profits, of course," von Alten said. "His Lordship the Bishop got other motives, but us, we want profits. We make you a pretty good deal to get them, too."

Tsandi nodded. *This* he could understand. But there was Ifnoka's Union group and the coup he was undoubtedly planning in the army. . . .

"Another thing," von Alten snorted. "Seems I got me forty, fifty thousand submachine guns. Some good rifles, too. I wonder, Mr. Prime Minister of Rondidi, if you want some of those guns for your own party people, for your police too, *ja?*"

"What?" The monosyllable was jerked from Tsandi's lips. He looked fearfully at Ifnoka.

"*Ja*, we got the guns," von Alten said. "Already in Rondidi we got them. When Mr. Adams says smuggle in guns to Rondidi, me, I do it. I think maybe we organize a coup, only now I see what he really wants, *ja?*"

Adams smiled tightly. "They can be distributed before either of you gentlemen get back to your capital. By the way, I'm sorry but the airfield's got some problems. Undermined by an aquifer, I understand. Unusable . . . ."

"An aquifer?" Father Percy said carefully. He looked out at the barren desert. "I see." He suppressed a chuckle, but it was very loud in the still room.

"All you have to do is name the Cabinet people you want to distribute the guns," Adams said. "We'll see that they get them."

Ifnoka roared and charged out of the room. The door slammed behind him but didn't catch. Courtney went over to close it.

"Well, Mr. Prime Minister?" Adams said. "Of course we'd like your Minister of Trade to have a say in who gets those guns. Good man, that."

"What do you want?" Tsandi demanded. His tone was listless, flat.

"For the guns?" von Alten asked.

"You can't arm Rondidi!" Bloomfort exploded. "What's to keep Tsandi from taking the guns and still getting together with Ifnoka? Using them against Namibia?"

"Oh, he wouldn't do that," Adams said carefully. "Invasion of Namibia's a dream anyway. The Republic of South Africa wouldn't care to see an actual armed invasion of their showpiece descendant. Infiltration's one thing, open war's quite another."

"And who'd develop the iron ore?" Joe Bentley asked.

"Yeah. It does Rondidi no good." Adams stood at the head of the table. His smile was cordial and he spoke warmly to Tsandi, but Courtney saw his pale blue eyes were as cold as ice. "The Station was deliberately put a long way from cities. It won't fall to small arms. And everyone gains from the Station except Ifnoka. His whole power structure's built on poverty and promises. Now we're not in business to eliminate poverty, but there's no way to make a profit without leaving money behind us, and that upsets him. For the Premier of Rondidi, though, the Station's quite a good thing. What's it to be, sir? A chance to put Rondidi into the modern world, or life in Ifnoka's shadow forever?"

"I haven't even that choice," Tsandi said. "He's gone to order the military coup he's been planning for months. With me out of the country it will succeed."

Adams chuckled. "I wonder if Ifnoka's going to be surprised when he finds out somebody's broken the transmitter he brought with him. . . ."

"And the telephone's out, too," Courtney said. She was sure it was.

"Somebody's been jamming the whole Station," Jeff Franklin reported. "Strangest thing . . ."

"But we can get a signal through for our friends," Adams said. "Of course your instructions for distributing the weapons will upset the army. I'd suggest you ask your Minister of Trade to arrest the top Ifnoka people before they cause trouble, right?"

"And your price? Merely closing the borders?" Tsandi asked.

"Yeah, for the guns. But if you want Nuclear General and our combine to invest in Rondidi, you'll have to show enough political stability to convince the others. You heard the meeting."

"So that's why I was there," Tsandi mused. "You make a persuasive case."

Courtney held her breath. It was von Alten as much as Bill, she thought. Profits—Tsandi could understand that motive easily, but he distrusted altruism.

The door burst open. Ifnoka hurried in, his robes askew, a perplexed technician behind him. "What have you done?" he demanded.

Before Adams could answer, Tsandi stood. He looked at Ifnoka with contempt. "What they are doing, Henry Carter, is what you have demanded but never wanted." He pointed through the window to the huge reactors, the tractors, and water pumps. The faint hum of turbines came even to this sound-proofed room. "They are giving power to the people!"

Enforcer

Grey water crashed over the bows, throwing spray droplets high in the air, where they were caught by the
screaming wind and whipped down the ship's length.
The tug plunged into the trough of the wave, seeming
to stand on her bows, then leveled off and began the
climb up the next wave. That one broke across the deck
with a crashing shudder felt in every compartment.
Another wave advanced inexorably from the west. There
was always another wave.

"The 'Screaming Fifties,' " Captain Jellicic announced
to no one in particular. "Christ pity a seaman."

His companion didn't answer, possibly because he
hadn't heard him. He was inches shorter than the captain, a round man, overweight, but his face was angular
and craggy, the jaw set. Michael Alden wore earphones,

and he was listening intently. The ship pitched again, and a rogue wave caught her to roll her over until it seemed the bridge would go under water. Alden looked up in excitement. "Hold her steady, Captain! He's found something!"

"Here?" The captain curled his lip. "Bloody lot of good it'd do if you hit a strike here, Alden. 'Tis the worst place in the world!" He waved expansively at the grey waters. The sun was invisible above dark, brooding clouds that filled the skies from horizon to horizon. To the west a line of dark waves approached in a stately march, endless waves with curling white tops. Wind screamed unceasingly through the tug's rigging until the sound became part of the universe itself.

"Come right a touch," said Alden.

Jellicic scowled, but barked orders to the helmsman. The ship moved across the face of a wave, presenting the angle of the bow to the white water on its top, and more sea broke across her decks. Spray crashed like hail against the bridge windows.

"Steady," Alden said. He lifted a microphone. "Position fix. As good as you can get it. This looks like it."

Microwave antennae on the mast made tiny movements. High-frequency signals winged upward, where they made contact with a navigation satellite, and information flashed downward. Again. And again.

Captain Jellicic released a collapsing chart table hinged against the bulkhead. When it folded down, it nearly filled the bridge. He bent over it, scowling, and took a small instrument from a rack in the space the table had covered. He moved that about on the map, and his scowl darkened. He straightened to speak to Alden, but the engineer wasn't listening, and Jellicic impatiently poked the supercargo in the ribs. "We're *here*, ye daft fool! Look!"

Fifty-three degrees south latitude; the Falkland Islands were seven hundred miles due west, and another four hundred miles that way lay the entrance to the Straits of Magellan. The nearest land was two hundred and fifty miles southeast of the point Jellicic indicated. South Georgia Island, good for nothing, and owned by the British to boot.

"Not for nothing," Alden said.

Jellicic looked up, unaware that he'd been muttering. "Eh?"

Alden's face was grim. A tinge of green was visible around his cheekbones. "South Georgia. Not good for nothing. They render whales there. They're good for exterminating whales."

Jellicic shrugged. In his opinion anyone who sailed these Antarctic seas deserved whatever profit he could make; but Alden was a fanatic on that. There was no reasoning with him. "What have your lads found?" Jellicic asked.

"Mass concentrations. Veining down there. Thick veins. Manganese nodules to the deep floor. Veins in the sides of the crevasse. Just what we were looking for, Captain. And we've found it." He listened again for a moment. "Can you bring her about and over the same course again?"

Jellicic looked out at the crashing seas and thought of his little tug broad onto them. He pointed. Alden glanced up, then back at the chart. The captain shrugged and went back to the wheel. He wanted to be near the helm for this. As he watched the seas, waiting for a calm moment when he dared bring her around, he shook his head again. So they'd found metals. Copper, tin, gold perhaps. How could they bring anything up from fourteen hundred fathoms below the Southern Seas? The discoveries were of no value. He looked back at Alden's grim features and caught himself.

Perhaps they'd do it at that. But how?

It took Michael Alden two years. First he had to invent the technology to bring in mines for profit at two-thousand feet below the stormiest seas on earth, then he had to convince investors to put their money in it.

Technology, he found, wasn't his problem. The investors were ready for that. Howard Hughes mined the seas for twenty years before, and Hughes hadn't risked money on vigia. Alden's techniques were new, but the concept wasn't; and he'd found the richest source of ores ever discovered.

Economists waxed ecstatic over the potential markets: all of Latin America, and most of southern Africa. The minerals would come from the sea onto boats—onto the cheapest form of bulk transportation known. Given the minerals, Latin America was a fertile field for industries. Labor was cheap, investment costs low, taxes lower. The United States had become a horrible place for risk investment, with its unpopular governments, powerful unions, bad schools, and confiscatory taxes. U.S. investors were ready to move their capital.

It wasn't technology or economics that frightened investors away from Alden's mineral finds. It was politics.

Who owned the bottom of the sea?

Eventually ways to avoid the legal problems were found. They always are when enough money is at stake.

Ten years went by. . . .

There was bright sunshine overhead and new powder beneath his skis. Mont Blanc rose above him, brilliant in the new-fallen stuff, untouched; and there weren't many people out. Superintendent Enoch Doyle released the tension on his poles and plunged forward, *schussing* down the fall line, waiting until he was moving dangerously fast before bringing his shoulders around in perfect form, turning again in a series of christies, then back to the fall line, *wedeln* down with wagging hips. There was a mogul ahead and he took it perfectly, lift, springiness in the knees. Who said he'd forgotten and he ought to take it easy his first time out after so long behind a desk?

He had just cleared the mogul when the beeper screeched insistently. "No!" Doyle shouted into the rushing wind. He scrabbled at his parka, trying to find the off switch on the condemned thing, but he was moving too fast, it wasn't possible, and on he went, the enjoyment gone, past the turnoff to the high lift, around the logging road, through a narrow trail, now that was fun again and the hell with the bleep-bleep from under his parka.

Pole down, turn, turn again, cliff to his left, a long drop to doom, and Enoch laughed. The trail led to a steep bowl crowded with snow bunnies in tight trousers and tighter sweaters, gay colors against churned snow. Doyle threaded through them as fast as he dared. His wife was waiting outside the lodge. Enoch clipped a pole and mitt under one arm and used his free hand to turn off the bleeper.

She knew. He saw it as soon as he neared her. Her heart-shaped face, ringed with dark hair, incredible that she was so lovely and yet a grandmother twice now.

"They can't do this to you," she said. "It's your first vacation in four years. Tell them no, Enoch."

"Tell them no to what, *liebchen?* What is it they want?"

"Oh," she said, her mouth perfect roundness, holding it for a moment. "They did not warn you? You must call them."

"You wanted me to say no," he reminded her.

"But first you must know what it is that you are to say no about," she said. Her accent was faint, but it always came through in her English. Her French and Italian had none at all, but Enoch was born on the Scottish border, and Erica would speak to her man in his own language. Always. As if his German were not as good as hers, and his French and Spanish better. He put an arm around her waist to steady himself as he bent with chilled fingers to release the safety bindings and martinets of the skis. He kept his arm around her as they went into the lodge.

It was too warm inside, he had overheated on the slopes, only his hands were cold. He caught the eye of the counterman and was let inside the manager's office, took a seat at the desk, and called.

"International Security Systems," a pleasant voice answered.

"Doyle reporting in."

"Oh. Ja, Herr Superintendent. A moment, *bitte.*" The phone hummed and clicked. American telephones didn't do that, he thought sourly. Nothing else in America worked anymore, except the telephones; but they always worked. Best in the world. An epitaph of pride. They had the best telephones in the world.

"Van Hartmann," the phone said. "Doyle?"

"Ja, Herr Hartmann."

They spoke German by tacit consent. "The Argentine has boiled over," Van Hartmann said. "You must go there at once. Herr Alden has called five times."

"But the *residentes*," Doyle protested. "And Chief Inspector Menderez. . . ."

"Arrested. There is a new military junta in the Argentine. Molina is out, on his way to Portugal. And all our people are arrested. There are Argentine soldiers and police in Santa Rosa. Herr Alden is not the only one upset. He has called his board, and they are calling us."

Doyle was silent for a moment. It was stuffy in the little office with its frosted windows. Erica was standing in the doorway, no secrets from his wife, none that he would talk of on a telephone anyway. He made a drinking motion and she nodded and went out.

"I am not an Argentine specialist," Doyle said. "You would do better to send—"

"No. There is no one to send," Van Hartmann said flatly. "I will not plague you with the troubles our special assignment teams have at this moment. Be assured that you are the senior man available." The harsh voice softened a trifle. "You would be within your rights to refuse this, but I ask you not to. It is important. Very important. The stockholders will be concerned."

Erica came into the office with a cold beer. Doyle took it and thanked her with his eyes, but his thoughts were far away. Finally he spoke into the phone. "Have they attempted to board Malvinas Station?"

"Not yet."

Doyle drank the beer, a sip, then more, finally tilted back the glass and drained it. Then he sighed. "I will return to Zurich within four hours. Please have my people ready, and arrange transportation. I will need the full briefing, and the contracts."

"*Danke. Danke schön,*" Van Hartmann said. "It will be done. Please before you go, see me in my office."

×   ×   ×

The plane winged over the Atlantic. Doyle found a sheaf of computer printouts in his office behind the wing and began to read.

MALVINAS: DEEP SEA MINING AND REFINING STATION OPERATED BY OCEANIQUE INC. OF ZURICH. OCEANIQUE OWNERS OF RECORD ARE THREE MAJOR SWISS BANKS. SEE CLASSIFIED APPENDIX FOR STOCKHOLDERS.

MALVINAS IS LOCATED OVER THE MALVINAS TRENCH 1,850 KILOMETERS EAST OF THE ARGENTINE COAST INTERNATIONAL WATERS. THE STATION IS UNIQUE AMONG OCEAN MINING OPERATIONS IN THAT THE ABOVE-SURFACE INSTALLATIONS INCLUDING A WESTINGHOUSE-OERLIKON 50 MEGAWATT PRESSURIZED WATER REACTOR REST ON A CAPTURED ICEBERG. ICEBERGS ARE CHANGED AT INTERVALS DICTATED BY ECONOMIC FACTORS AND ARE GENERALLY 20 KILOMETERS LONG BY 2 TO 4 KILOMETERS WIDE.

THE PRINCIPAL PRODUCTS OF MALVINAS ARE COPPER, NICKEL, MANGANESE, AND GOLD. PRELIMINARY REFINING IS ACCOMPLISHED ON SITE USING FRESH WATER FROM THE ICEBERG. THE TOTAL VALUE OF REFINED ORES SHIPPED AMOUNTS TO 60 MILLION SWISS FRANCS OR $284 MILLION U.S. ANNUALLY.

And I can remember when a dollar bought four francs, Doyle thought. And when "sound as a dollar" meant the opposite of what it does now.

×   ×   ×

MANGANESE COLLECTION IS CONVEN-
TIONAL THROUGH SUBMERGING BARGES AND
DREDGES. THE MAJOR COPPER AND NICKEL
PRODUCTION COMES FROM MINING THE
WALLS OF THE TRENCH ITSELF. THE PLATEAU
DIVIDED BY THE TRENCH EXTENDS EAST-
WARD FROM THE FALKLAND (OR MALVINAS)
ISLANDS WITH DEPTHS RANGING FROM 300 TO
1,000 METERS. MINES AND STRIP-MINING
OPERATIONS TAKE PLACE FROM 350 TO 1,000
METER DEPTHS. THE DEEPEST PART OF THE
TRENCH WHERE MANGANESE NODULES ARE
FOUND IS 4,500 METERS.

THE FALKLAND PLATEAU IS CLAIMED BY
BOTH UNITED KINGDOM AND ARGENTINA.
THE UNITED KINGDOM HAS POSSESSION OF
THE FALKLAND ISLANDS. DISPUTE OVER OWN-
ERSHIP OF THOSE ISLANDS DATES TO THE 19TH
CENTURY AND WAS FIRST PLACED BEFORE THE
U.N. IN 1948. ISSUE TEMPORARILY SETTLED BY
FALKLANDS WARS OF 1980'S.

And it's still there, Doyle thought. He reached for a
beer. It'll be there when I'm dead. The plane winged on
toward Brazil.

OCEANIQUE PAYS ROYALTIES TO BOTH
ARGENTINA AND THE UNITED KINGDOM FOR
EXPLORATION RIGHTS TO THE FRENCH. THE
PAYMENTS ARE SMALL AS THERE APPEARS TO
BE NO POSSIBLE COMPETITOR WITH THE REQ-
UISITE TECHNOLOGY. EXPLOITATION CON-
TRACTS HAVE A TERM OF 30 YEARS AND ARE

GUARANTEED BY INTERNATIONAL SECURITY SYSTEMS LIMITED (ZURICH OFFICE).

ALSO BY CONTRACT WITH OCEANIQUE, INTERSECS PROVIDES LAW ENFORCEMENT AND JUDICIAL SERVICES ON THE STATION AND ALL VESSELS BASED THERE. A SEPARATE CONTRACT AMONG OCEANIQUE, INTERSECS, AND THE ARGENTINE GOVERNMENT GIVES OCEANIQUE EXTRATERRITORIAL RIGHTS IN THE PORT OF SANTA ROSA ON THE ARGENTINE COAST. WITHIN THE DEFINED AREA OCEANIQUE REGULATIONS AS ENFORCED AND ADJUDICATED BY INTERSECS HAVE THE FORCE OF LAW.

The plane reached the Brazilian coast as Enoch finished reading the summary and detailed attachments. The converted military transport landed in Recife for fuel and was on its way south again when the steward came into Doyle's crowded office space.

"*Telefono,* Superintendent. Zurich."

"*Gracias.*" Enoch Doyle lifted the instrument. There was no vision screen, "*Ja?*"

"Van Hartmann. You cannot land in the Argentine, Herr Doyle. The new government is arresting all INTERSEC people."

"I will divert the flight to Malvinas. Can you arrange for our reception there?"

"*Ja.* As we predicted, the Argentine is sending a warship to Malvinas. These men are not reasonable, Herr Doyle, and I must so inform the Board when it meets this afternoon."

Doyle cursed in English. There were more satisfying languages for cursing, but he generally reverted to the speech of his youth when pressed that far. "I suppose you must, but I will ask you to please impress upon the stockholders' representatives that this matter may yet be settled to our satisfaction. Restrain them."

Van Hartmann paused. "I will try. Not much is known of the new government. A military junta has made a coup against General Molina. They have given the usual pledges of democratic elections and promised the usual reforms. Many of the reforms have to do with what they call ending the exploitation of their nation by international imperialist corporations. The Directors will not care for this."

"No, I don't expect they will," Doyle said, but to himself. "What more do we know of the new government?"

"We have not yet identified the strongest man among the junta, and they have not yet announced their new President. I will have the dossiers sent to your computer when they are assembled. The junta has requested recognition from all the major nations."

"We have taken the standard measures, one presumes?" Doyle asked dryly.

"*Ja.* There will be delays in recognition. We are ready to bribe their diplomats if you think it required."

"I doubt it would do any good." Doyle thought for a moment. "South American nationalists place pride above all else. Their present diplomats will not be of their sympathies, of course, but the men they send to replace them may not be rational. I think it will be better if we merely assemble the dossiers."

"*Ja.* But do not forget, Herr Doyle, the Directors will be anxious."

"I understand. I will report when I know more. I must now instruct my pilot to change course." Enoch Doyle laid the receiver in its hook and turned back to his briefing forms. He did not like this at all.

These contracts, he thought. Now useless. Perhaps they were not so fair to the Argentines as they might be, but without contracts and enforcement of them, how could there be business? Argentine patriotism was a very fine thing, but the new leaders must be made to understand that contracts must be enforced.

Once upon a time men evolved a system called international law. For a short period it was taken very seriously. Until the end of the first quarter of the twentieth century, the Counsel for the Department of State was the second-ranking diplomatic official in America. International disputes had a decidedly legal air to them.

In general, only Great Powers could enforce international law, and then usually only against smaller powers; yet, oddly enough, the Great Powers took international law seriously among themselves. Legal disputes were cheaper than war. Scholars were paid large sums to prepare briefs quoting musty volumes of Grotius and Vattel, and phrases such as *"pacta sunt servanda"* and *"clausula rebus six standibus"* were traded in the chanceries of Europe.

Diplomats debated questions of real as opposed to paper blockades. The Powers signed conventions for the treatment of prisoners of war, and even Adolf Hitler invited the International Red Cross to inspect his POW camps. As trustees of the international legal systems the Great Powers were far from perfect, but international law was often upheld.

The rattletrap system survived World War I, but when World War II began, all bets were off. In 1918 the

United States of America went to war because German unrestricted submarine warfare was a violation of international law. On December 8, 1941, the United States of America ordered her submarines to sink enemy merchant vessels without warning and wherever found.

By the 1960s, the authorities could write that peace was more important than law. Enforcement of international law was entrusted to the United Nations—whose charter stated that no power could interfere in the internal affairs of another, and made self-defense the only permitted reason for resorting to force.

A small country could seize the property of a Great Power; murder her citizens; defy every contract and convention; and the authorities would gravely pronounce that the Great Power had no right to take military action. The powers could only sue before a court that could not enforce its judgments.

Pretty soon, nobody paid much attention to international law.

The runway was two kilometers long, but the iceberg lay north-south, nearly crosswinds; the landing was rough. Doyle had a brief glimpse of icy crags and, incredibly, gaily clothed skiers winding down the sides of the ice toward a plastic lodge decorated as an Austrian castle. The plane taxied to a semi-cylindrical hangar, ugly in its functional simplicity, yet certainly more honest than the frilly trim of the ski lodge. There were a number of people waiting for Doyle and his team.

"Inspector Jiminez Ortega," the first man introduced himself. Enoch recognized the INTERSECS chief agent at Malvinas. "And this is Mr. Michael Alden, the Director here."

Doyle took Alden's extended hand. The American engineer had dark patches beneath his eyes, and his look was grim.

"Glad to see you, Superintendent," Alden said. "But I don't know what you're going to do. I've had three calls from the junta, all from a Colonel Ortiz, but he won't discuss anything except how fast we're willing to turn over the station and everything else to him. They won't negotiate."

Doyle smiled lazily. "We'll see." His face showed confidence he didn't feel as they went to Alden's office through cylindrical tunnels laid above the ice. The office complex was a cube of a building, held together by girders so that it could be moved as a single unit.

Alden's office itself was sparsely furnished, with cellulose panel walls and steel furniture. Models of ocean craft and undersea vehicles filled shelving along one wall. Alden's desk was an old steel model with plenty of space for papers as well as the computer console. His drafting table was the latest model IBM, but next to it stood a wood table with T-square, unchanged in forty years except for the small console bolted to one edge. A mounted sailfish hung over the table.

The wall opposite Alden's desk was covered with screens showing TV pictures of underwater mining operations. The waters were murky, with bright yellow lights illuminating the drowned world. At the edge of the illuminated area Doyle saw grotesque shapes, some motionless, some moving.

Disc-shaped subs darted about the sheer wall of the Trench, which stretched upwards and down until there was no more light. Ledges had been cut into the convoluted sides of that infinite cliff, and enormous digging machines sliced out segments for vacuum dredge-heads to suck up and carry away. Another screen showed the ores loaded into an underwater barge suspended by cables from something unseen above.

An inside shot of the barge showed pulverization and suspension-sorting machinery. Constant streams of muck spewed forth from the sorting barges to drift with the current, and a dark cloud settled slowly toward the invisible abyssal floor below.

Doyle felt a growing admiration for the American engineer who had built all this. "Doesn't that sediment give your manganese dredges some problems?" Enoch asked.

"Uh?" Alden glanced at the screen. "No. It settles too slowly, and there's a fast current." He grimaced slightly; that current made it difficult to anchor the iceberg. "We only dredge a few miles downwind of the berg. Seas get too high for the surface equipment outside the wind shadow. We let the refining discharges out near the surface—oddly enough, the stuff stimulates plankton blooms. Lots of fish. Sports fish, too."

"Ummm. Oh. Thank you." Doyle accepted a drink Alden took from a cabinet next to his cluttered desk and sniffed. Scotch. Alden would have heard that Enoch Doyle came from the Scots border country, but his deduction was wrong. Doyle hated Scotch and its iodine flavor.

"It seems you are operating," Enoch said.

"Sure. But where will I send the crews for rest-up?" Alden asked. "The shift patterns are complicated, Superintendent. The underwater crews stay down there for six weeks, then they get three off. Surface crews rotate by the week. They all have to live somewhere. Southern part of Chile's no good. Costs too much to send 'em to Uruguay or Brazil."

"So you need Santa Rosa. A pity."

"Yeah, that's what I thought when we put in the station. I wanted to be self-sufficient here. Couldn't do it. Installation got too big, human factors killed me. We keep finding more and more minerals, and developing new capabilities for on-site processing, and that needs more workers." Alden's fingers played across the computer console and pictures on the TV monitors changed to show grey crashing seas and bleak lead-grey skies. "How long can workmen put up with that?" The question was rhetorical, of course. OCEANIQUE, like every other country, would long since have tested just what conditions would get maximum productivity at minimum cost. There weren't any labor unions in this business, and with a hundred nations clamoring for the hard currencies international corporations paid taxable workmen, there wouldn't be. Not real ones.

"We can't keep people here anyway," Alden said. "Logistics of feeding a big crew are just too expensive." The pictures changed again, to show a lavish casino, where couples in evening clothes played roulette, craps, blackjack, other games. A famous Canadian couple sang a duet in a bar furnished like 1928 America. "And yet we get tourists here. They don't stay too long, though. Go over to the mainland after a few days, but a lot of 'em come back every year. Jet set, idle rich. They like it. I can't imagine why."

"How long have you been here?" Doyle asked.

"Eight years." Alden shrugged and grinned lopsidedly. "Yeah. Well, I don't like it much either, but this operation's got me. Last-minute technology. My own development budget. Where else are the resources to come from, Doyle? Everybody wants to live it up, but we used up all the resources. Ocean mining's the only way we can do anything about—" he stopped, embarrassed. "What the hell happened? You're supposed to have intelligence operations. You were suppose to warn us!"

"Obviously, someone failed," Doyle said. "Well. It is time to work. Can you call this Colonel Ortiz?"

"I can try. He'll keep us waiting to show how trivial we are and how important he is, of course."

Enoch shrugged. "We have time." Wasted time, which I could be spending on the Mont Blanc slopes with Erica. Wonder what it's like to ski an iceberg?

Colonel Ortiz wore formal uniform, with polished leather shoulder belt and pistol holder. He was a big man, with a thin, clipped mustache, and he looked as much German as Latin. Doyle regarded him with satisfaction; at least Ortiz dressed like a gentleman. It might not make him easier to deal with, but it should be less unpleasant while they negotiated.

"You have spoken to your directors and are now ready to be reasonable?" Ortiz demanded.

"I have called to introduce a representative of the International Security System Company," Alden replied. "Colonel, I have the honor to present Superintendent Enoch Doyle."

Ortiz's lip curled. "INTERSECS." He said it with contempt. "I have nothing to say to you. Whatever arrangements we make with Señor Alden, you will have no further part to play. Your slave trading is finished."

"You refer to the men convicted under the contractual arrangements between INTERSECS and your government?" Doyle asked.

"There are no contracts between INTERSECS and my government!" Ortiz was shouting now. "The Dictator Molina purported to make such contracts, but they are void. We repudiate them all!"

"It is not so easy a matter as that, *Coronel*," Doyle said smoothly. "Surely your government does not yet appreciate how serious this is? INTERSECS has guaranteed this contract. There is a great deal of money at stake. A very great deal."

"Money!" Ortiz visibly struggled to control himself. "You bleed us and you enslave our people, and you speak of money! You would not know the word, Superintendent, but there is such a thing as honor, and it cannot be bought for money."

"I had always been persuaded that honor included keeping one's pledges, *Coronel*. But perhaps you are correct. Government can afford honor. Businesses cannot. We have only contracts and agreements, and those must be kept."

The screen went blank. Alden looked up in alarm. "I told you. He won't talk to you."

"Yes, a very difficult man," Doyle said thoughtfully. "But perhaps something can be done."

"What? They won't even negotiate." Alden toyed nervously at a bald spot forming at the back of his head. "Superintendent Doyle—"

"Enoch. Call me Enoch, it's much simpler." Americans like to be on a first-name basis, he thought. Never did understand why.

"Enoch. And they call me Duke, usually. Enoch, this thing's just money to you, but it's been my whole life. Ever since I first realized just how thoroughly the United States raped this planet for minerals so we could have a few years of what we thought was prosperity, I've wanted to—well, to try to do something to make up for it." Alden spoke defiantly. "I think I have. And now it's coming apart. Nobody'll ever invest that kind of money in sea mining again."

"Then we'll just have to keep your station operating, won't we, Duke?" Doyle stood and moved toward the door. "No, no, I can find my own way. I'd best go to the INTERSECS offices and use our computer. Zurich was to send me data you won't have. Cheer up, Duke. You're not stopped yet."

As he went through the rather dingy corridors Enoch thought about Alden. Incomprehensible, like all Americans. The whole country seemed to have a collective guilt complex about its past successes. The world struggled after the impossible goal of obtaining a way of life that the Americans have achieved, while the Americans grimly hung onto what they had and covered themselves with self-reproach. Incomprehensible people, all of them.

Inspector Ortega was a small, wiry man, utterly unlike Doyle; but his eyes held the same hard look, and there was no humor in them despite the smile he attempted for his superior. Ortega's office was paneled in wood, and the computer consoles were out of sight, as were the wall screens. Ortega opened a small cabinet and produced cold beer.

"You have been studying my dossier," Enoch said as he took the glass. "Thank you."

"It is nothing." Ortega offered Doyle the desk, then sat at it when Enoch took a chair. "Superintendent, I do not understand. We had no warning. The chief Inspector was on the mainland, and with all the INTERSECS people he is under arrest. Why did he not know? Surely you had warning in Zurich. We have men in Buenos Aires—"

Enoch shrugged. "Had we known, General Molina would have known as well. The conspirators were shrewd. Excuse me a moment. I would like quiet, to think."

Enoch leaned back in his comfortable chair and wiggled his ears. There was no movement visible, but the motion activated his implant. A voice came into his head. "ON LINE. PLEASE GIVE YOUR CODE." It was a very impersonal voice.

Enoch formed words in his head, a letter at a time. It was slow work. First a code identity establishing himself as cleared for all INTERSECS information. Then: "D-O-S-S-I-E-R-S."

"READY."

"I-N-S-P-E-C-T-O-R X-X J-I-M-I-N-E-Z X-X O-R-T-E-G-A."

"SUMMARY OR DETAIL INTERROGATIVE?"

"S-U-M."

"ORTEGA, JIMINEZ. INSPECTOR SENIOR GRADE. NO SECURITY FAULTS. LAST LOYALTY REVIEW 34 DAYS AGO. MAY BE ENTRUSTED WITH ALL COMPANY INFORMATION BELOW LEVEL OF COSMIC. KNOWS IDENTITY OF MAJOR STOCKHOLDERS. FORMERLY CITIZEN OF MEXICO. RECRUITED INTERSECS AT AGE TWELVE. EDUCATED INTERSECS ACADEMY MADRID. LENGTH OF SERVICE EIGHTEEN YEARS ELEVEN MONTHS FOUR DAYS. SPECIALTY SERVICE COURSES—"

"SUFFICIENT. THANK YOU." Which is silly, Doyle thought. Being polite to a machine. But it was a difficult habit to break. The machines talked to him. . . . "Inspector Ortega, would you please call Herr Van Hartmann in Zurich? I assume you have taken security measures with this office."

"Of course." Ortega lifted a telephone instrument and spoke a few short phrases. "What else, Superintendent?"

"Some information, please. How many convict laborers have we at this station?"

"One hundred forty-three, of whom twenty are in close confinement," Ortega answered immediately.

"And the total value owing by all of them?"

Ortega spoke with a distinct change in the pitch and timbre of his voice. "Dolores. Information. Convict labor. Total current value of contracts at Malvinas station."

"EIGHTY-SEVEN THOUSAND FOUR HUNDRED AND NINE FRANCS THIRTY-FOUR CENTIMES, DARLING," a wall panel said. The voice was a rich contralto, totally unlike the impersonal tones Doyle had heard. Ortega looked embarrassed.

"I will change the voice, Superintendent. When I am alone I prefer—"

"No, no, make no changes," Enoch insisted. He grinned. "What crimes have we here?"

Ortega spoke to the computer again. The contralto voice replied, "THREE MURDERS. TWENTY-FOUR GRAND THEFT. ONE HUNDRED AND THREE PROPERTY DESTRUCTION DUE TO CARELESS OPERATION OF MACHINERY. TWENTY-THREE INJURY TO FELLOW WORKMEN. OF THE LATTER TWO CATEGORIES, EIGHTY-SIX ARE DUE TO ABUSE OF ALCOHOL OR DRUGS. DETAIL. SEVEN—"

"Sufficient. Thank you," Doyle said.

"YES, DEAR."

Ortega looked up, surprised. "I had not known Dolores was keyed to your voice—Ah." He looked closely at Doyle. "Implant."

"Of course. If you are ever promoted to Superintendent, you will have one also. Not that they are as useful as is thought, but sometimes it is a great convenience. How many convict laborers on the mainland?" he asked in the tones recognized by office computers. There was no answer.

"Dolores does not have the key-word program," Ortega explained. He translated: "Information. Santa Rosa. Convict labor. Total number and value of contracts."

"TWO HUNDRED FORTY-SEVEN CONVICTS. VALUE OF CONTRACTS SEVENTY THOUSAND FRANCS NINETY CENTIMES. ADDITIONAL. TOTAL VALUE OF CONTRACTS ON MAINLAND PROBABLE VALUE ZERO. SOMEBODY BLEW IT, DARLING."

"Your accountant has a sense of humor," Doyle said dryly. "It may get him in trouble someday."

"But a good man," Ortega said. "Are you ordering me to discipline him?"

"Good Lord, no! How you run this station is your business, and Chief Inspector Menderez's business, and perhaps Zurich's business, but it's certainly not mine." Enoch lifted his beer and drank deeply. There was a low buzz.

"ZURICH ON THE LINE, DARLING," the computer announced.

"SPEAKER," Enoch ordered. "Herr Hartmann? Superintendent Doyle here."

"*Ja.* Have you more information, Superintendent?"

"No. Have you information for me? We're secure here."

"There are strange developments, Superintendent. The Argentine junta is coming to terms with other companies. It is only with OCEANIQUE that they threaten total confiscation."

"Hmm." Enoch slugged back more beer and thought about that. "Does INTERSECS have contracts with other Argentine based companies?"

"Only minor ventures, and none with enforcement clauses. They are not threatened, in any event."

"Curiouser and curiouser. So why OCEANIQUE?"

"We do not know."

"I see. What have you got for me on the rebel government, then?"

There was a pause and a rustle of printout papers, then Van Hartmann's voice again. "The junta is composed of seven officers who have agreed to ignore their differences in rank. They have informed the Zurich office that all contracts with INTERSECS are void, and there are no negotiations required. They will release our people when they please."

"Damned nice of them," Enoch said. Ortega muttered inaudible curses.

"Of the junta, two are vulnerable. A Colonel Mendoza has gambling debts and owes much money to Recreacion, S.A., as well as to others. The other, a General Rasmussen, has sexual appetites which would not appeal to his military associates. Colonel Mendoza is aware that we know of his problems and has privately assured us that he would be pleased to cooperate but cannot. The General does not know that we have any suspicions. On the others we have nothing of importance, but our agents are looking."

"What about a Colonel Ortiz?" Doyle asked.

"Incorruptible. Superintendent, these dossiers have been relayed to Malvinas. It is not necessary to ask me about them."

"Sure, but it's easier this way. Have you got any suggestions about how we can get to Ortiz? He seems to be in charge of negotiations with OCEANIQUE."

"Colonel Ortiz is thirty-four years old. He is an extreme patriot. Affiliated with Opus Dei and Catholic Action. Outspoken. He has always opposed any concessions to other nations or companies. He demands immediate high technology for his country and protests that only second-rate equipment is sold to the Argentine. General Molina had scheduled him for early retirement, but Ortiz is popular with his men and was thought to be necessary. I believe we recommended that Ortiz be given a diplomatic post abroad, but Molina did not act on it in time."

"I see. Incorruptible. A pity," Doyle said thoughtfully.

"Our associates have already marked him dangerous," Van Hartmann said. "Should I inform them that Ortiz is a man beyond reason?" Van Hartmann was casual, as if he were discussing the falling price of manganese.

"No, please."

"The stockholders are extremely concerned," Van Hartmann said. His voice took on a note of warning. "The Board has authorized you to take whatever measures may be required. You may request action by stockholder associates as you think best. They want immediate results."

"I understand," Enoch said quietly.

"Immediate results," Van Hartmann repeated. "It should not be necessary for you to call us again."

"Yes. A request, Herr Van Hartmann. It will be easier for you than me until I have placed new agents in Buenos Aires. Please have someone approach General Rasmussen and Colonel Mendoza to arrange for the junta to meet with me. Colonel Ortiz will not negotiate, and I cannot persuade them until they will talk to me. I would prefer that the request for a meeting come from them."

"It can be arranged," Van Hartmann said. "Anything more than that you must do yourself. Is that all?"

"Yes."

"The stockholders will expect to hear of results. Soon." The line went dead, and there was a long silence.

"I have known Colonel Ortiz," Inspector Ortega said. "He is a good man. It is a pity."

"Yes."

"I suppose there is no possibility of legal action? Eventually we might obtain compensation—"

"No." Doyle shook his head positively. "The security of the contracts between OCEANIQUE and the Argentine was directly and absolutely guaranteed by INTERSECS. If we let this outfit get away with confiscation of Santa Rosa, the whole structure of international trade will be affected. Contracts must be honored."

Ortega sighed. "I am a policeman. I suppose I might also be described as a soldier. I do not make company policy. But I cannot help but think that—"

"If you are wise, you will not finish that sentence," Enoch said quietly. "Do you think there's a man among us who hasn't thought the same bloody thing? Do I have to give you the usual pep talk about international law enforcement?"

"No. Intellectually I am convinced. And I remain loyal. But I do not like it, Superintendent."

"None of us do. I've got a few hours before Zurich gets those buzzards to call me. Where can I get some skis?"

The slopes were not good, Enoch decided. The snow was artificial, and the slopes too gentle. He gave it up as a bad job, wondering why anyone would pay the prices the gaming and recreation concessionaires charged. It was just as well that he quit early, because the call from Buenos Aires came not long after he returned to Inspector Ortega's office.

The screen showed five officers in Argentine uniform. Doyle recognized Colonel Ortiz, and was introduced to the others. Ortiz seemed to be the spokesman.

"My compatriots believe it would be useful to meet with you," Ortiz said without preliminaries. "I do not, but they have persuaded me to discuss it."

"*Señor Coronel,* are you familiar with the terms of the contracts your government has signed?" Doyle asked carefully. "Let me refresh your memories, *señores.* You have over twenty million gold francs on deposit in Zurich to back your currency. All of that is forfeit upon abrogation of our contracts. Surely this is a sufficient reason for negotiations? Argentine cannot be overly endowed with hard currency reserves." Doyle knew to the centime what currencies were held by the central banks of Buenos Aires.

"We had written that off," Ortiz said. There was a buzz of conversation behind him. Evidently his colleagues hadn't. Ortiz turned to confer with them, then spoke to Doyle again. "When do you suggest we hold this meeting? We are willing to grant you safe conduct."

"I much regret that I cannot come to Buenos Aires," Enoch said carefully. "It is not that I do not trust your word, but we hold contracts with the Argentine, yet my people are under arrest in your country at this moment. It would serve no useful purpose for me to join them."

Ortiz flushed and opened his mouth to shout, but he was interrupted by General Rasmussen. "We can understand that view, Superintendent Doyle. Yet surely you do not suggest that the ruling council of a sovereign nation should travel to an iceberg and confer with the representatives of a private company!"

A company with a bigger budget than a lot of nations, Doyle thought. But no matter. "Would Montevideo be convenient?"

General Rasmussen shrugged. "It is a matter of principle, *Señor* Doyle. It would not appear proper for us to come to you, even if we wished to do so. It would enrage our people—"

"We will not come to you," Ortiz said coldly. "We are the ruling council of the Argentine Republic. We do not travel to meet the lackeys of a corporation which exists on slavery."

"Then we are at an impasse already," Doyle said. "A pity. I think that when the news of your, ah, currency difficulties becomes widely known there is very likely to be a loss of confidence in your peso. Widespread selling. A few million francs in gold is not so much, but these things always seem to snowball."

"I see. You threaten us with economic war if we do not come to meet you. You would do that in any event, whether we meet or not," Ortiz said.

"A moment." The new man was tall and slender, and superficially resembled Ortiz. Colonel Mendoza. "If, perhaps, we released your colleagues as a gesture of good faith, would you then be willing to come here?"

Doyle smiled. That's round one, he thought. "Certainly, *Coronel*. You see, we are not so difficult to do business with. . . ."

There were soldiers in the streets of Buenos Aires. Enoch saw them as an Army staff car took him from the airport to the Casa Rosada. As they hustled him into the Presidential Palace, he barely had time to mark the contrasts on the Plaza del Mayo: palm trees and fountains, impressive nineteenth-century granite buildings with air conditioners protruding from the windows, a Gothic cathedral. Between the old buildings were modern steel and glass structures; and there were tanks on the broad white walkways under the palm trees.

Enoch went first to the office of General Rasmussen. *El General* was stocky, built like a wedge, with thick meaty lips and dark eyes. He eyed Doyle warily. When the aides left the room, and Enoch had declined a drink, the general leaned forward confidentially. "You understand that I am in sympathy with your efforts, but that I do not control the council?" he asked anxiously.

"Certainly, General," Enoch said. "We appreciate your efforts. What I don't understand is, why have we been singled out? Your council isn't giving the other companies nearly this much trouble."

Rasmussen shrugged. "It is Colonel Ortiz," he said. "He is a maniac, Superintendent! No compromise. The holdings of OCEANIQUE must be seized, and all contracts with INTERSECS cancelled. He is willing to release your people, but it was difficult to persuade him even that far."

"Hmm. And if his opposition ceased?"

"Then, I think, it would be well between us. He is the leader of Opus Dei, and that is three votes in the junta. But he will not be persuaded, Superintendent. It is not my fault. I have done the best I can for you; to go further would accomplish nothing except that I would be called a traitor to the revolution and a tool of the corporations. . . ."

"We understand, General. We believe these contracts are in the interests of your country. It is gratifying to know that you share that belief. Certainly we will have disagreements, but we are both reasonable men. . . ."

The damn fool, Enoch thought. If Ortiz doesn't have this office bugged, *he's* a fool. Rasmussen was a non-political official under Molina, put on the junta for national unity. But how did a creature like that get to be a general? "I suppose, then, that I should speak with Colonel Ortiz. Can I be taken to his office?"

"Certainly." Rasmussen rang for an orderly. "It has been pleasant to meet with you, Superintendent. And you will not forget that—"

"That you are a reasonable man. No, certainly not. Thank you, General."

Ortiz had offices directly across from the ornate Presidential suite; and the President's offices were empty. Symbolic, Enoch thought. And dangerous. He was kept waiting in an anteroom.

"I-N-F-O-R-M-A-T-I-O-N," he thought.

"ON LINE."

"O-R-T-I-Z X-X J-E-S-U-S M-A-R-I-A X-X C-O-N-N-E-C-T-I-O-N-S W-I-T-H O-C-E-A-N-I-Q-U-E."

"NONE SIGNIFICANT."

"R-E-L-A-T-I-V-E-S C-O-N-V-I-C-T-E-D U-N-D-E-R C-O-N-T-R-A-C-T."

"NONE IN RECORDS."

"P-U-T M-Y A-S-S-I-S-T-A-N-T I-N T-H-E L-O-O-P."

"I'M ON, BOSS." The voice wasn't different, of course; but now Enoch could ask questions in normal language and Timothy would program them into the computer—provided the Argentines didn't do something about his communications. Implant to Enoch's briefcase, briefcase to the aircraft he'd come in; aircraft to Zurich and Malvinas, via satellites; any of the lines were vulnerable to jamming. The codes were supposed to be unbreakable, though. He might be jammed, but he wouldn't be overheard. He hoped.

The office had been ornately furnished for one of General Molina's assistants, and Ortiz hadn't changed the decor. The colonel wore the same uniform as before, or a newly pressed copy of it. Neat, Enoch thought. Best description of him. Mustache seems to have been clipped one hair at a time. No religious memorabilia in evidence—is that normal for a Catholic Action type?

The dossier had been complete. Ortiz was intelligent, well-educated, popular with his troops and the communities they'd been stationed in. He seemed to have an understanding of international economics. INTERSECS consultants thought he'd be a stabilizing force and might be the best leader Argentina had come up with since before the multiple Peron regimes. Except for one point. He hated INTERSECS.

"You saw General Rasmussen before you came to me. I am surprised. I had thought you would consult with Colonel Mendoza," Ortiz said. There was no trace of a smile.

"I do not comprehend, _Coronel_."

"We will pay his gambling debts, of course. Colonel Mendoza will be a very useful man when he no longer has reason to fear or love you. Now I must investigate General Rasmussen. You see, I am a realist, Superintendent Doyle."

Enoch showed no surprise, but his features were locked in a rigid mask. "*Coronel* Ortiz, why is this necessary? There is so little to negotiate. Your threat to seize Malvinas, for example. A bargaining point, but not one of consequence. I dealt with it before leaving Zurich. We simply pay higher royalties to the United Kingdom. The British lion is toothless, perhaps, but not so helpless that he cannot defend the Falkland Islands and their offshore sea bottom, as Argentina found once before."

Ortiz's eyes narrowed slightly. Then he shrugged. "I had not expected quite such prompt action. I had hoped to present England and the UN with a *fait accompli.* Very well, you have taken one bargaining counter, but what will you do about Santa Rosa? That, Superintendent, is entirely an internal affair of the Argentine Republic."

"But conceded on lease to OCEANIQUE," Doyle said. "At your former government's request, I remind you. You receive the taxes, but have no necessity to provide government. Not even to operate jails and prisons—"

"Yes. You enslave people—"

"We collect the economic costs of their crimes for the victims. And we permit them to work. They keep a portion of their wages, and if they have dependents another portion is sent to their families. To be frank, *Señor Coronel,* foreign technicians would not entrust themselves to General Molina's justice. Even the Argentine citizens who work for us prefer our justice to yours. Only the incorrigibles, those who will not work at all, would rather be in an Argentine prison."

"There will be changes in the Ministry of Justice," Ortiz said coldly.

"Your pardon, *Coronel*, but all that has been said before. Here and elsewhere, and many times."

Ortiz said nothing.

"And what value is Santa Rosa to you?" Doyle asked. "You harm OCEANIQUE, but do no good for your country. Without Santa Rosa, Malvinas cannot operate. Without Malvinas, you have problems obtaining minerals. Without low-cost minerals—how soon before Chrysler begins laying off auto workers in La Plata? Where will GE get the copper for the radios they make in Montevideo? Your neighbors will not be pleased to see Malvinas harmed, *Señor Coronel*. Uruguay and Chile need the products sold by OCEANIQUE. You risk your whole economy, and for what?"

"Those contracts are not fair, Superintendent. OCEANIQUE makes enormous profits and we get none of them. Yet it is our people who work in those death-traps of undersea mines."

Doyle nodded. "The profits are high, but the risks were enormous. It took a great deal of capital, and in these days of high taxes, risk capital is always very careful. Nobody would finance Malvinas without the chances of high profit."

Ortiz made a gesture of dismissal. "These matters may be adjusted. But INTERSECS will leave the Argentine, and immediately. There will be no more extraterritorial rights, as if our Republic were composed of barbarians not fit to enforce its own laws against European technicians. INTERSECS must go."

Enoch looked up with interest. "C-O-N-N-E-C-T O-R-T-I-Z T-O I-N-T-E-R-S-E-C-S."

"TRYING EVERYTHING, BOSS."

"Why do you dislike us so?" Doyle asked.

Ortiz sniffed coldly. "A private company with pretentions of sovereign rights. Company judges decided the fate of our people after company police arrested them for violation of company regulations. And you have the temerity to guarantee the pledged word of the Argentine Republic!"

"I do not wish to be impolite, *Coronel,* but the Argentine Republic is not keeping its word—"

"It was not the action of my people! General Molina made those pledges."

"Are they so unreasonable? There were, it is true, payments made in special form directly to the President of the Republic. Perhaps you will be good enough to tell me how those should be made in future?"

"You offer me bribes?"

"Of course not. But the payments were understood, if not part of the formal contracts, and your government should have them—"

"Get out," Ortiz said. "You and your slavers. Leave."

"A-N-Y L-E-V-E-R O-N O-R-T-I-Z INTERROGATIVE."

"NOT A DAMN THING, BOSS."

"Coronel," Doyle said carefully. "I beg you to reconsider. To many corporations, INTERSECS is their only guarantee of international contracts. Our guarantees are always enforced. A government cannot be sued in any court unless it wishes to be. It can always escape an agreement it no longer cares for, or defy an International Court award it does not like. INTERSECS takes no part in the negotiation of contracts, and never guarantees any agreement unless asked by the governments concerned,

but our guarantees are known to be reliable. You threaten more than the interests of OCEANIQUE and your economy. You threaten the structure of international trade."

"Then it is time that rotten structure is destroyed. There is no place for such as you among sovereign governments. There is no more to discuss."

"A-N-Y-T-H-I-N-G A-T A-L-L INTERROGATIVE URGENT."

"NOTHING WE CAN USE."

Doyle stood slowly. He had been thoroughly searched before entering the Casa Rosada, of course; but even the best detection equipment cannot find a weapon whose nature is unsuspected. "I remind you, *Coronel,* that it is to the interest of every government that the great corporations believe contracts will be enforced. I am sorry we cannot act as reasonable men." Enoch looked casually around the room and fixed his attention on a wall plaque. "Very nice."

Ortiz looked around. As he did, Enoch's hands came together and applied pressure to his class ring. The stone fell out. The exposed part of the stone was hermetically sealed, as had been the back side until now. As he left the office, the volatile back of the stone began to sublimate.

The plane winged across the Atlantic toward Zurich.

Another small scar on my conscience, Doyle thought. In the old days, gunboats might have bombarded Argentine ports, and marines landed to collect Argentine customs duties until all payments were satisfied. Certainly we are more *civilized* than in the old days.

The phone buzzed insistently. Enoch lifted it. "Superintendent Doyle."

"We found it, Boss," his assistant said. "Trouble was, there were name changes involved. We had to feed Ortiz's fingerprints into the system. Here it goes.

"ORTIZ, JESUS MARIA, DEFINITELY INDENTI-FIED AS JESUS MARIA RUIZ, ORPHAN AT SANTA YNEZ CONVENT BHIA BLANCA. AT AGE TWELVE RUIZ APPLIED FOR ADMISSION TO INTERSECS ACADEMY. REJECTED.

MARGINAL ACADEMIC TEST SCORES AND PSY-CHO DOWN-CHECK DIAGNOSIS RIGID PERSON-ALITY. REAPPLIED AGE SEVENTEEN REJECTED ACADEMIC TEST SCORES SATISFACTORY BUT PERSONALITY DIAGNOSIS UNCHANGED. ADD HOSTILITY TO INTERNATIONAL CORPORATIONS PARTICULARLY INTERSEC. HOSTILITY WAS CON-CEALED AND SUBJECT POSSIBLY UNAWARE AT CONSCIOUS LEVEL.

ENTERED ARMY AS JESUS MARIA ORTIZ PRO-MOTED SERGEANT POSTED TO MILITARY ACAD-EMY ARGENTINA. BACKGROUND RECORDS FALSIFIED, REASONS UNKNOWN. GRADUATED UPPER QUARTER OF CLASS NO OUTSTANDING HONORS.

EMPLOYEE MALVINAS STATION HERNANDO RUIZ NOW SERVING 5TH YEAR OF 9–YEAR SEN-TENCE FOR DESTRUCTION OF COMPANY PROP-ERTY AND MAN-SLAUGHTER WHILE UNDER INFLUENCE OF ALCOHOL DEFINITELY IDEN-TIFIED AS BROTHER OF JESUS MARIA RUIZ AKA ORTIZ."

✕   ✕   ✕

"That's enough. Thank you," Enoch said. So it was

there all the time. Personal hatred for INTERSECS. With good reason. A twelve-year-old kid told he wasn't good enough to get citizenship with an international, he'd have to make do with the country he was born in. Tried again, rejected again. Then his brother jailed . . .

"Have somebody review the Hernando Ruiz case," Doyle said. "We owe him that much."

But it's too late for Jesus Maria Ortiz, Doyle thought. Perhaps I could have made a bargain with him if I'd known about his brother. Probably not. But Colonel Ortiz would already be in a mental hospital now, with all the symptoms of paranoid schizophrenia.

The drug was temporary, but the effects on Ortiz would be permanent. He'd never be trusted with authority again. "How's Van Hartmann doing with the junta?" Enoch asked.

"OK. We'll have to make a few concessions, but they'll bargain."

"Right." Enoch Doyle gently replaced the phone. In a few hours he'd be in Zurich, and after that the slopes of Mont Blanc. His face was expressionless as he stared at the dark waters of the Atlantic far below.

High Justice

His name was Aeneas MacKenzie, he was thirty-eight years old, and his life no longer had a purpose. He was skilled in the law and could easily join some firm where he could spend his life protecting the wealth of clients he detested; and he thought it would be better if a Mafia contract, or a CIA termination order, prevented that.

Either rescue was possible, but neither was very likely. He was no longer a threat to the Mafia, no matter that he had done them much harm in the past. Revenge was seldom profitable. His murder might create problems and alive he was no problem to them at all.

There was a better chance that a professional would be sent from the Agency. Aeneas would be a threat to President Gregory Tolland as long as he lived. Aeneas knew there were dedicated and loyal men who would make any sacrifice to protect the President; the man who killed him might be Aeneas' friend. Tears would not spoil his aim; they would not have made Aeneas miss.

Melodrama, he told himself. And yet: Aeneas Mac-Kenzie had destroyed a President. Years of corruption had been swept away by Greg Tolland and his dedicated young man; but then Aeneas had traced the tentacles of the Equity Trust right into the anteroom of the White House. His grand jury had emptied the Executive Office of the President as efficiently as plague. Neither Equity Trust nor President Tolland would ever forgive that, but for different reasons. Tolland was honest. Aeneas believed that still.

"Why?" the President had demanded. "You've been with me for sixteen years, Aeneas. You elected me! Why did you do this to me?"

"When you made me Solicitor General, you ordered me to clean house. Duty and honor, Greg. Remember?" And Aeneas had writhed at the pain in Tolland's eyes, but his gaze never wavered, and his face never lost the grim, dedicated stare that had become familiar to every American with a TV set.

"You could have told me first, Aeneas. We could have worked quietly. God Almighty, did you think I was part of that? But now you've ruined me. The people have no confidence in me—three more years I'll be in this office, and the people hate me. Do you know exactly what you've done?"

And Aeneas wanted to shout that he did, but he said nothing.

"You've robbed the young people of their birthright. You took away their confidence. You've told the people of this nation that there's no one they can trust, and probably assured the election of that gang of crooks we spent all our lives trying to break. . . . You could have come to me, Aeneas."

"No. I tried that. I couldn't see you, Greg. I couldn't get past that barrier you built. I tried."

"But not hard enough. I should have known better than to trust a fanatic. . . . Get out of here, Aeneas. Just leave."

And Aeneas had walked away, leaving his only friend sitting in the Oval Office with his plans in ruin.

But with the country no better off, Aeneas told himself bitterly. We have no goals beyond comfort. The people are decadent and expect corruption. You have to rub their faces in dirt before they get upset. Then, of course, *then* they demand blood; but how much of their righteous indignation comes from guilt? How much is sorrow because no one ever offered them a price?

The jet began its gut-wrenching descent into La Paz. Below were the sparkling colors of the Sea of Cortez, dark blue for deep water, lighter blue in the shallows, the brilliant white of the shores; incredible reds where the coral reefs were close to the surface, creamy white wakes in the great bay where ships endlessly came and went. Beyond the bay was the sprawl of a city, ugly, filthy, but *alive*, growing and feeling greatness.

"The harbor is large enough to hold all the navies of Christendom," the conquistadores had reported to the king of Spain; and it was all of that. Giant cargo vessels, tramp steamers, ferry boats from the mainland; ships everywhere. Industries had sprouted around the bay, and great haciendas with red-tiled roofs dominated the heights of Espiritu Santo Island. Railroads snaked north to the Estados Unidos del Norte, that colossus which so

dominated Mexican thoughts and so thoroughly dominated the Mexican economy. . . .

Only not this time. Aeneas smiled bitterly. That had
been one of his defeats. The miracle of Baja California
was wrought by a power independent of the United
States . . . or of Mexico, or anyone else.

It was hot on the runway. The airport, rebuilt when
the expansion began, was still too small; and there was
a bewildering variety of temporary sheds. MacKenzie felt
heat rising from the runway to meet the hot sun from
above; in August the trade winds do not blow in La Paz.
He saw the high-rising buildings, but he remembered
another Baja and another La Paz. It was all long ago,
and the boy and girl who had struggled over rutted dirt
roads, dove in the clean blue waters among crimson reefs
and darting fish, camped under bright tropical
stars—they were gone like the cobblestone streets.

"*Señor? Señor* MacKenzie?"

The man wore expensive clothing, and there was the
bulge of a pistol beneath the embroidered shirt which
hung loose below his belt. He displayed a badge: not the
serpent and eagle of Mexico, but the design of Hansen
Enterprises. Not far away were men in uniform and
weapons belts, both the khaki of the Mexican police and
the light blue of Hansen service. Aeneas smiled ruefully.
Getting Mexican permission to have her own police on
duty at La Paz airport must have taxed even Laurie
Jo's ingenuity; but little she did surprised him now.

"The *Doña* Laura Hansen regrets that she could not
meet your aircraft, and asks that you come with me," his
guide said. "She is inside the terminal." He led the way
through Customs so quickly that Aeneas wasn't sure they
had passed them; and that was strange, because now

that *los turistas* were not Baja's only source of income, Americans were none too popular here.

The terminal was a maze of marble and concrete and wooden scaffolds and aproned workmen, art treasures, and unfinished masonry blended in a potpourri of sights and smells like every expanding airport, but different. Aeneas wasn't sure how, the differences were subtle, but they were there: in the attitudes and postures of the workmen, in the quality of the work, even the smells of the paint.

Pride, Aeneas thought. They have pride in what they are building. The nation has pride and so do these craftsmen; and we've lost all that.

They went upstairs and through one of the unmarked doors that seem to be standard features at airports. Suddenly they were in a luxurious VIP lounge: and she was there.

Aeneas stood silently looking at her. Her hair was red now; it had been red when he knew her before, but most of her recent pictures showed her as a blonde. Not terribly pretty, but yes, more beautiful than she'd been when he knew her. Filled out. She'd always been very thin. She still was, but it was graceful now, and more feminine. Proper exercises and the most expensive clothes in the world wouldn't make a plain girl beautiful, but there were few women who wouldn't be improved by them.

He knew she was only two years younger than he was, but she looked ten years younger. Money had done that.

His guide stood embarrassed as they looked wordlessly at each other. "*Señor* MacKenzie, *Doña* Laura. Or—he led me to believe he was the *Señor* MacKenzie." He put his hand very close to his pistol, and he eyed Aeneas warily.

Her laugh was as fresh as when they'd come out of the waters of Bahia Concepcion to lie on the beach. "'*Sta bien*, Miguel. *Gracias*."

Miguel looked from Aeneas to his *patrona*, and backed toward the door. "*Con su permission, Doña* Laura."

She nodded, and he left them alone in the elegant room. A jet thundered off the runway outside, but there was no sound here. There was nothing he could hear except his own heart, and the memory of her laugh erased sixteen years of defenses. The heart pounded loudly, and hearts can break, despite what surgeons say. Aeneas knew.

"Hello, Laurie Jo."

She moved toward him, and he hoped she would come to him; yet he prayed that she wouldn't—not again. It was long forgotten, and better so. "You wanted me *Doña* Hansen?"

"I've always wanted you with me, Aeneas. I thought this time you'd burned so many bridges you'd have to come."

"And you were right. I've no place left."

"You should have stayed with me. What have you accomplished with your crusades?" She saw the pain in his eyes. "No. I didn't mean that. Will you believe me when I say that I wish I'd been wrong? I've always wished I'd been wrong about Greg Tolland." She turned and swept a hand around the paneled room. "I'm forgetting my manners. Is there anything I can get you? A drink? You—I wish you wouldn't stand there with that suitcase."

So she remembered that too. That was how he'd stood the last time; but it hadn't been in an ornately paneled room with deep carpets, only the cheap student apartment in Los Angeles that they'd shared. And how does she remember those days, when she wasn't *Doña* Laura Hansen, and we sang and made love and hitchhiked around the country? . . . "What did you have in mind, Laurie Jo? What does Hansen Enterprises have for me?"

"Anything, Aeneas. Anything you'll take."

And she meant it, he knew. But the offer wasn't as generous as it seemed: she wouldn't attach any strings, but his daemon would. It was the only public story about him that was completely true: Aeneas MacKenzie, the man who never accepted a job he wouldn't do, the single-minded robot who'd sacrifice everything to duty. . . .

"If you don't want a drink, we should be leaving," she said. "We're due in Cabo San Lucas in three hours, and that's two hundred kilometers . . . but you know that."

"I know that."

It was all changed. There had been a paved road south from La Paz to Cabo San Lucas for as long as Aeneas could remember, but it had been the only one in lower Baja; now there were dozens. The city of Todos Santos was sending out tentacles onto the surrounding hills, and there were no longer burros on dirt roads; now, huge trucks loaded with agricultural products roared past.

"But there are still horses," Laurie Jo told him. "Horses with great leather saddles and silver trim, and the vaqueros ride them proudly. . . . Remember when we thought how grand it would be if every rancher had a fine horse and saddle? Now they all do."

"And you did that."

"And I did that."

But at what a cost, Aeneas said silently. What price a proud and honest culture? A way of life? But it was a way of life that included disease and early death, children carrying well water in buckets because there wasn't enough money for piping and pumps, and the withe and mud houses with palm thatch roofs were very quaint and kind to the ecology, but they didn't keep the bugs from gnawing the children at night. . . .

Now those were gone. Concrete block, poured concrete, aluminum roofs, floors of concrete and not dirt, screen doors—they had come to Baja. And the children sang in schoolyards, and they were healthy, and the land was dying as land always dies when desert is irrigated.

"They're mining the soil, Laurie Jo. It can't last, and you know it."

She nodded. They drove smoothly on black pavement past straight green furrows of cotton and soybeans; once they had come here in a Jeep, and the land had been chaparral and sentinel cactus and incredibly thin cattle whose bones jutted out as if they were dying, but they weren't, they were a hardy breed who could live on the scrub brush. . . . "It can't last, but *something* can. We've brought hope and progress, and we'll see that—" but she couldn't finish and he knew why. There was no cure for dead soil but time; and these people's grandchildren would live among strangers. Not even Hansen Enterprises could keep Baja fertile for more than a few generations.

"Remember this grade?" she asked. Miguel drove the big Cadillac smoothly so that it hardly faltered; but they had babied the Jeep up that rocky hill with its interminable switchbacks, some so narrow that the rear of the car hung far out over the edge as they reversed to ease around the sharp turns.

At the top of the rise they saw the end of Baja laid out like a map: the grey Pacific to their right, and beyond land's end a sharp line where the Pacific waters met the bright blue of the Sea of Cortez. Hills along the shore, and the red tile and palm trees of resort hotels everywhere, green oases on the sandy beaches.

The town of Cabo San Lucas was at the very tip of the peninsula: just beyond it were high, rocky hills, and over them the stormy Pacific. The hills curled around a bay that had once been so lovely Aeneas had cried when he saw it.

He could cry again: the bay was choked with ships, and the pueblo was gone, replaced by rows of town houses, high-bay industrial sheds, a city with the heart and soul of Los Angeles in its days of frantic expansion. And north of Cabo, along the Pacific shore, where the water came in cool and clear, were the reactors: domes fifty meters high, twelve of them, each with its attendant blockhouses and power plants and sea-water ponds where the chemicals of the sea were extracted. There was a vast jungle of insulators and spidery cube towers and finned transformers spewing forth a web of thick cables leading to a line of transmission towers marching inland and northward toward La Paz and ultimately the whole 1600 kilometers to the energy-starved United States.

Laurie Jo moved her head in a sidewise jerk, a peculiar tic to her left ear. She'd done that before, and she saw Aeneas looking at her curiously. "Implant," she said. "I was asking for the time. Miguel, take us to the observation tower."

"*Si, Doña* Laura."

"I hadn't known," said Aeneas. "But I should have guessed. How do you ask questions?"

"I merely think them." She indicated a little console in her purse, and a panel at her side in the car. The panel swung down to reveal a computer input console. "My implant is keyed to these, and there's a data link from the car to any of my plants. I've asked them when the next scheduled launchings are, and we're just in time. You've never seen one, have you?"

"Not live." He wanted to think about what she'd told him. The implants weren't common—at over a million dollars each, they wouldn't be. A little transceiver, wired directly into the nervous system, a short-range computer link. Provided that she had access to a transmitter—the one in her purse was very small and could be manipulated without anyone seeing it—Laurie Jo could know everything known to the largest computer net on earth.

She could ask it to solve any equation, look up any dossier, find the commercial strength of any company, and hear the output directly and silently. "That must be useful at board meetings," said Aeneas.

"Yes. Most of my colleagues don't know about it. Will you keep my secret?"

"Of course."

"And my other secrets? If I show you everything, will—will you use it again? Or are your crusades against me ended?" Her eyes were very blue and she was very close; and Aeneas knew what she was doing. She had deliberately driven him over a route they'd taken seventeen years ago, and she'd done her hair the way she had then. The linen suit she now wore wasn't like the jeans and chambray shirts of years past, and she'd never again have the eyes that Laurie Jo Preston had; Laurie Jo Hansen had seen too much. But she could try.

"What would be the point?" Aeneas asked. "I won my crusade. We liberated Jerusalem." And it had been as it must have been for a true knight of the Middle Ages:

how could he rejoice when he saw his comrades wade
in blood to the altar of the Prince of Peace? When he
saw the Chivalry of the West grubbing for lands in the
Kingdom of Jerusalem? "I no longer have weapons to
fight you with."

"It's not enough. Aeneas, I want you to look at what
I've done. I want you to see the choices I have. The *real*
choices, not the theoretical ones. And when you've seen
all that, I want you to join me. But I can't even try to
convince you unless—Aeneas, I owe it to my colleagues
not to bring a spy into their councils."

"I see." And he did see. She had always been as certain
that she was right as he'd been convinced that her way
was wrong; and his way had fallen. He had no duties.
The thought broke over him like one of the great grey
curling rollers from the Pacific. *I have no duties.* It made
him feel alone and uneasy. "I promise. Your secrets
are safe."

"No matter what you see? And no matter what you
decide?"

"Yes." And that was that, as they both knew. Aeneas
cursed himself for allowing his emotions to betray him
. . . but she was Laurie Jo, and she couldn't have changed
that much. She couldn't.

God, let me be able to join her. Let it always be like
this. Because the last two hours have been the happiest
I've had in sixteen years.

The tower overlooked a valley ringed by low hills. A
forest of *cardones*, the great sentinel cactus, marched
down the sides of the hills to the leveled plain below.
Rail lines and huge electric cables snaked through at
either end; the plain was filled with concrete blockhouses

where the power cables terminated. At the end of each blockhouse was a flat mirror a meter in diameter, and they all pointed toward the installation below them where streamlined cylinders squatted on railroad cars.

The spacecraft were two meters in diameter and five times that tall, and as they waited in neat lines for their turn they reminded Aeneas of machine gun ammunition grown swollen and pregnant; but their progeny was not war.

Everyone in the tower had been politely respectful, but harried; now they had no time for visitors. Hansen Enterprises carried no dead weight. There were no explainers, not even when the owner came to watch the operations; perhaps especially when Laurie Jo Hansen was present. Aeneas and Laurie Jo were alone in a small, glass-enclosed room, while below a dozen hard-eyed young men sat at consoles.

A clock ticked off the seconds. "We have to be very precise," she told him. "The MHD engines give us half the power we need, but we have to draw the rest directly from the line. There'll be dimouts all over Baja."

"And it costs," Aeneas said.

"Yes. Three thousand megawatts for an hour. At twenty cents a kilowatt hour."

"But you get part of the power directly."

"From burning hydrogen in old rocket engines and sending it through an MHD system. Yes. But the hydrogen and oxygen have to be made. That part of the operation is less efficient than just taking the power from the line, but we have to do it. We can't take everything off the line when we launch." She looked fondly at the capsules below. "We get a lot for my six hundred thousand dollars, Aeneas. Eighty tons go into orbit in the next hour."

The first of the capsules moved over the embankment enclosing the launch area. A roar from beyond the low hills signaled the beginning of the rocket engines: giant engines, but they lay on their sides, their exhaust directed down ceramic tubes protecting copper coils that drew power directly from the hot gasses.

Aeneas couldn't see the launching mirror below the capsule, but suddenly the spacecraft rose and there was a blinding green beam, a solid rod of light over a meter thick extending from the capsule to the ground. The sound rolled past: two hundred and fifty explosions each second as the laser expanded the air in the parabolic chamber below the capsule, and the air rushed out to propel it upward. The two hundred and fifty-cycle note was oddly musical, but very loud at first, then dying away. The spacecraft soon vanished, but the light stayed on for half a minute, tracking the capsule; then it vanished as well.

The mirrors at each blockhouse pivoted slightly, and a second capsule rose from another launch station. The green light tore through roiled air, and there was a humming roar that vibrated the glass of the observation room until the spacecraft was gone and there was only the silent power of the green light. In the half minute that the second capsule absorbed power, a new spacecraft had been placed on the first launch station. The mirrors pivoted again, and it rose; then another, and another.

The laser launchings had been impressive on TV; live they were unbelievable. The long lines of capsules moved toward the earth and concrete emplacements protecting the launching mirror; they reached them; and seconds later, each capsule vanished at 300 gees, shoved upward by a meter-thick column that was nothing more than light, but which looked like a great green growing plant.

"About a thousand kilograms each?" Aeneas asked.

"Exactly a thousand kilos total weight," she said. "We lose fifty kilos of ablating material. The rest goes into orbit, and that's all payload. Any mass is payload. That's what we need up there, Aeneas, mass, any mass—metal, fuel, gases, tankage, even human wastes. We can convert and modify if we have something to start with."

"And you can launch eighty thousand kilos in one hour . . ."

"Yes. We lose some. Each one of those capsules has to be picked up, somehow. That costs mass. We guide some into rendezvous with *Heimdall,* but they have to go after most. Still it's cheaper this way—once we start launching, the power scheduling's such that it's better to go on for a full hour."

The lines of capsules had ended; now new ones were brought up. These were longer and slimmer than the others; and when they took their places over the launching mirrors, they rose more slowly.

"Ten gees," she said. "Crew capsules. Ten gees for a minute and a half."

"Isn't that close to human tolerance?"

"Not really." Her voice was cold and distant. "I took it. And if I can—"

He finished the thought for her. "Hansen Enterprises employees will damn well have to. Or starve."

"I want no one who goes only for the money."

They watched the three personnel capsules rise; then the trains brought up more of the unmanned thirty-g cargo capsules, and the pregnant machine gun began again. "And this was what it was all for. Your crusade," he said.

Her smile was wistful, full of triumph and regret. "Yes. I'm not proud of all I've done, Aeneas. You've seen La

Paz. Todos Santos. Cabo. Ugly, changed, not what they were when we—not what they were. But the men in Cabo don't go to the mainland looking for work while their families starve. I've done that."

"Yes. You've done that."

"But it was all only fallout, Aeneas. *This* is what it was for. *Heimdall.* The rainbow bridge to the stars! And by God it was worth it! You haven't seen the station, Aeneas. And I want you to."

He said nothing, but he looked out at the launching field. The lasers were off now. The great crippled rocket engines were silent. The power from the reactors was back on line, fed to the Baja industries, to Southern California; to the pumps even now cooling the laser installations. To the water-makers that made Baja fertile, for a while. But all that was incidental, because she hadn't lost the dream they'd shared, a dream she'd learned from him in his anger when America retreated from adventure. . . .

She hadn't lost it. He thought he had, once. Not entirely; but he'd been willing to sacrifice it to a larger dream.

Yet what dream was larger than a bridge to the stars?

"And now what?" he asked.

"You've seen what I've done. You don't know what I do to keep it."

"And?"

"And when you do—when you know everything that's happened in the last sixteen years—we'll talk. Not until then." And her eyes were on his, and he saw the hunger and the loneliness, and he prayed to a God he'd half forgotten that it wasn't just a reflection of his own.

✕   .   ✕   ✕

They flew high over the Pacific. There were no luxuries in this aircraft; Aeneas and Laurie Jo sat uncomfortably in bucket seats over the wing, and Miguel sat far behind them. Neither the pilot nor the air crew paid them any attention. The pilot was not pleased to have them aboard, no matter that the plane belonged to Laurie Jo Hansen.

Two armed jets flew high above them. They bore the markings of Hansen Enterprises and were registered in Mexico; and the bribes required to keep permission for a private air force were as staggering as the cost of operating them.

"Why?" Aeneas asked, pointing to the slim black delta shapes above.

"Pirates," she said. "Each capsule holds a thousand kilos of cargo." She took papers from her briefcase and handed them to him. "Computer chips, four thousand dollars a kilo. Water-maker membranes, six thousand dollars a kilo if we'd sell them. We won't until we've enough for ourselves. Concentrated vitamins, forty-five hundred dollars a kilo. And other things. Chemicals, vaccines. Some not for sale at any price."

The value of each capsule in the current drop was nearly seven million dollars. Even in these inflated times that was enough money to make a man wealthy for life. And there would be no problem selling the cargo. . . .

"But how would pirates find them?" he asked. "You can bring them down anywhere in the world."

"They can be tracked. So can my recovery planes. The NORAD radar system watches us very closely."

"But they don't give information to pirates! Not anymore! I put a stop to that sort of thing!" ·

"Did you, Aeneas? For a while, after Greg became President, the losses stopped; but they started again. Do you want proof?"

"No." She'd never lied to him. "How long have you had proof? Why didn't you tell someone?"

"Who'd listen? Greg Tolland is President of the United States."

"Why didn't you tell me?"

She was silent for a long time. There was only the thunder of the jet, and the chatter of the crew as they watched for the cargo capsules to parachute down from orbit. Finally: "What would I have been to you if I'd given you the proof about Greg, Aeneas? If I'd done that, I'd have lost you forever."

And the White House itself had become the abattoir of his dreams. . . . "We fought you, Laurie Jo. I fought you. I think it gave Greg a perverted satisfaction to have me as his general against you. But—was he right? Laurie Jo, should power like yours exist?"

"Without power, none of this would happen. You can't do anything without power."

"Yes." They'd been through it before, endlessly. "But it must be responsible power! It must be directed for—"

"For what, Aeneas? Something trite, like 'the betterment of mankind'? Who chooses the goals? And how do you see the choice is kept, once made? Responsible, Aeneas? To the people? You tried that."

And that was the new thing in their eternal argument. Before, there had always been Greg Tolland and his People's Alliance. There had been the hope that power would be controlled. Could be controlled.

"Greg was right, you know," she said. "Power like mine can't be neutral. It must be used or it dissipates.

He assumed that because I wasn't with him, I was against him—and he was right."

"Or made himself right—" The plane banked sharply and there were shouts. They ducked low to see out forward between the pilots; and far ahead was an orange billow in the sky.

The plane moved swiftly. Hatches opened behind them, and a hook on a long cable trailed out. It caught the shrouds with a jolt perceptible even in that large ship; then the motors sang as the cable was reeled in.

The plane banked onto a new course toward the next parachute. There would be five in all.

"We don't dare miss," she said. "If one of them falls into the sea, there'll be swarms of ships and planes out to get it, and we can't do anything about it. Salvage, the courts call it."

"My doing. It seemed right at the time. I—The enemy was Hansen Enterprises, not you. But why the fighters?"

"To keep this plane from being shot down. There's too little time for the Equity people to get to the capsules before we do. They don't know when and where they're coming down until the retros fire. But there's enough time to intercept my recovery planes."

Her voice was without drama, but Aeneas was startled. "Who flies the interceptors, Laurie Jo?"

"They don't have any markings. Somehow the ships that salvage my wrecked planes always belong to Equity or one of their dummies; but the interceptors are unmarked. I doubt they'll bother this time. We're close to Mexico, and the cargo's only worth thirty-five million dollars."

Only thirty-five million. Not so very much to Hansen Enterprises. But more than enough to buy souls. Most had a far lower price. "And NORAD tells them where to look?"

"Sometimes. Other governments too. Greg Tolland will help any enemy of mine. Look at the situation with Peru and Ecuador. They steal my cargoes with the help of the United States." She was bitter now. The national claims to space above and water beyond the small countries her satellites and cargo drops passed through had been rejected by every international authority: until Greg Tolland had used the power of the United States. "It would have been different if I'd stayed with you."

How different, he wondered. Sixteen years ago: she'd been Laurie Jo Preston, then. An orphan girl, with memories of her mother living far beyond the income she made as a night-club entertainer. And her mother had died, and Laurie Jo knew only a succession of governesses paid by bankers; and a trust fund that dictated what schools she would attend, what courses she would take. At first the bankers ruled her life; but they interfered with her very little after she was sixteen. They'd met at UCLA, the shy girl with her mysterious bankers and no parentage; Aeneas, already consumed with the daemon that drove him to change the world; and Greg Tolland, a young California Congressman with a political heritage that might someday take him to the White House, if he could keep his seat in Congress.

At first, Greg Tolland had worked very hard for his election; but after Aeneas MacKenzie became his field deputy and manager, Tolland did not need to campaign any longer. They had won their second election together when Laurie Jo came into Aeneas's life.

Two years. Two years she'd lived with Aeneas. The bankers didn't care. No one did. They traveled, and sang, and drank too much, and made love too little, and one day the bankers came to say that her name was Hansen, not Preston, and to tell her she had inherited control of the greatest fiscal empire on earth.

Aeneas had gasped at the size of her fortune. All through the day they'd sat at the battered kitchen table of his apartment and looked at the marvels she owned. Greg Tolland flew back from Washington to join them: and came the disaster.

"It must be broken up, of course," Aeneas had said. "It's exactly what's wrong with the world—irresponsible power like that. Economic imperialism."

"I'm not so sure," Greg Tolland had said., "Think of what we can do with a fortune like that. What the People's Alliance can do. Aeneas is right, it's too much power; but we shouldn't be too hasty in deciding."

"I won't be," Laurie Jo said. They looked at her in surprise. "I don't understand what power like this means; but before I use it, I will."

That was the beginning. Greg Tolland saw her fortune as the ladder to short-cut the long road to the White House. Aeneas saw it as the kind of power no person should have. Laurie Jo Preston had no opinions. She'd always agreed with Aeneas. But Laurie Jo Hansen was otherwise.

"Greg only despises power he can't control," she said later. "He'll let me keep mine to use for him. No. I won't break up Hansen Enterprises, and I won't help Greg Tolland gather all power into government."

"Where it will be used for the people!" Aeneas protested.

"Where it will be used. How is not as obvious as that it would exist."

"What do you mean?"

"You want to build something so powerful that nothing can oppose it and hand it over to Greg Tolland. Aeneas, I've always thought you could do that. I've never laughed at your abilities. And I've been terrified every day that you'd succeed."

"You've helped me!"

"Yes. I love you. And I've told myself that by staying with you, I'd have some control over what you two will do when you've won. Now I've got something more substantial."

"You'll fight Greg?"

"No. Unless he deserves it. But I won't help him, either."

And then had come the terrible words. That she saw things differently now that she was rich. That she'd got hers, and to hell with their dreams . . .

The plane banked sharply, bringing him from his reverie. "You chose Greg Tolland," she said. "I couldn't."

He shook his head. "I chose—what? My country? I always thought so." And how must the true knights have felt when their crusade succeeded, and they saw the actuality, not the dreams? Was it true that some went to the Saracens because they had no place else to go?

When the plane landed near Cabo San Lucas, Miguel drove them to the Hansen hacienda. He seemed to go everywhere with Laurie Jo. Inside she said, "Miguel is nearly the only man I trust. He guards me well."

"*Con mi vida, Doña* Laura."

"You will protect this man the same way."

"*Si, Doña* Laura."

She left, and they stood in the low-ceilinged library, Aeneas and Miguel, and Aeneas looked at him for the first time. He seemed vaguely familiar, but he looked like any Baja rancher with an ageless, lined face that could be forty or sixty.

"Welcome, *Don* Aeneas," Miguel said.

Aeneas frowned. "I ask for no titles."

"Those who do do not often deserve them. It would be enough that *Doña* Laura says you are a good man; but I have reason to know. You do not remember me, *Don* Aeneas."

"No."

"It was here. Within a kilometer. You gave me a shotgun."

"Oh—the vaquero. You helped us with the Jeep."

"Si. You never returned. There was no reason why you should. But Doña Laura came here the year after you left, and I have been with her ever since."

"And why the titles?"

Miguel shrugged. "I prefer to serve those I believe may deserve them. I have no education, *Don* Aeneas. I am not a man who benefits from schools. But my sons will never row boats for drunken Americans."

"I see."

"I hope you see. My sons tell me I am a peasant, and they are right. They will not be peasants, and I am happy for them. I hope they will be as happy in their work as I am."

"I of all people should understand, Miguel." Aeneas found the bar and poured a tall drink for himself. Miguel accepted beer. They drank deeply. "She does many things she cannot be proud of?" Aeneas asked.

Miguel spread his hands. "You must ask her."

"I have."

Another shrug. "Some men take pride in acts that make others die of shame. Power like hers must not be judged by men like me."

"But it must be!" Aeneas shouted.

Miguel shrugged and said nothing.

The weeks passed. Aeneas learned that Hansen Enterprises reached places even he'd never suspected. Mines, factories, shipping—everywhere she was entangled with other international firms in enterprises so scattered that no one could ever understand them all. Most were operated by managers, and she saw only summaries of results; and even those took time she barely had.

"You'll kill yourself," Aeneas said.

"I don't work any harder than you did."

"No." But *I worked for—for what?* The memory of those years was slipping away from him. He recalled the fanatical young man he'd been, but he saw him almost as a stranger. *I have no duties,* he told himself. *I can relax.* But he could not. He buried himself in her reports.

"Why do you do it?" he asked another time. "Bribes to keep your mines open. Your agents block labor legislation, or bribe officials not to enforce the laws. . . ."

"Do you think they are good laws? Do you like this fine net of regulations that is settling over the earth?"

He had no answer to that. "Why do you do it?" he asked again. "You'll never need money. You couldn't spend what you have if you devoted your life to it."

"*Heimdall* absorbs everything. . . ."

"It makes money too!"

"Does it?" she asked. "Barely. Aeneas, even I couldn't have built the power plants. I don't own them, I'm only part of a syndicate. Without the power plants we can't launch, and it takes nearly everything I make to keep up the interest payments on those power installations."

He looked closer at the reports, then, and saw that it was true. Between the power plants and the laser launchers there was so much capital investment that it wouldn't be paid off for fifty years. There were other places the syndicate could have invested its money, operations with a far higher immediate profit; and Laurie Jo had to make up the difference. If she ever failed, she'd lose control.

"Now do you see?" she asked. "In the long run, *Heimdall* has a greater potential than any investment ever made; but it took so much capital—"

"You're at the thin edge," Aeneas said wonderingly. "It wouldn't take much and you'd lose all this."

"Yes. I'd be a very rich lady; but I wouldn't be Laurie Jo Hansen any longer. I wouldn't have the power."

Without the power of Hansen Enterprises—what?

"*Heimdall* would still exist. It's already profitable. It would ruin your partners to shut it down."

"Certainly. Or they can sell it. Who would you like to see have it, Aeneas? A hundred nations would like to own my bridge to the stars. The United States perhaps? The Equity Trust? Another company? It would be damn easy to get out from under all this and enjoy myself again!" She had become shrill; but whether because of regret at what she'd paid to hold this empire, or terror at the thought of losing it, Aeneas didn't know. He thought it was both. "There's more," she said. "You've seen the books."

"Yes. You're investing in expansions of *Heimdall*. Sending up mass instead of taking out profits."

She smiled. He hadn't spent long examining her accounts; but he hadn't disappointed her. "Have you wondered why I built the launching station in Baja?" she asked. "It wasn't just sentiment, or politics. We're on a Tropic—and that makes it easier to launch into an ecliptic orbit. Heimdall was the god who guarded the bridge to the stars, but my *Heimdall* will build one!"

He looked up in wonder. "Where are you sending them?" he asked.

"Not sending. Going. An interplanetary explorer ship. And a Moon colony. A Moon colony can be self-supporting. It can support exploration of the other planets. It will be free of Earth and everything here!"

"Even you don't have that much money."

"I will have. *Heimdall* will make it for me."

"But you're very near losing it. Your deliveries are behind schedule. Haven't you risked everything on some shaky technology?"

The terror crept around her eyes again, but her voice was firm. She had no regrets. "I had to. And it wasn't technology that failed me. Aeneas, how do you keep discipline in space?"

"I never thought about it—how does any company control workers? Hire people who like to work, and pay them well to do it."

"And if someone pays agents to sabotage your factories? There are no laws in space, Aeneas. Captain Shorey has managed to keep things under control, but only barely. Most of our people are loyal—but some others slip through, and the worst we can do to them is send them down without pay. Suppose they've been offered higher pay to make mistakes aboard *Heimdall?* What can I do to them? Mexican courts won't prosecute non-Mexicans for crimes in space. American courts won't prosecute at all without trials and witnesses. If I have to send half a crew down to sit around a courtroom for years, I'm ruined anyway."

She came to the window next to him and looked out into the night. "But we're winning. We will win. *Heimdall. Valkyrie.* The Moon and planets, Aeneas. And now you know it all."

They were in the hacienda atop Finisterre, the rocky hills that overlook the town of Cabo San Lucas. On one side were the lights of the town; on the other, grey water with flashing fluorescent whitecaps. Ships moved in the harbor even this late at night, and factory lights were ablaze below.

Out beyond, in the dark of the inland hills, a green light stabbed upward; more capsules fired into orbit, raw materials for the factories in the satellite, structural materials for expansion, fuel, oxygen, the expendables that ate so much profit despite recycling. The sun was long over the horizon and *Heimdall* wouldn't be visible; but soon it would be coming overhead. The supply pods were always as close to the satellite as her engineers dared.

"It's time for our talk, then," Aeneas said. "Is there anything to talk about? You're what I've opposed all my life."

"Yes. But you love me. And if you fight me—who are you fighting *for*?"

He didn't answer.

"I love you, Aeneas. I always have, and you've always known it. Tell me what to do."

"Will you—would you throw all this away if I asked you to?"

"I don't know. Will you ask it? Remember, Aeneas. You can't destroy power. You can fragment mine, but someone else will move into the vacuum. Power doesn't vanish."

"No." And she had a dream. A dream that had been his.

"You don't trust me with all this. Would you trust yourself?"

"No."

"Then someone else. Who?"

"No one, of course."

There was no change in her pose or voice, but he sensed triumph.

"Then tell me what I should do," she said.

This time she meant it. He felt that whatever he said, she'd do. She knew him well. She was taking no chances, because she knew what he must say. Forty billion dollars was ten dollars for every human on Earth—or the key to the planets. "I can't."

"Then join me. I need you."

"Yes."

There were no longer barriers, and sixteen years vanished as if they'd never been.

For a week there were only the two of them—and Miguel, silent, invisibly near. They slipped away from Cabo San Lucas and its power plants and factories, to find still lonely beaches where they swam to brilliant coral reefs. Afterwards they made love on the sand and desperately tried to forget the years they'd wasted.

One week and a little more; and then the phones in the camper buzzed insistently and they had to return.

She told him what she could as they drove back. "Captain Shorey has been all the authority I have up there," she said. "The station depends on the ground launching system to survive, but there's nothing I can do to control it."

"You think there's mutiny on *Heimdall?*" Aeneas asked incredulously.

"I don't know. I only know Shorey is dead, and Herman Eliot says he can't meet the manufacturing schedule. Without the finished goods from the station I can't pay the syndicate. I'll lose *Heimdall.*"

There would be any number of people who might benefit from that. With over a hundred men and women in space, the odds were good that several organizations had agents aboard the satellite factory complex. "How do you select crew for *Heimdall?*" Aeneas asked.

The Jeep camper bounced across rutted roads toward the main highway. Ten kilometers ahead they'd meet a helicopter.

"I try to pick them myself," she said. "The pay is good, of course. Almost two hundred thousand dollars at the end of a two-year tour in space. We have plenty of volunteers, but not just for the money. I choose generalists, adaptable people, and I try to keep a balance between the intellectuals and factory people. There's a lot of construction work, and production runs mean repetitive labor that bores the big brains. I also look for people who might want to go on to the Moon colony, or be crew aboard *Valkyrie.* So far it's worked, but Captain Shorey was the key to it. Now he's gone."

"Tell me about Herman Eliot."

"He's been second in command. A mechanical genius. He's in charge of production and research."

"Do you think he's loyal to you?"

"I'm almost sure of it. He wants to go with *Valkyrie.* But he didn't tell the ground station much. Maybe he'll tell me directly. Aeneas, if I don't keep the manufacturing schedule, I'll lose the station and everything else!" She was near panic; and he'd never seen her frightened before. It upset him more than he'd thought possible.

The Jeep bounced through a dust bowl laced with a myriad of ruts. Wind blew a torrent of fine powder across the windshield, and Miguel had to start the wipers to remove it. The dust ran like rivulets of water.

Dr. Herman Eliot was nervous. It came through in his voice as he reported to Laurie Jo. "We have a nasty situation up here, Miss Hansen. Captain Shorey was murdered and the crew knows it. There's been sabotage all along, now this. Some of the engineers are saying that the Equity Trust is going to gain control of this satellite, and they'll remember who their friends were. There's even talk that people who won't help the Equity cause will be stranded, or have accidents on reentry."

"Tell them Equity will never control *Heimdall!*" Laurie Jo shouted into the microphone.

"I can tell them, but will they believe it? I repeat, Miss Hansen, Captain Shorey was murdered, and we all know there's no chance the killer will be punished. Who's next?"

"Do you know who did it?"

"I'm fairly sure it was an engineer named Martin Holloway."

"If you know he killed the captain, why don't you do something?" Laurie Jo demanded.

"Do what? I'm no policeman. Suppose we put Holloway under arrest. Then what? We have no jails here, and there's no court that will take jurisdiction over him. I doubt he was the only man involved in this; what if he won't go when I order him down? It could start a mutiny. The crew thinks Equity will gain control here; nobody wants that, but there aren't many who'll risk their necks for a lost cause."

"If you meet the delivery schedules, I keep *Heimdall!* Don't they know that?"

"If you were only fighting the Equity Trust, Miss Hansen, we could believe you'd win. But not against the United States as well."

She was silent for a long time. Since the United States had thrown away her investments in space, or had them stolen and sold out by corruption, *Heimdall* had been the key to regaining that position. . . . "Will you try?" she asked.

"I'll do what I can," Eliot said. The speaker went dead.

Tears welled at the corners of Laurie Jo's eyes, but her voice was firm. "I'll go up there myself with a squad of company police!"

Aeneas shook his head. "If things are that bad, they won't even meet your capsule; you can't afford to provoke an open break. Besides, you have to stay here. No one else can control your partners. With you out and away up there you'd certainly lose the station."

"Then what will I do?"

Aeneas drew in a deep breath and let it out slowly. It was time to repay the Saracens for their hospitality. . . . "Send up Holloway's file, to begin with. Let's see who we're up against."

He took out the photographs of Martin Holloway as Laurie Jo began to read. "Five feet eleven inches, 175 pounds, hair brown, eyes green, graduated from—"

"It will be lies," Aeneas said. "His name is David Hindler."

"You know him?" Laurie Jo asked.

Aeneas smiled wistfully. "Long ago. Before Greg was President. You remember that Greg's enemies tried to have him killed. . . . David was very valuable then. He saved my life." And I his; we have no debts to each other. But once there was a bond . . . "Dr. Eliot implies that the Equity Trust is behind your difficulties. David is Greg Tolland's man. He wouldn't kill for anyone else."

She said nothing, but there was concern in her eyes; not hatred for Tolland, although that was deserved; but sorrow because she knew the pain Aeneas must now feel. He could never convince himself that Greg Tolland hadn't known. . . .

"Have your people make me a space suit and whatever else I'll need," Aeneas said.

Hope came to her—then it was gone. "You've never been in space. How can you stay alive there?"

"I'm a careful man, Laurie Jo. And I think I see what must be done."

"But I just found you again! It isn't fair, not so soon."

"I'll be back," he promised. "You've always meant to go out with *Valkyrie*. How can I go with you without experience? Have you anyone else you can trust with this?"

"No."

"I'll be back. Soon."

Ten gravities for ninety seconds is easily within the tolerance of a healthy man; but Aeneas had no wish to prolong the experience. He was laid flat on his back in a nylon web, encased in baggy reflective coverall and under that a tight garment resembling a diver's wet suit. The neckseal and helmet were uncomfortable, and it was an effort to exhale against the higher pressures in the helmet.

He had thought waiting for the launch the most unpleasant experience he'd ever had: lying awkwardly on his back, with no control of his destiny, enclosed in steel; then the laser cut in.

He weighed far too much. His guts ached. Like the worst case of indigestion imaginable, he thought. There was no way to estimate the time. He tried counting, but it was too difficult, and he lost count somewhere. Surely he had been at eighty seconds? He started over again.

There was noise, the loud, almost musical two-hundred-fifty-cycle tone of the explosions produced as the laser heated the air in the chamber under him—how close? he wondered. That great stabbing beam that could slice through metal aimed directly at him; he squirmed against the high gravity, and the effort was torture.

The noises changed. The explosion tone drifted down the scale. He was beyond the atmosphere, and the laser was boiling off material from the thrust chamber, reaching closer and closer to him—

Silence. The crushing weight was gone. He was falling endlessly, with no way to know. Was he in orbit? Or was he plunging downward to his doom? He closed his eyes to wait, and then he felt he was truly falling, with the sick sensations of a boat in motion—he opened his eyes again to orient himself in the capsule.

Will they pick me up? There was no reason they shouldn't. New crewmen arrived weekly, and he was merely another. He listened for a voice, a signal, anything—

"Hullo, laddie. All right in there?"

Aeneas grabbed for the microphone and pressed the talk switch. "That was one hell of a ride." He fought for control of his voice. "I think I'm all right now."

"Except that you feel like letting the world's record fart, right?" the voice said. "Go ahead. You'll feel better."

He tried it. It helped.

"Hang on there, mate. Be alongside in a minute," the voice said. It took less than that. There were clunks and thuds, and the capsule jarred with some impact. "Righto. You're new in this game, they tell me."

"Yes, very," Aeneas replied.

"Right. So we'll start by testing your suit. I've got a bottle attached to the outlet, crack the atmosphere evac valve a half turn, there's a good chap."

A short moment of panic. The capsule held half an atmosphere. When the capsule was evacuated, only his helmet above the neckseal would contain pressure. The tight garment he wore was supposed to reinforce his own skin so that it would be able to hold the pressure differences, and it had worked in the ground training chamber; but there had been physicians waiting there. Aeneas did as he was told. As the air hissed out, the pressure in his guts returned, but worse.

"Fart again, lad. How's the breathing?"

"All right." He carried out the instruction. Again it helped. It was hard work to breathe out, but there didn't seem to be any problems.

"Good. Open the valve the rest of the way and let's get you out of there." Pumps whirred, and he felt more sensations of internal pressure. The wetsuit was very tight around every part of his body. His heart pounded loudly, and he felt dizzy.

"Now unstrap and open the hatch."

The steel trap around him seemed comfortable and safe compared to what he might find outside. Aeneas gingerly unfastened the straps that held him to the D-frame-webbed bunk and immediately floated free. It took longer than he had thought it would to orient himself and get his feet braced so that he could turn the latches on the hatchway, but Aeneas was surprised to find that he had no trouble thinking of what had been the capsule "wall" as now "down" and the hatchway as "up." The falling sensation vanished as soon as there was something to do.

The man outside hadn't mentioned the tether line on its reel on his belt, but the ground briefing had stressed that before the hatch was open he should clip the tether to the ring by the hatchway. That took fumbling, but he managed it.

The hatch opened smoothly and he put his head outside. There was brilliant sunshine everywhere, and he was thankful for the sun visor and tinted faceplate of his helmet. Crisp shadows, Earth an enormous bulging circular mass of white clouds and blue sea, not below but just there; stars brilliant when he looked away from Earth and sun . . . he had seen the pictures a thousand times. It wasn't the same at all.

He used his hands to rotate himself. There was an odd vehicle about seven meters long at the aft end of the capsule. Its nose was shoved into the capsule thrust chamber, and it reminded Aeneas of dogs. An open framework of thin aluminum bars with—saddles? But why not? A mirrored helmet atop bulky metallic shining coveralls perched on the nearest saddle. Aeneas couldn't see a face inside it.

"One of the ones who listen, eh?" the voice said. "Jolly good. Now you see that line above you?" Aeneas looked up and saw an ordinary nylon rope. It seemed to be a solid rod. "Get hold of it and clip it on your belt. After that, reach inside and unclip your own line. And don't be slow about it." There was a pleasant note to the voice, but it expected to be obeyed.

Aeneas complied quickly. He was reeled very slowly toward the spindly personnel carrier, and with a lot of difficulty and help from the pilot managed to get astride one of the saddles. His feet slipped easily under loops in the thing's "floor"—Aeneas supplied the quotation marks because there was only a minuscule grillwork there—and a safety harness went around his waist.

Now that he was in the carrier, he could look around, and he did unashamedly.

The launch crew had cut it pretty fine, Aeneas told himself. *Heimdall* floated less than a kilometer away.

It looked like a junkyard. Two large curved cylindrical sausages on the ends of cables rotated around each other at a distance of nearly half a kilometer. The sausages had projections at crazy angles: solar cell arrays, shields, heat dissipation projectors connected to the station by piping, antennae. There was an inflated tube running from each cylinder to an amorphous blob between them, and part of the center structure rotated with the cylinders. Most of the center did not rotate.

Other junk—the pregnant machinegun shapes of supply capsules, cylinders of all sizes, inflated structures of no recognizable shape—floated without apparent attachment near the axis of spin. Solar panels and orange sunshades lay everywhere. *Heimdall* had no real form.

"Quite a sight, isn't it?" his companion said. "Name's Kit Penrose, old chap. Officer in charge of everything else. Weight control, atmosphere recycling, support systems, all the marvy things like that. Also the taxi driver. Who're you?"

"MacKenzie."

"Oh, Christ, a bloody Scot. You don't sound one. Engineer?"

Aeneas shrugged, realized the gesture couldn't be seen, and said, "Like you. Little of everything, I suppose. And I'm American."

"American, eh? Whoever or whatever you are, the ground crew seemed worried about you. Well, you're OK. Here we go." He did something to the panel in front of him and the spindly structure moved slowly toward the satellite. His capsule was still attached at the nose. "We'll just take this along, eh?" Penrose said.

"Yes, my kit's in there." And I may need everything in it, Aeneas thought.

It took a long time to cover the short distance to the station. Kittridge Penrose burned as little mass as possible. "Energy's cheap up here," he told Aeneas. He waved carelessly at the solar panels deployed everywhere and at mirrors fifty meters across that floated near the station. The mirrors were aluminized Mylar or something like it, very thin, supported by thin fiberglass wands to give them shape. "Plenty of energy. Not enough mass, though."

As they neared *Heimdall,* it looked even more like a floating junkyard. There was a large cage of wire netting floating a hundred meters from the hub, and it held everything: discarded cargo and personnel capsules, air tanks, crates, and cylinders of every kind. It had no door except an inward pointing cone—an enormous fish trap, Aeneas thought. They headed for that, and when they reached it and killed their approach velocity, Penrose unfastened himself from the saddle and dove into Aeneas' capsule.

He emerged with two sealed cylindrical fiberglass containers of gear Aeneas had brought up and clipped them to the wire net of the cage. He did the same with the spindle vehicle they'd crossed on, then did something that released the personnel capsule from its faintly obscene position on the taxi's nose. Penrose gripped the cage with one hand and strained to shove the discarded capsule with the other.

Nothing seemed to happen. Then the capsule moved, very slowly, down the tube into the cage; the motion was only barely apparent, but Penrose turned away. "Takes care of that. We'll have a crew come take it apart later. Now for you. I'll carry your luggage."

He reached down and pulled the safety line out of the reel on Aeneas' belt and clipped it to his own. "Now you're tethered to me, but if you drift off and I have to pull you in, I'll charge extra for the ride. Follow me, and the trick is, *don't* move fast. Keep it slow and easy."

They pulled themselves across the wire cage. It looked like ordinary chicken wire to Aeneas, a more or less sphere of it a hundred meters in diameter. There were other blobs of wire cage floating around the station. When they got to the side of the cage facing *Heimdall*, Aeneas saw a thin line running from the cage to the nonrotating hub between the cylinders. Up close the rotating cylinders on their cables and inflated tunnel looked much larger than before; twenty meters in diameter, and made of segments, each segment at least twenty meters long. They pulled themselves gingerly along the tether line to an opening ahead.

There was no air in the part of the hub they entered. Penrose explained that the interface between rotating and nonrotating parts was kept in vacuum. Once inside,

Aeneas felt a gentle tug as the long tube, leading to the capsules at the end of the tether line pushed against him until he was rotating with it.

Before Aeneas could ask, Penrose pointed up the tube away from the direction they were going. "Counter-weights up there," he said. "We run them up and down to conserve angular momentum. Don't have to spend mass to adjust rotation every time somebody leaves or comes aboard. Course we have to use mass to stop *our-selves* rotating when we leave, but I've got an idea for a way to fix that too."

As they descended, Aeneas felt more weight; it increased steadily. They passed into the first of a series of multiple airlocks. Then another, and another. "Hell of a lot easier than pumping all this gup every time," Penrose said. "Feel pressure now?"

"A little. It's easier to exhale."

"You could breathe here. Not well." They passed through another set of airlocks and felt increasing weight; after that it was necessary to climb down a ladder. The walls of the silo they were descending were about three meters in diameter. They stood out stiffly from the pressure and seemed to be made of the same rubberized cloth as his pressure suit, but not porous or permeable as his suit was.

Eventually they reached a final airlock, and below that the silo had metallic walls instead of the inflated nylon. The final airlock opened onto a circular staircase and they climbed down that into the cylindrical structure of the station itself.

Dr. Herman Eliot was a thin man, no more than thirty-five years old, with bifocal spectacles and long hair that curled at his neck; it was cut off short in front and at the sides so that it wouldn't get in his eyes, and it was uncombed: a thoroughly careless appearance. He had a harried expression, and his desk was littered with ledgers, papers, books, two pocket computers, and a dozen pencils. There were compartments in the desk for all that gear, but Eliot didn't use them.

Kit Penrose clucked his tongue as they entered. "Sloppy, Herman. Sloppy. Suppose I had to take spin off?"

Eliot looked annoyed. "You'd like to make up production schedules, then?" he demanded. He did not smile.

Penrose did. He recoiled in mock horror. "Easier to keep spin." He pulled off his helmet and turned to Aeneas. "Want some help with that?"

"Thank you." There had been little time for practice with the suit on Earth, but the procedure seemed simple enough; still, there was no harm in getting assistance. Aeneas worked slowly and carefully to undog the helmet and disconnect it from the neckseal. He lifted it off.

Penrose stared. "MacKenzie, eh?" he said sourly. His friendly expression was gone, replaced by a mask of emotional control that couldn't conceal dislike. His voice was strained and overmodulated. "*Aeneas* MacKenzie. If you'd told me that, I'd have left you out there."

Aeneas said nothing.

"He is the owners' agent," Eliot said.

"I doubt it." Penrose curled his lip into a twisted sneer. "I never did believe that lot about his break with Tolland. I think he is another goddam CIA man."

"Then why would Miss Hansen send him?" Eliot asked. His voice and gestures were very precise, in contrast to the litter on his desk.

"Probably had to. Tolland can get to her partners. God knows what kind of deals he's made."

"I do not think anyone has ever accused Aeneas Mac-Kenzie of personal corruption," Eliot said. "Precisely the opposite, in fact."

"I still think he belongs to Tolland." Penrose stalked to the door. "Tolland and MacKenzie tried to break Miss Hansen with legal tricks. That didn't work, so they're trying something else. I'll leave you with your little pet, Herman. Mind he doesn't bite you. And keep these doors closed." He swung the lightweight oval airtight door closed behind him. There were chairs bolted to the deck opposite Eliot's desk. Aeneas sat in one of them. He felt a peculiar sensation each time he moved up or down, but he was growing accustomed to it. Experimentally he took a pencil from Eliot's desk and dropped it to the floor. It followed a lazy, curved arc and landed inches away from where his eye expected it to fall. He nodded to himself and turned to Dr. Eliot. "I don't bite," he said.

"That's about the only thing I know about you, then. Just what are you doing here, Mr. MacKenzie? You're no spaceman."

"Of course not. Was everyone here experienced in space when he first arrived?"

"No. But they had some technical value. We knew what they would do here."

"I will learn whatever is needed." Aeneas spoke dogmatically. There had never been a task he had failed to learn if he had to know it. "I can help with your administrative work now."

"It's only make-work anyway. We aren't likely to last long enough to need work schedules." Eliot turned a pencil slowly in his fingers and gave Aeneas a searching look. "My instructions were to give you complete cooperation. What do you want?"

"You can begin by telling me how Captain Shorey died."

"How he was murdered, you mean." Eliot's face still showed little emotion, but he clinched the pencil in fingers suddenly gone white with strain.

"What makes you so sure he was murdered?"

"Amos Shorey had ten years experience in space. He was found outside—it was only an accident that he was found at all. His faceplate was open. His features were relaxed. That's not the way a spaceman dies, Mr. MacKenzie. Amos was drugged and put out an airlock."

"And Martin Holloway killed him?"

Eliot pursued his lips tightly. "I shouldn't have told Miss Hansen that." He was silent for a moment—"But you'll find out, now that you're here. Yes. I couldn't prove it, but Holloway did it."

"If you can't prove it, how do you know?"

"I have a witness." Eliot's features twisted into an involuntary thin smile—wistful, sad, amused? Aeneas couldn't tell. "And a fat lot of good it'd be taking *her* into a courtroom. Not that Holloway will ever come to trial. Who'd prosecute?"

Aeneas nodded. Mexico wanted no jurisdiction over *Heimdall*. The United States was unlikely to prosecute one of President Tolland's agents—if the victim had been Tolland's man, that would be different. "Send for the witness, please," Aeneas said.

Eliot glanced at the clock above his desk, then at his wristwatch. Crew schedules were posted on the bulkhead, but he didn't seem to need to look at them. "She'll be off duty." He lifted a telephone.

✕   ✕   ✕

The girl wore white coveralls. She had a mass of brown curls, all cut short, and no makeup; but she walked with the grace of a dancer, making use of the low gravity. Her features were finely carved and relaxed into no expression at all, but Aeneas thought that she would have as much control over them as she did of her body. She was very young, possibly no more than twenty, and she didn't need makeup to be pretty. "Ann Raisters," Eliot said. "Ann, this is—"

"I know who he is. If I hadn't recognized him, Penrose has told everyone in the station anyway. Kit Penrose doesn't like you, Mr. MacKenzie. Should anyone?" She cocked her head to one side and smiled, but it didn't seem genuine.

"I'm told you were a witness to the murder of Captain Amos Shorey," Aeneas said.

Ann turned a suddenly expressionless face towards Dr. Eliot. "Why did you tell him that?"

"You told me you were."

"I should have known better," she said. Her voice was bitter. "Occupational disease with whores, Mr. MacKenzie. It's no less lonely for us than for the men who talk to us. Sometimes we make the mistake of thinking we have friends."

"If you were a witness to murder, you should tell about it," Herman Eliot said. "It was your duty to come to me."

The girl laughed. The sound was hard, but it might have been a nice laugh at another time and place. She ignored Eliot as she spoke to Aeneas. "Suppose I did see murder done? So what? Who'd try the case—not that a court would pay much attention to a whore anyway."

"You're registered as a biology technician," Aeneas said.

"Yeah. Mister, there are ninety-three men and twenty-six women on this satellite. Twenty of those women are engineers and technicians and whatever, and they sleep with one man at a time or none at all. Men serve a two-year hitch up here. Now what would happen if my friends and I weren't aboard? There are six whores on this ship. Call me an entertainer if you want to. Or a mother confessor. Or just friendly. I like it better that way. But if I get in front of a jury, I'm a whore."

"You sound rather bitter, Miss Raisters."

"I liked Captain Shorey."

"Do you want this station he gave his life to handed over to the people who hired him killed?"

Her lips tightened. "There's nothing I can do."

"There is. First, I have to know what happened."

"Who the hell are you, Mister? Kit Penrose says you're working for the same outfit that killed Amos. Everybody knows the U.S. government wants to see Equity take control here. I don't know how to fight that combination, Mister."

"Miss Hansen does. Dr. Eliot, tell Miss Raisters your orders concerning me."

Herman Eliot frowned. "Miss Hansen said to give him complete cooperation."

"Tell her the rest."

"Do you think that's wise? All right. She also said that Mr. MacKenzie is in command of this station if he says he is. Are you taking command, then?"

"Not precisely. Now, what did you see, Miss Raisters?"

Ann shrugged. "What difference does it make? You can't do anything about it. I thought I could, but I'm just not a murderer. Neither is Kit. Or Dr. Eliot." Her voice tightened. "That's rich, isn't it, Mister? We don't even have the guts to knock off the bastard who killed our friend. Some of the short-termers might, but what'd happen to them when they went home? They'd be up for it."

"Vengeance murder won't solve the problems of this station," Aeneas said. "You may as well tell me what happened. Everyone else seems to know."

"Yeah. Why not?" She sat across from Aeneas, every movement graceful and lovely, in stark contrast to the angry expression of her eyes. "It started a long time ago. Men get lonesome up here, Mister. They need a girl. Not just a lay, either. It took Marty Holloway longer than most, but he started coming to see me after six months. You will too if you stay long enough. Me or one of the other girls." She looked defiantly at him.

Aeneas said nothing.

"You will. Anyway, after about a year, Holloway starts talking to me a lot. I liked him. He's pretty cheerful and he seemed like a good worker. But he tells me how he's going to be rich when he gets down. Well, what the hell, we all are, but he meant rich and famous. Going to retire from the whole rat race and spend his life hiking in the woods. Maybe buy some mountain land and put together an animal preserve. Or be the top man in a really big national park. Does this make sense?"

Aeneas remembered long nights when he and David Hindler stood watch together, and they talked of the things they would do when they'd taken Jerusalem. . . . "Yes."

"Then he starts telling me Hansen won't own this place much longer, but I shouldn't worry because he can fix it so I go on *Valkyrie* anyway. . . . I want on that,

Mister. And I want in the Moon colony. So I listened. Pretty soon Marty had me convinced. He had me wondering if Miss Hansen could last a year. But I didn't say anything to anybody until he asked me to help him."

"What did he want?"

"I'm a pretty good biotech, Mister. I do my share of that work up here. Marty wanted me to poison the vaccine cultures so the yields would go down. Nothing drastic, nothing that would really hurt the station, just cut down production. So I told Amos."

"What did the captain do?" Aeneas asked.

"Amos wanted me to cooperate with Marty, but I wanted no part of that. I told Marty to go to hell. The next day when I was coming off shift I saw Marty go into my lab, so I went to the captain and told him about it. Amos went in after Marty. An hour later one of the construction people saw the captain drifting away from the airlock."

"Were there any other witnesses?"

She wouldn't answer. "There's no point in this," she said.

"We'll see." Aeneas turned to Dr. Eliot. "Is there any place you can assemble the entire crew?"

"Yes—"

"Please call them together in one hour. Until then, leave me alone here." His voice carried command, and when Eliot looked into his eyes they seemed as deep as the stars outside the viewport.

The messroom was large enough to hold the hundred men and women with room to spare. It was the full width of the central section of the crew quarters, twenty meters across and more than twice that in length. Thin aluminum flooring made the floor flat across its width and curved gently along the length. The walls were curving sections of a cylinder, with a metallic shine of impervious synthetic cloth. There were several viewports, deep, proving that the inner walls were covered with something outside them.

Aeneas let Kit Penrose lead him into the room. He noted small groups of crewmen clumped together, nervous little groups speaking in low voices that died away as they saw him.

"You know who I am." His voice, raised to carry through the messroom, sounded tinny and high-pitched. He had been told that the gas mixtures in the station would do that, but he hadn't noticed when he spoke in normal tones.

"What the hell are you doing here?" a man demanded. He came across the room to Aeneas: a tall man, sandy-haired and square-jawed, his muscles hard. He had the confidence of a man long in space, and more; a man who made his own destiny and controlled the destinies of others. It was a confidence that Aeneas recognized easily. . . .

"Hello, David," Aeneas said quietly.

"Eh?" Penrose said. "That's Martin Holloway."

"His name is David Hindler," Aeneas said. "He is, or was until very recently, an agent of the CIA."

Holloway-Hindler smiled with half his face. "And Aeneas MacKenzie is, or was until recently, political and legal advisor to the President of the United States."

"I work for Miss Hansen now," Aeneas said. The room was still; everyone was listening.

Holloway shrugged. "You betrayed Greg after damn near twenty years with him—how long before you double-cross Hansen, Aeneas? Just what the hell are you doing here, anyway?"

"I have come to try a case of murder," Aeneas said.

Holloway looked up in surprise. "By what authority?"

"My own. I am commander of this station." He looked to Eliot.

"That's what Miss Hansen says," Eliot announced. "She appointed MacKenzie in Captain Shorey's place."

"That's stupid," Holloway said. "You've got no authority. Companies don't make law and courts and appoint judges—"

"Then I appoint myself. Sit down, David. You are charged with the willful murder of Captain Amos Shorey. How do you plead?"

"Go to hell! You've got no authority over me." He looked around for support.

"But I do." The quiet voice demanded attention. Holloway looked back to Aeneas and saw that he had taken an odd-looking gun from inside his coveralls. Holloway started to reach for his own—

"Don't!"

The command halted his move for a second.

"The first dart contains a tranquilizer," Aeneas said. "The rest have cyanide. And I've practiced in this gravity. Keep your hands where I can see them, David. And please sit down."

"I'll sit." Holloway eyed the gun warily. "But you can't make me accept the authority of your court. You're no better than any other gunman—don't the rest of you see that? You let him do this to me, and which one of you's next? Do something!"

There were murmurs of assent, and several crewmen stood menacingly.

"Wait," Aeneas commanded. The helium in the atmosphere in the station made his voice shrill, but the timbre of command remained. "You may as well hear me out. How many of you hope to go with *Valkyrie?* Or to the Moon colony?"

About half. Kittridge Penrose was among them.

"And why?" Aeneas asked.

"Because we've had enough of Earth and bureaucrats and laws and regulations," Penrose said. "We can't breathe down there! We've had it with the Martin Holloways—and people like you, MacKenzie!"

"Yet you cannot live without law," Aeneas said. "There is no civilization without justice."

"Law? Justice?" Penrose was contemptuous. "Rules, regulations, taxes, traps for people minding their own business."

"Those are perversions of law." Aeneas deliberately kept his voice low so that they had to strain to listen. "There can be no civilization without law and no civilized men without justice. Earth's law cannot govern here. It cannot even govern Earth. But that does not mean you can dispense with law altogether."

"So you'll give us laws?" Holloway said contemptuously.

"No. But this satellite is not independent of Earth. It is not sovereign. It must have government. Miss Hansen has given me that task."

"Are you going to put up with this?" Holloway demanded. "You don't know this son of a bitch. Law! He's a goddam computer. He'll have you marching around under regulations like you've never seen." He turned to the crew. "Help me!"

"Help him and you give *Heimdall* to the Equity Trust. Or to Greg Tolland," Aeneas said. "I do not think you will care for either master. Even those who are here for short tours only—and those who want a new life in space will be finished."

There was a buzz of conversation. "Hansen's been decent enough."

"Hell, he's got the gun. . . ."

"I don't owe Holloway nothing."

"Let Penrose and Eliot decide, that's their job, I mind my own business. . . ."

Aeneas raised his voice to cut through the chatter. "The prohibition against murder is as old as man. Are any safe here? Who had more friends than Captain Shorey? Who will avenge you if you are wronged?"

"What do you intend to do with Holloway?" one engineer demanded.

"I intend to try him for murder."

"Some trial!" Holloway shouted. "A kangaroo court."

"Yes. You prefer a court which you know will never convict you. I think, David, you have forgotten what a trial is for. It is not a show, but a means of discovering what has happened. I think we can do that here. The crew will be the jury."

"What happens if we say guilty?" Penrose demanded.

"Sentence is the responsibility of the judge. Martin Holloway, as you are known here, how do you plead?"

"You goddam fools!" Holloway shouted. "You're really going to let him do this, aren't you? By God, you touch me and the Agency'll track every one of you down. You've got to go back to Earth sometime—"

"Not everyone," Aeneas said quietly.

"They've got families," Holloway said grimly.

Aeneas shook his head sadly. "This is beneath you, David. And I warn you, you are not helping your case. I advise you to say nothing else." Still carefully holding the pistol ready, Aeneas took a seat across the table from Holloway. "I wish you had not threatened the crew."

Because, Aeneas thought, you force me to act alone. But he had always known it would come to this. He had become—what? "Your plea is not necessary," Aeneas said. "I call the first witness. Miss Raisters, your oath. Do you swear—"

"His people will kill me," Ann said. "He wasn't alone. There are more of them here—"

"You told me Amos Shorey was your friend. And there will be justice here, and on *Valkyrie*."

Her lips tightened. She took a deep breath and began to tell her story.

In two hours they had heard it all: Holloway's threats and promises to various crewmen; sabotage plans, promises of money and position when Equity took control of *Heimdall*. There were five witnesses to those acts; and Ann Raisters and another woman had seen Holloway enter the laboratory. They saw Captain Shorey go in after him; and Shorey never returned.

The station physician told them that Shorey died of explosive decompression, but that he had been drugged first. "I don't know the drug," he told them. "Not precisely. One of the curare derivatives, I'd think. Certainly something at least that powerful, to leave a man's muscles relaxed as he explodes. Not even unconsciousness could have done that."

When it was finished, Aeneas spoke to Holloway. "You may present your defense."

"I don't have to make any defense!"

"I advise you to do so. At the moment the evidence is much against you."

"You used to be my friend," David said.

"Make your defense," Aeneas replied. His voice was even, and no one could tell if that had cost him much or little.

"Crap. I didn't kill Shorey!"

"How did he die?"

"It was an accident. He—"

"Yes?"

Holloway thought for a moment. There was no possible explanation. Drugged, Shorey could not have operated the airlock; yet he had certainly been outside it. "You've got no authority here. I demand you send me down!"

"No. Have you completed your defense?"

"I've said all I'm going to say to you."

"Then this court finds you guilty. I would have put this to a jury, but your threats prevent that. David Hindler, alias Martin Holloway, this court finds you guilty of sabotage, attempted bribery, and willful murder. On the minor charges you are sentenced to forfeiture of all pay and allowances and one year at hard labor. You will not serve that sentence. On the charge of murder you are sentenced to death."

There was an excited babble in the room.

"Who'll kill me, Aeneas?" Holloway said. "You?"

"Of course. I would not ask anyone else to do it." I never wanted the high justice, but I accepted refuge with the Saracens. . . . "Stand up, David."

"No. I won't help you."

"You have five minutes."

Penrose and Eliot crowded around Aeneas. "You can't do this," Dr. Eliot said.

"Why the hell not?" Penrose demanded. "The bastard's got it coming."

"This is no better than murder," Eliot insisted. "You have no authority. . . ."

"If I have none, there's none here," Aeneas said. "And you can't live that way. If you object, Doctor, you can get the crew to stop me. I'm only one man."

"Two," Penrose growled.

"Three." Ann Raisters stood behind him.

"Your five minutes are up. Have you anything to say, David?"

Holloway turned to the others. The crew hadn't moved; they stood or sat in small groups, watching, saying very little, speaking in the hushed tones used in cemeteries and at funerals. "You're all next!" Holloway shouted. "You let him get away with this and you're next! They'll send up company cops, and you'll all be slaves."

No one moved. They may have believed him; but Aeneas stood there as the figure of—

What am I? he thought. Justice in person? The high justice? Why should they accept me? But what can they accept? In these days when no one trusts anyone or anything—there is only power. I would like to believe I am more than that.

"They'll have you for murder, Aeneas," Holloway said. "Greg Tolland will have extradition warrants in every country on Earth. But don't worry about that, because the Agency won't forget either. You're a dead man, Aeneas. You won't live an hour after you get to ground."

"I believe you." Almost, Aeneas envied David; Aeneas had once been part of that brotherhood of dedicated young men, and he missed their camaraderie. But now he served the Saracens.

Must I do this? What choices have I? There had been a time when David's threat would have been welcome;

now, Aeneas would never see Laurie Jo on their lonely beach. She wouldn't be safe for long, either. Earth was not a place of safety for anyone, great or small.

The Station turned slowly and through the ports he saw the spindly framework and tankage that would some-day be *Valkyrie*. Earth was lovely beyond it. But she will come here, and we will take that ship together. . . .

"Lost your goddam nerve?" Holloway demanded. The fear was unmistakable in his voice, and beyond it was pleading. "Get it over." The pistol coughed twice.

Afterwards, Aeneas stood again at the viewport and looked at *Valkyrie;* but did not look at Earth.

Extreme Prejudice

There were only nine people on the airplane, but the stewardess forgot to serve me coffee. I should have been flattered. In my job, being inconspicuous is an important talent, but I hadn't been trying to be invisible, and it infuriated me. By the time we were six hundred miles southwest of the southern tip of Baja California, I'd made a scene and the girl wouldn't forget me, ever.

I was ashamed of myself long before it was over. The whole point to my job is to make the United States a better place to live. We've no business spreading unhappiness for our own gratification. We do enough of that as official duties.

Dansworth Station sits seven hundred miles southwest of Baja, and we'd been flying over blue water for hours. I remembered the old days of fast jets and squirmed around uncomfortably, cursing the fuel shortages and the people who'd lit a match to all that oil. There wasn't anything to look at below, no islands, and from our cruising altitude I couldn't see waves or white-caps. There was just that deep blue and the steady rumbling whine of the engines to lull me toward sleepiness but keep me from sleeping. Then the water changed color.

It was many shades of blue, and green, and red, and yellow, all boiling up blue-white in the center of each patch and then the colors spreading outwards in great streaks. Most of Dansworth is under water, so those enormous color patches were all I could see.

The plane circled lower as the stewardess, still not looking at me, gave her little spiel about seat belts and having a pleasant trip. There was an airstrip floating in the water. It wasn't very wide, but over 3000 feet long, and there were buildings along its sides at the lee end. A dirigible mooring mast floated on its own platform not far away. The plane rolled to a stop at that end of the runway.

A regular grid of concrete domes dotted the sea around the airstrip, and further away were big floating docks. A couple of newly painted ocean-going ships were alongside. The whole place was clean and bright, different from any city I'd been in recently. Somehow the new planned cities, the "arcologies," never seem to look this bright and new; but we're getting there. We have to.

Dark kelp patches grew between the isolated domes, and the water was so clear that I could see platforms about fifty feet below the surface. Silvery torpedo shapes flashed through the kelp, and sailboats cruised among the domes, their bows throwing up white spumes as they raced with the wind. They didn't have the look of yachts. Just a means of transportation.

Dr. Peterson himself was there to meet me. I strutted a bit for the benefit of the other passengers, and the stewardess looked worried, as she should have. Ignoring passengers who rate a planesides meeting from the civilian director could get her in a lot of trouble, and jobs are pretty scarce. She wasn't wearing any rings, so she was reasonably safe from the new "One Job Per Family" program, but I understand the Federal Employment Commission is looking into that, too. Married women voters don't appreciate single girls who have jobs when there are still many families with no job at all. . . .

Peterson wasn't wearing anything but a pair of shorts and a wide-brimmed hat, and he looked at my light-weight drip-dry suit with sympathy. I've worn it on so many assignments that it seems like an old friend, and even in hot weather I'm comfortable in it. I thought I'd lost it once when Hertzog's blood spurted all over me, but it washed out all right. I've never got any of my own on it, maybe that's why I like it. A good luck charm.

I was surprised at how cool it seemed here in the tropic midafternoon. The sun was high and bright overhead, the sky impossibly blue with only tiny white fleecy clouds scudding across. I haven't seen a sky like that since I last went hiking in the Sierras. Yet, despite the hot sun, the west wind was cold.

Peterson had a tan like old leather. So did everyone else moving around the floating airstrip. It made me feel that I must look like something that had crawled from under a rock. A part of me said that might not be too bad a description, and I thrust it away. It's bad enough getting doubts in the middle of the night; I can't afford them in bright daylight. I wondered if that was what happened to the man I'd come to see.

Dr. Peterson had a funny habit of brushing his beard with the tips of his fingers, the way a man might test a wall to see if it had fresh paint. He had no mustache, and I found out later that few people at Dansworth do, although beards are common. Mustaches get in the way of your diving mask. They cause leaks.

I shook hands with Peterson and walked over to the edge of the airstrip to look down into the kelp. I hadn't expected anything like that in the middle of the Pacific, and I said so. "It only grows in cold, shallow water, doesn't it?" I asked.

"Right." Peterson seemed pleased that I knew that much. "That *is* cold, shallow water, Mr. Starr. The kelp's anchored to platforms below the surface, and the water's pumped up from the deep bottom. The kelp is brought in from all over the world so we can experiment with different varieties. The stuff right here comes from the Los Angeles area."

I couldn't look away. The water was clear, and millions of fish swam in the thick kelp beds. There were long, thin, torpedo-shaped fish with bright blue stripes down their sides, moving dartingly in schools, every fish turning at precisely the same instant. Each thick clump of kelp held a brilliant orange damselfish warily guarding its territory. There were few sea urchins among the kelp bed, and as I watched, a swiftly moving shape darted past to snatch one—an otter, I thought.

A school of dolphins played among the fish. Two detached themselves from the rest and came over to examine me. One rose high on his tail, lifting himself out of the water to stand there churning while he splashed water on me. I ducked back in alarm, but it was too late. I was dripping wet.

Peterson clucked and whistled, then shouted, "Jolly! That's not nice."

The dolphin whistled something, and then, kind of garbled but clear enough so I could understand it, it said "Sorry, boss." And laughed.

Peterson was still trying to explain when we got to Admiral Kingsley's office.

"They've always been able to imitate speech," Peterson said. "The stories about dolphins talking and singing go back to classical Greek times. But nobody ever took the trouble to systematically teach them before."

"Yeah, well, look," I protested. "We get stories about intelligent fish all the time. Used to take 'em pretty seriously, and I know about how useful the dolphins are. But does that thing understand what he's saying?"

"They aren't fish," Peterson said.

"OK. Cetaceans. Toothed sea-going mammals. They breathe through lungs, and they've never been known to attack a man, and the Navy and fishermen have been systematically using them as messengers and herders since the fifties anyway. I've had the standard briefing, Dr. Peterson. But nobody told me the damned things could talk!"

"Not many can," Peterson said. "At least not so that an untrained man can understand them. Tell me, Mr. Starr, do you speak any foreign language?"

"Yeah." It was safe to admit that. I wasn't about to tell him just how many I could get along in. He wouldn't have believed me anyway.

"And was it difficult to learn it?"

"Sure."

"Well, to a dolphin, any human language is much more difficult. You'd find it easier to learn Urgic or Yakutsk

than Jolly did to learn English. Dolphin grammar isn't
like any language we speak. Couple that with the fact
that he has to suppress over half the frequencies and
sounds he normally makes to communicate, and maybe
you'll appreciate why so few dolphins ever manage to
be understood."

We'd reached the Admiral's office ten fathoms below
the surface, and the conversation trailed off. There was
a watertight door to the office and a Navy yeoman as
receptionist. Admiral Kingsley didn't have a beard, and
his tan looked pasty, as if he'd been out of the sun for a
while after a long stint outdoors. I was told he'd just
come up from a seven-week tour of duty with the deep-
mining operation below Dansworth.

The pallor bothered me. I'd had one like that myself
after the worst assignment I ever drew. The FBI caught
an economic saboteur and put him away at Lewisburg.
Our Director decided he knew too much and would
probably be exchanged, so they sent me in after him. I
tagged him in two weeks, but it took another six to spring
me, and by the time I came out I looked like a slug. I
felt like one, too. Ever since, I've been sure prisons don't
rehabilitate anyone. Problem is, what does?

"This is Gideon Starr," Peterson said. "Admiral
Kingsley."

We exchanged pleasantries and Kingsley offered
drinks. I took mine and sat in a big government-issue
easy chair, the kind they have in the Pentagon, or at
Langley. It seemed like an old friend.

"Mr. Starr," said Kingsley, "you've got real pull. We've
never had a visitor here with an endorsement from the
Secretary like yours."

And if you're lucky you won't again, I thought, but I
said, "Well, it's coming up on budget review time. A few

enthusiastic articles wouldn't hurt your research appropriation."

He smiled at that, and Peterson practically beamed. "That's a fact," Peterson muttered. "Actually, if they'd just let us keep some of the profits, we'd be all right. How many research efforts actually make money?"

I shrugged. "I'll do my best, anyway."

Kingsley beamed this time. "Well. We're to show you around and then let you direct yourself," he said. "Orientation'll take a while, though. There's a lot here, Mr. Starr. And a lot of ways for a man who doesn't know what he's doing to get killed."

"Yeah." There were a lot of ways for a man who did know what he was doing to get killed, too. Most of 'em had been tried on me at one time or another. "I've got a diver's card, and some underwater experience," I said. "I think I know what to look out for."

"It's a start," Kingsley agreed. "Well, you may as well begin sightseeing." He reached out to his desk console and pushed a button. Curtains opened on the wall behind him.

There were artificial lights as well as the sunlight filtering down this low. Big fronds waved in slow motion, an underwater forest just outside his office. I could barely see the grid that held the kelp below us. There were shelves sticking out of every structure and shaft, and lots of shafts. Coral in bright reds and blues grew from the shelves, and barnacles, and shellfish there and on long lines that dangled down from the surface. Fish darted through the kelp fronds. It was a dynamic color picture that would never come through on a TV screen. I couldn't wait to get out there in it, and I told them so.

They exchanged grins. I expect every tourist says the same thing. If anybody could visit that place and not want to get outside, he was dead or might as well be.

"Yes. Well, perhaps first an orientation tour?" Peterson said. "I really don't know how familiar you are with what we're doing here at Dansworth."

"Not at all," I told him. "I'm primarily an aerospace writer. I've done some diving, but not much serious study of sea power stations. You'd better assume I don't know anything at all."

The nice part about it was I was telling the truth. Not all of it, but no lies.

The admiral hit another button and more curtains opened. There was a 3–D map behind them, a holograph tank, and by manipulating his desk console he could show things at different levels. He started with the bare floor of the Pacific. It was crosshatched with very regular lines, a checkerboard of cracks in the bottom, and about sixteen thousand feet deep. Dansworth Seamount rose steeply from the floor to within seven hundred feet of the surface. It stood there all by itself, with nothing around, at least not on that map.

"Dansworth," Peterson said. "The deep gash next to it is Shatterton Fissure. The geologists are having a field day here."

"Um." I wasn't really interested in the geology. The theories change every year, so what's the point in studying up on them? I like technology, though, and I'm a pretty good writer. I think I could make a living at it even if Langley didn't use influence to get my stuff placed in important magazines. I'll never find out, of course. You don't quit in my job. I didn't want to, anyway.

Kingsley did something to the console and the scale changed to show only Dansworth Seamount and a little area around it. A grid appeared, a 3–D space-chessboard, with part of the grid below the top of the mountain, and the rest above that going on to the surface. "Dansworth Station," Kingsley said. "Our city in the sea."

"Impressive." I meant it. "What's the grid?"

"Corridors, mostly. Concrete cylinders strung together. Labs, quarters, processing plants."

The place was big, and they had color codes on the different structures in the map. It would take a long time to learn everything, but I wouldn't have to. We'd found the traitor after five years, and I wouldn't be here long at all. It seemed a pity, because Dansworth was a very interesting place. I wondered what it would be like to live here.

"Now for your guide," Dr. Peterson said. "I understand you asked for Hank Shields. Any reason why?"

I shrugged. "A couple of sailors in San Diego told the editor he was a good man who knew a lot about Dansworth. Anybody else would do, if it's inconvenient."

"No, nothing like that," Peterson said. "Just that Hank doesn't want any publicity. Something about his wife. He'll be glad to show you around if you won't put him in the story."

"Suits me." I needed to think that one over, and cursed the damn fools who'd asked for Shields in the first place. I like to plan my own operations, and I don't need help from the goddam desk men. I'll take their orders, but I don't need them trying to run my life. "When do I meet him?"

Hank Shields was about five eleven, a good three inches shorter than me, but he weighed nearly as much, a hundred and ninety pounds. He matched the description perfectly: blond, blue eyes, thick matty beard like most people have at Dansworth. Except for the beard he hadn't made any attempt to change his face. The pictures at Langley might have been taken last week, once the artists had airbrushed on the beard.

He looked me over carefully, then we shook hands and stood there sizing each other up. I looked to see anything in his eyes—recognition of my face, or my name, but if he'd ever heard of me he was pretty good at hiding it. That didn't mean anything, of course. So was I. He had a powerful grip, as good as mine, and that figured too. He'd had my job once. Finally we let go and Peterson waved us out of the admiral's office.

"What would you like to see first?" Shields asked.

I shrugged. "Better let you decide, Mr. Shields."

"Hank," he said automatically.

"Fine. I'm Gideon. Where we going? I can't wait to get outside."

"We'll put today in the inside tour and go out tomorrow. OK?"

"Sure." As we talked he was leading me through the maze of corridors. There were watertight doors at intervals, some open, some closed and we'd have to stop and open them, step through, and seal up behind. The corridors were about ten feet high, rounded on top and rough inside. He pointed out different laboratories as we passed.

"How long does it take to learn your way around here?" I asked.

"Years. And they keep adding to it. Well, they used to keep adding to it," he caught himself. "Budget's been rotten the last couple of years."

He had a hearty voice and was eager to explain things to me. Hank Shields would be an easy man to like. I decided he didn't know anything about me or why I was here, and I could relax.

We reached an elevator shaft and went down. "I'm taking you to the number one power plant," Hank said. "It's the only one at sea-level pressure. The rest are just like it, only they're pressurized to ambient. Saves construction costs."

We went through another watertight door and out onto a catwalk. There were turbines below, big Westinghouse jobs, and it was noisy as hell, but otherwise it didn't look a lot different from the generator house at a dam. I said so.

He motioned me back into the elevator shaft and closed the door so it was quiet. "It isn't any different, really," he told me. "Surface water, 25°C. Seventy-seven if you like it in Fahrenheit. Down at the bottom the water's 5°C. We take the warm water down to heat exchangers and boil propane with it. Propane steam goes through the turbines. On the other side we've got condensers. They get cooled by another set of heat exchangers with water pumped up from the bottom. Turbines spin, and out comes electricity. Works like a charm, and no fuel costs."

"Sounds like perpetual motion."

"It is. There's a power source, of course. The sun. It heats water pretty good in the Tropics. What it amounts to, Gideon, is we have a temperature difference with the same power potential as a ninety-foot water drop. Lots of dams with a smaller pressure head than that. And we've got all the hot water we could ever want."

"Yeah, OK." We started up in the elevator. It sounded impressive as hell but there hadn't been anything to see. "Just a minute. The water by the airstrip was cold."

"Right. That's used cooling water. We dump it high because it's full of nutrients. Artificial upwelling. You know, like Peru? Over half the fish caught anywhere in the world are at natural upwellings. We've made our own. Lot of profit in fish, fish meal, frozen fish, gamefish, you name it."

I could appreciate that. With meat prices where they were in the U.S., we're getting to be a nation of fish eaters anyway, and Dansworth supplies a lot of the fish. "But where do you get the hot water, then?"

"Bring it in from up-current of the station, where there are black platforms below the surface to help get it hotter. No problem. It has to be pumped anyway. With dolphin-hide liners on the pipes, it's about as easy to pump the water a long way as a short."

I gave him a blank look. "I must be dense—dolphin hides? You kill them for that?"

He laughed. It was a real long laugh, hearty, and after a second I joined in because it was infectious, even if it was obviously on me. "What're we laughing about?" I asked him.

"Dolphin-hide's a process name," Hank wheezed. "You'll see. We've got a way to duplicate the effect that dolphins use to control water flow across their skin. They get true laminar flow, if that means anything to you."

I nodded. It did, just. "Smooth water flow, no friction."

"Yeah. We haven't got it worked out for boats yet, but we're trying. Easy to make it work with steady flows, like pipes. You'll see tomorrow."

We toured the Station. Fisheries, where they used graded nets to catch fish at just the right sizes and let the others through. There were dolphins involved in that too. They chased the fish into the nets. The men in charge used little boxes with keys to play dolphin-sound tunes and direct their partners. The dolphins seemed to be having more fun than the men, but nobody was working very hard and I could see a lot of grins.

In another place they had plant research farms. Different kinds of kelp and other seaweeds, and different creatures living in them. Shrimp, fish, shellfish—anything that might be edible, and some that weren't. Everything grew like crazy, and Hank said it was because of the nutrients in the water they brought up from the bottom. "Infinite supply of that, too. All free since we need it in the power plants to begin with."

We took an elevator to the surface at the down-wind end of the airstrip, and watched the big ships loading up at the floating docks. I asked how they'd survive in storms, big structures like that exposed to the waves.

"They wouldn't," Hank said. "So we sink 'em if there's a big enough blow coming. Ships stay the hell away unless there's good weather. We get good predictions from the satellites."

It was a whole new world. Everything was bright and clean. The shops along the airstrip had no iron bars or reinforced doors. I hadn't seen a policeman since I arrived. Hank told me the Navy Shore Patrol did all the policing they needed—mostly drying out sailors who'd had one too many.

I'd never known people could live like that. Why can't we, back in the States? One day we will, if we can hang on long enough.

We went through hydrogen plants, where they electrolyzed water into its parts and liquefied the hydrogen and oxygen. The compression and electrolysis made heat, and they pumped that back into the system with heat exchangers. No stage of the Dansworth operation was very efficient, but overall it was fabulous. I knew the hydrogen was important to California, where they pipe it through the old natural gas pipelines and people burn it in floor furnaces and stoves.

"We're starting to get salable quantities of metals out of sea water, too," Hank said. "That wouldn't be economic if it was the only reason for the system, but we pump a *lot* of water through here. Power's free except for building the equipment to get it." He went on about Dansworth and how it was the wave of the future until he stopped suddenly and grinned.

"I'm an enthusiast," he said.

"I've noticed." I grinned back. "You're making me one."

"Yeah. Now let's go home and have dinner. Judy's expecting you to put up with us while you're here."

"Well, I'll be all right at the VOQ. Wouldn't want to put you to any trouble."

"Crap. No trouble. Only problem with Dansworth is we don't get many visitors. There's three thousand people here and we know every one of them, or it seems like it anyway. Judy'd kill me if I didn't give her a chance to hear the latest gossip from the States."

"Yeah, I suppose—Look, you're sure it's no problem?" I wasn't being polite. My father had a big thing about hospitality. It was about the only thing my father taught me that I hadn't sacrificed to the Job; but Hank gave me no choice, just as the Job gave me no choice. No choice at all.

Judy Shields was a willowy brunette, thin but with muscles. She had an aristocratic look and the same deep tan everyone seemed to have, but the effect was partly spoiled by freckles on her nose. My kid sister had freckles like that, and she hated them. I can remember her making unhappy sounds at the bathroom mirror while the rest of us waited outside for our turn. A rapist finished her on her eighteenth birthday.

Judy Shields was happy to meet someone from Outside, as they called it. I also got introduced to Albert Shields, age nine, and called "Hose-nose" for no reason I could understand.

"Mr. Starr's a science writer," Hank told the kid.

"Sure! I've seen some of your books, Mr. Starr. You going to put Dad in a book?"

I lifted an eyebrow and looked at Hank. "According to Dr. Peterson, your father doesn't want in a book."

"Aw, why not? I'd sure like to be in a book. Jimmy Peterson's father's in a lot of books, and he'll never let you forget it, either."

"Off to your room, Hose-nose," Judy said. "Out, out, out."

"So you can drink, huh?" The lad winked and went out.

"He's got a point, you know," I said. "A little publicity never hurt anybody's career." I looked over at Hank with complete innocence. It seemed like the right thing to say. He looked back helplessly.

"It's my fault, Gideon," Judy said. "My family never wanted me to marry Hank. It's—Well, it's all very unpleasant, and I'd rather they didn't know we were here, that's all. I suppose it would do Hank some good to be written up."

"Not as much as that, and by damn I don't need your mother dropping in for a visit," Hank said. He poured me another drink.

"Well, forget it, then." I hoisted the martini. "Here's to Dansworth. It's quite a place."

It was, too. Although we were a hundred feet under water, the Shield's apartment wasn't small or gloomy. There was a big window looking out, just like the admiral's, and the same unending color swarms of fish around the coral. Inside, the walls were concrete, and they'd hung them over with woven mats, needlework tapestries, pictures, and the like. There was a shelf of books on one wall and a shelf of ship models on another. It was nothing like homes in the States where the TV dominates the room. You could tell that the people who lived here liked to talk, and read, and do things together.

"We like it," Judy said. "Now. What's the latest gossip? Is Gregory Tolland going to hang on as President? Whatever happened to Aeneas MacKenzie?"

I shrugged, and told her what the press people were saying. "MacKenzie's gone off to Baja. Probably joined up with Hansen Enterprises," I told them. "And they say Tolland's going to hang in there. The press supports him—Don't you get any news here at all?"

"Very little," Judy said. "We like it that way. No TV, and we don't read the stateside papers. Is it true that MacKenzie found Equity Trust people in the White House itself?"

"It looks that way." I didn't really want to talk about it, although I suppose half the people in the country were having the same conversation at just that moment. Usually Agency people have about as much interest in politics as they do in Donald Duck, but some of us really thought Tolland and his People's Alliance would put some new pride into the United States. He'd started off well, and certainly MacKenzie's investigations had cleaned up a lot of dirt accumulated in Washington for thirty years. We'd helped in that. And then MacKenzie got too close to the White House, and he was out, and Tolland sat there alone in the Oval Office. "The consensus is that President Tolland was as surprised as anyone. At least the press thinks so."

Hank laughed unpleasantly. He clearly didn't believe it. Maybe he was trying to justify something, like running out.

"I'd rather talk about Dansworth," I told them. "Hank, you never did tell me what you do here."

"I'm a generalist. Sea farming methods, mostly. Some clumsy engineering. Diving—Academic training's not worth a hoot compared to just getting down there and fooling around. We've still got a lot to learn."

"Do you dive too?" I asked Judy.

"Oh, sure. I have to. I'm the schoolteacher. A lot of the classes are out on the reefs."

"Isn't that dangerous for the kids?"

"A little. Traffic accidents are bad for children too. And we don't have gangs and muggings or smog or enriched white flour."

"Yeah." Paradise. There was something else about Dansworth. Everybody was doing something he was interested in. I wondered when I'd last met anybody like that. There are a lot of go-getters with the big international corporations, but they're in short supply back home.

And yet. It's my country. We *built* Dansworth. The arcology projects in the Midwest haven't worked so well, but we'll lick that too. We're finding ourselves again.

Dinner was fish, of course. All kinds of fish. There was one thing that tasted like steak, and I asked about it, "Whale?"

They all shuddered. "No, it's beef. Dr. Peterson sent steaks over in your honor," Judy said. Her throat seemed tight. Hank didn't look too good either, and I thought the kid was going to throw up. It was very quiet in the room.

"OK, what's wrong?" I asked. "Obviously I put my foot in it."

"You wouldn't really *eat* a whale, would you?" Hose-nose asked. His eyes were as big as saucers. "I mean not *really.*"

"I never have, as far as I know," I answered. "But—I thought they were raising whales for food out here."

"No. That's over," Hank said. "Gideon—did you meet Jolly? Dr. Peterson's talking dolphin?"

"Sure."

"Would you eat him?"

"Good Lord, no."

"Whales may be at least as smart as dolphins. Killer whales certainly are—of course they're a kind of dolphin anyway. But even if the bigger whales aren't as intelligent as we are, they're more like apes or gorillas than cattle. They're *aware.* Would you eat monkeys?"

"I see what you're getting at." I saw it, but I didn't have the emotions they did. It really disturbed them.

"The reason we can let the children swim without worrying about them is the dolphins watch out for them," Judy said. "We wouldn't be able to operate this place without them."

"But whales eat dolphins," I protested. "Don't they?"

"Killer whales do," Hank said. "OK. I grant that, and the dolphins have no use for their overgrown cousins. But dogs eat sheep too, until they're taught to take care of them. It's the same thing."

"You have killer whales here?"

"No. They'd be too hard to take care of," Hank said. "We're concentrating on training the dolphins right now. But there'll come a time—"

"And what about sharks?" I asked. "Any chance of taming them?"

"No. They're vicious and stupid, and you can't even hate them. I suppose they have a place in nature, but there's none for them here."

Hank's voice had an edge to it when he said that. I wondered if he was thinking the same thing I was. He'd been a shark, and he'd found a place here. A bloody traitor to the Agency, a man who'd run out, making it just that much harder for the rest of us.

After dinner, we sat around watching the fish look in at us. They were attracted to the lights. There were dolphins too, including a baby that kept perfect station just behind and under her mother. I was told I'd meet them the next day.

Hank and Judy kept asking me about the States, and they didn't like what I told them. That didn't surprise me. Even after a few hours here, I could feel the contrast with the way we lived at home. Everyone at Dansworth had a purpose, but back home we all seem to be like a man hanging on to a rope over the edge of a cliff, and nobody seems to quite know what to do about it. Until somebody does, it's my job to keep some charlie from sawing the rope in two. God knows there are enough trying it.

They'd listen to stories about the Outside for a while, then they'd get off onto something else going on at Dansworth. Minerals. Ecological farming, fish, and plants, pollution-free power, talking to dolphins. Hank was working on all of it, trying to keep track of the big picture, but there was so much going on he always had more to do than he had time for.

That's when I really hated Hank Shields. He was enthusiastic about his work. He had a wife and family. He had a job he really believed in. He slept nights, with none of those little doubts that grow and grow in the quiet darkness until you get up and turn on the lights. He had all the things I'd never have, and why should he?

He'd been one of us. He'd quit. We can't quit, but Hank Shields had tried it. Now he sat smugly in his living room, with his lovely wife, and thought about this Paradise he lived in. He thought he was safe.

He'd soon learn different.

For our first day's diving we used only masks and snorkels and fins. The water was clear, and there were fish everywhere. I was surprised to see Pacific barracuda swimming near us, and they made me nervous, but Hank said they wouldn't hurt anyone. They hardly ever did back in the States, of course, and here they were well fed and the vicious ones weeded out.

The dolphins did that. We'd no sooner gone off the platform into the water, Hank and me and Hose-nose, than five dolphins came around. Hank had a little box attached to his belt, and he played a tune on some keys sticking out of it. The dolphins arranged themselves in front of us, and I'd swear they were laughing at us.

"This is Jill," Hank said, pointing to the mother I'd seen the night before. "And the little one's Sarah. Jill, meet Gideon Starr." He also made clicks and wheezes on the box.

"You telling me she understands English?" I asked.

"Quite a lot. So does Jumbo, the big male there," Hank said. The dolphins laughed again. "But none of these can speak English, at least not so that you could understand them. We're teaching Sarah, but she's very young. Actually she doesn't speak dolphin very well either. She's learning both languages together."

Hose-nose was swimming around the big female dolphin, pushing Sarah away from her mother. Jill turned in a tight circle, Sarah following exactly, leaving Hose-nose behind and then coming up face-to-face with the boy. The dolphin chattered loudly.

"Stop it, Albert," Hank said wearily. "You know better." He turned to me. "Kids. He knows that dolphins don't like people messing with their children. Jill won't actually hurt him, and Hose-nose counts on it. Well, Gideon, you ready for a wild ride?"

Hank produced harness things, big rigid rings with trapeze bars hanging behind them. The dolphins stuck their bills into the rings, and we each grabbed a bar. Hose-nose had Jill, and I drew Jumbo, while another male called Fonso towed Hank. We moved through the kelp beds at about five knots, with a kaleidoscope of colors flashing below us. The other two dolphins ranged around us in tight circles, charging toward me and then diving under just as it seemed a collision was inevitable. It took me a while to get used to it, and I saw Hank watching me out of the corner of his eye, while Hose-nose was openly laughing.

I was damned if I'd give them anything to laugh about, but there were a couple of times I held my breath. A six-hundred-pound dolphin is *big*, and when he comes straight at you moving about twenty knots, it's scary.

It was also hard to manage my snorkel at those speeds. We made enough of a wake to swamp the thing quite often, so I was pretty busy keeping my mask clear of water and trying not to inhale too much brine. Eventually Hank made more clicks and wheezes on his box and the dolphins slowed down a bit. I was sure I'd been tested, and wondered if it were standard treatment for visitors. Dudes are fair game anywhere.

I saw how the barracuda-management program worked about an hour out. We were free swimming in kelp beds, the giant fronded stuff that grows off Catalina Island, diving down among the fish and watching sea otters collect the spiny sea-urchins to take them up to the surface and crack them. One of the barracuda got too interested in an otter, and the dolphins converged around it. The barracuda realized its mistake immediately and darted off, doing maybe thirty-five knots, much faster than a dolphin, but one of the dolphins had anticipated that. It had started on a converging course before the barracuda saw him, and snap!

I began to have a healthy respect for dolphin teeth. The barracuda made a nice meal for the five of them, a tidbit apiece, with Sarah getting most of the innards.

Well, people keep dogs, and they have big teeth. Families will trust their babies to the temper of an Alsatian that could take the kid apart in three bites, yet puts up with being sat on and ridden . . . but dogs have been bred for that behavior for thousands of years. The dolphins are only wild animals.

Or are they? They aren't really wild, and is it fair to call anything that smart an animal?

We went out again the next morning. The Shields had a lock system so you could go out from their home, twenty fathoms down; at that depth we were below most of the kelp, although there were some giant fronds growing up from platforms attached to the deep-layer corridors and labs. A couple of sailors brought over equipment for me and got it fitted properly, while Hank and Hose-nose put on their own gear. The kid was enjoying his respite from classes, and Judy Shields was mad because she couldn't come with us. She had to teach the school her son was playing hooky from. . . .

They used helmets with a faceplate that covered the whole face, mouth and all. I'd never used that system before. The advantage was you could talk with it, and I could understand Hank a few feet away, although it was tough; but there was also a plug-in system to connect to the underwater sled, and when we were all attached to that, everything was easy. There was a little garbling, but not much.

The sled was a four-man job with two pairs of seats protected by what I'd have called wind-screens except that of course these were water-screens. It was powered by batteries, and held air tanks so we didn't have to use the backpack air while we traveled around the station. When we got outside and Hank showed me how the system worked, he used the dolphin-talker box to play a tune. Jumbo, Jill, and Sarah showed up.

"We'll only need Jumbo," Hank explained. His voice sounded heavy and a little mushy in my helmet phones. "Jill's off duty anyway, of course, because raising Sarah's a full-time job. The others have work to do."

It took a little while for our eyes to get accustomed to the light down that far, and I was surprised to see just how much filtered through to twenty fathoms. There weren't many reds or yellows, of course; water absorbs that end of the spectrum so that down that deep everything seems to be different shades of blues and greens.

We took the sled out to the edges of the great colored patches of diatoms and plankton that surrounded the upwelling cold water with its nutrients. There weren't any structures out here, and it was officially not part of Dansworth at all, but Hank wanted to show me the color changes. We were up to about sixty feet now, but we'd been down a couple of hours. On the way the dolphins played their game with the sled, darting ahead and then racing back to do a couple of tight turns around us, urging Hank to get up more speed.

Finally I asked Hank about decompression.

"No problem," he said. "Judy'll have the whole apartment pressurized when we get back. We'll go in and let the system take care of gradual decompression—or leave it pressurized if you want to go out tomorrow. That's one of the big advantages at Dansworth, the deep-water boys can get saturated and stay at pressure as long as they want."

"What do you do if you want to get down really deep?" I asked. As we'd cruised through the last of the experimental kelp farms a couple of miles back, I'd seen the winking lights of the mining operations far below, down at the top of the Seamount itself.

"Have to use special gas mixtures," Hank said. "Expensive. Helium's gone out of sight. We use rebreather systems so we won't waste it."

"I want to try that. The editors insist on coverage of the deep mines."

"Better to use the crabs," Hank said. "Little subs. The outside gear takes a lot of training."

"I've been down with Navy gear," I told him. "And out into space for that matter. It can't be all that different."

"It is, though. Well, OK, maybe next week. Can't bring the boy."

Hose-nose mumbled disappointment. He'd seen all this before, although he said he hadn't been this far from the Station itself before, and he wanted to see the mines.

We swam around the edges of color patches. The cold water spreading out to here made distinct layered patches in the warm tropic waters, each layer edging downward away from the upwelling point. There were different critters in each layer, and the layers were separated by twenty or thirty feet of water. The scene was fascinating.

We were about ready to turn back when we heard a shrill whistle and loud scream. I looked around, scared stiff, then decided it was the dolphins playing games on us.

Hank had his box out and played a series of clucks and gobbles on it. One of the dolphins answered. "Quick!" Hank shouted. "Into the sled! Shark!"

Hose-nose moved toward the sled fast. I was confused, not knowing what to do for a second, and stayed with Hank. We swam toward the sled, and then, just beyond it, I saw the thing.

It was a big blue shark, over twenty feet anyway, and it was charging toward little Sarah while Jill tried to stay between the shark and her daughter. I didn't see Jumbo at all.

The shark was beautiful. It raced through the deep water, a blue deadly torpedo, straight toward the baby dolphin. Jill would have had no trouble keeping away from it if she hadn't been worried about Sarah, but now she was right in its path.

Even from forty feet away I could hear the underwater crunch as the shark hit the big dolphin. Jill whirled away, tumbling and twirling, and the shark headed for the baby.

It was like watching a bad movie, all in slow motion it seemed, although nothing was moving slowly at all. We were kicking hard to get to the sled, and the shark took another tight turn and came back at the little dolphin and Hose-nose was screaming something and we couldn't get to the sled in time and even if we could I didn't know what to do—

Jumbo came from nowhere and struck the shark just behind its gills. He had come on at full tilt, seven-hundred pounds of dolphin moving at twenty-five knots, and the impact was terrific.

It didn't seem to affect the shark at all. The deadly blue shape was knocked off course and missed Sarah but that was all. It started another tight turn, while Jumbo whirled with it, trying to get up speed and at the same time keep the shark off the baby.

Sarah was making screaming clicks and kept trying to get to her usual station behind and below her mother, but Jill was tumbling out of control and I was sure she was dead.

We reached the sled and Hank took a long lance with a slender ice-pick tip from a rack along the sides. There were other lances there and I grabbed one and followed.

"Stay with the sled!" Hank shouted. "Button her up!"

"Yeah, do that!" I told Hose-nose. I kept right with Hank. He looked back for just a glance to see I was with him, a twisted look of pain and rage and thanks all at the same time.

We got to the two dolphins and took up positions on each side, lances held out toward the shark. Once we were there, Jumbo streaked off to get up momentum.

The shark didn't like the situation now. I don't know just how conscious these things are, but it had three functional enemies, none as big as it was, but all acting aggressively.

On the other hand, there was a faint trail of blood from Jill and that attracted the shark. I saw that Jill wasn't dead, but she wasn't under control either. The impact had done something to her, knocked her unconscious perhaps.

The shark circled. Jumbo flashed at it, and the shark dodged in a tight turn above us, then when he was past made up its mind and started straight toward me. I kept the lance pointed out at it. It seemed that I had plenty of time, although the whole battle hadn't lasted more than a minute.

The shark was moving fast and I didn't know if I could hit it straight on. Just before it got into range of the lance, Jumbo was there again, wham!, striking the shark at the same place, just aft of the gills, and diverting it. As it passed overhead I rammed the lance deep into its belly.

It was a charged lance, and it should have injected a full bottle of CO_2 into the shark. I cursed when nothing happened and realized I hadn't pulled the goddam safety pin out. All I'd done was give the shark a tiny puncture wound, nothing that would hurt it at all.

It did the job, though. The shark flinched in surprise and turned slightly. Hank was right there with his lance, and he hadn't forgotten. The needle went in and there was a loud whooshing sound. The shark wriggled for a second, then started floating upward, fast, its insides blown up and compressed and great bubbles of bloody gas coming from its mouth and gill slits. Jumbo came screaming around in another tight circle and rammed it amidships, forcing out more blood, but the monster was dead and headed topside, buoyed up by the gas injected into its innards.

Hank was still shouting. He was under the unconscious dolphin, pushing it upward toward the surface, kicking hard. Jill had neutral buoyancy; she wasn't heavy, but she was very massive, and it was slow work. I swam alongside and kicked upward, pushing at that great heavy body. She felt warm and hard, almost rigid. Sarah kept swimming around us, screaming plaintively. Then Jumbo was there pushing upward as well.

"Get back down!" Hank ordered. "You'll have the bends."

"So will you." I kept shoving upward. It seemed to take forever, but the light was getting brighter.

He didn't say anything else, and after a long time we broke surface. I had managed to keep the pressures equalized and breathe out steadily on the way up, only taking in a few breaths at intervals. It would be a while before we felt anything, I decided. We didn't have any embolism problems. Or if we did, I didn't feel anything. Yet.

When we got the blow-hole above water, Jill let out a long whistle of breath and started breathing again. She was thrashing around feebly, unable to keep herself above water without help. The only blood I could see was from an irregular tear just below her fin, whether shark-bite or just abrasion from the sandpaper sides of the blue shark I couldn't tell.

Hank played another tune on his call-box and Jumbo darted away from us, swimming in a big circle that kept widening before coming back and making clicking grunts. "No more sharks in sight," Hank translated. He stuck his helmet down below the surface and shouted. "Hose-nose!"

"Yes, sir." The kid's voice was faint but we could hear it. I couldn't make out any expression in it, but I could imagine what the boy was thinking. He was well-trained, to stay down there while his father brought his friend—Jill was certainly more than a pet—up to the surface.

"Go get help. Jumbo will stay with us."

"Yes, sir." There was a pause. "Is Jill all right?"

"She's alive. Get going."

"Yes, sir."

I heard the sled motor start up, a high-pitched whine, and then it receded. We were alone up there, saturated with nitrogen and holding up a bleeding dolphin, while more sharks might come around at any moment. I thought I remembered that blues hunt alone. I also remembered that sharks can smell blood for miles.

"All right, get back down to forty feet," Hank ordered. "Jumbo and I'll hold her up. Stay five minutes and then come up and relieve me. Your lance is still armed, isn't it?"

"Yes. OK." I let air out of the buoyancy compensator and sank slowly. It didn't need two to hold up the dolphin. At least not two men; Jumbo was doing most of the work anyway, but he couldn't quite hold Jill alone. It took someone on the other side to do that, to keep her from rotating and falling away.

The five minutes took forever, then I surfaced again. Hank made more noises on his call-box, sending Jumbo on another long patrol out around us. When the dolphin returned, Hank gave me his place. He seemed a bit grey and sweaty under his faceplate and I thought he had a touch of the bends, or an embolism, or both. The only thing we could do for that was to get him down again, and I pointed emphatically. He nodded.

"Thanks," he said. Then he sank out of sight, and I was alone on the surface.

Not really alone, I decided. There was Jumbo on the other side of our burden, and Sarah just under us, still clicking and whistling but not so plaintively now. Jumbo clicked at her, and she was quiet. There were swells, about five feet high, with tiny whitecaps on them, and it was hard to hold the dolphin upright so the blow-hole was above water. I kept getting salt water into my mask and it was hard to clear. I was still on tanks; a snorkel would have been flooded. The sun was hot, but the water was only warm, friendly, comfortable except for the waves. I cursed them.

We floated there, Jumbo and I, holding up the wounded dolphin, and I thought about Hank Shields. We'd worked well together, and the only mistake had been mine. A stupid one at that. Shields had been a good man. He was doing a good job here at Dansworth. He wasn't hurting anyone. He and the work at Dansworth were helping make life better for people in the States.

That wasn't a profitable way of thinking. Shields was a goddam traitor. He'd run out on the team. Maybe what he was doing now was more important, but that wasn't my decision.

Jumbo made more sounds at me, but I couldn't understand them. *"No comprende,"* I said, then laughed at myself. For some reason I'd used a language foreign to me, thinking Jumbo might know that. Of course he wouldn't understand any language I knew. Except perhaps English. "I don't understand," I said as clearly as I could.

"OK," the dolphin replied. It was quite clear and distinct. He began nudging Jill, and she responded a bit, moving her tail about to help keep herself above water. She breathed noisily. After a while she could hold herself up with only a little help. I pointed out toward the sea and made a big circular movement with my arm. "Sharks?" I called.

Jill clicked something that sounded scared. Sarah clicked back.

"No. OK," Jumbo said. Again it was quite clear enough to understand. He darted away, leaving me to hold Jill with her help. He tore off in a big circle and stayed out there a long time. When he got back, he made clicking noises.

"Another shark out there," I heard. "Probably a lot of them. They'll eat the dead one first." This wasn't from the dolphin but it took a moment to realize I was hearing Hank's voice from seventy feet down. "I can't come up, I'm afraid. Can you hold on?"

"Sure!" I called. I wondered. But Jumbo was racing around us in a tight circle now, and I had my lance. I took the bright red ribbon hanging on the safety pin and pulled it out, then held the lance warily. The thing was as dangerous to humans and dolphins as it was to sharks.

I thought about the sharks. Come to blood from miles away. Eat each other. Stupid, single-minded killers. I didn't like the thought.

After a while I saw Hank rising from below. He hadn't given me any warning, and my lance was pointed slantingly downward, just where he'd come up, the point probably invisible because he'd be looking up at the bright surface and the lance was shadowed by the dolphin and her daughter. . . .

It was simple. An accident, and no questions. He was swimming badly, and I was sure he was suffering, how bad I couldn't tell.

An accident. No witnesses. Terminate with extreme prejudice. He was almost to the point of my lance now. A tiny movement and he'd be a closed file entry—

No. He was a goddam traitor, but he'd fought to keep the dolphin alive. He'd earned that much. The sharks might come back, and I'd need him. The Job could come later. Right now, I wasn't risking the dolphin. It made an ironic joke, because my supervisor hates dolphins more than he hated Hank Shields.

"Get your ass down there under pressure!" I shouted. "You're in no goddam condition to come to the top." I shifted the lance point so that it missed him. "And give me warning when you come up. You almost impaled yourself."

He looked at me funny. It was a knowing look, and it said a lot. I frowned. "Get below!"

He sank back down without a word. A Navy recovery boat with a compression chamber reached us about twenty minutes later, but it was only ten minutes before a whole school of angry dolphins was around us, looking for sharks to kill. They found two.

They let Hank come home for dinner. He'd suffered a painful emphysema, but nothing permanent. We ate dinner in the Shield's apartment pressurized to fifty feet. It was a quiet dinner, and afterwards he sent the boy off to his room.

"Thanks," he said. "Don't think I could have saved Jill by myself. The babies always die if they lose their mothers, and Sarah's the best prospect we've ever had. You did a good job of work today."

"So did you."

"I try. Maybe I'll earn my way back into the human race."

Before I could say anything, Judy came back into the room. She looked at Hank sprawled out in a reclining chair and clucked at him. A bubble had formed inside his chest cavity, and another under the skin at his neck. Recompression forced them back into solution, and now we were paying the penalty by being confined while the pressure was slowly reduced. It wasn't really a problem, since large parts of Dansworth stay under pressure all the time.

"Guess you can't take me diving tomorrow," I said.

"No. Surgeon says it'll be a week. I expect you don't want to go without me," Hank said slowly. "Be no point to it. Right?"

I looked up sharply. Judy was frowning, not really understanding. I couldn't keep from watching her. She reminded me of my sister, all right, but even more of the last girl I'd really been serious about. The one I'd driven away because of the Job. It would be easy to be in love with her, and she was going to be alone pretty soon.

"We'll dive together next week," Hank said. "Can't put it off forever. If I don't take you, there'll be somebody else show up for the same dive. Right?"

"Yes." So he understood. I wondered what had given me away.

"We're pretty heavily insured here," Hank said slowly. "The Navy pays staggering premiums, but our families are well provided for if there's an accident." He saw Judy about to say something, and continued, "So if you haven't filled out the forms yet, you ought to. You'll be covered, be a pity if you haven't set things up properly. Morbid subject, of course. Let's change it."

We did, talking about dolphins, and about sea farms and the power plants. And sharks.

"They adapt," Hank said. "We've tried the lot. Electric signals, noises, chemicals—nothing stops them all. But most avoid this place. The dolphins hunt them. If sharks weren't so stupid, they wouldn't come around at all; but there're so many fish here, and the wastes from the processing plant can't be completely disposed of without getting some blood and guts in the water. We were upcurrent of that, and usually the sharks don't come there. I doubt it would have attacked us anyway, except for Sarah. Baby dolphin's a tasty dish to a shark."

Judy shuddered. "I've never seen a shark attack," she said. "But Hank, you were out of your mind to take Albert out beyond the perimeter. Close to the Station we've always got plenty of dolphins on patrol, but out there with just Jumbo—I wish you wouldn't take the boy out that far again."

"I won't," he said. He stood and put his arm lightly around her. "It's been a good five years," he said. He wasn't talking to anyone in particular. He kissed her. "I'm a little tired. Gideon, if you'll excuse me, I'm sure Judy can entertain you—"

"No, of course not," I said, and went off to my own room. I had a lot to think about, and I didn't want Judy's company just then. I wasn't sure I wanted my own.

They put me through a week of training before they'd let me take a deep dive to the mine sites. It was another week after that before the surgeons would let Hank go with me.

We went down in a concrete shaft that contained a series of elevators. Every hundred feet we'd have to get out and pass through a pressure tight door. Not only did the pressures change at each depth, but the gas mixtures as well, and at the third we had to put on our hearing aids.

They weren't really hearing aids, of course. They were tiny computers and electronic speech-filtering devices. The gas mixtures used to let men live at the lower depths and higher pressures contained a lot of helium, and a man talking in a helium-oxygen mixture sounds like Donald Duck. Some of the old-timers could understand each other without hearing aids, or claimed to, but most people can't make out a word.

The hearing aids take that gobble-gobble and suppress some of the frequencies while amplifying others, so that the result sounds like normal speech in a flat monotone. It's impossible to get much expression into a voice, but you can be intelligible.

We went on down until we were at the lowest level, 780 feet below the surface. There was a large structure there, with laboratories and quarters for the workmen, mostly Navy people.

It was also cold. They heated the structures, and they had plenty of power to do it with, but helium conducts heat better than normal air. You feel heat losses and feel them fast. When we went outside we'd need heated wet suits too. The water at that depth is quite cold.

The first couple of days we took it easy, going out with a gang of Navy men to watch the mining operations. They were just getting started good, sinking shafts into the sides of the Seamount, taking samples for the scientists as they dug. Everybody was excited about what they were learning. This was the United States' first chance to catch up with the big international corporations who had a big edge in undersea mining technology.

On the third day we went out alone. It was dark and gloomy except where our lights pointed, and there were ghastly streaks of phosphorescence everywhere. It reminded me of some big city, deserted at night, and it had the same air of indefinable menace. The dolphins couldn't come with us, although Jumbo and Fonso were overhead, and once in a while one or the other would dive down to our level, chatter at Hank for a second and get a reply from his belt call-box, then head back topside. The depth was extreme for dolphins, Hank said, and although they were breathing surface air rather than high-pressure stuff as we did, so they could go up and down without decompression problems, at that depth nitrogen will go into solution quite rapidly; the dolphins had to watch out for embolisms and bends themselves.

It wasn't quiet down there, and we weren't alone. There were hundreds of tiny clicking sounds, which I didn't understand until Hank took me to the Seamount itself and I saw little shrimp, or things that looked like them, scuttling along on the bottom. They made snapping noises with their pincers.

There were also things like eels, not very large, and strange-looking fish, also small. The real deep-bottom monsters are much farther down, of course, down where men can't get to them without bathyscaphes and protective equipment; but these were strange enough. There was one thing about seven inches long, dark blue in the yellow-glaring lights, and it seemed to be all teeth and eyes. I'm told it can swallow fish larger than itself. Nothing seemed interested in us one way or another.

We could get quite close to the fish—not that I'd want to touch any of them. It was a fascinating scene, but a little scary, and the knowledge that anything going wrong with the gear would kill us instantly didn't help. I don't like situations where I have to rely on equipment some unknown tech has made.

We swam around the bottom until we were out of sight of the lights of the station and mining operations. The top of the Seamount was fairly flat, and rocky, scoured clean of mud, with small pebbles between the larger rocks. Even down this far were anemones and barnacles with feathery flowers waving gently in the current. Once in a while larger fish up to a couple of feet long would cruise by. I kept watching for squid or octopus, but I didn't see any.

There was a light far ahead of us and Hank waved me toward it. We cruised gently along, conserving energy. The rebreather apparatus didn't even leave bubbles behind, and despite our lights nothing paid much attention to us; I began to feel like a ghostly intruder, unable to affect anything, an observer in a plane of existence I didn't belong to.

The light turned out to be a shelter. It was a hemispheric dome held up from the bottom on stilts. The hatchway underneath swung upward and opened at a touch. We came up inside a space about thirty feet in diameter and fifteen high. Cabinets lined the walls, and there were more lockers under low benches. Plexiglas windows looked out onto the Seamount and its surprising inhabitants.

The shelter was heated, and we could disconnect our batteries. I took a seat, and gratefully removed the scuba gear with Hank's help. Then he was taking off his own, his back toward me, and I had the long shark dart, safety still on because I didn't want him to float. I aimed it just under the diaphragm and my hand wouldn't move.

He finished taking off his gear and sat across from me. We didn't say anything for a long time.

"It's not going to do either one of us any good," he said finally. "Why the hell don't you get it over?"

"Get what over?"

"I've had you made since you came here. Gideon Starr. Science reporter, able to move around and interview almost anybody—Great cover, Gideon. I knew about you before I left the Agency."

"I see. They don't know that, back at Langley." I watched him warily now. We couldn't just leave here and go swimming again, not with it out in the open like this.

"I thought they might not. I can't run, you know. Where could I go? And I'm sure your people are watching the transports."

"Humph." I didn't say anything else, but he knew what I was thinking. Anybody as good as he was wouldn't have any trouble outwitting gate-watchers.

"Yeah. OK, I'm tired of running. I like it here, Gideon. And what good does it do Judy? That how you spotted us? She's not too good at this game."

"No, it was the dolphins," I said. "Turner. You remember Turner?"

He grimaced. "Sure. Holier than thou. America for the Good Americans, whoever the hell they are. I think he likes termination orders. What's he got to do with this?"

"He hates dolphins," I said. "Afraid they'll replace people or something. Reads everything he can find on them. Something he read made him wonder if you were out here at Dansworth. I don't know what it was, but he had Plans take a look. *Then* we spotted your wife."

"I see. Yeah, there was a *Science* article that might have given me away, but I didn't think anybody in the Company would read it. . . ."

"He did. And really got mad. Double traitor, he called you. Traitor to the Agency, and traitor to the whole

human race. Not that the dolphins made any difference.
Harold Braden. OK, you cut and ran. There's a few get
away with that. But not when they warn their subject
first. We can't allow that, Braden." I shifted the shark
dart in my hand, turning it over and over, wondering
what would happen if he decided to fight. He was nearly
as big as I am, and he'd been a good man in his day. But
he was out of training, and he seemed to have given up.

I had to remember that a man hasn't really given up
until he's dead. Not a real man.

"Call me Hank," he said. "I killed Harold Braden five
years ago. Did they tell you who the subject was? The
man I warned?"

"No."

"Aeneas MacKenzie."

I whistled. It didn't come out as much; the hearing
aids weren't designed for that. The whole conversation
had an eerie quality, as we talked of life and death in
flat monotones. "MacKenzie. Greg Tolland's manager.
If you'd got him, Tolland wouldn't have been
President. . . ." I thought for a moment. Five years. "It
was *after* the election! Tolland's orders!" Again the excla-
mation points didn't come through. All Hank could have
heard was another monotone.

"Yeah. I know."

But I'd believed the story. Tolland made Aeneas Mac-
Kenzie his Solicitor General, and MacKenzie found graft
and corruption all through Tolland's People's Alliance.
It had nearly destroyed President Tolland, but we all
believed he hadn't known any of it until MacKenzie
uncovered the mess.

Only Tolland ordered MacKenzie terminated with
extreme prejudice before he even started his investigations.

"You know MacKenzie's gone over to Hansen Enterprises?" I asked.

"You told me." Hank kept watching me, and every now and then he'd look away, out the windows, to watch the fish and shrimp cruising past; and when he'd look back again, he did it with surprise that he was still alive. "I guess it figures. Laurie Jo Hansen never had much use for Greg Tolland to begin with." He laughed. The hearing aids made it come out "Ha. Ha. Ha." And a snort. "Funny. We always thought the big corporations were the enemy."

"They are. You know how they work."

"Sure. How do we work?"

"It's different. We've got no choices. We're soldiers. How else can the people fight that kind of power? Don't play games with my head, Shields. It won't work."

"Didn't think it would. You can't admit you're wrong. You've spilled too much blood for the cause. Admit you're wrong and you're a monster. I know, Gideon. I *know*."

We were quiet for a while. Finally I said, "Hansen's got a set-up like this in the Sea of Cortez. Experimental. Not full production scale."

Hank nodded. "Pity I didn't run to her in the first place. You'd have had your problems getting to me. Too late now. Not even Hansen could keep your people away from me. Not forever. And I'd always come out in the open if the family was involved."

Family. I thought about Judy. She'd be alone soon. And that was stupid, because I'd always be alone. "Nobody'd look for a dead man."

I don't know why I said that. In my business you do your job and that's all. Hank was right, you can't question your orders. If the people at the top don't know what they're doing, if it isn't worth it, what are you? A goddam hired killer, a criminal, and I'm not that, I'm a patriot. A soldier.

Hank gave me another funny look. "If you report me dead and I turn up again—"

"Yeah." If that happened, I was meat, I *should* be. One day I'd find myself across a room from somebody like Gideon Starr. Get it over, my mind said. Hank was looking out the window again. One quick thrust. Or the right blow, and push him out without the SCUBA gear. Without the gear he'd go straight up, and nobody had ever survived a free ascent from those depths. He'd float, lungs ruptured, embolisms all through his blood and brain. Quick, painless, and easy to explain.

And I knew I wasn't going to do it. "If a man bought it with his gear on down here, he'd go right to the bottom," I said. "No way ever to find a body."

"But he'd have to leave Dansworth. You think I'd get past your people?" He turned to face me again, but this time he didn't look surprised. Just tired. "I told you, Gideon, I killed Harold Braden. Hank Shields doesn't let his friends trade their lives for him."

"Friends?"

"By me, yeah." He didn't say anything else, but I remembered how it was with the two of us swimming Jill to the surface, watching for sharks, waiting for the flash of pain in the head that signals embolism, or the crippling stab in the joint from bends. . . .

We sat there some more, thinking. "If you got to Hansen's outfit off the Baja coast, you'd be OK," I said finally. "Seven hundred miles. Open water. Don't dolphins go that far?"

This time he really looked at me.

"There are spare air bottles in here, aren't there?" I asked. "Air and helium-oxy? Enough to let you decompress? And you've got the call-box. Trust the dolphins to take you seven hundred miles?"

He thought about it. "We'd make about ten knots. Three days. Warm water." He started rooting around in the lockers and came up with canteens. "Fresh water. I won't need food. The dolphins can catch fish, and a man can live a long time on fresh raw fish. How'll you explain the supplies missing from here?"

"Who's to know we were ever here? I'll have good stories, for the Navy and for the Agency. You're down in that muck, in five hundred fathoms."

"You're crazy. They'll watch Judy. I have to send for her, Gideon. When she comes to Hansen's outfit, they'll suspect. Then we've both had it."

"They won't bother with her. Not if you're dead."

"Why, Gideon?" he asked.

"Get the hell out of here. Just do it." Please. Before I change my mind, before I get my sanity back. For God's sake, Hank, go, please, go.

He put on the SCUBA gear and gathered up water bottles. Then he made a neat towing package of the other stuff, helium-oxy bottles, and some pure oxygen for when he got closer to the surface and wouldn't get oxygen poisoning. He could stay down a long time with those. Much longer than the decompression time he'd need. If there were storms, he'd just go under. The dolphins would take care of him.

"Dr. Peterson's going to hate losing Jill and Sarah." He looked back at me for a second. "You'll tell Judy?"

"She'll know. Not at First. Later."

He winced. It was going to be tough on the family. His only other choice would be tougher. He waved, just a quick flash of the hand, and dropped through the bottom of the shelter.

A long time after, as I swam alone back to the mining station, I saw a whole school of sharks. One was wounded, and the others were tearing him to pieces, eating him while he was still alive.

I wondered if they'd see me, but I didn't really care.

Consort

The senator looked from the bureau with its chipped paint and cracked mirror to the expensive woman seated on the sagging bed. My God, he thought. What if one of my constituents could see me now? Or the press people got wind of this?

He opened the leather attaché case and turned knobs on the console inside. Green lights winked reassuringly. He took a deep breath and turned to the girl.

"Laurie Jo, would it surprise you to know I don't give a damn whether the President is a crook or not?" the senator asked.

"Then why are you here?" Her voice was soft, with a note of confidence, almost triumphant.

Senator Hayden shook his head. This is a hell of a thing. The Senate Majority Leader meets with the richest woman in the whole goddam world, and the only way we can trust each other is to come to a place like this. She picks the highway and I pick the motel. Both of us have scramblers goin', and we're still not sure nobody's makin' a tape. Hell of a thing.

"Because you might be able to *prove* President Tolland's a crook. Maybe make a lot of people believe it," Hayden said. "I can."

"Yeah." She sounds so damned confident, and if what she sent me's a good sample of what she's got, she can do it, all right. "That's what scares me, Laurie Jo. The country can't take it again."

He drew in a lungful of air. It smelled faintly of gin. Hayden exhaled heavily and sank into the room's only chair. One of the springs was loose, and it jabbed him. "Christ Almighty!" he exploded.

"First Watergate. No sooner'n we get over that, and we're in a depression. Inflation. Oil crisis. The Equity Trust business. One damn thing after another. And when the Party gets together a real reform wing and wins the election, Tolland's own Solicitor General finds the Equity people right next to the President!

"So half the White House staff goes, and we get past that somehow and people still got something to believe in, and you're tellin' me you can prove the President was in on all of it. Laurie Jo, you just can't do that to the country!"

She spread her skirts across her knees and wished she'd taken the chair. She never liked sitting without a backrest. The interview was distasteful, and she wished there were another way, but she didn't know one. We're so nearly out of all this, she thought. So very near.

"DING."

It was a sound in her mind, but not one the senator could hear. He was saying something about public confidence. She half listened to him, while she thought, "I WAS NOT TO BE DISTURBED."

"MISTER MC CARTNEY SAYS IT IS VERY IMPORTANT. SIGNOR ANTONELLI IS CONCERNED ABOUT HIS NEXT SHIPMENT."

"WILL IT BE ON TIME?" she thought.

"ONLY HALF. HIS BIOLOGICALS WILL BE TWO DAYS LATE," the computer link told her. The system was a luxury she sometimes regretted: not the cost, because a million dollars was very little to her; but although the implanted transceiver link gave her access to all of her holdings and allowed her to control the empire she owned, it gave her no peace.

"TELL MC CARTNEY TO STALL. I WILL CALL ANTONELLI IN TWO HOURS," she thought.

"MISTER MC CARTNEY SAYS ANTONELLI WILL NOT WAIT."

"TELL MC CARTNEY TO DORK HIMSELF."

"ACKNOWLEDGED."

"AND LEAVE ME ALONE."

"OUT."

And that takes care of that, she thought. The computer was programmed to take her insulting commands and translate them into something more polite; it wouldn't do to annoy one of her most important executives. If he needed to be disciplined, she'd do it face to face.

The senator had stopped talking and was looking at her. "I can prove it, Barry. All of it. But I don't want to."

Senator Hayden felt very old. "We're almost out of the slump," he said. He wasn't speaking directly to Laurie Jo any longer, and he didn't look at her. "Got the biggest

R&D budget in twenty years. Unemployment's down a point. People are beginning to have some confidence again." There was peeling wallpaper in one corner of the room. Senator Hayden balled his hands into fists and the nails dug into his palms.

When he had control of himself, he met her eyes and was startled again at how blue they were. *Dark red hair, oval face, blue eyes, expensive clothes; she's damn near every man's dream of a woman, and she's got me. I never made a dishonest deal in my life, but God help me, she's got me.*

I have to deal, but—"Has MacKenzie seen your stuff? Does he know?"

Laurie Jo nodded. "Aeneas didn't want to believe it. Your media friends aren't the only ones who want to think Greg Tolland's an honest man. But he's got no choice now. He has to believe it."

"Then we can't deal," Hayden said. "What the hell are you wasting my time for? MacKenzie won't deal. He'll kamikaze." *And do I admire him or hate him for that?*

There's something inhuman about a man who thinks he's justice personified. The last guy who got tagged as "The Incorruptible" was that Robespierre character, and his own cronies cut his head off when they couldn't take him any longer.

"I'll take care of Aeneas," Laurie Jo said.

"How?"

"You'll have to trust me."

"I've already trusted you. I'm here, aren't I?" But he shook his head sadly. "Maybe I know more'n you think. I know MacKenzie connected up with you after he left the White House. God knows you're enough woman to turn any man around, but you don't know him, Laurie Jo, you don't know him at all if you think—"

"I have known Aeneas MacKenzie for almost twenty years," she said. "And I've been in love with him since the first day I met him. The two years we lived together were the happiest either of us ever had."

"Sure," Barry Hayden said. "Sure. You knew him back in the old days before Greg Tolland was anything much. So did I. I told you, maybe I know more'n you think. But goddam it, you didn't see him for ten, twelve years—"

"Sixteen years," she said. "And we had only a few weeks after that." Glorious weeks, but Greg Tolland couldn't leave us alone. He had to spoil even that. Damn him! I have more than one reason to hate Greg Tolland—"Why don't you listen instead of talking all the time? I can handle Aeneas. You want political peace and quiet for a few years, and I can give them to you."

I don't listen because I'm afraid of what I'll hear, the senator thought. Because I never wanted this day to come, and I knew it would when I went into politics, but I managed for this long, and it got to lookin' like it never would come and now I'm in a cheap motel room about to be told the price of whatever honor I've got left.

God help us, she's got all the cards. If anybody can shut MacKenzie up—

The room still smelled of cheap gin, and the senator tasted bile at the back of his throat. "OK, Laurie Jo, what do I have to do?"

Aeneas MacKenzie switched off the newscast and stared vacantly at the blank screen. There had been nothing about President Greg Tolland, and it disturbed him.

His office was a small cubicle off the main corridor. It was large enough for a desk as well as the viewscreen and console that not only gave him instant access to every file and data bank on *Heimdall* Station, but also a link with the master Hansen data banks on Earth below. He disliked microfilm and readout screens and would greatly have preferred to work with printed reports and documents, but that wasn't possible. Every kilogram of mass was important when it had to go into orbit.

There was never enough mass at *Heimdall.* Energy was no problem; through the viewport he could see solar cells plastered over every surface, and further away was the power station, a large mirror reflecting onto a boiler and turbine. Everything could be recycled except reaction mass: but whenever the scooters went out to collect supply pods boosted up from Earth, that mass was lost forever. The recent survey team sent to the Moon had cost hideously, leaving the station short of fuel for its own operations.

He worked steadily on the production schedules, balancing the station's inadequate manpower reserves to fill the most critical orders without taking anyone off the *Valkyrie* project. It was an impossible task, and he felt a sense of pride in his partial success. It was a strange job for the former Solicitor General of the United States, but he believed his legal training helped; and he was able to get the crew to work harder than they had thought they could.

Get *Valkyrie* finished, Laurie Jo had said. It must be done as quickly as possible, no matter what it does to the production schedules. She'd said that, but she couldn't have meant it; Aeneas knew what would happen if *Heimdall* didn't continue sending down space-manufactured products. *Heimdall* was a valuable installation, now that there were no risks left in building it, and Laurie Jo's partners were ruthless; if she defaulted on deliveries, they'd take it away from her.

Eventually the assignments were done. By taking a construction shift himself (he estimated his value at 65% as productive as a trained rigger, double what it had been when he first tried the work), he could put another man on completing the new biological production compartment. The schedule would work, but there was no slack in it.

When he was done, he left the small compartment and strode through the corridor outside. He was careful to close and dog the airtight entryway into his office, as he was careful about everything he did. As he walked, his eyes automatically scanned the shining metallic cloth of *Heimdall's* inner walls, but he was no more aware of that than he was of the low spin gravity and Coriolis effect.

The corridor curved upwards in front of and behind him. When he reached the doorway to the Chief Engineer's office, it stood open in defiance of regulations. Aeneas nodded wryly and ignored it. Kittridge Penrose made the regulations in the first place, and Aeneas only enforced them. Presumably Penrose knew what he was doing. If he doesn't, Aeneas thought, we're all in trouble.

Penrose was in the office, as Aeneas knew he would be; one of his prerogatives was to know where everyone was. The engineer was at his desk. A complex diagram filled the screen to his left, and Penrose was carefully drawing lines with a light pen. He looked up as Aeneas came into the office. "What's up, boss?"

"I don't know." Aeneas peered at the screen. Penrose noticed the puzzled look and touched buttons on the console below the picture. The diagram changed, not blinking out to be replaced, but rearranging itself until it showed an isometric view which Aeneas recognized instantly.

"Right on schedule," Penrose said. "Just playing about with some possible improvements. There she is, *Valkyrie,* all ready to go."

"Except for the engines."

Penrose shrugged. "You can't have everything. Nothing new from Miss Hansen about getting that little item taken care of?"

"Not yet."

"Heh. She'll manage it." Penrose went back to his game with the light pen. "I used to think my part of this was the real work," the engineer said. He sketched in another line. "But it isn't. I just design the stuff. It's you people who get it built."

"Thanks." And it's true enough: Laurie Jo put together the syndicate to finance this whole station.

"Sure. Meant that, you know," Penrose said. "You've done about as well as Captain Shorey. Didn't think you'd be much as commander here, but I was wrong." Now that, Aeneas thought, is high praise indeed. And I suppose it's even true. I do fill a needed function here. Something I didn't do when I was down there with Laurie Jo. Down there I was a Prince Consort, and nothing else.

True enough I came here because I was the only one she could trust to take control, but I've been more than just her agent.

"Sit down, boss," Penrose said. "Have a drink. You look like you're in need of one."

"Thanks, I'll pass on the drink." He took the other chair and watched as Penrose worked. I could never do

that, he thought, but there aren't a lot of jobs up here
that I can't do now. . . .

The newscast haunted him. Laurie Jo had the whole
story, all the evidence needed to bring Greg Tolland
down. *We can prove the President of the United States
is a criminal. Why hasn't she done it? Why?*

*I don't even dare call and ask her. We can't know
someone isn't listening in. We can't trust codes, we can't
even trust our own computer banks, and how have things
come to this for the United States?*

"Got a couple of new reports from the Lunatics," Penrose said. "Had a chance to go over them?"

"No. That's what I came to talk to you about." The
console would have given him instant communications
with Penrose or anyone else aboard *Heimdall,* but
Aeneas always preferred to go to his people rather than
speak to them as an impersonal voice.

"Pretty good strike," Penrose said. "Another deposit
of hydrides and quite a lot of mica. No question about
it, we've got everything we need."

Aeneas nodded. It was curious: hydrogen is by orders
of magnitude the most common element in the universe,
but it had been hard to find on the Moon. There were
oxides, and given the plentiful energy available in space
that meant plenty of oxygen to breathe, but hydrogen
was rare.

Now the Lunar Survey Team sent up from *Heimdall*
had found hydrogen locked into various minerals. It was
available, and the colony was possible—if they could get
there. The survey team's fuel requirements had eaten
up a lot of the mass boosted up to *Heimdall,* and without
more efficient Earth-orbit-to-lunar-orbit transport it
would take a long time to make a colony self-sustaining.

"We've either got to bring the survey party home or send another supply capsule," Penrose was saying. "Which is it?"

"Like to hold off that decision as long as we can." And please don't ask why. I don't know why. Just that Laurie Jo says do it this way.

Penrose frowned. "If you'll authorize some monkey motion, we can do the preliminaries for going either way. That'll hold off the decision another couple of weeks. No more than that, though."

"All right. Do it that way."

"What's eating you, Aeneas?"

"Nothing. I've been up here too long."

"Sure." Kit Penrose didn't say that he'd been aboard *Heimdall* nearly two years longer than MacKenzie's eighteen months, but he didn't have to.

Of course, Penrose thought, I've had my girl here with me; and MacKenzie's seen his precisely twice since he's been here, a couple of weekends and back she went to look after the money. Wonder what it's like to sleep with the big boss? What a silly thing to wonder about.

The diagram faded and another view came on the screen. "There she is," Penrose said. "Lovely, isn't she?"

Valkyrie may have been lovely to an engineer, but she was hardly a work of art. There was no symmetry to the ship. Since she would never land, she had neither top nor bottom, only fore and aft. "All we need is the NERVA, and we're all set," Penrose said. "No reason why the whole Moon colony staff can't go out a week after we have the engines."

"Yes."

"Christ, how can you be so cold about it? Moon base. Plenty of mass. Metals to work with. Who knows, maybe even radioactives. We can cut loose from those bastards down there!" He waved at the viewport where Earth filled the sky before the station slowly turned again to show the sequined black velvet of space. "And we've very nearly done it."

"Very nearly." But we haven't done it, and I don't see how we can.

"What we need are those military aerospace-planes," Penrose said. His voice became more serious. "I expect they'll be coming round for visits whether we invite them or not, you know."

"Yes. Well, we got on with their chaps all right—"

"Sure," Penrose said. "Sure. Visiting astronauts and all that lot. Proud to show them around. Even so, I can't say I'm happy they can get up here whenever they like. . . ."

"Nor I." Aeneas opened a hinged panel beside the desk and took out a coffee cup. He filled it from a spigot near Penrose's hand. "Cannonshot," he said.

"I beg your pardon?"

"In the old days, national law reached out to sea as far as cannonballs could be fired from shore. Three miles, more or less. It became the legal boundary of a nation's sovereignty. There used to be a lot of talk about international law in space, and the rest of it, but it will probably be settled by something like cannonshot again. When the national governments can get up here easily, they'll assert control."

"Like to be gone when that happens," Penrose said. "Can't say I want more regulations and red tape and committees. Had enough of that lot."

"So have we all." Aeneas drank the coffee. "So have we all."

Penrose laughed. "That's a strange thing to say, considering that you were one of the prime movers of the People's Alliance."

"Maybe I've learned something from the experience." Aeneas stared moodily into his coffee cup. *I wasn't wrong*, he thought. *But I wasn't right either. There's got to be more than comfort and security, and we didn't think of that, because the Cause was all the adventure* we *needed.*

I wonder how long it will take them to make space tame? Forms to fill out, regulations always enforced, not because of safety but because they're regulations . . .

Penrose looked at the digital readouts above his drafting console: Greenwich time, and Mountain Daylight time. "Big shipment coming up next pass over Baja. I'd best be getting ready for it."

"Yes." Aeneas listened without paying much attention as Penrose told him what the big lasers in southern Baja would send up this time. It didn't really concern him yet, and when he needed to know more, the information would be available through his desk console.

As the engineer talked, Aeneas remembered what it had been like to watch the launches: the field covered with lasers, their mirrors all focusing onto the one large mirror beneath the tramway. The squat shapes of the capsules on the tramway, each waiting to be brought over the launching mirror and thrust upward by the stabbing light, looking as if they were lifted by a fantastically swift-growing tree rising out of the desert; the thrumming note of the pulsed beam singing in hot desert air.

It had been the most magnificent sight he had ever seen, and Laurie Jo had built it all. Now she was ready to move onward, but her partners were not. They were content to own *Heimdall* and sell its products, raking in billions from the miracles that could be wrought in space.

Biologicals of every conceivable kind. Crystals of an ultimate purity grown in mass production and infected with precisely the right contaminants, all grown in mass production.

Heimdall had revolutionized more than one industry. Already there were hand calculators with thousands of words of memory space, all made from the chips grown in orbit. Deserts bloomed as the production crews sent down membranes that would pass fresh water and keep salt back; they too could be made cheaply only in zero gravity conditions.

Why take high risks on a Moon base when there was so much more potential to exploit in orbital production? The investors could prove that more money was to be made through expanding *Heimdall* than through sending *Valkyrie* exploring. They remembered that they would never have invested in space production at all if Laurie Jo hadn't bullied them into it, and that had been enough to give her some freedom of action; but they could not see profits in the Moon for many years to come.

And they're right, Aeneas thought. Laurie Jo doesn't plan for the next phase to make profits, not for a long time.

She wants the stars for herself. And what do I want? Lord God, I miss her. But I'm *needed* here. I have work to do, and I'd better get at it.

The airline reception lounge was no longer crowded. A few minutes before, it had been filled with Secret Service men and Hansen Security agents. Now there was only one of each in the room with Laurie Jo. They stayed at opposite ends of the big room, and they eyed each other like hostile dogs.

"Relax, Miguel," Laurie Jo said. "Between us there are enough security people to protect an army. The President will be safe enough—"

"Si, *Doña* Laura." The elderly man's eyes never left the long-haired younger man at the other end of the room. "I am willing to believe *he* is safe enough."

"For heaven's sake, I'm meeting the President of the United States!"

"Si, *Doña* Laura. *Don* Aeneas has told me of this man who has become President here. I do not care for this."

"Jesus." The Secret Service man curled his lip in contempt. "How did you do it?" he demanded.

"How did I do what, Mr. Coleman?" she asked.

"Turn MacKenzie against the President! Fifteen years he was with the Chief. Fifteen years with the People's Alliance. Now you've got him telling tales about the Chief to your peasant friend there—"

"Miguel is not a peasant."

"Ah, *Doña* Laura, but I am. Go on, *Señor.* Tell us of this strange thing you do not understand." There was amusement in the old vaquero's eyes.

"Skip it. It just doesn't make sense, that's all."

"Perhaps my *patrona* bribed *Don* Aeneas," Miguel said.

"That will do," Laurie Jo said. Miguel nodded and was silent.

"Bullshit," Coleman said. "Nobody ever got to MacKenzie. Nobody has *his* price. Not in money, anyway." He looked at Laurie Jo in disbelief. He didn't think her unattractive, but he couldn't believe she was enough woman to drive a man insane.

"You're rather young to know Aeneas that well," Laurie Jo said.

"I joined the People's Alliance before the campaign." There was pride in the agent's voice. "Stood guard watches over the Chief. Helped in the office. MacKenzie was with us every day. He's not hard to know, not like some party types."

"INFORMATION," Laurie Jo thought. "COLEMAN FIRST NAME UNKNOWN, SECRET SERVICE AGENT. RECENTLY APPOINTED. SUMMARY."

"COLEMAN, THEODORE RAYMOND. AGE 25. PAID STAFF, PEOPLE'S ALLIANCE UNTIL INAUGURATION OF PRESIDENT GREGORY TOLLAND. APPOINTED TO SECRET SERVICE BY ORDERS OF PRESIDENT TO TAKE EFFECT INAUGURAL DAY. EDUCATION—"

"SUFFICIENT." Laurie Jo nodded to herself. Coleman hadn't been like the career Secret Service men. There were a lot of young people like Coleman in the undercover services lately, party loyalists who had known Greg before the election.

Personally loyal bodyguards have been the mark of tyrants for three thousand years, she thought. But some of the really great leaders have had them as well. Can any President do without them? Can I?

Not here. But I won't need guards on the Moon. I won't—

"DING."

"WHAT NOW?"

"THERE IS A GENERAL STRIKE PLANNED IN BOLIVIA. TWO HANSEN AGENTS HAVE INFILTRATED THE UNION. THEY HAVE FOUND OUT

THE DATE OF THE STRIKE, AND WERE DISCOV-
ERED WHEN TRANSMITTING THEIR INFORMA-
TION. SUPERINTENDENT HARLOW WISHES TO
TAKE IMMEDIATE ACTION TO RESCUE THEM.
WILL YOU APPROVE?"

"GIVE HARLOW FULL AUTHORIZATION TO
TAKE WHATEVER ACTION HE THINKS
REQUIRED. REPORT WHEN HIS PLANS ARE
COMPLETE BUT BEFORE EXECUTION."

"ACKNOWLEDGED."

Another damned problem, she thought. Harlow was a
good man, but he thought in pretty drastic terms. What
will that do to our other holdings in Bolivia? One thing,
it will hurt my partner worse than it will hurt me. I'll
have to think about this. Later, now I've got something
more important.

The door opened to admit another Secret Service
man. "Chief's on the way," he said.

"DO NOT CALL ME FOR ANY PURPOSE," she
thought.

"ACKNOWLEDGED."

It was almost comical. The Secret Service men
wouldn't leave until Miguel had gone, and Miguel
wouldn't leave his *patrona* alone with the Secret Service
men. Finally they all backed out together, and Laurie Jo
was alone for a moment. Then President Greg Tolland
came in.

He's still President, she thought. No matter that I've
known him twenty years and fought him for half that
time. There's an aura that goes with the office, and Greg
wears it well. "Good afternoon, Mr. President."

"Senator Hayden says I should talk to you," Tolland
said.

"Aren't you even going to say hello?" She thought he looked very old; yet she knew he was only a few years older than herself, one of the youngest men ever to be elected to the office.

"What should I say, Laurie Jo? That I wish you well? I do, but you wouldn't believe that. That I'd like to be friends? Would you believe me if I said that? I do wish we could be friends, but I hate everything you stand for."

"Well said, sir!" She applauded. "But there's no audience here." And you only hate that the fortune I inherited wasn't used to help your political ambitions, not that I have it. You always were more comfortable with wealthy people than Aeneas was.

He grinned wryly. It was a famous grin, and Laurie Jo could remember when Congressman Tolland had practiced it with Aeneas and herself as his only audience. It seemed so very long ago, back in the days when her life was simple and she hadn't known who her father was, or that one day she would inherit his wealth.

"Mind if I sit down?"

She shrugged. "Why ask? But please do."

He took one of the expensively covered lounge chairs and waited until she'd done the same. "I ask because this is your place."

True enough. I own the airline. But it's hardly my home and this is hardly a social visit. "Can I get you anything? Your agents have sampled everything at the bar—"

"I'll have a bourbon, then. They shouldn't have done that. Here, I'll get—"

"It's all right. I know where everything is." She poured drinks for both of them. "Your young men don't trust me. One of them even accused me of seducing Aeneas away from you."

"Didn't you."

She handed him the drink. "Oh good God, Greg. You don't have to be careful what you say to me. Nothing I could tape could make things worse than I can make them right now. And I give you my word, nobody's listening."

His eyes narrowed. For a moment he resembled a trapped animal.

"Believe that, Greg. There's no way out," she said. "With what I already had and what Aeneas knows—"

"I'll never know how I put up with that fanatic S.O.B. for so long."

"That's beneath you, Greg. You wouldn't be President if Aeneas hadn't helped you."

"Not true."

It is true, but why go on? And yet—"Why have you turned so hard against him? Because he wouldn't sell out and you did?"

"Maybe I had no choice, Laurie Jo. Maybe I'd got so far out on so many limbs that I couldn't retreat, and when I came crashing down the Alliance would come down with me. Maybe I thought it was better that we win however we had to than go on leading a noble lost cause. This isn't what we came here to talk about. Senator Hayden says you've got a proposition for me."

"Yes." And how Barry Hayden hates all of this. Another victim of patriotism. Another? Am I including Greg Tolland in that category? And what difference does it make? "It's simple enough, Greg. I can see that you'll be allowed to finish your term without any problems from me. Or from Aeneas. I can have the Hansen papers and network stop their campaigns against you. I won't switch to your support."

"Wouldn't want it. That would look too fishy. What's your price for all this?"

"You weren't always this direct."

"What the hell do you want, Laurie Jo? You've got the President of the United States asking your favor. You want me to crawl too?"

"No. All right, the first price is your total retirement from politics when your term is over. You don't make that promise to me. You'll give it to Barry Hayden."

"Maybe. I'll think about it. What do you want for yourself?"

"I want a big payload delivered to *Heimdall*."

"What the hell?"

"You've got those big military aerospace planes. I want something carried to orbit."

"I'll think about it."

"You'll do it."

"I don't know." He stared into his glass. "If it means this much to you, it's important. I'd guess it's tied in with that lunar survey party, right? Your Moon colony plans?"

She didn't answer.

"That's got to be it." He drained the cocktail and began laughing. "You can't throw me out because you'd never get anyone else to agree to this! It's pretty funny, Laurie Jo. You and Mr. Clean. You *need* me! More than just this once, too, I expect—What is it you want delivered?"

"Just a big payload."

Tolland laughed again. "I can find out, you know. I've still got a few people inside your operation."

"I suppose you do. All right, I've got a working NERVA engine for *Valkyrie*. It's too big for the laser launching system. We could send it up in pieces, but it would take a long time to get it assembled and checked out." And I don't have a long time. I'm running out of time. . . .

"So you want me to hand over the Moon to a private company. That's what it amounts to, isn't it? The People's Alliance was formed to break up irresponsible power like yours, and you want me to hand you the Moon."

"That's my price, Greg. You won't like the alternative."

"Yeah. It's still pretty funny. A couple more years and you won't have a goddam monopoly on manned space stations. So you want me to help you get away."

"Something like that. We see things differently."

"You know you're doomed, don't you? Laurie Jo, it's over. You sit there in your big office and decide things for the whole world. Who asked you to? It's time the people had a say over their lives. You think I'm ambitious. Maybe. But for all of it, everything I've done has been in the right direction. At least I'm not building up a personal empire that's as anachronistic as a dinosaur!"

"Spare me the political speeches, Greg." God, he means it. Or he thinks he does. He can justify anything he does because he's the agent for the people, but what does it mean in the real world? Just how much comfort is it to know it's all for the good of the people when you're caught in the machinery? "I won't argue with you. I've got something you need, and I'm willing to sell."

"And you get the Moon as a private fief."

"If you want to think of it that way, go ahead. But if you want to be President three months from now, you'll do as I ask."

"And why should I think you'll keep your bargain?"

"When have I ever broken my promises?" Laurie Jo asked.

"Don't know. Tell you what, get MacKenzie to promise. That way I'll be sure you mean it."

"I'll do better than that. Aeneas and I are both going to the Moon. We can hardly interfere with you from there."

"You are crazy, aren't you?" Tolland's face showed wonder but not doubt. "You know you're going to lose a lot. You can't manage your empire from the Moon."

"I know." And how long could I hold out to begin with? And for what? "Greg, you just don't understand that power's no use, money's no use, unless it's for something that counts."

"And getting to the Moon is that big?" He shook his head in disbelief. "You're crazy."

"So are a lot of us, then. I've got ten volunteers for every opening. Pretty good people, too—as you should know."

"Yeah. I know." Tolland got up and wandered around the big room until he came to the bar. He filled his glass with ice cubes and water, then added a tiny splash of whiskey. "You've got some of my best people away from me. You can pay them more—"

"I can, but I don't have to. You still don't understand, do you? It's not my money, and it's not my control over the Moon colony that counts. What's important is this will be one place that you don't control."

"Hah. I hadn't thought I was that unpopular with the engineers."

"I don't mean you personally," Laurie Jo said. "Your image control people have done well. But, Greg, can't you understand that some of us want out of your system?"

"Aeneas too?"

"Yes." More than any of us, because he knows better than any of us what it's going to be like—

"I should have known he'd go to you after I threw him out."

"There wasn't anywhere else he could go. Mr. President, this isn't getting us anywhere. You'll never understand us, so why try? Just send up that payload and you'll be rid of us. You may even be lucky. We'll lose people in the lunar colony. Maybe we'll all be killed."

"And you're willing to chance that—"

"I told you, you won't understand us. Don't try. Just send up my payload."

"I'll think about it," Tolland said. "But your other conditions are off. No promises. No political deals." The President stood and went to the door. He turned defiantly. "You get the Moon. That ought to be enough."

He felt dizzy and it was hard to breathe in the high gravity of Earth. When he poured a drink, he almost spilled it, because he was unconsciously allowing for the displacement usual in *Heimdall's* centrifugal gravity. Now he sat weakly in the large chair.

The Atlantic Ocean lay outside his window, and he watched the moving lights of ships. The room lights came on suddenly, startling him.

"What—*Miguel!*" Laurie Jo shouted. Then she laughed foolishly. "*No esta nada. Deseo solamente estar, por favor.*" She came into the room as Miguel closed the door behind her. "Hello, Aeneas. I might have known. No one else could get in here without someone telling me—"

He stood with an effort. "Didn't mean to startle you." He stood uncomfortably, wishing for her, cursing himself for not telling her he was coming. But I wanted to shock you, he thought.

"You didn't really. I think Greg has called off his dogs. I'm safe enough. But—you're not!"

"I'll take my chances."

"Why are we standing here like this?" she asked. She moved toward him. He stood rigidly for a moment, but then stepped across the tiny space that separated them, and they were together again.

For how long? he thought. How long do we have this time? But then it didn't matter any more.

"Laurie Jo—"

"Not yet." She poured coffee for both of them and yawned. Her outstretched arms waved toward the blue waters far below their terrace. "Let's have a few minutes more."

They sat in silence. She tried to watch the Atlantic, but the silence stretched on. "All right, darling. What is it?"

"There's been nothing on the newscasts about Greg. And then I got a signal. Prepare *Valkyrie* at once. The engines will be up, intact."

"And you wondered if there was a connection?" she asked.

"I knew there was a connection." There was no emotion in his voice, and that frightened her.

"I've bought us the stars, Aeneas. The engines will go up in a week. Tested, ready for installation. And you've done the rest, you and Kit. We can go to the Moon, with all the equipment for the colony—"

"Yes. And Greg Tolland stays on."

She wanted to shout. What is that to you? she wanted to say. But she couldn't. "It was his price. The only one he'd take."

"It's too high."

She drew the thin silk robe around herself. Despite the bright sun she felt suddenly cold. "I've already agreed. I've given Greg my word."

"But I haven't. And you didn't tell me you were doing this."

"How could I? You wouldn't have agreed!"

"Precisely—"

"I can't lie to you, Aeneas." And now what do I lose? You? Everything I've worked for? Both? "The deal hasn't been made. Greg wants your word too."

"And if I don't give it?"

"Then he won't send up the engines. You're close enough to know what happens then. I'm at the edge of losing control of *Heimdall* to my partners. This is my only chance."

But it didn't have to be, he thought. You're in trouble because you insisted on speeding up the schedule, no matter what that cost, and it cost a lot. Technicians pulled off production work for *Valkyrie*. The Lunatic expedition. "You've put me in a hell of a fix, Laurie Jo."

"Damn you! Aeneas MacKenzie, damn you anyway!" He tried to speak, but the rush of words stopped him as she shouted in anger. "Who appointed you guardian of the people? You and your damned honor! You're ready to throw away everything, and for what? For revenge on Greg Tolland!"

"But that's not true! I don't want revenge."

"Then what do you want, Aeneas?"

"I wanted out, Laurie Jo. It was you who insisted that I direct your agents in the investigation. I was finished with all that. I was willing to leave well enough alone, until we found—" Until it was clear that Greg Tolland had known everything. Until it was clear that he wasn't an honest man betrayed, that he was corrupt to the core, and had been for years. Until I couldn't help knowing that I'd spent most of my life electing—"You intended this all along, didn't you?" His voice was gentle and very sad.

Her anger was gone. It was impossible to keep it when he failed to respond. "Yes," she said. "It was the only way."

"The only way—"

"For us." She wouldn't meet his eyes. "What was I supposed to do, Aeneas? What kind of life do we have here? It takes every minute I have to keep Hansen Enterprises. Greg Tolland has already tried to have you killed. You were safe enough in *Heimdall*, but what good was that? With you there and me here? And I couldn't keep the station if I lived there." And we've got so little time. We lost so many years, and there are so few left.

They were silent for a moment. Gulls cried in the wind, and overhead a jet thundered.

"And now I've done it," she said. "We can go to the Moon. I can arrange more supplies. *Valkyrie* doesn't cost so much to operate, and we'll have nearly everything we need to build the colony anyway. We can do it, Aeneas. We can found the first lunar colony, and be free of all this."

"But only if I agree—"

"Yes."

"Laurie Jo, would you give up the Moon venture for me?"

"Don't ask me to. Would you give up your vendetta against Greg for the Moon?"

He stood and came around the table. She seemed helpless and vulnerable, and he put his hands on her shoulders. She looked up in surprise: his face was quite calm now.

"No," he said. "But I'll do as you ask. Not for the Moon, Laurie Jo. For you."

She stood and embraced him, but as they clung to each other she couldn't help thinking, thank God, he's not incorruptible after all. He's not more than human.

She felt almost sad.

Two delta shapes, one above the other; below both was the enormous bulk of the expendable fuel tank which powered the ramjet of the atmospheric booster. The big ships sat atop a thick, solid rocket that would boost them to ram speed.

All that, Laurie Jo thought. All that, merely to get into orbit. And before the spaceplanes and shuttles, there were the disintegrating totem poles. No wonder space was an unattractive gamble until I built my lasers.

The lasers had not been a gamble for her. A great part of the investment was in the power plants, and they made huge profits. The price she paid for *Heimdall* and *Valkyrie* hadn't been in money.

There were other costs, though, she thought. Officials bribed to expedite construction permits. Endless meetings to hold together a syndicate of international bankers. Deals with people who needed their money laundered. It would have been so easy to be part of the idle rich. Instead of parties I went to meetings, and I've yet to live with a man I love except for those few weeks we had.

And now I'm almost forty years old, and I have no children. But we will have! The doctors tell me I have a few years left, and we'll make the most of them.

They were taken up the elevator into the upper ship. It was huge, a squat triangle that could carry forty thousand kilos in one payload, and do it without the 30-g stresses of the laser system. They entered by the crew access door, but she could see her technicians making a final examination of the nuclear engine in the cargo compartment.

She was placed in the acceleration couch by an Air Force officer. Aeneas was across a narrow passageway, and there were no other passengers. The young A.F. captain had a worried frown, as if he couldn't understand why this mission had suddenly been ordered, and why two strange civilians were going with a cargo for *Heimdall*.

You wouldn't want to know, my young friend, Laurie Jo thought. You wouldn't want to know at all.

Motors whined as the big clamshell doors of the cargo compartment were closed down. The A.F. officer went forward into the crew compartment. Lights flashed on the instrument board mounted in the forward part of the passenger bay, but Laurie Jo didn't understand what they meant.

"DING."

"MY GOD, WHAT NOW?"

"SIGNOR ANTONELLI HAS JUST NOW HEARD THAT YOU ARE GOING UP TO HEIMDALL. HE IS VERY DISTURBED."

I'll just bet he is, Laurie Jo thought. She glanced across the aisle at Aeneas. He was watching the display.

"TELL SIGNOR ANTONELLI TO GO PLAY WITH HIMSELF."

"I HAVE NO TRANSLATION ROUTINE FOR THAT EXPRESSION."

"I DON'T WANT IT TRANSLATED. TELL HIM TO GO PLAY WITH HIMSELF."

There was a long pause. Something rumbled in the ship, then there were clanking noises as the gantries were drawn away.

"MISTER MC CARTNEY IS VERY DISTURBED ABOUT YOUR LAST MESSAGE AND ASKS THAT YOU RECONSIDER."

"TELL MC CARTNEY TO GO PLAY WITH HIMSELF TOO. CANCEL THAT. ASK MISTER MC CARTNEY TO SPEAK WITH SIGNOR ANTONELLI. I AM TAKING A VACATION. MC CARTNEY IS IN CHARGE. HE WILL HAVE TO MANAGE AS BEST HE CAN."

"ACKNOWLEDGED."

"Hear this. Liftoff in thirty seconds. Twenty-nine. Twenty-eight. Twenty seven . . . "

The count reached zero, and there was nothing for an eternity. Then the ship lifted, pushing her into the couch. After a few moments there was nothing, another agonizing moment before the ramjets caught. Even inside the compartment they could hear the roaring thunder before that, too, began to fade. The ship lifted, leveled, and banked to go on course for the trajectory that would take it into an orbit matching *Heimdall's.*

"GET MC CARTNEY ON THE LINE."

There was silence.

Out of range, she thought. She smiled and turned to Aeneas. "We did it," she said.

"Yes."

"You don't sound very excited."

He turned and smiled, and his hand reached out for hers, but they were too far apart. The ship angled steeply upward, and the roar of the ramjets grew louder again, then there was more weight as the rockets cut in. Seconds later the orbital vehicle separated from the carrier.

Laurie Jo looked through the thick viewport. The islands below were laid out like a map, their outlines obscured by cotton clouds far below them. The carrier ship banked off steeply and began its descent as the orbiter continued to climb.

Done, she thought. But she looked again at Aeneas, and he was staring back toward the United States and the world they had left behind.

"They don't need us, Aeneas," she said carefully.

"No. They don't need me at all."

She smiled softly. "But I need you. I always will."

Tinker

"The tinker came astridin', astridin' over the Strand, with his bullocks—"

"Rollo!"

"Yes, ma'am." I'd been singing at the top of my lungs, as I do when I've got a difficult piloting job, and I'd forgotten that my wife was in the control cab. I went back to the problem of setting our sixteen thousand tons of ship onto the rock.

It wasn't much of a rock. Jefferson is an irregular-shaped asteroid about twice as far out as Earth. It measures maybe seventy kilometers by fifty kilometers, and from far enough away it looks like an old mud brick somebody used for a shotgun target. It has a screwy rotation pattern that's hard to match with, and since I couldn't use the main engines, setting down was a tricky job.

Janet wasn't finished. "Roland Kephart, I've told you about those songs."

"Yeah, sure, hon." There are two inertial platforms in *Slingshot*, and they were giving me different readings. We were closing faster than I liked.

"It's bad enough that you teach them to the boys. Now the girls are—"

I motioned toward the open intercom switch, and Janet blushed. We fight a lot, but that's our private business.

The attitude jets popped. "Hear this," I said. "I think we're coming in too fast. Brace yourselves." The jets popped again, short bursts that stirred up dust storms on the rocky surface below. "But I don't think—" the ship jolted into place with a loud clang. We hit hard enough to shake things, but none of the red lights came on "—we'll break anything. Welcome to Jefferson. We're down."

Janet came over and cut off the intercom switch, and we hugged each other for a second. "Made it again," she said, and I grinned.

There wasn't much doubt on the last few trips, but when we first put *Slingshot* together out of the wreckage of two salvaged ships, every time we boosted out there'd been a good chance we'd never set down again. There's a lot that can go wrong in the Belt, and not many ships to rescue you.

I pulled her over to me and kissed her. "Sixteen years," I said. "You don't look a day older."

She didn't, either. She still had dark red hair, same color as when I met her at Elysium Mons Station on

Mars, and if she got it out of a bottle she never told me, not that I'd want to know. She was wearing the same thing I was, a skintight body stocking that looked as if it had been sprayed on. The purpose was strictly functional, to keep you alive if *Slinger* sprung a leak, but on her it produced some interesting curves. I let my hands wander to a couple of the more fascinating conic sections, and she snuggled against me.

She put her head close to my ear and whispered breathlessly, "Comm panel's lit."

"Bat puckey." There was a winking orange light, showing an outside call on our hailing frequency. Janet handed me the mike with a wicked grin. "Lock up your wives and hide your daughters, the tinker's come to town," I told it.

"*Slingshot,* this is Freedom Station. Welcome back, Cap'n Rollo."

"Jed?" I asked.

"Who the hell'd you think it was?"

"Anybody. Thought maybe you'd fried yourself in the solar furnace. How are things?" Jed's an old friend. Like a lot of asteroid Port Captains, he's a publican. The owner of the bar nearest the landing area generally gets the job, since there's not enough traffic to make Port Captains a fulltime deal. Jed used to be a miner in Pallas, and we'd worked together before I got out of the mining business.

We chatted about our families, but Jed didn't seem as interested as he usually is. I figured business wasn't too good. Unlike most asteroid colonies, Jefferson's independent. There's no big corporation to pay taxes to, but on the other hand there's no big organization to bail the Jeffersonians out if they get in too deep.

"Got a passenger this trip," I said.

"Yeah? Rockrat?" Jed asked.

"Nope. Just passing through. Oswald Dalquist. Insurance adjuster. He's got some kind of policy settlement to make here, then he's with us to Marsport."

There was a long pause, and I wondered what Jed was thinking about. "I'll be aboard in a little," he said. "Freedom Station out."

Janet frowned. "That was abrupt."

"Sure was." I shrugged and began securing the ship. There wasn't much to do. The big work is shutting down the main engines, and we'd done that a long way out from Jefferson. You don't run an ion engine toward an inhabited rock if you care about your customers.

"Better get the big'uns to look at the inertial platforms, hon," I said. "They don't read the same."

"Sure. Hal thinks it's the computer."

"Whatever it is, we better get it fixed." That would be a job for the oldest children. Our family divides nicely into the Big Ones, the Little Ones, and the Baby, with various subgroups and pecking orders that Janet and I don't understand. With nine kids aboard, five ours and four adopted, the system can get confusing. Jan and I find it's easier to let them work out the chain of command for themselves.

I unbuckled from the seat and pushed away. You can't walk on Jefferson, or any of the small rocks. You can't quite swim through the air, either. Locomotion is mostly a matter of jumps.

As I sailed across the cabin, a big grey shape sailed up to meet me, and we met in a tangle of arms and claws. I pushed the tomcat away. "Damn it—"

"Can't you do anything without cursing?"

"Blast it, then. I've told you to keep that animal out of the control lab."

"I didn't let him in." She was snappish, and for that matter so was I. We'd spent better than six hundred hours cooped up in a small space with just ourselves, the kids, and our passenger, and it was time we had some outside company.

The passenger had made it more difficult. We don't fight much in front of the kids, but with Oswald Dalquist aboard, the atmosphere was different from what we're used to. He was always very formal and polite, which meant we had to be, which meant our usual practice of getting the minor irritations over with had been exchanged for bottling them up.

Jan and I had a major fight coming, and the sooner it happened the better it would be for both of us.

Slingshot is built up out of a number of compartments. We add to the ship as we have to—and when we can afford it. I left Jan to finish shutting down and went below to the living quarters. We'd been down fifteen minutes, and the children were loose.

Papers, games, crayons, toys, kids' clothing, and books had all more or less settled on the "down" side. Raquel, a big bluejay the kids had picked up somewhere, screamed from a cage mounted on one bulkhead. The compartment smelled of bird droppings.

Two of the kids were watching a TV program beamed out of Marsport. Their technique was to push themselves upward with their arms and float up to the top of the compartment, then float downward again until they caught themselves just before they landed. It took nearly a minute to make a full circuit in Jefferson's weak gravity.

I went over and switched off the set. The program was a western, some horse opera made in the 1940s.

Jennifer and Craig wailed in unison. "That's *educational,* Dad."

They had a point, but we'd been through this before. For kids who've never seen Earth and may never go there, *anything* about Terra can probably be educational, but I wasn't in a mood to argue. "Get this place cleaned up."

"It's Roger's turn. He made the mess." Jennifer, being eight and two years older than Craig, tends to be spokesman and chief petty officer for the Little Ones.

"Get him to help, then. But get cleaned up."

"Yes, sir." They worked sullenly, flinging the clothing into corner bins, putting the books into the clips, and the games into lockers. There really is a place for everything in *Slingshot,* although most of the time you wouldn't know it.

I left them to their work and went down to the next level. My office is on one side of that, balanced by the "passenger suite" which the second oldest boy uses when we don't have paying customers. Oswald Dalquist was just coming out of his cabin.

"Good morning, Captain," he said. In all the time he'd been aboard he'd never called me anything but "Captain," although he accepted Janet's invitation to use her first name. A very formal man, Mr. Oswald Dalquist.

"I'm just going down to reception," I told him. "The Port Captain will be aboard with the health officer in a minute. You'd better come down, there will be forms to fill out."

"Certainly. Thank you, Captain." He followed me through the airlock to the level below, which was shops, labs, and the big compartment that serves as a main entryway to *Slingshot*.

Dalquist had been a good passenger, if a little distant. He stayed in his compartment most of the time, did what he was told, and never complained. He had very polished manners, and everything he did was precise, as if he thought out every gesture and word in advance.

I thought of him as a little man, but he wasn't really. I stand about six three, and Dalquist wasn't a lot smaller than me, but he *acted* little. He worked for Butterworth Insurance, which I'd never heard of, and he said he was a claims adjuster, but I thought he was probably an accountant sent out because they didn't want to send anyone more important to a nothing rock like Jefferson.

Still, he'd been around. He didn't talk much about himself, but every now and then he'd let slip a story that showed he'd been on more rocks than most people; and he knew ship routines pretty well. Nobody had to show him things more than once. Since a lot of life-support gadgetry in *Slingshot* is Janet's design, or mine, and certainly isn't standard, he had to be pretty sharp to catch on so quick.

He had expensive gear, too. Nothing flashy, but his helmet was one of Goodyear's latest models, his skintight was David Clark's best with "stretch steel" threads woven in with the nylon, and his coveralls were a special design by Abercrombie & Fitch, with lots of gadget pockets and a self-cleaning low-friction surface. It gave him a pretty natty appearance, rather than the battered look the old rockrats have.

I figured Butterworth Insurance must pay their adjusters more than I thought, or else he had a hell of an expense account.

The entryway is a big compartment. It's filled with nearly everything you can think of: dresses, art objects, gadgets and gizmos, spare parts for air bottles, sewing machines, and anything else Janet or I think we can sell in the way-stops we make with *Slingshot*. Janet calls it the "boutique," and she's been pretty clever about what she buys. It makes a profit, but like everything we do, just barely.

I've heard a lot of stories about tramp ships making a lot of money. Their skippers tell me whenever we meet. Before Jan and I fixed up *Slingshot* I used to believe them. Now I tell the same stories about fortunes made and lost, but the truth is we haven't seen any fortune.

We could use one. Hal, our oldest, wants to go to Marsport Tech, and that's expensive. Worse, he's just the first of nine. Meanwhile, Barclay's wants the payments kept up on the mortgage they hold on *Slinger*, fuel prices go up all the time, and the big Corporations are making it harder for little one-ship outfits like mine to compete.

We got to the boutique just in time to see two figures bounding like wallabies across the big flat area that serves as Jefferson's landing field. Every time one of the men would hit ground he'd fling up a burst of dust that fell like slow-motion bullets to make tiny craters around his footsteps. The landscape was bleak, nothing but rocks and craters, with the big steel airlock entrance to Freedom Port the only thing to remind you that several thousand souls lived here.

We couldn't see it, because the horizon's pretty close on Jefferson, but out beyond the airlock there'd be the usual solar furnaces, big parabolic mirrors to melt down ores. There was also a big trench shimmering just at the horizon: ice. One of Jefferson's main assets is water. About ten thousand years ago Jefferson collided with the head of a comet and a lot of the ice stayed aboard.

The two figures reached *Slingshot* and began the long climb up the ladder to the entrance. They moved fast, and I hit the buttons to open the outer door so they could let themselves in.

Jed was at least twice my age, but like all of us who live in low gravity it's hard to tell just how old that is. He has some wrinkles, but he could pass for fifty. The other guy was a Dr. Stewart, and I didn't know him. There'd been another doctor, about my age, the last time I was in Jefferson, but he'd been a contract man and the Jeffersonians couldn't afford him. Stewart was a young chap, no more than twenty, born in Jefferson back when they called it Grubstake and Blackjack Dan was running the colony. He'd got his training the way most people get an education in the Belt, in front of a TV screen.

The TV classes are all right, but they have their limits. I hoped we wouldn't have any family emergencies here. Janet's a TV Doc, but unlike this Stewart chap she's had a year residency in Marsport General, and she knows the limits of TV training. We've got a family policy that she doesn't treat the kids for anything serious if there's another doctor around, but between her and a new TV-trained MD there wasn't much choice.

"Everybody healthy?" Jed asked.

"Sure." I took out the log and showed where Janet had entered "NO COMMUNICABLE DISEASES" and signed it.

Stewart looked doubtful. "I'm supposed to examine everyone myself. . . ."

"For Christ's sake," Jed told him. He pulled at his bristly mustache and glared at the young doc. Stewart glared back. "Well, 'least you can see if they're still warm," Jed conceded. "Cap'n Rollo, you got somebody to take him up while we get the immigration forms taken care of?"

"Sure." I called Pam on the intercom. She's second oldest. When she got to the boutique, Jed sent Dr. Stewart up with her. When they were gone, he took out a big book of forms.

For some reason every rock wants to know your entire life history before you can get out of your ship. I never have found out what they do with all the information. Dalquist and I began filling out forms while Jed muttered.

"Butterworth Insurance, eh?" Jed asked. "Got much business here?"

Dalquist looked up from the forms. "Very little. Perhaps you can help me. The insured was a Mr. Joseph Colella. I will need to find the beneficiary, a Mrs. Barbara Morrison Colella."

"Joe Colella?" I must have sounded surprised because they both looked at me. "I brought Joe and Barbara to Jefferson. Nice people. What happened to him?"

"Death certificate said accident." Jed said it just that way, flat, with no feeling. Then he added, "Signed by Dr. Stewart."

Jed sounded as if he wanted Dalquist to ask him a question, but the insurance man went back to his forms. When it was obvious that he wasn't going to say anything more, I asked Jed, "Something wrong with the accident?"

Jed shrugged. His lips were tightly drawn. The mood in my ship had definitely changed for the worse, and I was sure Jed had more to say. Why wasn't Dalquist asking questions?

Something else puzzled me. Joe and Barbara were more than just former passengers. They were friends we were looking forward to seeing when we got to Jefferson. I was sure we'd mentioned them several times in front of Dalquist, but he'd never said a word.

We'd taken them to Jefferson about five Earth years before. They were newly married, Joe pushing sixty and Barbara less than half that. He'd just retired as a field agent for Hansen Enterprises, with a big bonus he'd earned in breaking up some kind of insurance scam. They were looking forward to buying into the Jefferson co-op system. I'd seen them every trip since, the last time two years ago, and they were short of ready money like everyone else in Jefferson, but they seemed happy enough.

"Where's Barbara now?" I asked Jed.

"Working for Westinghouse. Johnny Peregrine's office."

"She all right? And the kids?"

Jed shrugged. "Everybody helps out when help's needed. Nobody's rich."

"They put a lot of money into Jefferson stock," I said. "And didn't they have a mining claim?"

"Dividends on Jefferson Corporation stock won't even pay air taxes." Jed sounded more beat down than I'd ever known him. Even when things had looked pretty bad for us in the old days he'd kept all our spirits up with stupid jokes and puns. Not now. "Their claim wasn't much good to start with, and without Joe to work it—"

His voice trailed off as Pam brought Dr. Stewart back into our compartment. Stewart countersigned the log to certify that we were all healthy. "That's it, then," he said. "Ready to go ashore?"

"People waitin' for you in the Doghouse, Captain Rollo," Jed said. "Big meeting."

"I'll just get my hat."

"If there is no objection, I will come too," Dalquist said. "I wonder if a meeting with Mrs. Colella can be arranged?"

"Sure," I told him. "We'll send for her. Doghouse is pretty well the center of things in Jefferson anyway. Have her come for dinner."

"Got nothing good to serve." Jed's voice was gruff with a note of irritated apology.

"We'll see." I gave him a grin and opened the airlock.

There aren't any dogs at the Doghouse. Jed had one when he first came to Jefferson, which is why the name, but dogs don't do very well in low gravs. Like everything else in the Belt, the furniture in Jed's bar is iron and glass except for what's aluminum and titanium. The place is a big cave hollowed out of the rock. There's no outside view, and the only things to look at are the TV and the customers.

There was a big crowd, as there always is in the Port Captain's place when a ship comes in. More business is done in bars than offices out here, which was why Janet and the kids hadn't come dirtside with me. The crowd can get rough sometimes.

The Doghouse has a big bar running all the way across on the side opposite the entryway from the main corridor. The bar's got a suction surface to hold down anything set on it, but no stools. The rest of the big room has tables and chairs, and the tables have little clips to hold drinks and papers in place. There are also little booths around the outside perimeter for privacy. It's a typical layout. You can hold auctions in the big central area and make private deals in the booths.

Drinks are served with covers and straws because when you put anything down fast it sloshes out the top. You can spend years learning to drink beer in low gee if you don't want to sip it through a straw or squirt it out of a bulb.

The place was packed. Most of the customers were miners and shopkeepers, but a couple of tables were taken by company reps. I pointed out Johnny Peregrine to Dalquist. "He'll know how to find Barbara."

Dalquist smiled that tight little accountant's smile of his and went over to Peregrine's table.

There were a lot of others. The most important was Habib al Shamlan, the Iris Company factor. He was sitting with two hard cases, probably company cops.

The Jefferson Corporation people didn't have a table. They were at the bar, and the space between them and the other Company reps was clear, a little island of neutral area in the crowded room.

I'd drawn Jefferson's head honcho. Rhoda Hendrix was Chairman of the Board of the Jefferson Corporation, which made her the closest thing they had to a government. There was a big ugly guy with her. Joe Hornbinder had been around since Blackjack Dan's time. He still dug away at the rocks, hoping to get rich. Most people called him Horny for more than one reason.

It looked like this might be a good day. Everyone stared at us when we came in, but they didn't pay much attention to Dalquist. He was obviously a feather merchant, somebody they might have some fun with later on, and I'd have to watch out for him then, but right now we had important business.

Dalquist talked to Johnny Peregrine for a minute and they seemed to agree on something because Johnny nodded and sent one of his troops out. Dalquist went over into a corner and ordered a drink.

There's a protocol to doing business out here. I had a table all to myself, off to one side of the clear area in the middle, and Jed's boy brought me a big mug of beer with a hinged cap. When I'd had a good slug I took messages out of my pouch and scaled them out to people. Somebody bought me another drink, and there was a general gossip about what was happening around the Belt.

Al Shamlan was impatient. After a half hour, which is really rushing things for an Arab, he called across, his voice very casual, "And what have you brought us, Captain Kephart?"

I took copies of my manifest out of my pouch and passed them around. Everyone began reading, but Johnny Peregrine gave a big grin at the first item.

"Beef!" Peregrine looked happy. He had five hundred workers to feed.

"Nine tons," I agreed.

"Ten francs," Johnny said. "I'll take the whole lot."

"Fifteen," al Shamlan said.

I took a big glug of beer and relaxed. Jan and I'd taken a chance and won. Suppose somebody had flung a shipment of beef into transfer orbit a couple of years ago? A hundred tons could be arriving any minute, and mine wouldn't be worth anything.

Janet and I can keep track of scheduled ships, and we know pretty well where most of the tramps like us are going, but there's no way to be sure about goods in the pipeline. You can go broke in this racket.

There was more bidding, with some of the storekeepers getting in the act. I stood to make a good profit, but only the big corporations were bidding on the whole lot. The Jefferson Corporation people hadn't said a word. I'd heard things weren't going too well for them, but this made it certain. If miners have any money, they'll buy beef. Beef tastes like cow. The stuff you can make from algae is nutritious, but at best it's not appetizing, and Jefferson doesn't even have the plant to make textured vegetable proteins—not that TVP is any substitute for the real thing.

Eventually the price got up to where only Iris and Westinghouse were interested in the whole lot, and I broke the cargo up, seven tons to the big boys and the rest in small lots. I didn't forget to save out a couple hundred kilos for Jed, and I donated half a ton for the Jefferson city hall people to throw a feed with. The rest went for about thirty francs a kilo.

That would just about pay for the deuterium I burned up coming to Jefferson. There was some other stuff, lightweight items they don't make outside the big rocks like Pallas, and that was all pure profit. I felt pretty good when the auction ended. It was only the preliminaries, of course, and the main event was what would let me make a couple of payments to Barclay's on *Slinger's* mortgage, but it's a good feeling to know you can't lose money no matter what happens.

There was another round of drinks. Rockrats came over to my table to ask about friends I might have run into. Some of the storekeepers were making new deals, trading around things they'd bought from me. Dalquist came over to sit with me.

"Johnny finding your client for you?" I asked.

He nodded. "Yes. As you suggested, I have invited her to dinner here with us."

"Good enough. Jan and the kids will be in when the business is over."

Johnny Peregrine came over to the table. "Boosting cargo this trip?"

"Sure." The babble in the room faded out. It was time to start the main event.

The launch window to Luna was open and would be for another couple hundred hours. After that, the fuel needed to give cargo pods enough velocity to put them in transfer orbit to the Earth-Moon system would go up to where nobody could afford to send down anything massy.

There's a lot of traffic to Luna. It's cheaper, at the right time, to send ice down from the Belt than it is to carry it up from Earth. Of course, the Lunatics have to wait a couple of years for their water to get there, but there's always plenty in the pipeline. Luna buys metals, too, although they don't pay as much as Earth does.

"I'm ready if there's anything to boost," I said.

"I think something can be arranged," al Shamlan said.

"Hah!" Hornbinder was listening to us from his place at the bar. He laughed again. "Iris doesn't have any dee for a big shipment. Neither does Westinghouse. You want to boost, you'll deal with us."

I looked to al Shamlan. It's hard to tell what he's thinking, and not a lot easier to read Johnny Peregrine, but they didn't look very happy. "That true?" I asked.

Hornbinder and Rhoda Hendrix came over to the table. "Remember, we sent for you," Rhoda said.

"Sure." I had their guarantee in my pouch. Five thousand francs up front, and another five thousand if I got here on time. I'd beaten their deadline by twenty hours, which isn't bad considering how many million kilometers I had to come. "Sounds like you've got a deal in mind."

She grinned. She's a big woman, and as hard as the inside of an asteroid. I knew she had to be sixty, but she had spent most of that time in low gee. There wasn't much cheer in her smile. It looked more like the tomcat does when he's trapped a rat. "Like Horny says, we have all the deuterium. If you want to boost for Iris and Westinghouse, you'll have to deal with us."

"Bloody hell." I wasn't going to do as well out of this trip as I'd thought.

Hornbinder grinned. "How you like it now, you goddam bloodsucker?"

"You mean me?" I asked.

"Fucking A. You come out here and use your goddam ship a hundred hours, and you take more than we get for busting our balls a whole year. Fucking A, I mean you."

I'd forgotten Dalquist was at the table. "If you think boostship captains charge too much, why don't you buy your own ship?" he asked.

"Who the hell are you?" Horny demanded.

Dalquist ignored him. "You don't buy your own ships because you can't afford them. Ship owners have to make enormous investments. If they don't make good profits, they won't buy ships, and you won't get your cargo boosted at any price."

He sounded like a professor. He was right, of course, but he talked in a way that I'd heard the older kids use on the little ones. It always starts fights in our family and it looked like it was having the same result here.

"Shut up and sit down, Horny." Rhoda Hendrix was used to being obeyed. Hornbinder glared at Dalquist, but he took a chair. "Now let's talk business," Rhoda said. "Captain, it's simple enough. We'll charter your ship for the next seven hundred hours."

"That can get expensive."

She looked to al Shamlan and Peregrine. They didn't look very happy. "I think I know how to get our money back."

"There are times when it is best to give in gracefully," al Shamlan said. He looked to Johnny Peregrine and got a nod. "We are prepared to make a fair agreement with you, Rhoda. After all, you've got to boost your ice. We must send our cargo. It will be much cheaper for all of us if the cargoes go out in one capsule. What are your terms?"

"No deal," Rhoda said. "We'll charter Cap'n Rollo's ship, and you deal with us."

"Don't I get a say in this?" I asked.

"You'll get yours," Hornbinder muttered.

"Fifty thousand," Rhoda said. "Fifty thousand to charter your ship. Plus the ten thousand we promised to get you here."

"That's no more than I'd make boosting your ice," I said. I usually get five percent of cargo value, and the customer furnishes the dee and reaction mass. That ice was worth a couple of million when it arrived at Luna. Jefferson would probably have to sell it before then, but even with discounts, futures in that much water would sell at over a million new francs.

"Seventy thousand, then," Rhoda said.

There was something wrong here. I picked up my beer and took a long swallow. When I put it down, Rhoda was talking again. "Ninety thousand. Plus your ten. An even hundred thousand francs, and you get another one percent of whatever we get for the ice after we sell it."

"A counteroffer may be appropriate," al Shamlan said. He was talking to Johnny Peregrine, but he said it loud enough to be sure that everyone else heard him. "Will Westinghouse go halves with Iris on a charter?" Johnny nodded.

Al Shamlan's smile was deadly. "Charter your ship to us, Captain Kephart. One hundred and forty thousand francs, for exclusive use for the next six hundred hours. That price includes boosting a cargo capsule, provided that we furnish you the deuterium and reaction mass."

"One fifty. Same deal," Rhoda said.

"One seventy-five."

"Two hundred." Somebody grabbed her shoulder and tried to say something to her, but Rhoda pushed him away. "I know what I'm doing. Two hundred thousand."

Al Shamlan shrugged. "You win. We can wait for the next launch window." He got up from the table. "Coming, Johnny?"

"In a minute." Peregrine had a worried look. "Ms. Hendrix, how do you expect to make a profit? I assure you that we won't pay what you seem to think we will."

"Leave that to me," she said. She still had that look: triumphant. The price didn't seem to bother her at all.

"Hum." Al Shamlan made a gesture of bafflement. "One thing, Captain. Before you sign with Rhoda, you might ask to see the money. I would be much surprised if Jefferson Corporation has two hundred thousand." He pushed himself away and sailed across the bar to the corridor door. "You know where to find me if things don't work out, Captain Kephart."

He went out, and his company cops came right after him. After a moment Peregrine and the other corporation people followed.

I wondered what the hell I'd got myself into this time.

✕   ✕   ✕

Rhoda Hendrix was trying to be friendly. It didn't really suit her style.

I knew she'd come to Jefferson back when it was called Grubstake and Blackjack Dan was trying to set up an independent colony. Sometime in her first year she'd moved in with him, and pretty soon she was handling all his financial deals. There wasn't any nonsense about freedom and democracy back then. Grubstake was a big opportunity to get rich or get killed, and not much more.

When they found Blackjack Dan outside without a helmet, it turned out that Rhoda was his heir. She was the only one who knew what kind of deals he'd made anyway, so she took over his place. A year later she invented the Jefferson Corporation. Everybody living on the rock had to buy stock, and she talked a lot about sovereign rights and government by the people. It takes a lot of something to govern a few thousand rockrats, and whatever it is, she had plenty. The idea caught on.

Now things didn't seem to be going too well, and her face showed it when she tried to smile. "Glad that's all settled," she said. "How's Janet?"

"The family is fine, the ship's fine, and I'm fine," I said.

She let the phony grin fade out. "OK, if that's the way you want it. Shall we move over to a booth?"

"Why bother? I've got nothing to hide," I told her.

"Watch it," Hornbinder growled.

"And I've had about enough of him," I told Rhoda. "If you've got cargo to boost, let's get it boosted."

"In time." She pulled some papers out of her pouch. "First, here's the charter contract."

It was all drawn up in advance. I didn't like it at all. The money was good, but none of this sounded right. "Maybe I should take al Shamlan's advice and—"

"You're not taking the Arab's advice or their money either," Hornbinder said.

"—and ask to see your money first," I finished.

"Our credit's good," Rhoda said.

"So is mine as long as I keep my payments up. I can't pay off Barclay's with promises." I lifted my beer and flipped the top just enough to suck down a big gulp. Beer's lousy if you have to sip it.

"What can you lose?" Rhoda asked. "OK, so we don't have much cash. We've got a contract for the ice. Ten percent as soon as the Lloyd's man certifies the stuff's in transfer orbit. We'll pay you out of that. We've got the dee, we've got reaction mass, what the hell else do you want?"

"Your radiogram said cash," I reminded her. "I don't even have the retainer you promised. Just paper."

"Things are hard out here." Rhoda nodded to herself. She was thinking just how hard things were. "It's not like the old days. Everything's organized. Big companies. As soon as we get a little ahead, the big outfits move in and cut prices on everything we sell. Outbid us on everything we have to buy. Like your beef."

"Sure," I said. "I'm facing tough competition from the big shipping fleets, too."

"So this time we've got a chance to hold up the big boys," Rhoda said. "Get a little profit. You aren't hurt. You get more than you expected." She looked around to the other miners. There were a lot of people listening to us. "Kephart, all we have to do is get a little ahead, and we can turn this rock into a decent place to live. A place for people, not corporation clients!" Her voice rose and her eyes flashed. She meant every word, and the others nodded approval.

"You lied to me," I said.

"So what? How are you hurt?" She pushed the contract papers toward me.

"Excuse me." Dalquist hadn't spoken very loudly, but everyone looked at him. "Why is there such a hurry about this?" he asked.

"What the hell's it to you?" Hornbinder demanded.

"You want cash?" Rhoda asked. "All right, I'll give you cash." She took a document out of her pouch and slammed it onto the table. She hit hard enough to raise herself a couple of feet out of her chair. It would have been funny if she wasn't dead serious. Nobody laughed. "There's a deposit certificate for every goddam cent we have!" she shouted. "You want it? Take it all. Take the savings of every family in Jefferson. Pump us dry. Grind the faces of the poor! But sign that charter!"

" 'Cause if you don't," Hornbinder said, "your ship won't ever leave this rock. And don't think we can't stop you."

"Easy." I tried to look relaxed, but the sea of faces around me wasn't friendly at all. I didn't want to look at them so I looked at the deposit paper. It was genuine enough: you can't fake the molecular documents Zurich banks use. With the Jefferson Corporation Seal and the right signatures and thumbprints that thing was worth exactly 78,500 francs.

It would be a lot of money if I owned it for myself. It wasn't so much compared to the mortgage on *Slinger*. It was nothing at all for the total assets of a whole community.

"This is our chance to get out from under," Rhoda was saying. She wasn't talking to me. "We can squeeze the goddam corporation people for a change. All we need is that charter and we've got Westinghouse and the Arabs where we want them!"

Everybody in the bar was shouting now. It looked ugly, and I didn't see any way out.

"OK," I told Rhoda. "Sign over that deposit certificate, and make me out a lien on future assets for the rest. I'll boost your cargo—"

"Boost hell, sign that charter contract," Rhoda said.

"Yeah, I'll do that too. Make out the documents."

"Captain Kephart, is this wise?" Dalquist asked.

"Keep out of this, you little son of a bitch." Horny moved toward Dalquist. "You got no stake in this. Now shut up before I take off the top—"

Dalquist hardly looked up. "Five hundred francs to the first man who coldcocks him," he said carefully. He took his hand out of his pouch, and there was a bill in it. There was a moment's silence, then four big miners started for Horny.

When it was over, Dalquist was out a thousand, because nobody could decide who got to Hornbinder first.

Even Rhoda was laughing after that was over. The mood changed a little; Hornbinder had never been very popular, and Dalquist was buying for the house. It didn't make any difference about the rest of it, of course. They weren't going to let me off Jefferson without signing that charter contract.

Rhoda sent over to city hall to have the documents made out. When they came, I signed, and half the people in the place signed as witnesses. Dalquist didn't like it, but he ended up as a witness too. For better or worse, *Slingshot* was chartered to the Jefferson Corporation for seven hundred hours. The surprise came after I'd signed. I asked Rhoda when she'd be ready to boost.

"Don't worry about it. You'll get the capsule when you need it."

"Bloody hell! You can't wait to get me to sign—"

"Aww, just relax, Kephart."

"I don't think you understand. You have half a million tons to boost up to what, five, six kilometers a second?" I took out my pocket calculator. "Sixteen tons of deuterium and eleven thousand reaction mass. That's a bloody big load. The fuel feed system's got to be built. It's not something I can just strap on and push off—"

"You'll get what you need," Rhoda said. "We'll let you know when it's time to start work."

Jed put us in a private dining room. Janet came in later and I told her about the afternoon. I didn't think she'd like it, but she wasn't as upset as I was.

"We have the money," she said. "And we got a good price on the cargo, and if they ever pay off we'll get more than we expected on the boost charges. If they don't pay up—well, so what?"

"Except that we've got a couple of major companies unhappy, and they'll be here long after Jefferson folds up. Sorry, Jed, but—"

He bristled his mustache. "Could be. I figure on gettin' along with the corporations too. Just in case."

"But what did all that lot mean?" Dalquist asked.

"Beats me." Jed shook his head. "Rhoda's been making noises about how rich we're going to be. New furnace, another power plant, maybe even a ship of our own. Nobody knows how she's planning on doing it."

"Could there have been a big strike?" Dalquist asked. "Iridium, one of the really valuable metals?"

"Don't see how," Jed told him. "Look, mister, if Rhoda's goin' to bail this place out of the hole the big boys have dug for us, that's great with me. I don't ask questions."

Jed's boy came in. "There's a lady to see you." Barbara Morrison Colella was a small blonde girl, pug nose, blue eyes. She looks like somebody you'd see on Earthside TV playing a dumb blonde.

Her degrees said "family economics," which I guess on Earth doesn't amount to much. Out here it's a specialty. To keep a family going out here you better know a lot of environment and life-support engineering, something about prices that depend on orbits and launch windows, a lot about how to get something to eat out of rocks, and maybe something about power systems, too. She was glad enough to see us, especially Janet, but we got another surprise. She looked at Dalquist and said, "Hello, Buck."

"Hello. Surprised, Bobby?"

"No. I knew you'd be along as soon as you heard."

"You know each other, then," I said.

"Yes." Dalquist hadn't moved, but he didn't look like a little man any longer. "How did it happen, Bobby?"

Her face didn't change. She'd lost most of her smile when she saw Dalquist. She looked at the rest of us, and pointed at Jed. "Ask him. He knows more than I do."

"Mr. Anderson?" Dalquist prompted. His tone made it sound as if he'd done this before, and he expected to be answered.

If Jed resented that, he didn't show it. "Simple enough. Joe always seemed happy enough when he came in here after his shift—"

Dalquist looked from Jed to Barbara. She nodded.

"—until the last time. That night he got stinking drunk. Kept mutterin' something about 'Not that way. There's got to be another way.' "

"Do you know what that meant?"

"No," Jed said. "But he kept saying it. Then he got really stinking and I sent him home with a couple of the guys he worked with."

"What happened when he got home?" Dalquist asked.

"He never came home, Buck," Barbara said. "I got worried about him, but I couldn't find him. The men he'd left here with said he'd got to feeling better and left them—"

"Damn fools," Jed muttered. "He was right out of it. Nobody should go outside with that much to drink."

"And they found him outside?"

"At the refinery. Helmet busted open. Been dead five, six hours. Held the inquest right in here, at that table al Shamlan was sitting at this afternoon."

"Who held the inquest?" Dalquist asked.

"Rhoda."

"Doesn't make sense," I said.

"No." Janet didn't like it much either. "Barbara, don't you have any idea of what Joe meant? Was he worried about something?"

"Nothing he told me about. He wasn't—we weren't fighting, or anything like that. I'm sure he didn't—"

"Humpf." Dalquist shook his head. "What damned fool suggested suicide?"

"Well," Jed said, "you know how it is. If a man takes on a big load and wanders around outside, it might as well be suicide. Hornbinder said we were doing Barbara a favor, voting it an accident."

Dalquist took papers out of his pouch. "He was right, of course. I wonder if Hornbinder knew that all Hansen employees receive a paid-up insurance policy as one of their retirement benefits?"

"I didn't know it," I said.

Janet was more practical. "How much is it worth?"

"I am not sure of the exact amounts," Dalquist said. "There are trust accounts involved also. Sufficient to get Barbara and the children back to Mars and pay for their living expenses there. Assuming you want to go?"

"I don't know," Barbara said. "Let me think about it. Joe and I came here to get away from the big companies. I don't have to like Rhoda and the city hall crowd to appreciate what we've got in Jefferson. Independence is worth something."

"Indeed," Dalquist said. He wasn't agreeing with her, and suddenly we all knew he and Barbara had been through this argument before. I wondered when.

"Janet, what would you do?" Barbara asked.

Jan shrugged. "Not a fair question. Roland and I made that decision a long time ago. But neither of us is alone." She reached for my hand across the table.

As she said, we had made our choice. We've had plenty of offers for *Slingshot,* from outfits that would be happy to hire us as crew for *Slinger.* It would mean no more hustle to meet the mortgage payments, and not a lot of change in the way we live—but we wouldn't be our own people anymore. We've never seriously considered taking any of the offers.

"You don't have to be alone," Dalquist said.

"I know, Buck." There was a wistful note in Barbara's voice. They looked at each other for a long time. Then we sat down to dinner.

I was in my office aboard *Slingshot.* Thirty hours had gone by since I'd signed the charter contract, and I still didn't know what I was boosting, or when. It didn't make sense.

Janet refused to worry about it. We'd cabled the money on to Marsport, all of Jefferson's treasury and what we'd got for our cargo, so Barclay's was happy for a while. We had enough deuterium aboard *Slinger* to get where we could buy more. She kept asking what there was to worry about, and I didn't have any answer. I was still brooding about it when Oswald Dalquist tapped on the door.

I hadn't seen him much since the dinner at the Doghouse, and he didn't look any different, but he wasn't the same man. I suppose the change was in me. You can't think of a man named "Buck" the same way you think of an Oswald.

"Sit down," I said. That was formality, of course. It's no harder to stand than sit in the tiny gravity we felt. "I've been meaning to say something about the way you handled Horny. I don't think I've ever seen anybody do that."

His smile was thin, and I guess it hadn't changed either, but it didn't seem like an accountant's smile any more. "It's an interesting story, actually," he said. "A long time ago I was in a big colony ship. Long passage, nothing to do. Discovered the other colonists didn't know much about playing poker."

We exchanged grins again.

"I won so much it made me worry that someone would take it away from me, so I hired the biggest man in the bay to watch my back. Sure enough, some chap accused me of cheating, so I called on my big friend—"

"Yeah?"

"And he shouted 'Fifty to the first guy that decks him.' Worked splendidly, although it wasn't precisely what I'd expected when I hired him—"

We had our laugh.

"When are we leaving, Captain Kephart?"

"Beats me. When they get the cargo ready to boost, I guess."

"That might be a long time," Dalquist said.

"What is that supposed to mean?"

"I've been asking around. To the best of my knowledge, there are no preparations for boosting a big cargo pod."

"That's stupid," I said. "Well, it's their business. When we go, how many passengers am I going to have?"

His little smile faded entirely. "I wish I knew. You've guessed that Joe Colella and I were old friends. And rivals for the same girl."

"Yeah. I'm wondering why you—hell, we talked about them on the way in. You never let on you'd ever heard of them."

He nodded carefully. "I wanted to be certain. I only know that Joe was supposed to have died in an accident. He was not the kind of man accidents happen to. Not even out here."

"What is that supposed to mean?"

"Only that Joe Colella was one of the most careful men you will ever meet, and I didn't care to discuss my business with Barbara until I knew more about the situation in Jefferson. Now I'm beginning to wonder—"

"Dad!" Pam was on watch, and she sounded excited. The intercom box said again, "Dad!"

"Right, sweetheart."

"You better come up quick. There's a message coming through. You better hurry."

×   ×   ×

"MAYDAY MAYDAY MAYDAY." The voice was cold and unemotional, the way they are when they really mean it. It rolled off the tape Pam had made.

MAYDAY MAYDAY MAYDAY. THIS IS PEGASUS LINES BOOSTSHIP AGAMEMNON OUTBOUND EARTH TO PALLAS.

OUR MAIN ENGINES ARE DISABLED. I SAY AGAIN, MAIN ENGINES DISABLED. OUR VELOCITY RELATIVE TO SOL IS ONE FOUR ZERO KILOMETERS PER SECOND, I SAY AGAIN, ONE HUNDRED FORTY KILOMETERS PER SECOND. AUXILIARY POWER IS FAILING. MAIN ENGINES CANNOT BE REPAIRED. PRESENT SHIP MASS IS 54,000 TONS. SEVENTEEN HUNDRED PASSENGERS ABOARD. MAYDAY MAYDAY MAYDAY.

"Lord God." I wasn't really aware that I was talking. The kids had crowded into the control cabin, and we listened as the tape went on to give a string of numbers, the vectors to locate _Agamemnon_ precisely. I started to punch them into the plotting tanks, but Pam stopped me.

"I already did that, Dad." She hit the activation switch to bring the screen to life.

It showed a picture of our side of the solar system, the inner planets and inhabited rocks, along with a block of numbers and a long thin line with a dot at the end to represent _Agamemnon_. Other dots winked on and off: boostships.

We were the only one that stood a prayer of a chance of catching up with _Agamemnon_.

The other screen lit, giving us what the *Register* knew about *Agamemnon*. It didn't look good. She was an enormous old cargo-passenger ship, over thirty years old—and out here that's old indeed. She'd been built for a useful life of half that, and sold off to Pegasus Lines when P&L decided she wasn't safe.

Her auxiliary power was furnished by a plutonium pile. If something went wrong with it, there was no way to repair it in space. Without auxiliary power, the life-support systems couldn't function. I was still looking at her specs when the comm panel lit. Local call, Port Captain's frequency.

"Yeah, Jed?" I said.

"You've got the Mayday?"

"Sure. I figure we've got about sixty hours max to fuel up and still let me catch her. I've got to try it, of course."

"Certainly, Captain." The voice was Rhoda's. "I've already sent a crew to start work on the fuel pod. I suggest you work with them to be sure it's right."

"Yeah. They'll have to work damned fast." *Slingshot* doesn't carry anything like the tankage a run like this would need.

"One more thing, Captain," Rhoda said, "Remember that your ship is under exclusive charter to the Jefferson Corporation. We'll make the legal arrangements with Pegasus. You concentrate on getting your ship ready."

"Yeah, OK. Out." I switched the comm system to *Record*. "*Agamemnon*, this is cargo tug *Slingshot*. I have your Mayday. Intercept is possible, but I cannot carry sufficient fuel and mass to decelerate your ship. I must vampire your dee and mass. I say again, we must transfer your fuel and reaction mass to my ship.

"We have no facilities for taking your passengers aboard. We will attempt to take your ship in tow and decelerate using your deuterium and reaction mass. Our engines are modified General Electric Model five-niner ion-fusion. Preparations for coming to your assistance are under way. Suggest your crew begin preparations for fuel transfer. Over."

Then I looked around the cabin. Janet and our oldest were ashore. "Pam, you're in charge. Send that, and record the reply. You can start the checklist for boost. I make it about two-hundred centimeters acceleration, but you'd better check that. Whatever it is, we'll need to secure for it. Also, get in a call to find your mother. God knows where she is."

"Sure, Dad." She looked very serious, and I wasn't worried. Hal's the oldest, but Pam's a lot more thorough.

The *Register* didn't give anywhere near enough data about *Agamemnon*. I could see from the recognition pix that she carried her reaction mass in strap-ons alongside the main hull, rather than in detachable pods right forward the way *Slinger* does. That meant we might have to transfer the whole lot before we could start deceleration.

She had been built as a general-purpose ship, so her hull structure forward was beefy enough to take the thrust of a cargo pod—but how *much* thrust? If we were going to get her down, we'd have to push like hell on her bows, and there was no way to tell if they were strong enough to take it.

I looked over to where Pam was aiming our high-gain antenna for the message to *Agamemnon*. She looked like she'd been doing this all her life, which I guess she had been, but mostly for drills. It gave me a funny feeling to know she'd grown up sometime in the last couple of years and Janet and I hadn't really noticed.

"Pamela, I'm going to need more information on *Aga-memnon*," I told her. "The kids had a TV cast out of

Marsport, so you ought to be able to get through. Ask for anything they have on that ship. Structural strength, fuel-handling equipment, everything they've got."

"Yes, sir."

"OK. I'm going ashore to see about the fuel pods. Call me when we get some answers, but if there's nothing important from *Agamemnon* just hang onto it."

"What happens if we can't catch them?" Philip asked.

Pam and Jennifer were trying to explain it to him as I went down to the lock.

Jed had lunch waiting in the Doghouse. "How's it going?" he asked when I came in.

"Pretty good. Damned good, all things considered." The refinery crew had built up fuel pods for *Slinger* before, so they knew what I needed, but they'd never made one that had to stand up to a full fifth of a gee. A couple of centimeters is hefty acceleration when you boost big cargo, but we'd have to go out at a hundred times that.

"Get the stuff from Marsport?"

"Some of it." I shook my head. The whole operation would be tricky. There wasn't a lot of risk for me, but *Agamemnon* was in big trouble.

"Rhoda's waiting for you. Back room."

"You don't look happy."

Jed shrugged. "Guess she's right, but it's kind of ghoulish."

"What—?"

"Go see."

Rhoda was sitting with a trim chap who wore a clipped mustache. I'd met him before, of course: B. Elton, Esq., the Lloyd's rep in Jefferson. He hated the place and couldn't wait for a transfer.

"I consider this reprehensible," Elton was saying when I came in. "I hate to think you are a party to this, Captain Kephart."

"Party to what?"

"Ms. Hendrix has asked for thirty million francs as salvage fee. Ten million in advance."

I whistled. "That's heavy."

"The ship is worth far more than that," Rhoda said.

"If I can get her down. There are plenty of problems—hell, she may not be fit for more than salvage," I said.

"Then there are the passengers. How much is Lloyd's out if you have to pay off their policies? And lawsuits?" Rhoda had the tomcat's grin again. "We're saving you money, Mr. Elton."

I realized what she was doing. "I don't know how to say this, but it's my ship you're risking."

"You'll be paid well," Rhoda said. "Ten percent of what we get."

That would just about pay off the whole mortgage. It was also a hell of a lot more than the commissioners in Marsport would award for a salvage job.

"We've got heavy expenses up front," Rhoda was saying. "That fuel pod costs like crazy. We're going to miss the launch window to Luna."

"Certainly you deserve reasonable compensation, but—"

"But nothing!" Rhoda's grin was triumphant. "Captain Kephart can't boost without fuel, and we have it all. That fuel goes aboard his ship when you've signed my contract, Elton, and not before."

Elton looked sad and disgusted. "It seems a cheap—"

"Cheap!" Rhoda got up and went to the door. "What the hell do you know about cheap? How goddam many times have we heard you people say there's no such thing as an excess profit? Well, this time *we* got the breaks, Elton, and *we'll* take the excess profits. Think about that."

Out in the bar somebody cheered. Another began singing a tune I'd heard in Jefferson before. Pam says the music is very old, she's heard it on TV casts, but the words fit Jefferson. The chorus goes, *"There's gonna be a great day!"* and everybody out there shouted it.

"Marsport will never give you that much money," Elton said.

"Sure they will." Rhoda's grin got even wider, if that was possible. "We'll hold onto the cargo until they do—"

"Be damned if I will!" I said.

"Not you at all. I'm sending Mr. Hornbinder to take charge of that. Don't worry, Captain Kephart, I've got you covered. The big boys won't bite you."

"Hornbinder?"

"Sure. You'll have some extra passengers this run—"

"Not him. Not in my ship," I said.

"Sure he's going. You can use some help—"

Like hell. "I don't need any."

She shrugged. "Sorry you feel that way. Just remember, you're under charter." She gave the tomcat grin again and left.

When she was gone, Jed came in with beer for me and something else for Elton. They were still singing and cheering in the other room. "Do you think this is fair?" Elton demanded.

Jed shrugged. "Doesn't matter what I think. Or what Rollo thinks. Determined woman, Rhoda Hendrix."

"You'd have no trouble over ignoring that charter contract," Elton told me. "In fact, we could find a reasonable bonus for you—"

"Forget it." I took the beer from Jed and drank it all. Welding up that fuel pod had been hot work, and I was ready for three more. "Listen to them out there," I said. "Think I want them mad at me? They see this as the end of their troubles."

"Which it could be," Jed said. "With a few million to invest we can make Jefferson into a pretty good place."

Elton wasn't having any. "Lloyd's is not in the business of subsidizing colonies that cannot make a living—"

"So what?" I said. "Rhoda's got the dee and nobody else has enough. She means it, you know."

"There's less than forty hours," Jed reminded him. "I think I'd get on the line to my bosses, was I you."

"Yes." Elton had recovered his polish, but his eyes were narrow. "I'll just do that."

They launched the big fuel pod with strap-on solids, just enough thrust to get it away from the rock so I could catch it and lock on. We had hours to spare, and I took my time matching velocities. Then Hal and I went outside to make sure everything was connected right.

Hornbinder and two friends were aboard against all my protests. They wanted to come out with us, but I wasn't having any. We don't need help from ground-pounders. Janet and Pam took them to the gallery for coffee while I made my inspection.

Slingshot is basically a strongly built hollow tube with engines at one end and clamps at the other. The cabins are rings around the outside of the tube. We also carry some deuterium and reaction mass strapped on to the main hull, but for big jobs there's not nearly enough room there. Instead, we build a special fuel pod that straps onto the bow. The reaction mass can be lowered through the central tube when we're boosting.

Boost cargo goes on forward of the fuel pod. This time we didn't have any going out, but when we caught up to *Agamemnon* she'd ride there, no different from any other cargo capsule. That was the plan, anyway. Taking another ship in tow isn't precisely common out here.

Everything matched up. Deuterium lines, and the elevator system for handling the mass and getting it into the boiling pots aft; it all fit. Hal and I took our time, even after we were sure it was working, while the Jefferson miners who'd come up with the pod fussed and worried. Eventually I was satisfied, and they got onto their bikes to head for home. I was still waiting for a call from Janet.

Just before they were ready to start up she halted us. She used an open frequency so the miners could hear. "Rollo, I'm afraid those crewmen Rhoda loaned us will have to go home with the others."

"Eh?" One of the miners turned around in the saddle. "What's the problem, Jan?" I asked.

"It seems Mr. Hornbinder and his friends have very bad stomach problems. It could be quite serious. I think they'd better see Dr. Stewart as soon as possible."

"Goddam. Rhoda's not going to like this," the foreman said. He maneuvered his little open-frame scooter over to the airlock. Pam brought his friends out and saw they were strapped in.

"Hurry up!" Hornbinder said. "Get moving!"

"Sure, Horny." There was a puzzled note in the foreman's voice. He started up the bike. At maximum thrust it might make a twentieth of a gee. There was no enclosed space, it was just a small chemical rocket with saddles, and you rode it in your suit.

"Goddamit, get moving," Hornbinder was shouting. If there'd been air you might have heard him a klick away. "You can make better time than this!"

I got inside and went up to the control cabin. Jan was grinning.

"Amazing what calomel can do," she said.

"Amazing." We took time off for a quick kiss before I strapped in. I didn't feel much sympathy for Horny, but the other two hadn't been so bad. The one to feel sorry for was whoever had to clean up their suits.

Ship's engines are complicated things. First you take deuterium pellets and zap them with a big laser. The dee fuses to helium. Now you've got far too much hot gas at far too high a temperature, so it goes into an MHD system that cools it and turns the energy into electricity.

Some of that powers the lasers to zap more dee. The rest powers the ion drive system. Take a metal, preferably something with a low boiling point like cesium, but since that's rare out here cadmium generally has to do. Boil it to a vapor. Put the vapor through ionizing screens that you keep charged with power from the fusion system.

Squirt the charged vapor through more charged plates to accelerate it, and you've got a drive. You've also got a charge on your ship, so you need an electron gun to get rid of that.

There are only about nine hundred things to go wrong with the system. Superconductors for the magnetic fields and charge plates: those take cryogenic systems, and *those* have auxiliary systems to keep them going. Nothing's simple, and nothing's small, so out of *Slingshot's* sixteen hundred metric tons, well over a thousand tons is engine.

Now you know why there aren't any space yachts flitting around out here. *Slinger's* one of the smallest ships in commission, and she's bloody big. If Jan and I hadn't happened to hit lucky by being the only possible buyers for a couple of wrecks, and hadn't had friends at Barclay's who thought we might make a go of it, we'd never have owned our own ship.

When I tell people about the engines, they don't ask what we do aboard *Slinger* when we're on long passages, but they're only partly right. You *can't* do anything to an engine while it's on. It either works or it doesn't, and all you have to do with it is see it gets fed.

It's when the damned things are shut down that the work starts, and that takes so much time that you make sure you've done everything *else* in the ship when you can't work on the engines. There's a lot of maintenance, as you might guess when you think that we've got to make everything we need, from air to zweiback. Living in a ship makes you appreciate planets.

Space operations go smooth, or generally they don't go at all. I looked at Jan and we gave each other a quick wink. It's a good luck charm we've developed. Then I hit the keys, and we were off.

It wasn't a long boost to catch up with *Agamemnon*. I spent most of it in the contoured chair in front of the control screens. A fifth of a gee isn't much for dirtsiders, but out here it's ten times what we're used to. Even the cats hate it.

The high gees saved us on high calcium foods and the drugs we need to keep going in low gravs, and of course we didn't have to put in so much time in the exercise harnesses, but the only one happy about it was Dalquist.

He came up to the control cap about an hour out from Jefferson.

"I thought there would be other passengers," he said.

"Really? Barbara made it pretty clear that she wasn't interested in Pallas. Might go to Mars, but—"

"No, I meant Mr. Hornbinder."

"He, uh, seems to have become ill. So did his friends. Happened quite suddenly."

Dalquist frowned. "I wish you hadn't done that."

"Really? Why?"

"It might not have been wise, Captain."

I turned away from the screens to face him. "Look, Mr. Dalquist, I'm not sure what *you're* doing on this trip. I sure didn't need Rhoda's goons along."

"Yes. Well, there's nothing to be done now in any event."

"Just why are you aboard? I thought you were in a hurry to get back to Marsport—"

"Butterworth interests may be affected, Captain. And I'm in no hurry."

That's all he had to say about it, too, no matter how hard I pressed him on it.

I didn't have time to worry about it. As we boosted, I was talking with *Agamemnon.* She passed about half a million kilometers from Jefferson, which is awfully close out here. We'd started boosting before she was abreast of the rock, and now we were chasing her. The idea was to catch up to her just as we matched her velocity. Meanwhile, *Agamemnon's* crew had their work cut out.

When we were fifty kilometers behind, I cut the engines to minimum power. I didn't dare shut them down entirely. The fusion power system has no difficulty with restarts, but the ion screens are fouled if they're cooled. Unless they're cleaned or replaced we can lose as much as half our thrust—and we were going to need every dyne.

We could just make out *Agamemnon* with our telescope. She was too far away to let us see any details. We could see a bright spot of light approaching us, though: Captain Jason Ewert-James and two of his engineering officers. They were using one of *Agamemnon's* scooters.

There wasn't anything larger aboard. It's not practical to carry lifeboats for the entire crew and passenger list, so they have none at all on the larger boostships. Earthside politicians are forever talking about "requiring" lifeboats on passenger-carrying ships, but they'll never do it. Even if they pass such laws, how could they enforce them? Earth has no cops in space. The U.S. and Soviet Air Forces keep a few ships, but not enough to make an effective police force even if anyone out here recognized their jurisdiction, which we don't. Captain Ewert-James was a typical ship captain. He'd formerly been with one of the big British-Swiss lines and had to transfer over to Pegasus when his ship was sold out from under him. The larger lines like younger skippers, which I think is a mistake, but they don't ask my advice.

Ewert-James was tall and thin, with a clipped mustache and greying hair. He wore uniform coveralls over his skintights, and in the pocket he carried a large pipe which he lit as soon as he'd asked permission.

"Thank you. Didn't dare smoke aboard *Agamemnon*—"

"Air that short?" I asked.

"No, but some of the passengers think it might be. Wouldn't care to annoy them, you know." His lips twitched just a trifle, something less than a conspirator's grin but more than a deadpan.

We went into the office. Jan came in, making it a bit crowded. I introduced her as physician and chief officer. "How large a crew do you keep, Captain Kephart?" Ewert-James asked.

"Just us. And the kids. My oldest two are on watch at the moment."

His face didn't change. "Experienced cadets, eh? Well, we'd best be down to it. Mr. Haply will show you what we've been able to accomplish."

They'd done quite a lot. There was a lot of expensive alloy bar-stock in the cargo, and somehow they'd got a good bit of it forward and used it to brace up the bows of the ship so she could take the thrust. "Haven't been able to weld it properly, though," Haply said. He was a young third engineer, not too long from being a cadet himself. "We don't have enough power to do welding and run the life support too."

Agamemnon's image was a blur on the screen across from my desk. It looked like a gigantic hydra, or a bull-whip with three short lashes standing out from the handle. The three arms rotated slowly. I pointed to it. "Still got spin on her."

"Yes." Ewert-James was grim. "We've been running the ship with that power. Spin her up with attitude jets and take power off the flywheel motor as she slows down."

I was impressed. Spin is usually given by running a big flywheel with an electric motor. Since any motor is a generator, Ewert-James's people had found a novel way to get some auxiliary power for life-support systems.

"Can you run for a while without doing that?" Jan asked. "It won't be easy transferring reaction mass if you can't." We'd already explained why we didn't want to shut down our engines, and there'd be no way to supply *Agamemnon* with power from *Slingshot* until we were coupled together.

"Certainly. Part of the cargo is liquid oxygen. We can run twenty, thirty hours without ship's power. Possibly longer."

"Good." I hit the keys to bring the plot tank results onto my office screen. "There's what I get," I told them. "Our outside time limit is *Slinger's* maximum thrust. I'd make that twenty centimeters for this load—"

"Which is more than I'd care to see exerted against the bows, Captain Kephart. Even with our bracing." Ewert-James looked to his engineers. They nodded gravely.

"We can't do less than ten," I reminded them. "Anything much lower and we won't make Pallas at all."

"She'll take ten," Haply said. "I think."

The others nodded agreement. I was sure they'd been over this a hundred times as we were closing.

I looked at the plot again. "At the outside, then, we've got one hundred and seventy hours to transfer twenty-five thousand tons of reaction mass. And we can't work steadily because you'll have to spin up *Agamemnon* for power, and I can't stop engines—"

Ewert-James turned up both corners of his mouth at that. It was the closest thing to a smile he ever gave. "I'd say we best get at it, wouldn't you?"

Agamemnon didn't look much like *Slingshot*. We'd closed to a quarter of a klick, and steadily drew ahead of her; when we were past her, we'd turn over and decelerate, dropping behind so that we could do the whole cycle over again.

Some features were the same, of course. The engines were not much larger than *Slingshot's* and looked much the same, a big cylinder covered over with tankage and coils, acceleration outports at the aft end. A smaller tube ran from the engines forward, but you couldn't see all of it because big rounded reaction mass canisters covered part of it.

Up forward the arms grew out of another cylinder. They jutted out at equal angles around the hull, three big arms to contain passenger decks and auxiliary systems. The arms could be folded in between the reaction mass canisters, and would be when we started boosting. All told she was over four hundred meters long, and with the hundred-meter arms thrust out she looked like a monstrous hydra slowly spinning in space.

"There doesn't seem to be anything wrong aft," Buck Dalquist said. He studied the ship from the screens, then pulled the telescope eyepiece toward himself for a direct look.

"Failure in the superconductor system," I told him. "Broken lines. They can't contain the fusion reaction long enough to get it into the MHD system."

He nodded. "So Captain Ewert-James told me. I've asked for a chance to inspect the damage as soon as it's convenient."

"Eh? Why?"

"Oh, come now, Captain." Dalquist was still looking through the telescope. "Surely you don't believe in Rhoda Hendrix as a good luck charm?"

"But—"

"But nothing." There was no humor in his voice, and when he looked across the cabin at me, there was none in his eyes. "She bid far too much for an exclusive charter, after first making certain that you'd be on Jefferson at precisely the proper time. She has bankrupted the corporate treasury to obtain a corner on deuterium. Why else would she do all that if she hadn't expected to collect it back with profit?"

"But—she was going to charge Westinghouse and Iris and the others to boost their cargo. And they had cargo of their own—"

"Did they? We saw no signs of it. And she bid far too much for your charter."

"Damn it, you can't mean this," I said, but I didn't mean it. I remembered the atmosphere back at Jefferson. "You think the whole outfit was in on it?"

He shrugged. "Does it matter?"

The fuel transfer was tough. We couldn't just come alongside and winch the stuff over. At first we caught it on the fly: *Agamemnon's* crew would fling out hundred-ton canisters, then use the attitude jets to boost away from them, not far, but just enough to stand clear.

Then I caught them with the bow pod. It wasn't easy. You don't need much closing velocity with a hundred tons before you've got a hell of a lot of energy to worry about. Weightless doesn't mean massless.

We could only transfer about four hundred tons an hour that way. After the first ten-hour stretch I decided it wouldn't work. There were just too many ways for things to go wrong.

"Get rigged for tow," I told Captain Ewert-James. "Once we're hooked up I can feed you power, so you don't have to do that crazy stunt with the spin. I'll start boost at about a tenth of a centimeter. It'll keep the screens hot, and we can winch the fuel pods down."

He was ready to agree. I think watching me try to catch those fuel canisters, knowing that if I made a mistake his ship was headed for Saturn and beyond, was giving him ulcers.

First he spun her hard to build up power, then slowed the spin to nothing. The long arms folded alongside, so that *Agamemnon* took on a trim shape. Meanwhile I worked around in front of her, turned over and boosted in the direction we were traveling, and turned again.

The dopplers worked fine for a change. We hardly felt the jolt as *Agamemnon* settled nose to nose with us. Her crewmen came out to work the clamps and string lines across to carry power. We were linked, and the rest of the trip was nothing but hard work.

We could still transfer no more than four hundred tons an hour, meaning bloody hard work to get the whole twenty-five thousand tons into *Slinger's* fuel pod, but at least it was all downhill. Each canister was lowered by winch, then swung into our own fuel-handling system, where *Slinger's* winches took over. Cadmium's heavy: a cube about two meters on a side holds a hundred tons of the stuff. It wasn't big, and it didn't *weigh* much in a tenth of a centimeter, but you don't drop the stuff either.

Finally it was finished, and we could start maximum boost: a whole ten centimeters, about a hundredth of a gee. That may not sound like much, but think of the mass involved. *Slinger's* sixteen hundred tons were nothing, but there was *Agamemnon* too. I worried about the bracing Ewert-James had put in the bows, but nothing happened.

Three hundred hours later we were down at Pallasport. As soon as we touched in, my ship was surrounded by Intertel cops.

The room was paneled in real wood. That doesn't sound like much unless you live in the Belt, but think about it: every bit of that paneling was brought across sixty million kilometers.

Pallas hasn't much for gravity, but there's enough to make sitting down worth doing. Besides, it's a habit we don't seem to be able to get out of. There was a big conference table across the middle of the room, and a dozen corporation reps sat at it. It was made of some kind of plastic that looks like wood; not even the Corporations Commission brings furniture from Earth.

Deputy Commissioner Ruth Carr sat at a table at the far end, across the big conference table from where I sat in the nominal custody of the Intertel guards. I wasn't happy about being arrested and my ship impounded. Not that it would do me any good to be unhappy. . . .

All the big outfits were represented at the conference table. Lloyd's and Pegasus Lines, of course, but there were others, Hansen Enterprises, Westinghouse, Iris, GE, and the rest.

"Definitely sabotage, then?" Commissioner Carr asked. She looked much older than she really was; the black coveralls and cap did that. She'd done a good job of conducting the hearings, though, even sending Captain Ewert-James and his engineers out to get new photographs of the damage to *Agamemnon's* engines. He passed them up from the witness box, and she handed them to her experts at their place to her right. They nodded over them.

"I'd say definitely so," Captain Ewert-James was saying. "There was an attempt to lay the charge pattern such that it might be mistaken for meteorite damage. In fact, had not Mr. Dalquist been so insistent on a thorough examination, we might have let it go at that. On close inspection, though, it seems very probable that a series of shaped charges were used."

Ruth Carr nodded to herself. She'd heard me tell about Rhoda's frantic efforts to charter my ship. One of Ewert-James's officers testified that an engineering crewman jumped ship just before *Agamemnon* boosted out of Earth orbit. The Intertel people had dug up the fact that he'd lived on Jefferson two years before, and were trying to track him down now—he'd vanished.

"The only possible beneficiary would be the Jefferson Corporation," Mrs. Carr said. "The concerns most harmed are Lloyd's and Pegasus Lines—"

"And Hansen Enterprises," the Hansen rep said. Ruth Carr looked annoyed, but she didn't say anything. I noticed that the big outfits felt free to interrupt her and wondered if they did that with all the commissioners, or just her because she hadn't been at the job very long.

The Hansen man was an older chap who looked as if he'd done his share of rock mining in his day, but he spoke with a Harvard accent. "There is a strong possibility that the Jefferson Corporation arranged the murder of a retired Hansen employee. As he was insured by a Hansen subsidiary, we are quite concerned."

"Quite right." Mrs. Carr jotted notes on the pad in front of her. She was the only one there I'd seen use note paper. The others whispered into wrist recorders. "Before we hear proposed actions, has anyone an objection to disposing of the matter concerning Captain Kephart?" Nobody said anything.

"I find that Captain Kephart has acted quite properly, and that the salvage fees should go to his ship."

I realized I'd been holding my breath. Nobody wanted my scalp so far as I knew, and Dalquist had been careful to show I wasn't involved in whatever Rhoda had planned—but still, you never know what'll happen when the big boys have their eye on you. It was a relief to hear her dismiss the whole business, and the salvage fees would pay off a big part of the mortgage. I wouldn't know just how much I'd get until the full Commission back in Marsport acted, but it couldn't come to less than a million francs. Maybe more.

"Now for the matter of the Jefferson Corporation."

"Move that we send sufficient Intertel agents to take possession of the whole damn rock," the Lloyd's man said.

"Second." Pegasus Lines.

"Discussion?" Ruth Carr asked.

"Hansen will speak against the motion," the Hansen rep said. "Mr. Dalquist will speak for us."

That surprised hell out of me. I wondered what would happen, and sat quite still, listening. I had no business in there, of course. If there hadn't been some suspicion that I might have been in on Rhoda's scheme I'd never have heard this much, and by rights I ought to have left when she made her ruling, but nobody seemed anxious to throw me out.

"First, let me state the obvious," Dalquist said. "An operation of this size will be costly. The use of naked force against an independent colony, no matter how justified, will have serious repercussions throughout the Belt—"

"Let 'em get away with it and it'll *really* be serious," the Pegasus man said.

"Hansen Enterprises has the floor, Mr. Papagorus," Commissioner Carr said.

Dalquist nodded his thanks. "My point is that we should consider alternatives. The proposed action is at least expensive and distasteful, if not positively undesirable."

"We'll concede that," the Lloyd's man said. The others muttered agreement. One of the people representing a whole slew of smaller outfits whispered, "Here comes the Hansen hooker. How's Dalquist going to make a profit from this?"

"I further point out," Dalquist said, "that Jefferson is no more valuable than many other asteroids. True, it has good minerals and water, but no richer resources than other rocks we've not developed. The real value of Jefferson is in its having a working colony and labor force—and it is highly unlikely that they will work very hard for us if we land company police and confiscate their homes."

Everybody was listening now. The chap who'd whispered earlier threw his neighbor an "I told you so" look.

"Secondly. If we take over the Jefferson holdings, the result will be a fight among ourselves over the division of the spoils."

There was another murmur of assent to that. They could all agree that something had to be done, but nobody wanted to let the others have the pie without a cut for himself.

"Finally. It is by no means clear that any large number of Jefferson inhabitants were involved in this conspiracy. Chairman Hendrix, certainly. I could name two or three others. For the rest—who knows?"

"All right," the Lloyd's man said. "You've made your point. If landing Intertel cops on Jefferson isn't advisable, what do we do? I am damned if we'll let them get away clean."

"I suggest that we invest in the Jefferson Corporation," Dalquist said.

The Doghouse hadn't changed. There was a crowd outside in the main room. They were all waiting to hear how rich they'd become. When I came in, even Horn-binder smiled at me.

They were getting wild drunk while Dalquist and I met with Rhoda in the back room. She didn't like what he was saying.

"Our syndicate will pay off the damage claims due to Pegasus Lines and Lloyd's," Dalquist told her. "And pay Captain Kephart's salvage fees. In addition, we will invest two million francs for new equipment. In return you will deliver forty percent of the Jefferson Corporation stock to us."

He wasn't being generous. With a forty percent bloc it was a cinch they could find enough more among the rockrats for a majority. Some of them hated everything Rhoda stood for.

"You've got to be crazy," Rhoda said. "Sell out to a goddam syndicate of corporations? We don't want *any* of you here!"

Dalquist's face was grim. "I am trying to remain polite, and it is not easy, Ms. Hendrix. You don't seem to appreciate your position. The corporation representatives have made their decision, and the Commission has ratified it. You will either sell or face something worse."

"I don't recognize any commissions," Rhoda said. "We've always been independent, we're not part of your goddam fascist commission. Christ almighty, you've found us guilty before we even knew there'd be a trial! We weren't even heard!"

"Why should you be? As you say, you're independent. Or have been up to now."

"We'll fight, Dalquist. Those company cops will never get here alive. Even if they do—"

"Oh, come now." Dalquist made an impatient gesture. "Do you really believe we'd take the trouble of sending

Intertel police, now that you're warned? Hardly. We'll merely seize all your cargo in the pipeline and see that no ship comes here for any reason. How long will it be before your own people throw you out and come to terms with us?"

That hit her hard. Her eyes narrowed as she thought about it. "I can see you don't live to enjoy what you've done—"

"Nonsense."

I figured it was my turn. "Rhoda, you may not believe this, but I heard him argue them out of sending the cops without any warning at all. They were ready to do it."

The shouts came from the bar as Jed opened the door to see if we wanted anything. "There's gonna be a great day!"

"Everything all right here?" Jed asked.

"No!" Rhoda shoved herself away from the table and glared at Dalquist. "Not all right at all! Jed, he's—"

"I know what he's saying, Rhoda," Jed told her. "Cap'n Rollo and I had a long talk with him last night."

"With the result that I'm speaking to you at all," Dalquist said. "Frankly, I'd rather see you dead." His face was a bitter mask of hatred, and the emotionless expression fell away. He hated Rhoda. "You've killed the best friend I ever had, and I find that I need you anyway. Captain Anderson has convinced me that it will be difficult to govern here without you, which is why you'll remain nominally in control after this sale is made."

"No. No sale."

"There will be. Who'll buy from you? Who'll sell to you? This was a unanimous decision. You're not independent, no matter how often you say you are. There's no place for your kind of nationalism out here."

"You bastards. The big boys. You think you can do anything you like to us."

Dalquist recovered his calm as quickly as he'd lost it. I think it was the tone Rhoda used; he didn't want to sound like her. I couldn't tell if I hated him or not.

"We can do whatever we can agree to do," Dalquist said. "You seem to think the Corporations Commission is some kind of government. It isn't. It's just a means for settling disputes. We've found it more profitable to have rules than to have fights. But we're not without power, and everyone's agreed that you can't be let off after trying what you did."

"So we pay for it," Jed said.

Dalquist shrugged. "There's no government out here. Are you ready to bring Rhoda to trial? Along with all the others involved?"

Jed shook his head. "Doubt it—"

"And there's the matter of restitution, which you can't make anyway. And you're bankrupt, since you sent no cargo to Luna and the launch window's closed."

"Just who the hell is this syndicate?" Rhoda demanded.

Dalquist's expression didn't change, but there was a note of triumph in his voice. He'd won, and he knew it. "The major sums are put up by Hansen Enterprises."

"And you'll be here as their rep."

He nodded. "Certainly. I've been with Hansen most of my life, Ms. Hendrix. The company trusts me to look out for its best interests. As I trusted Joe Colella. Until he retired he was my best field agent."

She didn't say anything, but her face was sour.

"You might have got away with this if you hadn't killed Joe," Dalquist said. "But retired or not, he was a Hansen man. As I'm sure you found when he discovered your plan. We take care of our people, Ms. Hendrix. Hansen is a good company."

"For company men." Jed's voice was flat. He looked around the small back room with its bare rock walls, but I think he was seeing through those walls, out through the corridors, beyond to the caves where the rockrats tried to make homes. "A good outfit for company men. But it won't be the same, for us."

Outside they were still singing about the great days coming.

EXILES TO GLORY

To Dan Alderson, the sane genius

CERES

Asteroid at average distance 257 million miles (2.767 AU) from sun.

Mass: 8 X 10^{23} grams

Radius: 370 kilometers

Surface area: somewhat larger than the state of Texas

Period: 4.6 years

Rotation: 9 hours, 5 minutes

Surface gravity: 38.9 centimeters/second = .04 Earth gravity

Escape Velocity: 5.37 X 10^4 centimeters/second

Path velocity in orbit: 17.9 kilometers/second

Largely composed of stone, Ceres has an easily accessible metallic core containing rich, commercially valuable deposits of gold, silver, tin, copper, nickel, and iron. The most valuable minerals are the super-heavy elements, particularly Arthurium, which exists in recoverable quantities. Water-ice has been found both in permafrost and underground deposits.

Chapter One

The first expedition to Ceres in 2007 was financed by Hansen Enterprises (Ltd. et cie, incorporated in and with General Headquarters at Hong Kong Luna). Interplanet of Zurich subsequently made extensive investments in mining and refinery operations on Ceres. The commercial future of this venture is uncertain due to general political and economic instability.

> *Falton's Encyclopedia*, 4th Edition
> (University of Bridgeport Press)

First he heard the click of the switchblade. Then the whining, feral voice. "Hey man, gimme money!"

There were four of them in his path: two slouching against the wall, two erect and staring. Westwood was deserted. The UCLA campus beyond showed lights, but it might have been in another city for all the good it did him. Kevin tasted sour bile, felt the sharp knot of fear in his stomach. They moved closer.

"Come on, hand it over, you sumbich." The spokesman's blade moved in intricate, blurringly fast passes inches from Kevin's face. It gleamed dully despite the power-saving partial blackout in the city. His tormentor laughed as Kevin cringed away. "Beg," he said. "Beg good."

Kevin was a well-muscled six-footer, had played football for UCLA and made his letter in his junior year before the pressure of studies made him drop from the team; he was certain he was more than a match for any of them—for any two—but the knife seemed hungry for his eyes, and he felt only fear and shame. His legs wouldn't move. He reached into his pocket and took out his wallet.

"Watch," the mugger said. "Take it off." The whining voice was filled with contempt and sadistic power-lust. Kevin felt it wash over him, and felt contempt for himself. "Turn out all your pockets. Deucey, rub him over."

Another of the young gangsters—they couldn't, Kevin thought, be more than sixteen—came up behind him and rubbed his hands over Kevin's clothes. The hands moved insultingly, paused in insulting places, then reached into his pockets and took out his lighter. "Aw, he's got cigarettes," Deucey said.

"Good for you, mother," the spokesman said. "We cut you if you don't have cigarettes. Cut you good. Now we miss the fun. Get in there." The knife jerked to indicate a dark alleyway.

Kevin was beyond terror. He had never experienced the feeling before, but he recognized it now, like something known previously from a faded photograph. They pushed him off the street and away from his last hope of rescue. The street lights dimmed even more just as they entered the alley; it was almost pitch black in the stinking passageway between buildings. His foot kicked something, trash or a dead cat, and insanely he thought of the city garbage strike—would anyone find him for weeks? He was certain the gangsters were going to kill him, and kept worrying about that: would the strike end in time for them to find his body?

Suddenly he was surrounded by the smell of naptha, strong enough to overpower the smells of urine and decay in the alley. He felt a chill on scalp and shoulders. Lighter fluid. They were going to burn him alive!

Desperation drove him forward, away from his captors for a moment. The knife had terrified him, but the threat of becoming a living torch did something else. He was no less afraid—more so if that were possible—but now there was rage and hatred as well. He cast about for a weapon, anything to defend himself. He was certain he was going to die, but now he wanted to take them with him, to end this humiliation and show them he was a man—

His hand struck a garbage can. It had a lid, and he seized that by the handle. Years before, when he was only seventeen—it was only five years ago, but at this moment it felt like two lifetimes—he had participated in a tournament held by the Society for Creative Anachronism. The SCA fighters used wooden swords, but their armor and other equipment had been real. He'd been fascinated by the use of shields as weapons. A hand grabbed his hair, and despair gave him strength of a different order than when he'd fought in the SCA tournament.

He swung the lid blindly, felt it clash, then swung it backhand against the spokesman's face. He felt bone crunch, and shouted his triumph.

As the first gangster screamed Kevin used the shield to deflect another half-seen knife attack, then again blindly swung the lid backhand with all his strength. He couldn't see anything, but he could feel when he connected, and he wanted to hurt them. He hated them with all his soul, and he wanted them to feel as humiliated as he had felt. He struck out again and again, felt the improvised shield strike home at least once more. Then he was past them and in the street.

The sight of freedom ahead robbed him of his rage; he turned and ran. Two of them followed him for a block, but they didn't have the wind to keep up.

He ran on and on, long after he could no longer hear their heel-beats behind him.

The Los Angeles policeman showing his badge at Kevin's door was big and burly, and looked as if he ought to be in uniform instead of neat civilian tunic and trousers. Kevin's landlady stood disapprovingly behind him in the hall.

"Detective Sergeant Mason," the policeman said. "May I come in?"

Kevin couldn't think of anything he had done. He was exhausted from standing in lines for his food ration stamps, and he wanted to send the policeman away, but he was afraid that his landlady would believe he was in trouble with the law. Mrs. Jeffries was a good friend to her student tenants. She would let them be late with the rent, but she didn't want police trouble in her rooming house. "What's it about?" Kevin asked. His voice sounded much more calm than he felt.

"This yours?" The policeman held up a wallet.

"Uh—"

"It's got your ID in it," the detective said. "I'm returning it. No big deal. Want to talk about how you lost it."

"Yes, sure, it's mine," Kevin said. He felt relief, and saw that Mrs. Jeffries had lost her worried look. Kevin winked at her and got a slight smile in return before she left and the policeman came in.

The room wasn't very large. There was a couch that could make into a bed, but it was long enough for Kevin to sleep on without unfolding it, and he never opened it. The walls were lined with bookshelves. Over the years the many students who'd lived there had added to the shelving until there wasn't a bare wall. There were two desks and a table that came from the Salvation Army Thrift Store. At the opposite end from the entrance was an opening onto an alcove where a stove, refrigerator and cat litter box filled what would not have been a very large closet. The room smelled of food and cats. The desks were littered with papers, pocket calculator, library reader-screen, opened books, drafting tools, and junk mail.

"Reminds me of my student days," Sergeant Mason said. "I stayed down the street in a room just like this. What class are you?"

"Senior, I think."

"Kevin Senecal," Mason said. "Senecal. Unusual name. Don't think I ever heard it before."

"It's Norman French. We think it used to be Seneschale," Kevin told him. "That'd be Stewart in English—you know, meant Steward." He wondered why he was so nervous with this policeman. The cop had brought back his wallet, and Kevin hadn't done anything to be afraid of. But the policeman's manner was unusual, cagey, as if he were trying to think of the right way to say something unpleasant. He didn't think the policeman would have come alone if he'd intended to make an arrest, but why was he acting this way?

Kevin had never had much contact with police: in the neighborhood where he grew up police were to be avoided. Cops didn't have much respect for people on welfare and unemployment. When Greg Tolland's People's Alliance won the White House and Congress that had changed for a while, but then Tolland was hounded by the press and the Alliance was smeared and things went back to politics as usual and—

His reverie was interrupted by the policeman. "Here." Mason tossed him the wallet. "Put it away. Officially, I never saw it."

"Uh?"

"Look, Kevin—you don't mind if I call you Kevin? We took this off some bad people last night. Guy carrying it had a broken jaw. His buddies were trying to get him to a doctor."

"You caught the bastards! Good work," Kevin said. He looked at the policemen with new respect. His mother, who had once had a better life, had always told him the police were all right. "But isn't the wallet evidence?"

"You don't want to prosecute."

"But—"

"No." The policeman was very firm. "Look, those guys belong to the Garvey Street Crips. If you identify them, you won't live until the trial. Actually, you're probably in trouble anyway; they wouldn't have kept the wallet if they didn't have something in mind. Usually they just take out the money, put the credit cards into an envelope and mail them to friends—and dump the wallet so there's no evidence if we shake them down. They kept yours. I don't have to be very smart to guess why. You did a good job on the guy with the broken jaw. And a better job on the other one."

The policeman was looking carefully at Kevin's face. Kevin didn't care. He was glad that he'd hurt those bastards.

Whatever the policeman saw seemed to please him. "You didn't know, did you?" the cop asked. "You killed one of them. That garbage can lid caught him just at the base of the skull. Clean and neat."

"Jeez—" Kevin felt a rush of shock, fear, and anger. "I never meant to kill anyone! Am I in trouble for that?"

"You would be if we knew who'd done it. But of course we don't. Never found anything at all. They must have ditched the wallet."

It took Kevin a moment to catch on. "But—"

"But nothing," Mason said. "We got ourselves a new DA, a real People's Alliance type, and we've got judges who don't approve of 'deadly force.' Somebody killed a juvenile last night, and you don't kill juvies in this town. That's bad news."

"But they were trying to kill me! They poured lighter fluid on me, to set me on fire!"

"Can you prove that?"

"How the hell could I prove—"

"Exactly," the policeman said. "You can't. And we can't do one damned thing for you, Kevin. If we give you protection the DA will want to know why, and we can't tell him or he'll have you up for manslaughter of a juvie. It gets worse. Those were black kids. Ever say anything about blacks? Africans taking jobs? Say anything against the quota system? Even if you didn't, the DA will likely go against you for hate crimes. You could get twenty years."

"That can't be true."

"I sure wish it couldn't. Look, Kevin, I don't make the rules. I'm breaking hell out of them coming here."

"Yeah. I know that. Thanks, but—"

"But it stinks. Look, the DA isn't the worst of your problems. He doesn't know who you are. The Crips do know, and they'll be looking for you. If you're smart they won't find you."

"You're telling me I ought to run because some muggers tried to kill me and I defended myself?"

Kevin's face showed anger. His fists clenched and he felt the blood rising—

"Nope." The detective's calm was maddening. "Remember, I don't even know who you are. I'm just returning some property I found while I was off duty. Which, by the way, I am now. You got any beer in that fridge?"

"Sure." Kevin went to the refrigerator. Snowdrop, his white kitten, was sitting guard on top of it. She mewed hopefully when Kevin opened the door, then looked resigned when no cat food or milk came out.

Mason popped the top of the beer bulb and made a face at it. "I liked this stuff in bottles or cans. Now we got biodegradable cardboard, and it don't taste the same." He drank it anyway, a long healthy glug. "Can you change apartments?"

"I'm a month behind here. There's no way I could get the money for a new place."

"Probably wouldn't help anyway. They'd follow you when you moved. What are your plans?"

"Well, I graduate this term . . ."

"You might last that long. Want some advice? Keep out of dark places. Don't have a routine. Come home at different times, and don't eat in the same place every day. Keep the shades down and keep your shadow off the shade. Lock up good when you go out. Get a better lock. Get *two* locks. And stay with people you know." Mason drank again. His lips tightened as he set the bulb on the couch arm. "Kevin, do you think I *like* this? I'm a cop. My job is protecting people. And I'm telling you that I can't protect you, that the bastards in City Hall won't let me. I don't like that much, but you tell me—what should I do?"

"I don't know," Kevin said.

"Yeah. Well, if you think of something, let me know."

It seemed appropriate that the lights dimmed just then. The experimental windmills never did deliver enough power, and many of the regular generators were down for maintenance. It always took a while to get the lights back on.

Long after the policeman left Kevin sat at his desk staring at a book. He read the same page three times, but none of it registered. He was afraid. His books said he lived in a post-industrial society and described the benefits in glowing words, but the police couldn't help him.

Out there somewhere a gang of nameless children—the DA would call them children, and Kevin a child-murderer—was looking for him, and those children would kill him if they could, and the police were helpless. The United States of America in all its awful majesty was no use at all. The police could give out tickets and harass taxpayer demonstrations but they couldn't protect Kevin's life.

His life had been settled and orderly, completely planned. He would get his degree and go to work for one of the big international corporations, perhaps even go out to one of the near-Earth space industries if he could get a post. Junior engineers weren't paid much for a starting salary, because nearly everyone graduated from state universities and had some kind of "professional" job—or didn't work at all—but when he got his degree Kevin would be eligible to join a strong union, and the union with its influence with the government would keep the pay raises coming. The unions would prevent smart-ass whiz kids from taking his job, too. Once Kevin had wanted to be a smart-ass whiz kid, but he'd seen what happened to them. Now Kevin looked forward to marriage, a house, a car, perhaps a camper and a small boat.

When he told his friends, they usually laughed and said it sounded dull, but Kevin didn't mind. Dull was fine, as long as it was secure. After the years of living with his mother and his brother on welfare checks and food stamps, split pea soup, chicken once a week when they were lucky, patched clothes and shoes bought from the Salvation Army, dull-but-secure was attractive. Dull meant buying food in private stores instead of standing in long lines at the cooperatives, even eating out once in a while. Dull meant living in a neighborhood where the police were polite and respectful. Dull meant all the things Kevin had never had and always wanted.

And his dream of dull security was vanishing with the memory of a garbage can lid smacking into human bone.

The book stared back at him. "The most crucial questions that will be faced by every post-industrial society will deal with education, talent, and science policy. The rapid expansion of a professional and technical class, and the increased dependence of the society on scientific manpower, suggest a new and absolutely unique dimension in social affairs: i.e., that the economic growth rate of a post-industrial society will be less dependent on money capital than on human capital."

The words blurred and the idea was silly to begin with. The most crucial question was: how would Kevin Senecal stay alive long enough to graduate and get his union card so that he could find a job?

The letter had been generated by a computer. It had his name spelled "Senegal," but the student ID number was correct. It was for him.

It told him that two summer classes he'd taken at California State University, Northridge, were not recognized as transferable for credit to UCLA. "As these classes are prerequisite to other classes required for graduation (see schedule 4 below) you may not hold credit in the classes named in schedule 4, and thus you have not completed the requirements for graduation. Your application for graduation is denied, and your present class status is second-year, commonly called sophomore. Upon completion of the required prerequisites, and following that completion, your successful completion of the courses noted in schedule 4 (see below) you may again make application for graduation."

He read it three times. It said the same thing each time. Instead of graduating in two months, he had two more years of school. He crumpled the letter in rage, but then carefully smoothed it out. These things happened. It was futile to get excited. Computers often made mistakes. He telephoned the UCLA Appointment Exchange. The Voice Mail system was slow and cumbersome, but eventually he was able to register a request to see his advisor.

"Your appointment with Ms. Rasmussen has been scheduled for two PM on the twenty-second of April," the computer told him.

"Two weeks. Can't you make it earlier?"

"To accept the appointment, press one. To reschedule your appointment for a later time press two," the machine said. Kevin raged silently at the phone, then pressed one.

"Thank you for calling the Appointment Exchange. If you have further business with the Exchange, press one."

He slammed down the phone, then felt ashamed for being so angry. It shouldn't be surprising that it would take a while to see his advisor. There were over 50,000 students at UCLA. It took time to arrange for a human interview.

Chapter Two

He took the policeman's advice: varied his schedule, stayed off streets at night, and always locked his doors. His friends didn't notice. He'd always been something of a loner and a bit of a bookworm since he dropped out of the football squad, so there was no one to miss him. The girl he'd been dating had found someone else two days before the muggers had caught him, and except for Wiley Ralston no one would care.

Wiley had graduated a year ahead of Kevin, staying on after graduation to specialize in space industry technology. Engineering students were never popular on campus, and those going to space were hated. The One Earth Society, and other anti-technology groups, picketed the engineering building nearly every day. Their lunchtime demonstrations seldom got out of hand, and

Kevin had become accustomed to their shouted insults whenever he went in or came out of his classrooms. Today they were getting on his nerves. When they ritually shouted "murderer!" at him, he remembered the crunch of bone that he'd felt that night in the alley.

"Hey, don't let those nuts shake you," Wiley said as they walked past the demonstrators.

"Aw, they don't," Kevin said. They hurried toward the cafeteria.

There was a long line waiting. "Not really anyway."

"You ever really listen to them?" Wiley asked.

"Once," Kevin said. "Didn't make much sense to me. They kept telling me we're wasting all that money in space when there's so much needed here, and I know better. Without space technology we'd be a lot worse off than we are now. What goes to space wouldn't help anyway. It's just not enough."

Wiley nodded, then waved at the line ahead of them. "Yeah, except sometimes I wonder."

"You?"

Wiley Ralston laughed. "Not very often. Just sometimes. Like this. Why're so many people lined up for lunch? Because you get a free lunch on your student ID card. Which is why most of these turkeys are students to begin with."

Kevin didn't say anything. It was one reason he'd decided to go to college. The state university was free, and the food at the UCLA cafeteria was better than anything his mother had ever been able to afford on straight welfare.

"Better to be a student and eat than be unemployed," Wiley said. "And hell, it's all this technology that keeps people unemployed. That's the way they see it, anyway."

"You know better," Kevin said. "What's important is production. High production means a lot to go around, and—" He stopped, because Wiley was laughing at him.

"Gotcha," his friend said. He tossed back a shock of unruly red hair and grinned broadly. "You know the trouble with you, old buddy? You care. These jokers say the world's got to learn to use low technology, be kind to the Earth, live with the land, or our great-grandchildren will have green tentacles or something—"

"They never—"

"And you really worry about whether they're right or not," Wiley finished.

"But they aren't, and I can prove it—"

"So-friggin-what?" Wiley Ralston demanded. "Look, Kev, maybe they're right. Look around you. Food lines in the US of A. Want in the middle of plenty. And that's here! All over the world people are breeding like mad, nobody's got enough of anything, and hell, maybe all this space effort *will* be the last straw, the push that makes the donkey lie down and die. So what? You say space will save the Earth, they say it will kill us, and I say—somebody's going to get rich out there, and that somebody is going to be Wiley Ralston. I'll get mine, and if they're so stupid they'd rather put on demonstrations than get in on a good thing, that's their lookout."

But Wiley had spoken too loudly, and others overheard. An alternate technology group came up to argue. A Zero-Growth group joined in, then some fanatics from the One Earth Society. If the various protestors hadn't got to arguing among themselves the scene might have gotten ugly; as it was, Kevin missed his lunch.

Even so, he preferred to be in crowds. Most of the anti-technology students wouldn't actually harm him.

None wanted to kill him. Better them than the Garvey Street Crips.

His advisor was a prim, rather prissy-looking woman in her thirties. She reminded Kevin of a sentence in his sociology book. "The post-industrial society is organized around *knowledge*, and this gives rise to new social relationships which have to be organized politically." Ms. Rasmussen was the embodiment of that: she had *knowledge*, or was supposed to have, and that gave her power.

As he faced her, Kevin thought that was a bunch of horse puckey. She had a job that gave her power, and she liked that a lot.

"What seems to be the trouble?" she asked. She shoved a form toward him. His student ID card embossed his name and ID number on the form, but he had to fill in the address by hand. She waited until he was finished before she picked up the computer letter Kevin had handed her in response to her question.

She read it through twice. "This seems to be in order," she said.

Kevin wanted to scream at her, but he held his temper. Years of watching his mother manipulate the welfare workers had given him both patience and technique. "Please ma'am," he said. He felt sick saying it, but forced himself to keep his tone respectful. "This costs me two years of my life. It isn't fair, ma'am. I worked hard, and they tell me I'm still not through. Please, can't you do something?"

She punched buttons on her console. "I'll need your ID card," she said. She inserted the plastic into the machine. Records flowed across the screen. She peered at it, adjusting her glasses with fussy little movements, smiling thinly, a superior smile, the smile of those with power. "It's all in order," she said, "just as the letter tells you. You took the courses without the proper prerequisites, and so of course you're not entitled to credit for them."

"But, ma'am, I had the prerequisites," Kevin whined. He tried to keep his voice pleading, showing that he appreciated all that Ms. Rasmussen was doing for him. The effort made him tense. He hated himself, and suddenly realized that this was the way he'd felt when the muggers had him: helpless and violated. And he felt that way a lot, lately.

Ms. Rasmussen didn't feel helpless. She was empowered. "You did not have prerequisites as recognized by this university," Miss Rasmussen said. "I'm sorry, but I can't help you." She sounded pleased. She began marking the form; it would be turned in to record that she'd had another interview. The accounting machines needed the completed form to justify her job to the regents. So many interviews satisfactorily completed, requiring so many person-hours, requiring an adjustment and increase in salaries and personnel for the counseling department; in these days of unemployment it was necessary to keep one's forms in order.

"But," Kevin stammered. He almost lost control of his voice, but regained it with effort, and continued to keep a respectful tone. "I got A's in those courses," Kevin said. "A's at Northridge, B's in the courses here. What difference does it make if I had the prerequisites if I got B's here? Even an A in one of them. Prerequisites are supposed to keep you out of work you can't handle, but it's obvious that I *can* handle the work, because I *did*. Please, ma'am, can't you do something to help me?"

She held her head high and her look of sympathy was patently artificial. "We have to go by the rules," Ms. Rasmussen said. "There was a mistake. You should never have been admitted to the courses here without proper prerequisites. Now, officially, you have never taken those courses at all. You'll have to go meet the prerequisite requirements, then take the courses over again. I'm very sorry." She wasn't.

"But that's two years of my life!" Kevin said. He wasn't deferential now. "You can't do that to me!"

Patiently Ms. Rasmussen punched in more numbers. A blur of fine print filled the screen. "Look," she said. "Here are the rules. You may read them for yourself—"

If I plead, Kevin thought. If I plead, I may, just may, get her to help. She wants to feel important, and I can help her. Just say the right words.

But the feeling of self-contempt was too strong. His control broke like an exploded dam. "Damn you to hell!" he shouted.

"You will not swear at me." Ms. Rasmussen stood. "Get out of here. Instantly. I will not have students shouting at me. I do not have to put up with that. If you don't leave I will call the Campus Police."

Police. He didn't want trouble with the police. Kevin stood. "I'm very sorry," he said "I should not have lost my temper—"

"Go." Now that she was in control, Ms. Rasmussen felt much better. "Go now."

"Yes," Kevin said. He turned.

"Wait." The counselor kept him standing for a long moment. Her smile, a thin wintry smile that showed the tiniest thin line of white teeth, played at her lips. "You forgot your ID card. That's very important, you will need it. Here." She laid it on the desk, although it would have been easier to hand it to him.

Kevin took the card and left. As he went out, Ms. Rasmussen was marking the time onto still another form. The form title was "Interviews Successfully Completed."

He walked home glumly, not knowing what to do. There was a Zero-Growth Movement rally on campus, and students were shouting. An alternate technology group was arguing with the Z-Gs, screaming that all technology wasn't bad, only the big industries. Another group of Social Technocrats appeared to argue for high technology owned by the people. The Campus Police stood by interestedly.

He walked in fury, not knowing whether to be angry with himself for losing his temper when he might have talked Ms. Rasmussen into doing something for him, or for not telling her exactly what he thought of her and her useless bureaucratic job; whether to be ashamed for not getting the results he wanted, or for trying when trying meant pretending respect for the Rasmussens of this world.

When he reached the top of the stairs he wasn't surprised to see the door to his room standing open. Mrs. Jeffries often brought food to the students' rooms and put it in their 'frigs. She said she cooked too much, but she did it often. Kevin went in without thinking.

The room was empty. All his books had been tumbled from the shelves onto the floor. His calculator was a heap of rubble in the center of the floor. The refrigerator door stood open, and everything that had been in it was poured into a hideous soup over his books.

When he went into the bathroom he found Snowdrop drowned in the toilet.

Chapter Three

"Dr. Farrington?"

"Yes, Kevin?"

"Can I see you for a moment, sir? I need help."

"Sure." Professor Farrington's grin was reassuring. Of all Kevin's professors, Farrington was the only one who seemed actually interested in the students. He was a bulky man, heavyset and going to fat; forty years before, he'd been a football star, but he had little time for physical activities now.

His classes were interesting. He taught what was in the books but he often spoke of other things as well, of a world remade by technology and engineering, of man's future. "We're in a bad phase right now," Farrington said many times, "but that won't last. These things come in waves. Right now the social theorists are on top, and they don't trust people. It won't last. You'll all live to see a new era, an era of freedom and individual responsibilities, and I want you to be ready for it."

He waved Kevin toward his office and followed along the hall. His steps were slow; Farrington seemed always physically tired, but he spoke with an animation that denied it. They went into the office, a large room lined with books, drafting table beneath the windows, an oversized flat computer monitor on the battered wood desk. "Have a seat," Farrington said. "Now, what can I do for you?"

Kevin showed him the computer letter and described his interview with Ms. Rasmussen. "And I can't afford two more years," he concluded. "It's just not fair."

"No, probably not. Fair play isn't the strongest point of our regulated competitive welfare state. Rules and order, that's our goal. Let me have your ID card, I need to look up your records."

Kevin handed it over. "Two years because a computer says so. That doesn't make sense."

"Makes more than you think." Farrington inserted the ID card into a slot in the desk console. He began punching in numbers. "When you admit everyone who wants to go to college, and you're not allowed to flunk anybody out, you have to have some way to keep from getting hip-deep in idiots-with-degrees," Farrington said. "Too bad it happened to the engineering school too. I remember when this kind of horse puckey was reserved for the Sociology and Education Departments. And law schools, of course."

"But can't you do something?"

Farrington studied the read-outs. "Probably not. Used to be the professors had some authority here, but not for a long time now. Rules are rules—"

"Not you too!"

"Easy. Doesn't do any good to get excited. Least not here, not with me. Kevin, I can understand why you young people get frustrated. If things like this had happened to me when I was your age I'd have been scheming on how to bring the whole mess down in blood. I don't suppose your generation even talks like that."

Kevin said nothing. Farrington was right. A couple of times Kevin had complained about some rule or another, tried to get a student protest together, and his classmates had thought he was crazy. The only student demonstrations to get involved in were those sponsored by one of the recognized outfits. Demonstrating for the right causes was a key to a good job after graduation. Making trouble was a way to welfare.

"I can't give you a degree by waving my hand," Farrington said. "But we can diddle the system a bit. You stay on. I'll see that you get admitted to graduate courses. You can enroll in these junk courses they want you to take again, but you won't have to go to class. Just show up on exam day. When you've touched all the bases you'll get your degree and have two years of advanced study to go with it. Get you a better job."

"It sounds good," Kevin said, "But I can't do it—"

"I wasn't through," Farrington said. "Look, I've got some buddies out at Systems Development Corporation. I can get you on part-time at SDC. Get you some experience programming, feeding problems into the computer, that sort of thing. Won't pay too bad, and you'll have job experience in your resume. Ought to about make up for the time this stupid system is costing you."

"But I still can't," Kevin said. "I'd love to. What you're offering is better than—Dr. Farrington, it would be great, and I really thank you, but I can't stay in Los Angeles."

Farrington frowned. "Why not?"

Kevin told him. "I might have thought it wasn't serious, but when I found Snowdrop in the toilet—" He couldn't finish. The memory of wet fur was in his nostrils.

Farrington's lips tightened. "You know, a few years ago—I guess it was longer than that. Back about 1990. I knew a guy named Turk. Sold custom car parts. One of those damned street gangs decided Turk ought to kick in to them. Pay protection.

"The cops couldn't do anything: judges didn't believe in juvenile criminals. 'No such thing as a bad child,' all that crap. Racial overtones. One day Turk came home and found his dog puking blood all over the carpet. Seems someone had fed it meat filled with ground glass. So Turk went hunting. He took a shotgun over to the gang headquarters and blew hell out of the place. Then he cruised around the city looking for their cars and blew off four or five. You know, old Turk lived another two, three years, finally died of a very natural heart attack. I understand that gang goes out to the cemetery every month to be sure Turk's still under ground."

"I couldn't do that!" There was horror in Kevin's voice.

"No, I don't reckon you could. Mind if I look up your psych records?"

"No, sir."

Farrington played with the console keys. A series of graphs came onto the screen. "Know what these mean?"

"No. They wouldn't let me take any advanced psych courses. I don't know why."

"I do," Farrington said. He pointed to a series of dips and valleys on one of the graphs. "Those little wiggles right there. Unstable. Potential for violence. You got a hot temper?"

"Sometimes. I try to control it," Kevin said.

"Yeah. You've got some other problems too. Kind of a misfit, aren't you?"

"No!" Kevin almost shouted it. "I get along!"

"Have many friends?"

"Yes—well, I don't have time to make many friends. But I get along."

"Sure," Farrington said. "But I expect you have to work on that individualist streak. I see they had you in for intensive counseling for a couple of years. Help any?"

"Sure. Sensitivity training is important, particularly for those who hope to be promoted into managerial positions—"

"You don't need to quote the goddam course prospectus to me," Farrington said. He leaned back in his big chair. "Kevin, when I was your age, an engineer built things. Took responsibilities. They'd give us a project and by God we'd get it done. Build a bridge. Design something. Start with paper and ideas and see it through until it worked. Nowadays they put you in a room full of people just like yourself, and you feed numbers into a computer. Somebody checks all your work, somebody else originated it, and a third type will supervise the hardware—do you think you'll like that?"

"No," Kevin admitted. "But what can I do?"

Farrington shrugged. "Not much. Not here, anyway."

"I mean," Kevin said, "the system's set up so that no one person can ruin things for everybody. Isn't that the way it's supposed to work?"

"Sure. How it's supposed to work." Farrington fingered the computer letter that lay on his desk, then looked back at the console. He seemed to be debating with himself. "Senecal, I'm going to tell you something that I don't want you to repeat. You say I told you this, and I'll deny it."

"Sir? I can—I don't have to tell people everything I know."

"No. I don't expect you do," Farrington said. "Look, that computer letter was no accident. The psych people have decided you're not ready to graduate. If they hadn't found problems with your prerequisites they'd have come up with something else."

"But—why?"

"You're not mature enough by their thinking. Individualist. Not group-adjusted. See those little code numbers? That's the clue."

Kevin leaned over the desk and looked at the readout screen. The numbers meant nothing to him. "I don't think those were on the printouts I got," Kevin said. "I sent for my records. Don't they have to tell us everything in them? I thought there was a law—"

"Oh, there are laws and laws," Farrington said. "One law says that if properly qualified human-resources specialists determine that giving a subject information would be damaging to the subject, the information can be withheld. There are some others, too. I'm not even supposed to be able to get this, not even with your ID card, but—well, a couple of my former students designed the computer security system. Anyway. The psych boys have decided you ought to stay on as a student a few more years. Then they'll decide if your new profile is good enough to let you have a degree. My guess is that it'll still be 'no,' and it won't matter if you stay on as an undergraduate until you're ninety."

"But what can I do?" Kevin demanded.

"I don't know. One of the unions might help you, but you can't join a good union without a degree. Got any pull? Political friends? Ever worked campaigns?"

"No."

"Then I can't think of anything. I wish I could help. I really do." Farrington opened his desk drawer and took out a printed brochure. "There's one thing. This outfit's looking for good general systems engineers, and they don't care about degrees. They want ability, and I think you've got signs of that. You did a good paper for me last term. I'll recommend you, if you like." He scaled the brochure across the desk.

The illustration on the front leaped out at him; space as black as night; the Milky Way a sparkling waterfall of stars. Against the backdrop hung a small rock. Men floated in the foreground. A large mirror focused solar energy onto the asteroid, boiling out metals.

"The Daedalus Corporation," Kevin said. "That's a deep-space outfit."

Farrington nodded. "One of them. And they're hungry. Want me to talk to them for you?"

Kevin knew there were companies operating in the Asteroid Belt, but he'd never thought of working for one of them. When he thought of going to space it was always in terms of one of the near-Earth orbiting factories, or possibly to work for Hansen-MacKenzie on the Moon. There was real money to be made in the industrial satellite factories—and you could come home to spend it.

"Nobody ever comes back from the Belt," Kevin said.

"Not many have, yet," Farrington agreed. "But maybe they don't want to come home. They're doing something real out there in the Belt, Kevin. Something important

for the whole human race, and it's not done with acres
of engineers sitting in bullpens. They're going to build a
whole new civilization out there—and maybe save this
one in the bargain. If I were your age I wouldn't hesitate
a minute."

For a moment the intensity of Farrington's tone, the
professor's sincerity and wistful expression, made it
sound attractive. Kevin thought again. He knew almost
nothing about the Belt. There were stories. That they'd
found fabulously rich sources of metals, millions of tons
of nearly pure iron and nickel and copper, with solar
energy to run the refineries. "But they've never brought
anything back," Kevin said aloud.

"No. And if they don't pretty soon things will be bad
for the asteroid industries," Farrington said. "But that's
just the point. They need people out there. People
who'll work—"

"How can they bring enough metal back to Earth to
matter? The asteroids are a long way out."

"There are ways," Farrington said.

"I just don't know—"

"Yes." Farrington sighed. "I know. You've been
brought up to think somebody will take care of you.
Social Security, National Health Plan, Federal Burial
Insurance, Family Assistance, Food Stamps, Welfare.
Union representatives to speak for you. And I'm talking
about a place where it's all up to you, where you take
care of yourself because nobody's going to do it for you.
I guess that can be scary to modern kids. You don't like
the idea, do you?"

"It's not that," Kevin said. "But I never really thought
about the Belt. It's not what I had in mind for
myself—I'm sorry."

"Nothing to be sorry about. It's an alien way of life. For you. Me, I wish I was young enough to go. Enough of that. Kevin, I'll think about your problem. Maybe we can come up with something. Now, if you'll excuse me, I've got to prepare for my next class."

"Yes, sir. Thank you."

"Nothing to thank me for. I wish I could have been some help. Nice seeing you. Drop in again—I mean that. Come see me again in a couple of days. Maybe I'll have thought of something."

"Thank you. I will." But you probably won't have thought of anything, Kevin thought as he left the office.

Alfred Farrington continued to stare at the computer screen. He took out a thin black notebook and copied some of the data into it, then frowned and opened another file, selected a name, and touched keys. The telephone beeped and rang twice.

"Yeah?" The phone showed a fat man about Farrington's age.

"Alf. How are you, Ben?"

"Fine, except for recruiting—"

"Yes. I thought I had you a good prospect, but he may not work out. Then again, he may."

"Something special about this one?"

"Good prospect. No family ties, nobody's going to worry about him, nothing here for him to spend money on. Engineering student. And a pretty good one compared to the lot we get now."

"Umm. The ship's leaving pretty soon. Think you can get him aboard? We're short on engineering talent. I've been thinking maybe we ought to ask Paul to send out a couple of the Order—"

"Possibly. I hope it doesn't come to that. I doubt if he'd do it," Farrington said. "We've few enough in the Fellowship. Better to hire some talent—"

"If we can. One way or another we've got to get moving *now*, or the whole thing's going to come apart. How good is this prospect?"

"Potentially quite good. And no family. No one will worry about where he's gone or when he's coming back. Or not coming back."

"Good."

"Of course his motivation's all wrong," Farrington said thoughtfully.

"To hell with motivation," Ben said. "Get him aboard. We'll motivate him. And if we can't, well, we can still get some use out of him."

"Yes. Well, I'll send you his records. If you like him, let me know. There may be more pressures I can put on him. Now what about those others I sent over?"

They talked for a long time.

The new locks to Kevin's room hadn't been disturbed. The door hadn't been opened. It hadn't had to be.

Kevin's black tomcat was nailed to the door. The cat mewed piteously. Kevin gulped hard and examined the wounds. He knew what had to be done, and after a moment he did it. Then he sat on the floor with tears streaming from his eyes.

After a while he heard steps behind him. Sergeant Mason came into the upstairs hallway.

"Your landlady called," the policeman said. "The deskman passed it on to me." He looked at the still body nailed to the door. "You got your keys?"

"Yes—"

"Go inside. Carefully. Here, let me open that. You get back over there." Mason used the keys, stood back and kicked the door open. The room hadn't been disturbed. "I'd say it's all right." Mason said. "They don't usually do anything final after a warning like—like that. Not for a couple of days. Go get your face cleaned up, son. Go on, get."

Kevin went to the washroom. When he came back the body was gone. Sergeant Mason was sponging off the dark spots on the door.

"That's not evidence either, I suppose," Kevin said. His voice held bitterness.

"Evidence? Sure it's evidence. Of childish pranks. Cruel, of course, but deprived children often express aggression in cruelty. It's relatively harmless. We must weigh the importance of human life against that of an animal, and of course there can be only one decision—look, kid, I'm not saying what I believe, I'm just quoting."

"Children! They're no better than animals! Bad animals."

"Sure. You know that. I know it. But make the DA and the judges believe it—look, son, the judges are picked by the lawyers, and the lawyers get paid by the government to defend these deprived kids. The lawyers all live in closed communities with rent-a-cops. So do the news-critters. Nobody kills *their* pets. It's the way things are. You just get your degree and get out of LA, go find a good job and live in a company town with company cops around, and you can forget all this—"

The policeman's face went hard. "Look, I don't like it either. I can give you some protection, but we've only got so many police. And the Garvey Street Crips are never going to forget that you killed one of theirs. They'll remember a long time. A *long* time, Kevin."

"But this is insane!" Kevin sat on the couch and looked at the familiar books—stained and damaged now—on all the walls. The world no longer made any sense. "You're telling me this gang is more powerful than the government!"

Mason shrugged. "Maybe. What do you want us to do? Go lean on those kids? Rig up evidence? Senecal, I've got nineteen years in. I can retire in another year. You got any idea what happens to cops who bend the rules that way? The Public Defender and the Civil Liberties Union and all the others would have my head on a platter! Sure, there's lots of us would like to get those scumbags off the streets any way we can. But we've learned better, Senecal. They got Lieutenant Mogowa for tampering with evidence and they sent him to prison. He lived about a week. Not me, son. Not me. I got a wife and three kids—and none of 'em cops either."

"So you'll wait until they kill me—"

"And then maybe I can nail 'em for it. And if I do they'll be on the streets in a year. Yeah. That's the way it is, Senecal. Got any more beer?"

"Yes, but you'll have to excuse me. I've got to go make a telephone call. Maybe I can catch Dr. Farrington in his office."

Chapter four

Kevin had never seen so many forms and tests. There were dozens of them, and they asked him for information that no sane person would know. Finally he threw down his pencil. "This is ridiculous!" he shouted.

Three other job applicants who were still working looked up in annoyance, then went back to their tests. The test monitor, a pretty girl in short skirts, frowned. "You must complete your tests—"

"I will be damned if I will," Kevin said. He stalked out of the room as the girl pleaded with him to go back and finish.

That blows that, Kevin thought. Damnation. I thought a deep-space-operations outfit would—

"Congratulations, Senecal. Come with me, please." An elderly fat man barred his path. "Come on, we're running low on time," the man said. His voice was filled with authority.

Kevin wanted to tell him to stuff it, but he had nothing to lose. He followed the man through twisting hallways, then into an elevator. The man didn't speak until they got off at the top floor of the Santa Monica office building.

Downstairs the building had been coldly professional: new, expensive, and utterly without warmth. Up here it was completely different. The carpets were old but comfortable. Holos of space mining operations hung along the walls. People were dressed casually, and worked in small groups, or alone, and some sat in their offices with their feet on the desk and eyes directed to the ceiling. One man was making a paper airplane.

They went to the end of the hall and into an office. It too was comfortably furnished, and reminded Kevin of Professor Farrington's room.

"I'm Ben Simington," the fat man said. "Have a seat."

The chairs were comfortable.

"Want a drink? Scotch. Yes. I recommend scotch whiskey, a double." Simington went to a wall panel, touched it, and let it swing open. An elaborate wet bar was behind it. He took out glasses carved with strange creatures and poured, then handed one to Kevin. The figure on Kevin's glass was a phoenix. "Cheers," Simington said.

Kevin lifted the glass and sipped. The whiskey was smooth, much better than any scotch he'd ever had before. "Confused?" Simington asked.

"Yes."

"Think about it."

Kevin did. What data had he? The contrast between the lower floor of the Daedalus building, coldly professional, like hundreds of others all over the city, and the relaxed attitudes of the people on this floor—all of them obviously high-ranking executives even if they didn't act like it—was indeed confusing. This office, plain, but with very expensive carpets and pictures and electronic equipment—Kevin realized that he had, in all his life put together, never spent as much money as this office must have cost, yet the impression was of comfort and utility, not ostentation.

Then there were the tests. Medical exams, of course, then the others. The first ones had been sensible, related to systems engineering, digging deep into his knowledge. Others were obviously psychological tests, and all big companies used those. But after that—those forms, which asked for things like grandmother's age at death, great-grandfather's occupation, every address at which he ever lived. They'd made no sense, and they got worse as he went along. Why? What would the Daedalus Corporation want with such information?

Nothing. They couldn't want it. So why ask for it?

"You expected me to give up on those tests," Kevin said.

"Let's say we hoped you would. But not too soon. Part of the test score is the time it takes for the applicants to tell us to go to hell. Quit too soon, we don't need you. Not enough motivation. Keep on after it's too obvious the things are useless, and—well, you came off pretty good."

"But—"

"Many of the chaps down there still wading through will get jobs," the fat man said. "We need paper shufflers too. But we wouldn't send them out to the Belt. I take it you do still want the job."

"Yes." Kevin's voice was unnecessarily strong. He realized that, but didn't explain.

"Why?" Ben Simington prompted.

"Because there's got to be something better than—" He didn't know how to finish. Better than here, where teenaged gangsters tortured cats and threatened people and the courts protected them. Better than a world where there were regulations upon regulations, where every detail of your working life was supervised by Federal inspectors and union officials, where you could get into trouble for working too hard, where they told you that all the regulation was the price of a stable world economy and then they couldn't protect you from street gangsters. Better than—"Better than always having forms to fill out and people who think the forms are important," he said.

Simington nodded. "Good. We need people who want their work to make sense. But don't get the idea that it always will, Kevin. Sometimes there's things to be done whether they make sense or not. Still, you won't find too much monkey motion out where you'll be going. You'll have to take care of yourself, but you won't mind that. Wish I could go along. Drink up."

Kevin took another healthy sip of excellent whiskey. It went down smoothly and warmed him from the inside out—that and the fat man's camaraderie. He liked the feeling. Kevin was intelligent enough to know it was all deliberate, that it was all planned to make him feel welcome, but he liked that too. These people wanted him, and they cared about how he felt.

They talked for an hour. The fat man looked at Kevin's test scores, his medical records, his file from UCLA—Kevin wondered how he'd gotten that, but didn't ask—and a lot of other subjects. Some didn't seem very important.

Finally Simington leaned back and looked pensively at the ceiling. "It's that time again," he said. "I have to make up my mind. Are you worth the investment?"

"I honestly don't know," Kevin said.

"Neither do I." The fat man sighed. "You'd think I'd have thousands of volunteers," he said. "And I do, but not qualified people. The Belt's not the same as a quick tour in orbit. Don't kid yourself that it is. They're spread thin out there. A couple of thousand people, mostly on Ceres, spread across billions of cubic miles. It's no picnic, Kevin."

"No." He hadn't expected a picnic. He thought about the vast emptiness of the Belt. It wasn't a place he'd go by choice—but what choices had he? There were *plenty* of volunteers for the factories orbiting Earth, and what use would Kevin Senecal be to one of them? Officially he was neither engineer nor good mill-hand. He was nothing. It wouldn't be that way in the Belt, and that was something to think about.

"*Wayfarer* leaves in four days," Simington said. "Can you be in her?"

"Four days! Mr. Simington, I don't really know anything about space industries, and I can't learn in four days!"

"We don't expect you to. Trip out takes nine months. You'll learn more about space operations than you really want to know. Nothing else to do aboard ship. There'll be a reader and plenty of tapes, and some good computing equipment. Simulation programs. Operations games. That's the intellectual stuff. On a practical level, the ship's crew drills you in equipment, p-suits, getting around outside. You'll learn to live in low gravity or you won't live at all. I'm not worried about what you'll know when you get to Ceres. It's whether you'll stick it out that bothers me."

"I generally finish what I start," Kevin said.

"Yep. One reason I'm talking to you is because your coach told me how you finished a game with two broken ribs. Didn't play too well, but you finished."

"That was in high school." Just how far back had Daedalus gone in checking his background? But it made sense: he was going to cost them a lot of money. "I still don't understand why you want me," Kevin said.

Simington shrugged. "Who do we send out, Kevin? Not superheroes trained for one mission; most of the astronauts came apart when their tour was over. Senior engineers? Why would they go? They're doing all right here. No, we've found our best people are misfits who don't like our modern welfare state. If they've got some other reason to get them headed for the Belt, that's fine; but it's what they do when they get there that counts." The fat man looked down at the data sheets on his desk. "Look, I don't believe in a lot of this psych garbage, but some of it's useful. In some ways I may know you better than you know yourself."

There wasn't anything Kevin could say to that.

"Contract's for five years," Simington said. "But we don't really make a lot of profit on five years. We need people who'll go the course." He went back to studying the read-outs.

Kevin suddenly wanted very badly to go. Partly it was a competitive urge. He didn't want to be told he wasn't good enough. But there was more, too. Out there he might find a meaningful job and a chance to do something important.

Earth was running out of metals, of oil, of coal, of everything. The anti-technology organizations had halted nuclear power development and eco-freak rioters had smashed the space-power antenna outside Bakersfield— and investment money to build another couldn't be found. Population was rising and food production wasn't. There were already famines in parts of the world, and the pinch was felt everywhere, even in the United States. And the lawyers continued to gum up everything—in the courts, permit hearings, environmental impact statements.

The One Earth Society said the answer was to eliminate technology, space industries, everything that wasn't "natural." The costs would be terrible: millions, billions dead, but there was nothing else. Earth must abide, and she could not support a plague of mankind, an epidemic of humanity.

Kevin remembered Professor Farrington's lecture on that. "Maybe they're right," Farrington had said. "Maybe. But it's for damn sure if there's an alternative this is the time to take it. We can get off the Earth and live in the solar system. Not on one planet, but on nine of them, nine planets, thirty-five moons, and a million asteroids. Right now we can go. If we wait a few years, things will be so desperate down here we'll never make it. This is the first and last opportunity for mankind to be something more than a carnivorous ape crawling on the surface of one insignificant planet."

Kevin, remembering, nodded to himself. "I want to go," he said. "And I can make it in four days."

Simington said nothing for a long time. Kevin held his breath. Finally the fat man spoke. "Okay. I can offer you a starting salary of fourteen thousand Swiss francs a year. Five-year contract."

Kevin made rapid mental calculations. About a hundred and fifty thousand U.S. dollars a year. It wasn't as high as he'd expected; not that high at all in these days of inflation and ultra-taxation. Engineers on Earth made more. Engineers in orbital factories made a *lot* more. But—it was more than he could get without degrees and a strong union.

"It's more than you think," Simington was saying. "We pay half that in francs in the Belt, the other half into your account in Zurich. We'll set that up for you. No point in letting Uncle Sugar get his hands on your money. If you don't have too much junk shipped out from Earth, you can save your return passage in about four years."

"And if I don't save?"

Simington shrugged. "Your problem. We pay your way out. If you stay ten years with us, we pay your way back in. Don't worry about it. Even if you can't cut it for us, you won't be out of a job. There's a lot more jobs than people in the Belt. You won't starve."

"I suppose not—"

"And we give you a sign-up bonus," Simington said. "Thirty-five thousand bucks. You can use that to clean up any Earth-side problems. We'll also provide you with a basic outfit."

"Sounds good," Kevin said.

"It is good. We take care of our people. Notice I haven't said anything about owing us for passage and bounty. Some outfits pay higher, but their people owe for passage out. Some never do save it back. We don't work that way."

Sure, Kevin thought. But you're out to make a profit like the others.

Profit. Most of his professors had acted as if profits were nasty. Only Farrington seemed to think differently. And Wiley Ralston, of course. Not that the professors had any control; international firms survived despite the intellectuals' contempt. The welfare state could tax U.S. corporations practically out of existence, but they couldn't get their hands on the internationals, or the space operations firms.

"What kind of work?" Kevin asked.

Simington's grin was wide. "Everything! Mining operations, living quarters, refinery design, ships and transport, agriculture—it all needs doing. Terrific opportunity."

If it's that great, why do you need me? Kevin wondered. But it sounded exciting, and besides, what other choice did he have? "I'll take it."

Simington nodded. "Report here, ready to leave, in two days."

They flew him down to the Baja California spaceport in a windowless transport. He crouched with his gear among empty cargo containers and tried not to think of what was coming next. There was only one other passenger, a man more than twice Kevin's age, shorter by five inches but weighing almost as much as Kevin did—built like a lineman rather than a half back. He had dark hair and brown eyes and a fine network of thin red lines around his mouth and across the bridge of his nose. He drank heavily from a hip flask.

"Drink?" he asked.

"No thanks."

The man shrugged. "Headed for *Wayfarer*?" When Kevin nodded the man's grin broadened. He put out his hand. "Me, too. Bill Dykes."

Kevin took the offered hand. Dykes's grip was firm. "Kevin Senecal." He waited for Dykes to comment on the name, but he didn't.

"Sure you don't want that drink? You look nervous."

"No, I'm not nervous," Kevin said. "Wish they had windows back here. I'd like to see Baja."

"Not much to see," Dykes said. "Railroads, power lines, highways, looks just like anyplace else now. Not like it was a few years ago when there wasn't but one road down here. Damndest thing. Of all the places in the world to put a spaceport, I'd have thought Baja would be the last."

The airplane engines thrummed on. Kevin was glad of someone to talk with. It took his mind off what was to come. Deep space, the Belt—but more terrifying was the way he'd get out there. "Good location," Kevin said. "Further south than Canaveral, so there's more eastward velocity. Takes less energy to get the pods in orbit. And it's on the ecliptic. Anything launched from there has an easier time of it getting to the Belt—" Kevin stopped, because he could see he was boring his companion. "Sorry. You know all this."

"Some," Dykes admitted.

"You've been up before?"

Dykes nodded. "Orbital factories. Three years in the General Motors satellite. Didn't want to join up for another hitch. Took my pay back to Earth."

"But—you must have saved a lot—"

"Sure, but the IRS got most of it." Dykes took another drink. "And I couldn't get a dirt-side job. My union's full of One Earthers. They say space technology takes jobs away from people on Earth. Sweet Lord, they fixed up an initiation fee that would've wiped me out! Tried working without a union, but you know how that is. Got beat up about as many times as I had a day's work."

Dykes didn't seem broken up about his problems. He smiled cheerfully and took another drink, a long one this time. "So I took what was left of my savings and headed for the Moon."

"Oh." The Moon might be a good place to work. "Hansen colony?" Kevin asked.

"Naw, couldn't get on there. If MacKenzie and Hansen had been hiring, I'd probably still be up. No Mickey Mouse crap with Hansen, they tell me. Just hard work. Naw, I tried a little prospecting, a little mining. Luna America's no good. Regulations, bureaucrats, lawyers, taxes—hell, it's no different from Earth. No chance to get anywhere."

"So you're going to the Belt?"

"Sure. So're you. What in hell are you so nervous about?"

Kevin laughed. "Didn't know it showed *that* much. I—have you been up in a laser pod before?"

"Yeah. Four times. Lived through all but the second one."

"Huh?"

"That one killed me." Dykes held his serious expression for a moment, then grinned. "Look, there's nothing to worry about."

"Sure," Kevin said. "Sure. Say, if you don't mind, I'll have a drink after all."

The plane set down in morning tropical heat. There was no wind. The airfield was located near the launching facility, but a large concrete terminal building blocked their view of the laser field beyond. They watched their baggage loaded onto a cart, then went into the terminal.

There were few formalities. Kevin showed his ticket and was checked off a list. "First time up?" the clerk asked. When Kevin admitted it, he was sent down a long stairway.

"See you," Dykes called.

The passage led to a waiting room. There were a dozen other people there, mostly men older than he was, but a few women, and one family with two children. There was also a remarkably pretty girl. Kevin tentatively smiled at her, but she didn't respond, so he took out a book and began reading.

Presently a man in white coveralls came in and waited for their attention. He didn't say anything, just stood there until they were all looking at him. He looked at the two children and shuddered.

"Anybody here can't follow instructions? I mean follow 'em to the letter?" he asked. "If so, speak up and save the company some money. Save your lives, for that matter. You can get killed doing something stupid."

There was still no response. He shrugged. "I'm Hal Winstein, and I'm supposed to tell you groundhogs how to get from here to the orbit station alive. After that you're somebody else's worry.

"You all have pressure suits and helmets that fit? You should have turned them in for inspection. Everybody do that?"

There were murmurs, but no one said anything.

"Okay. Next. Anybody seriously suffer from claustrophobia? Course not, you wouldn't be here, but I'm supposed to ask. Now here's the drill. You'll go get your suits on and get checked out. Checkout includes vacuum test to be *sure* your equipment works. When the techs are happy with your gear, you'll go to the loading area and climb into a capsule.

"The capsules hold two hundred kilos each. That's approximately two people and their gear. We strap you in the webbing and you'll be there a while. Eventually the capsules move to the launch area, you'll hear a warning, and off you'll go at three gravities.

"Three gees isn't all that much if you're lying flat in the webbing. It goes on for a lot longer than you think it will, so don't get worried. When it stops you'll be in orbit. No weight."

"Free fall," Kevin muttered. He wondered how he'd feel. People often got sick in space.

"That's the only tricky part," Winstein said. "You'll feel like you're falling forever. Don't panic and don't unstrap. Capsules with kids aboard will be taken into the orbiter airlock and opened there. The rest of you'll have to get to the orbiter through vacuum. There's only two important things to remember: do exactly what the crewman who comes for you says you should do, and never get completely unfastened. You'll have two safety lines. Be sure one is attached to something before you unclip the other. The crew will get you into the airlock if you cooperate. If you don't, you could get very dead. Understood?"

"I think I will walk," the family man said. The others didn't laugh.

"Don't want to scare you," Winstein said. "But you do want to take this serious. Any questions?"

There weren't many. Everyone there was a potential colonist or would work in one of the satellite factories. Laser launching was a lot cheaper than tickets on the shuttle, but the Hansen Company didn't particularly encourage passenger traffic on the laser system: they made bigger profits on freight. Finally Kevin raised his hand.

"Yeah?" Winstein said.

"Can we watch the launches? I've never seen one."

Winstein looked at his watch. "If you get through suit check fast, you can watch cargo go up for a few minutes. Then you'll have to get below and load on. Okay, through this door to the changing rooms. Find your own gear and get it on."

"What do we do with our clothes?" one man asked.

Winstein shrugged. "Carry 'em along if you don't go over the mass marked on your ticket. Or ship 'em to somebody. Or leave 'em here and we'll give 'em to local charities. Suit yourself. By the way—I don't advise anybody to fudge on total weight. You wouldn't really want us to think you mass less than you do. And we can't afford to lose the capsules."

Chapter five

There was very little privacy in the changing room. Only a screen separated men from women. The only facilities were a long bench and table on either side of the screen.

Kevin collected his pressure suit from the Hansen Company inspector who'd checked it out. "Nice gear," the technician said as he handed it over. "David Clark makes the best, in my book."

One more datum to file away, Kevin thought. Daedalus Corporation didn't stint on equipment. They'd given him the best. He had his suit, and helmet, with radios; a programmable pocket computer, the latest model he knew of, complete with a plug-in memory-reference unit that contained, along with much other data, just about every formula and table in the big Chemical Rubber Handbook; a lightweight Fiberglas suitcase, really more like a pressure-tight portable footlocker. It was all first class and it made him feel that he was important to the company.

The pressure suit went on like a diver's wet suit, and looked like one only not so thick. It fit very closely; he had to use talcum powder to get into it. Gloves dogged onto the ends of the sleeves, and a seal set firmly around his neck. He slipped into the boots, hung the small equipment bag over his shoulder, and reported back to the technicians. They pulled and pinched, looking for loose spots. They didn't find any in Kevin's, but the next to come up was the girl he'd seen before, and after a moment they handed her a lump of what looked like clay. "Shove that under your breasts," the technician said. "Yeah, right there. Don't leave any gaps."

"But—" She was obviously embarrassed.

"Lady, you're going into vacuum," the man explained. "Your innards will be pressured to about seven pounds by the air in your helmet. Outside is nothing. Your skin won't hold that. The suit will, but you've got to be flat against the suit, otherwise *you'll* swell up to fill any empty spaces. It won't do a lot of good for your figure."

"Oh. Thank you," she said. She turned away and used the clay as she'd been told.

The technician looked at Kevin and shook his head. "Don't get many small-town chicks here. Okay, sport, on with your helmet. See it's dogged right. Don't like to lose passengers in the test chamber."

The helmet fit snugly onto the neck seal. The technician checked the locking mechanism and seemed satisfied. "Okay, you and blondie there, into the next room and through the airlock." He raised his voice. "Sending in the first two, Charlie."

"Right. Come on, come on, we got a full schedule today."

Kevin and the girl went through the door and were motioned to another, this one steel with a large locking wheel. Through that was a large chamber. There was a man in a pressure suit inside it. He motioned to hoses on the bulkhead. "Connect up to those."

They did, and the man checked the fittings. "Okay," he said. "We'll pump out this chamber. As we do, there'll come pressure into your helmets through those hoses. When the outside pressure's gone, you're going to be uncomfortable for a while. Any gas in your system will expand until you'll feel like a balloon. Don't be too damned polite to get rid of it, or you'll be sorry. If you feel really uncomfortable, or your ears hurt real bad, or you can't breathe, hit one of those panic buttons next to you there. Otherwise, don't do anything at all. Understood?"

"Yes," the girl said. Kevin nodded.

"Right." Charlie turned to his control panel and pressed buttons. The outside door had already been closed and sealed while he was talking.

Kevin felt the pressure drop. His ears clogged for a moment and he swallowed frantically until they popped and were clear. The pressure continued to fall and he felt his insides swelling as Charlie had said they would.

"OKAY." Charlie's voice was loud in his headset. "I've got your pressures here. Everything looks right to me. Any problems?"

"No," the girl's voice said.

"Good. Now comes the hard part. The worst thing that can happen to you is to run low on oxygen. You won't know it's happening. So, I'm gonna cut down on your oxygen supply to let you get used to what anoxia feels like. While I'm doing it I want you to write your name on that pad there in front of you. Every time I say 'write,' you write your name until I say to stop. Okay?"

"Yes," the girl's voice said in his headset.

"Sure," Kevin said.

"You, mister, I asked if it was understood," Charlie said.

"Oh." Kevin turned on his microphone. "Sorry. Understood."

"Okay. Here we go. Write."

It was no problem. He wrote carefully, then glanced over at the girl. "Ellen MacMillan." Her handwriting was neat and precise, unlike his own heavy scrawl.

"Write," Charlie said, and they did it again.

It seemed a silly game. Kevin felt an urgent impulse to laugh. Why? part of his mind wondered. But it didn't matter; of course he wanted to laugh, this was silly—

"Write."

His hand didn't work properly, but it was all right, he was tired of this silly game. He glanced over at Ellen's paper. Her neat hand had written "Coca-cola."

"Scotch and soda," Kevin wrote.

"Write."

"Will you have dinner with me?" he tried to write, but it didn't come out that way. He couldn't read it. Oh, well. Ellen looked at him and giggled. He responded, and they laughed together. "Hey, you're beautiful," Kevin shouted.

She laughed harder. Why was she laughing? Kevin wondered. It was true enough. Well, maybe not beautiful. But she was nice, a really pretty girl, blonde curls cut off short but still long enough to curl. He stared at her pressure suit, trying to see where her breasts left off and the clay began. She saw what he was doing and patted the spot, giggling again.

"Write your names. It is very important that you write your names. If you do not write your names legibly you will not be permitted to go up today," Charlie said. His voice was very stern, and that was funny too.

Only, part of his mind said, it wasn't funny. He tried very hard, but all he could produce was a scrawl. Ought to be good enough, though, he thought. They can read that—

His head began to clear suddenly, and he looked at the paper in front of him. It was awful. He wanted to cry—

He felt the chamber pressure rising. It became very warm in the capsule.

"Okay," Charlie said. "When I give the signal, disconnect from the hoses and go out the far door. Take those papers with you, and don't forget what you've learned. Anoxia sneaks up on you. You think you're doing all right, even when you're acting like a stupid drunk. If you remember that, you can function longer. Not a lot longer, but a little longer anyway."

The next stop was another supply counter, where he picked up his reflective coveralls and tool belt. When he put them on over his pressure suit, and slung the tool belt around his waist, Kevin felt like a spacer. He knew better. There was a lot to learn, and he wouldn't even begin learning it until he was aboard *Wayfarer*; but the tool kit and professional equipment was at least a start. He asked directions to the observation balcony and was shown a stairway.

The balcony was empty. It gave a view of the wide valley on the other side of the terminal building from the airfield. The upper parts of the valley sides were covered with the tall *cardones* cactus plants, giants twenty feet tall and more, looking like cartoons of the desert cactus. There were even vultures perched in the cactus. Below, on the valley floor, were the lasers.

At first it looked like a field of mirrors. Over a hundred lasers were scattered across the brown Baja desert sand. Each sent its output into a mirror. The mirrors were all arranged so that they reflected onto one very large mirror nearly a kilometer beyond the balcony.

A rail track ran onto a platform above the final mirror. Squat capsules, like enormously swollen artillery shells, sat on cars on the track, a long line of them waiting for launch. As he watched, one of the capsules was wheeled along the track until it stopped over the launching mirror.

The field became a blaze of blue-green light as the lasers went on. Somewhere nearby, Kevin knew, were two large nuclear power plants. They poured their entire output into the lasers below him, enough electricity to power a city, all turned into laser light. The mirrors pivoted slightly so that all their energy went to the one large mirror at the end of the field.

The capsule rose, suddenly and silently, as if pushed into the sky by a rapidly growing giant blue-green beanstalk. It vanished in seconds, but the laser beam continued to follow it, moving from vertical to an angle toward the east. Finally all the lasers went out together.

"My God," Kevin said aloud. "I'm going up like *that*?"

He heard a laugh behind him and turned quickly to see the girl who'd been in the altitude chamber with him. She smiled as he looked at her. "Yes, we are," she said. "Scared?"

"Damn betcha."

"Me too. I wish I'd taken the shuttle."

Another capsule was in position, and rose silently from the platform, vanishing into the clear blue sky, followed by the silent beam of intense light. If he listened carefully Kevin thought he could hear the hum of the beam. It was pulsed at something like two hundred times a second.

The laser system worked like a ram jet. Under each capsule was a bell-shaped chamber, open at the bottom. The laser energy entered the chamber and heated the air inside. The air rushed out, pushing the capsule upward. Then the beam was turned off just long enough for more air to get into the chamber, to be heated by the next pulse of the beam.

"I'm still not sure I believe it works," Kevin said. "It looks like black magic."

"Green magic," Ellen said.

There was a long pause in the launching sequence, then a trainload of capsules came out. Each capsule was accompanied by an armed guard. Four Mexican Army tanks rolled alongside the train.

"Ye gods, that must be a valuable cargo," Kevin said. He looked quickly at Ellen when she didn't answer. She was watching them with a look of satisfaction. "Do you know what's in them?" Kevin asked.

"No, do you?"

"I thought you were watching as if you did. No, I haven't a clue."

"As you said, it must be valuable." She continued to stare until all the capsules were launched, and the guards and tanks rolled away. Then she looked at her watch. "Maybe we ought to be getting down—"

"Yes. Hate to miss the ship. Where are you headed?"

"*Wayfarer.*" An appropriate enough name, Kevin thought: "*Das Wanderer.*"

Kevin had thought she would be going up to one of the orbital factories. "All the way to Ceres? Alone?"

"Yes, why not?"

Kevin shrugged. "No reason."

"Except that you don't approve of women going to the Belt," she said. "That's man's work. I suppose you want restrictive laws for space, too. 'One job per family' out in the Belt as well as here on Earth." There was anger in her voice. "Well, you had that in the United States, still do really, but you won't get it in space, and I'm going whether you approve or not." She turned and stalked down the stairwell.

"Hey," Kevin called. "Hey, I didn't mean anything. I'm sorry—"

She didn't turn. To hell with her, Kevin thought. He slowed down, wondering what to do next.

"Kev! Hey, buddy," someone called.

Kevin turned. It was Wiley Ralston. "Wiley! Hey, are you going up this round?" Wiley had left Los Angeles two weeks before to find a job in deep space. Kevin wasn't that surprised to see him.

"Sure, I'm in the afternoon wave. Ride up with me?"

"Can't," Kevin said. "I'm going right now—hey, where are you going?"

"Got some things to arrange," Wiley said.

"You going in *Wayfarer?*"

"Right—you too?" Wiley was hurrying away, and his manner indicated that he didn't want to be followed. "You're going up right now? Not in the first capsule, though—"

"Sure, get it over with," Kevin said. He had to shout now; Wiley was moving away fast.

"Not the first," Wiley said. "Get on the last one—"

"Why?"

"Can't stop to talk, old chum. I've really got to scoot. See you aboard *Wayfarer*." He vanished into a door marked AUTHORIZED PERSONNEL ONLY, leaving Kevin standing in the middle of the empty corridor.

Damn, Kevin thought. He walked slowly to the capsule loading area. If I wait, he thought, I'll be scared out of my wits before it happens. He knew the laser launching system was safe, but that didn't stop the butterflies in his stomach.

May as well get it over with, he thought. He collected his helmet from the technicians.

There was one couple, and Ellen MacMillan, in the loading area.

"Who's first?" the technician asked.

"We are," the couple said.

"Right. Let's see you get into your hats and seal up." When they had their helmets dogged down the technician attached a pressure gauge to the man, looked worried, and said, "Go back and get a recheck on this."

"Something wrong?"

"Probably not, but I like to be careful. Okay, you're down-checked. Next." He jerked a thumb at Kevin, then at Ellen MacMillan. "You two. Get your heads on and let's hook up air bottles. Come on, we haven't got all day. Orbits don't wait."

When they had donned helmets and air tanks the technician checked his gauges again. "Looks good," he said, and sent them through a door. Kevin hurried along, trying not to think of the ride ahead. No worse than a roller coaster, he kept telling himself.

The launching pods were waiting. They seemed much larger than the ones he'd seen being launched, but even so the capsule was too small. It looked like a bell-shaped steel coffin. Ellen was already inside, strapping herself into a nylon-webbing couch. Kevin got in and lay on the other couch.

"Hear me all right?" a voice asked.

"Yes." They both answered at once, speaking a little too loudly, a little too confidently. Kevin turned toward Ellen to see that she was looking at him. They grinned faintly at each other.

"Fine. Now you wait a while," the tech's voice said. "Then you go. There's nothing tricky about any of this. You're hooked into the capsule air supply. When you make orbit you wait until a crewman comes and opens the can. Then—and not before—you pull that big lever above you. It disconnects you from the capsule system and you'll be on your own air tanks. You got two hours of air in the capsule and another hour in your tanks. Okay, I'm closin' you in. *Bon voyage.*"

The capsule door closed. They watched the inside wheel turn as it was dogged shut. It already seemed close and cramped in the pod. Like a big steel coffin built for two, Kevin thought. He pushed the thought aside.

"We're moving," Ellen said.

There wasn't much sense of motion, but she was right. The capsule was moving along the track. Kevin tried to visualize its progress as it went inexorably toward the launch area. "Wonder how the kids will make out?"

"Better than us, I expect. At least we don't have to do anything—"

"I wish we did," Kevin said. "Better than just waiting for them."

"Sure—"

The warning tones sounded, then gravity seized them.

They were pressed hard into the seat webbing.

Three gravities isn't all that bad; a little like being on a water bed with another mattress on top of you and two people piled onto that. It was possible to breathe, but not to talk. The acceleration went on and on.

I'm really going, Kevin thought. I've left Earth, and I won't be back for a long time.

Eventually the weight diminished, then was gone entirely. There was a sensation of falling, endless falling.

"I wonder if we made it," Ellen said. Her voice was artificially calm.

"Well, this is free fall—"

"Which we would feel whether or not we have enough velocity to make orbit," Ellen said. "And we won't know for about half an hour."

"By then the crew people will be here." I hope, Kevin thought.

There was nothing to do. There ought to be some kind of instrument to tell them they were in orbit. Kevin thought about that. How could you design one? No air, of course; couldn't measure velocity by air speed. An accelerometer hooked into the capsule; add up all the accelerations and you'd have velocity. A micro-computer to decide whether that was the proper velocity for the job. Sure, it could be done. Why hadn't they done it? Another expense for an already expensive business.

"I'd think someone would have spoken to us by now," Ellen said. She moved her arm up so that she could see her watch. "Only five minutes. Seems longer."

"Sure does. Uh—by the way, my name is Kevin."

"I know. I saw it on your paper. In the chamber. You read mine, too. We were pretty silly, weren't we?"

"Yeah. What outfit are you with?"

"None. I'm paying my own way," she said.

Good Lord. She had to be fabulously wealthy. He looked at her suit and other gear. First class, but no frills.

"How come you're taking the hard way up instead of the shuttle?"

"I couldn't afford a shuttle ticket."

That didn't make sense. "But you can afford a ticket to Ceres. Why are you going there?"

"It seemed like a good idea at the time," she said. Then she giggled. "I'm not too bad at engineering, Kevin, even if you don't approve of women in your business—"

"I never said—"

"And I didn't like the offers I got from the orbital factories. Or the Luna companies either. So I took what I could scrape up and bought a ticket. There wasn't much to spare."

"Out to make your fortune pioneering," Kevin said.

"That's right. There'll be good jobs for me. For anyone who can do the work. I see you don't approve."

"Sure I approve. It just seems like a long way to go—"

"You're going," she pointed out. "Why can't I?"

Kevin didn't answer. It just didn't seem right. And you're a male chauvinist pig, he told himself. You hate to see a pretty girl working at something besides being a pretty girl.

Only that's not true. Dammit it's going to be rough out there, and—And, he thought, I've got about three million years of evolution that says women and children shouldn't get into tough situations. The world is no longer a place where we live in caves and go hunt tigers, and our instincts are all fouled up, but we've got them.

Of course it was pretty rough for unmarried women in the United States anyway. The feminist movement had gotten legal equality for women—for a while. But then came the Equity scandals, and the Great Recession, and rising unemployment. Women's rights weren't as thoroughly abandoned as were those with disabilities, but there were fundamental changes.

The unions put on the pressure, and Congress came up with the "One Job Per Family" law. The courts threw it out, but Congress passed it again, and its status was still undecided. And women weren't welcome in most unions whatever the courts said, not with so many men out of work.

And maybe, Kevin thought, maybe the whole idea is wrong, but there are plenty of women—married women—who approve the job restrictions and reserved occupations. For two thousand years "women's liberation" had meant that women with children didn't have to work outside the home. For a few years toward the end of the Twentieth Century that trend had been reversed, but now the pendulum was swinging back as everyone realized that raising children was a full-time—and difficult—job.

"It seemed a long time from when they launched the cargo to when they sent us up," Kevin said. "How can both batches get to the same satellite?"

"They can't. The cargo went directly to *Wayfarer*. We go to the orbital station," Ellen said. She frowned. "I make it twenty minutes since we were launched. Doesn't that seem like an excessively long time? We ought to have heard from someone."

"It does seem a while. Let's try calling out." He reached up to the radio panel above. There was a small card of instruction attached on its face. The first said, "FOR EMERGENCY USE ONLY" in five languages. "Is this an emergency?"

Ellen looked thoughtful. "I don't know—I'd hate to cause trouble, but I am getting a bit worried."

"Me too. To hell with them." He switched on the radio. Then he cursed. "There's no pilot light," he said. "Burned out—or does the set work?" There was only one way to find out. There was a jack on the face of the panel, and he plugged his mike into it. "Hey out there—anybody listening? This is Capsule—uh—nine-eight-four, hopefully in orbit. Anyone? Over."

"There isn't even static," Ellen said. "The receiver's not working. I doubt if the transmitter is working either."

Kevin looked at her with curiosity. She didn't seem scared. Or surprised, either. "What do we do?"

"You can try the transmitter again."

"Sure. Mayday. Mayday. This is Capsule nine-eight-four, Mayday, mayday. Over." Again he heard nothing. How long would it take for one of the crewmen to get to them, if the transmitter worked but the receiver didn't? "Mayday, Mayday, Mayday. This is Capsule nine-eight-four. Our receiver is not working. We cannot hear your reply. Please come help us. Mayday."

Ellen began unfastening her seat straps. Kevin watched with a frown. They'd been told not to do that. Of course they'd also been told someone would come get them. He felt a knot of fear in his stomach. Trapped in an orbiting steel coffin. The sensation of falling was overwhelming now. In a moment he'd panic if he couldn't do something constructive. But what? "MAYDAY. MAYDAY. SOMEBODY COME HELP US!"

"I don't think that's going to do much good," Ellen said. She inspected the emergency set. "I don't see anything obviously wrong. Should we take the cover off and look?"

Kevin doubted that would be any use. Integrated circuit chips all look alike; how could you tell if something was wrong with one of them? He began unfastening his own straps. When they were loose, he floated away from the acceleration couch. It was a strange sensation. He'd seen people in free fall on TV often enough, and had looked forward to experiencing it, to being able to swim in the air, but now all he wanted was to get back to having weight again.

"We have suit radios," Ellen said. "Is yours powered?"

"Yes. Fresh batteries, and it was checked out yesterday—Hey! If we get outside this thing, we might be able to raise somebody with it."

"We'll have to disconnect from the capsule air supply before we can open the hatch," Ellen said. "If the hatch will open at all—"

"Why shouldn't it?"

She shrugged. The motion set her twisting slightly, and she caromed into him in the confined space. They both grabbed handholds.

"We have to do something," Kevin said. "Let's open the hatch." He reached for the big emergency disconnect handle.

"Wait. Fasten your safety line to something."

"Oh. Right." He clipped the line to one of the couch pipe-frames. "Ready?"

"As I'll ever be. Go ahead."

He turned the red handle. It didn't turn; he did. Kevin cursed and got his feet planted against the couch, braced, and turned the handle again. It moved, slowly at first, then swung over. The ship's air hoses popped loose from their connections on their backpacks. They were now living on their air tanks.

"There's still pressure in here," Ellen said.

"Damn." She was right. The emergency disconnect was supposed to vent all the air from the capsule. The capsule hatch wouldn't open until the air was gone. There'd be no point in pulling on it; at seven pounds a square inch, hundreds of tons of air pressure held that hatch closed.

They couldn't open the hatch, and they had less than an hour of air.

Chapter Six

"I never thought they'd do it this way," Ellen said.

"Huh? Who'd do what this way?" Kevin asked.

"Nothing. We've got to bleed the pressure out of this capsule. Try to find the relief valve." She began searching her side of the capsule.

"This looks like it," Kevin said. There was a valve with a large handle. Remembering what happened the last time he'd tried to turn something in free fall, he braced himself before he twisted the handle.

It spun without effort. The handle wasn't splined to the valve stem. "Jesus Christ," he muttered. Ellen pulled herself over to watch as he futilely turned the handle. "No go," he announced. He was surprised at how calm he sounded.

"Your tool kit," Ellen said. "What's in it?"

Kevin didn't really know. He'd taken some of the items out to look them over, but that was something else he was supposed to learn about on the way out to the Belt, and there'd been so little time to prepare. He took the leather tool pack off his belt and opened it.

"There's a power head," he said. "I remember that. And drill bits. But is it enough to get through the capsule walls?"

"You won't know until you try," Ellen said.

He took out the power head and inspected it. Then he searched through the loops of the tool pack until he found the drill chuck. It wasn't obvious how that attached to the power unit, but he worked carefully to be sure he didn't bend or break anything, and eventually it snapped into place. He pulled the trigger experimentally. The whine of the motor was delightful music.

"Now for the bit. About six millimeters? Looks about right." He squinted in the dim capsule light, trying to read the tiny words on the shank of the bit. He couldn't make them out. He hoped all the bits were intended for drilling metal. At least they were sharp and new.

He put the bit in the chuck and tightened it, then looked for a place to drill, choosing a spot between two braces. "I wonder how thick these things are."

"No thicker than they have to be," Ellen said.

"True." The less structural weight, the more payload. "Here goes." He pressed the bit against the metal surface and turned on the drill. It whirred reassuringly, and the bit threw up tiny bright chips that floated in the compartment, dancing about when stirred by air currents kicked up by Kevin's movements.

"It's working," Ellen said. For the first time there was excitement in her voice. "It really is."

He continued to drill, trying not to think about why he was drilling and where he was. That was no good, so he tried to think about something else. Why was Ellen so calm? And why hadn't she been surprised?

The bit seemed to have gone awfully deep. Wouldn't it ever get through? But, even as he wondered, it jerked and pushed all the way to the chuck. Air whistled out past it. Kevin reversed the drill and withdrew it.

"Might take a long time to empty the capsule through that hole," Kevin said. "I'll do another hole, this time with a larger bit."

The second hole seemed to go easier. Now they could definitely feel the pressure dropping. He felt the familiar push of the neck seal as his air tanks pressurized his helmet in compensation. Then he glanced at his watch.

Fifteen minutes. They'd used a quarter of their air time in drilling the holes, and there was nothing they could do but wait.

"I have it," Ellen said. She turned the steel dogging wheel on the hatch. It seemed to turn easily, and the hatch opened inward.

Sunlight poured into the capsule. Kevin wondered how long that would last. They had to be in orbit, a very low orbit at that; it wouldn't be long before they were on Earth's night side. After making sure his safety line was still attached he slipped the pawl on the reel and worked his way out of the capsule. The sight was so glorious that for a moment he didn't move.

Earth was below, an enormous disc shrouded in wispy white clouds. They were above the Atlantic, and could see islands, and far at the horizon the west coast of Africa. It looked rather like an enormous circular map—they weren't high enough to see Earth as a sphere.

All around him—there was no "above" or "below"—there were capsules very close by. In the distance he saw what seemed to be a much larger structure that looked like a floating junk pile, without shape or form: a series of wheels and cylinders and shapes of no description at all held together by girders and cables. It had bright flashing lights. Kevin estimated it at about a mile away, although he found it was very hard to judge either its size or distance.

One of the channels of his suit radio was marked in red letters, for emergencies. Kevin turned to it, tongued the mike. "Mayday. Mayday, Mayday, this is Capsule—dammit!"

Ellen came beside him and put her helmet next to his. "Nine-eight-four."

"Mayday. This is Capsule nine-eight-four. Mayday! Dammit, where are you?"

"Maybe they aren't listening," Ellen said.

Her voice was the only thing he heard in his phones, and given that she was right next to him it didn't sound very loud at all; Kevin wondered if the batteries in his set were getting weak. But they couldn't be! They were new, the whole rig was new.

"Kevin, look! This is the only personnel capsule in this area. The others are all cargo."

She was right. There were plenty of capsules around, some only a few yards away, but the others were stubbier than theirs, and in contrast to the red-white checkerboard pattern on their own pod, these were yellow. Somehow they'd been launched into the cargo-pod recovery area. "Where are the others who came up with us?" Kevin demanded.

"Probably on the other side of the base station," Ellen said. "Where the crewmen are. No one will come over here until they have all the other passengers inside."

"But they damned well ought to know they're one pod and two people short," Kevin said angrily. "Now what? Mayday, dammit." They were conversing on the emergency channel. They shouldn't be doing that. Kevin laughed.

"What?"

"Hoping some communications monitor overhears us and comes out to slap us with a violation ticket." The joke seemed a little flat. He glanced at his watch. A little over half an hour of air. This was absurd! They were no more than a mile from the station—well, maybe two, Kevin thought; distances were hard to judge—and there wasn't any way they could get over there. Neither of them had a reaction pistol or a backpack jet. You can't swim in space: no air—nothing to push against! Kevin thought, sternly repressing an impulse to laugh hysterically. So what do we do? Have to do something!

"There are a lot of those capsules around here," Ellen said. "They seem to get pretty close to the station—"

Yes! Certainly they could get closer to the station. The nearest capsule in the right direction wasn't more than fifty meters off, possibly closer. It should be easy to jump that in free fall.

But if they missed, they'd drift forever.

He looked down at the reel on his safety line. Ninety meters. More than enough. "Look," he said. "I'm going to stay hooked on here and jump for that other capsule. If I hit, connect yourself to my line and I'll pull you over. Then we'll see about going on to the next one." He released the brake on his safety line reel.

She looked thoughtful for a moment, then nodded. "All right."

Kevin braced himself for the jump. No danger, not really. If he missed, she could pull him back. He crouched, got a hand-hold on the edge of the capsule hatch so he could get strain in his legs, and jumped.

He tumbled. Stars whirled above him, then Earth, the base station, Ellen, then more stars. He must have pushed harder with one leg than the other. He twisted to get a look at where he was going. The capsule he'd jumped for was a lot closer, moving up fast. He twisted again, instinctively spreading his arms and legs as wide as possible to slow his rotation.

His hand just brushed the capsule. He grabbed frantically and got hold of something. It almost yanked his arm off.

Have to remember that, he told himself: jump as hard as you can and you'll hit with the same force. "Okay, I'm aboard," he said. He clipped the other safety line to the protruding ring on the capsule. "Unsnap my other line and hang on—I'll pull you over."

"Right," she said. "Okay, I'm ready."

Kevin pulled gently. The temptation was to keep on pulling, but that wouldn't do: she'd just build up speed until she was moving too fast, maybe fast enough to get hurt. He let the line wind back onto its reel.

She turned just before she reached him and landed exactly feet first. She seemed pleased with herself. "Daddy made me study gymnastics," she said. "Always hated it, but now I'm glad I practiced."

"Yeah." Kevin pointed to another capsule, this one only twenty-five meters from their present position. "That one's a piece of cake. Here I go." He jumped, this time on center, and checked himself against his new perch.

It took time, but they were able to continue the process until they were only five hundred meters or so from the base. Then they ran out of capsules. Kevin prepared himself mentally for that final leap, one that he knew all too well would probably send him past the station, falling forever. . . . Better do it *now*—or he might not be able to do it at all. But wait—the station seemed enormous now; it had been farther away than he'd thought. He remembered that suit radios were deliberately underpowered so they wouldn't carry too far; otherwise all of space would be filled with chatter. But the emergency frequency? And they were a lot closer than the last time he'd tried. "Hell, it's worth a try. Mayday. *Mayday*, dammit!"

"Hello Mayday, identify yourself."

"By God!" he shouted. "We made it. Hello. We were passengers aboard capsule nine-eight-four. Air supply is going fast. We're on the leading side of the station, among the cargo capsules. Don't know which one. We abandoned the personnel pod and started hopping from cargo-pod to cargo-pod, trying to get to the base. I'd say we're about half a kilometer out."

"Nine-eight-four, can you make a light?" the voice asked. "I'll have a scooter out there in a moment. If you can show a light it will be easier to find you."

Kevin waved his flash. Down below he could see the sunset line stretching across East Africa. "Better hurry," he said. "We have about ten minutes of air left."

"No sweat. Be with you shortly."

"But how did it happen?" Kevin demanded.

The crewman shrugged. "I really don't know. There must have been a monumental foul-up down at ground control. Never happened before. Anyway, no harm done. Here you are in the station."

Foul-up at ground control. Sure, he thought. But why wasn't the capsule radio working? Or the emergency disconnect? Or even the manual pressure-bleed? It seemed like a lot of coincidences. It seemed like somebody was trying to kill him.

But that, he was sure, was silly. He couldn't think of anyone else who'd give a damn if he lived or died—and the Garvey Street Crips gang sure as hell couldn't reach out into space.

"I would appreciate it if you'd look into it," Ellen said. She seemed very calm. A lot calmer than Kevin was.

"Sure," the crewman said. "Luckily, no harm done. We've just time to send someone out for your gear and get you aboard the scooter for *Wayfarer*. Come this way, please."

"But—"

"Kevin," Ellen said. "If we raise a fuss they'll have to investigate. We'll have to stay here. And *Wayfarer* won't wait. I didn't spend ten thousand francs for a ticket just to miss the ship."

"All right." He let the crewman lead him through the base. They were both being damned nonchalant about something that had almost killed them. Maybe this was the way it's done in space, he thought. It doesn't take much to kill you out here so nobody's impressed with close calls.

The crewman stayed to the outer rim. The station rotated to give artificial gravity, about forty percent of Earth's. Kevin was surprised to find that it was hard to tell just how much gravity he felt. After that time in no-weight, any gravity felt good.

The deck curved up in front and behind them, but it always felt level. It was a strange experience to be walking on a curve. The walls of the station seemed to be made of some kind of rubberized cloth with a metallic thread in it. They didn't feel hard to the touch, not like steel.

They went through several airlocks and came finally to one that led outside. The crewman un-snapped four new air bottles from a rack. Kevin started to put his two into his backpack.

"Suggestion," the crewman said.

"Yes?"

He pointed to an air gauge on the rack of bottles. "It's a good idea always to check and see if they're full." He reached into his own belt pouch and came up with a gauge. "Me, I don't even trust the airmaster's gauge. Use my own."

Kevin found one in his tool kit. Just for luck he checked one bottle with all three gauges, his own, the airmaster's and the crewman's. He got the same reading each time. Ellen followed his example.

"Now you're thinking. Okay, close up helmets and into the airlock."

The "scooter" was no more than an open framework with a long line of saddles and a rudimentary control system at its front. The passengers sat astride fuel tanks, and baggage was strapped underneath. The other passengers for *Wayfarer* were already aboard. Somebody waved at Kevin, and he recognized Bill Dykes. Ellen and Kevin got the last seats aft, the only two left. They strapped in, and about then a smaller scooter came up with the baggage from their capsule. It was lashed aboard, and the pilot hit the throttles.

The motion was very gentle, hardly any acceleration at all. The view was marvelous. There was Earth below, night with brilliant points and squares of city lights. Everywhere else were stars, countless stars, endless stars, an endless fall of stars in the Milky way, brilliant stars, with bright colors.

They moved through a clutter of space-launch capsules and crewmen with lights unloading them. Kevin looked at his watch. Ellen, behind him, noticed the gesture. By now they would have both been dead. She nodded at him then pointed to a channel on her radio. Kevin switched to it and turned on his set.

"I've never been up before," she said. "It's beautiful, isn't it?"

"Yes." They were coming to the daylight line on Earth below. It ran through the Pacific. Behind them were the bright spots that were cities crowded with their millions of people. Ahead and below was blue water, fleecy clouds and a distant line that might have been more clouds, or maybe California. To the north was a tight spiral of clouds.

"Typhoon," Ellen said. She stared frankly at it. She seemed on edge, but the way a tourist is excited at seeing new and wondrous sights, not afraid. If she can do it, so can I, Kevin thought. He was more shaken than he cared to admit.

Then there was more industrial activity around them. They were moving into full daylight, and Kevin was surprised to see how far they'd come from the base station in such a short time. Up ahead was a mirror larger than a football field. It just hung there in space. It focused sunlight onto a rock somewhat larger than a house. Other big rocks nearby anchored what looked like big flat metal plates. Something—he supposed metal—boiled off the target rock and condensed onto the plates.

After that they saw a cage that looked as if it were made of ordinary chicken wire. It was big, half a kilometer in diameter, and it was filled with launching pods, tanks of all sizes, rocks, spare scooters, what looked like big garbage cans, plastic bags—anything that wasn't in use at the moment. It kept things from drifting away.

They went past other marvels, and eventually *Wayfarer* came into sight. The scooter pilot pointed it out to them. "Your home for a while," he said.

Their first impression was of a bundle of huge cigars. Those were the big fuel tanks almost a hundred meters long. They were so large that they dwarfed the rest of the ship, and ran the entire length of midsection. Behind the "cigars" was a solid ring that held three rocket motors. Then at the end of a spine as long as the main body of the ship was the nuclear reactor and another rocket motor.

This was the real drive. The three chemical rockets were only for steering and close maneuvering. *Wayfarer*'s power came from her atomic pile. The cigar-shaped tanks held hydrogen, which was pumped back to the reactor where it was heated up and spewed out through the rear nozzle. A ring of heavy shielding just forward of the reactor kept the pile's radiation from getting to the crew compartment. The rest of the pile wasn't shielded at all.

Despite the large size of the ship, the crew and cargo sections seemed quite small. There were some structures reaching back from the forward ring where the control room was. Two of those were passenger quarters. The other was another nuclear power unit to make electricity to run the environmental control equipment, furnish light for the plants, power to reprocess air, and all the other things the ship and passengers and crew would need. There was a big telescope and a number of radar antennae on the forward section.

The scooter pilot was careful not to get near the reactor in the ship's "stinger." He brought them in to the bow. The outer door of an airlock stood invitingly open. A crewman brought a cable over and attached it to the scooter, and then hauled the scooter in close. Then the passengers began the trip from their saddles into the airlock, crawling across the cable like so many spiders.

When it came his turn Kevin judged the distance and decided to jump. He had just crouched when the pilot grabbed him. "Hey, no!" the pilot shouted. "Not your first time in space!"

Kevin shrugged and grinned into his helmet. Probably he'd have to take extra-vehicular-activity training while on *Wayfarer.* As if he hadn't learned the hard way how to jump around in free fall . . .

He crawled across the cable behind the others.

Home at last, he thought. For nine months, A long time.

Chapter Seven

The ship had been designed for sixty passengers. She carried twice that number plus eight crew. Most of the passengers were already aboard; *Wayfarer* was crowded. No more than half the passengers had ever been into space before, and everyone drifted through the ship in total confusion.

The internal space was constructed in a series of circular decks. Each deck had an eight-foot hole in its center, so that from the forward end, just aft of the separately enclosed control cabin, Kevin could look all the way aft to the stern bulkhead. Although there was a long and rather flimsy-appearing steel ladder stretching from aft to forward bulkhead, no one used it. Passengers and crew dived from deck to deck in the null-gravity conditions of orbit. Most of the passengers weren't very good at it yet.

A harried crewman in red coveralls punched Kevin's name into a console. "F-12," he said.

"If that's supposed to mean something, it doesn't," Kevin said.

"F deck," the crewman said "A deck is the bridge. B is the wardroom. C, D, and E are the three aft of that. E happens to be the recreation and environmental control. Yours is the one beyond that. They're marked." Someone else had come up and the crewman turned away. "You'll find it," he said over his shoulder.

Kevin shrugged. It was a mistake, because it caused him to drift away from his handhold. He grabbed frantically at a protruding handle—the ship had plenty of those—and when he was stable, launched himself down through the central well. He got past C and D decks before he had to catch something and try again. Since he was carrying his bulky Fiberglas travel case with all his luggage, he felt he had a right to be proud of his first efforts.

Finally he reached F deck, which he found to be sectioned into slice-of-pie compartments arranged in a ring around the central well, fifteen of them in all. He found the one marked "12" and went in.

His "stateroom" was partitioned off with a flexible, bright blue material that Kevin thought was probably nylon. The door was of the same stuff and tied off with strings. It didn't provide much privacy.

Inside the cramped quarters were facilities for two people. There were no bunks, but two blanket rolls strapped against the bulkhead indicated the sleeping arrangements. It made sense, Kevin thought. You didn't need soft mattresses in space. "Sleeping on a cloud" was literally true here. You needed straps to keep you from drifting away, but that was all.

One viewscreen with control console, a small worktable, and two lockers about the size of large briefcases completed the furnishings. The cabin wasn't an encouraging sight. Kevin wondered what he should do with his gear. His Fiberglas travel case was stuffed with things he'd been told he'd probably need for the trip; another larger case had been stowed somewhere by the crew and was inaccessible. He wandered out into the central area of F deck and found that in other staterooms people were lashing their travel cases to the bulkheads. Kevin went back and did the same.

He wondered who his cabinmate would be. No one had asked him if he had any preferences. The only person he knew aboard *Wayfarer* was Ellen, and she wasn't likely to accept an offer to share quarters. While he was trying to convince himself that it couldn't hurt to ask, a middle-aged bearded man, quite heavyset, came in carrying two large travel cases. He looked up at Kevin apologetically.

"They told me to bunk here," he said. He blinked rapidly and looked around the small room. "It isn't very large, is it? I'm Jacob Norsedal." His voice wasn't very deep to begin with, and the low air pressure in the ship made it sound squeaky.

Kevin introduced himself. He tried to shake hands with Norsedal, but again got separated from his handhold and drifted across the cabin. Norsedal looked thoughtful, then, holding a wire conduit that ran through their stateroom, reached out and very gently pushed against Kevin. Kevin drifted to the bulkhead where he got himself back into control. Norsedal looked pleased.

The incident reminded Kevin that he was in free fall, and his stomach didn't like it much. He gulped hard.

"I'll be glad when we're under way," he said. "It won't last long, but it will be nice to have *some* weight again. Even for a day or so."

Norsedal frowned and rolled his eyes upward for a moment. "Not that long, I'm afraid," he said. "Let's see, total velocity change of about five kilometers a second, at a tenth of gravity acceleration—five thousand seconds." He took a pocket computer off his belt and punched numbers. "An hour and a half. Then we're back in zero-gravity." He restored the computer to its pouch. It was secured to it with a short elastic thong, as was everything else Norsedal carried.

Kevin was fascinated with the man. He went about everything methodically. First he strapped down his travel cases. Then he opened one. A geyser of clothing, papers, pencils, another and far more elaborate computer than the one he wore on his belt, chewing gum, bulbs of soft drinks, more clothing, a dozen magnetic-strip programs for his computer, and other small objects floated up into the room. They dispersed in the compartment.

"Oh, my," Norsedal said. He looked thoughtful. His hand snared the computer as it drifted by. Then he reached into the travel case again and got a shirt. "If you'll help me with this—"

Together they used the shirt like a seine to net all the gear. Norsedal produced a laundry bag to hold everything. Then he fished around in the travel case, more carefully this time, until he had a pleased expression. He came up with a small nylon-covered package that contained several rolls of Velcro, a pair of scissors, and a squeeze-tube of quick-drying glue. He began gluing Velcro hooks into his travel case and his locker. "I should have done this back on Earth," he said. His voice was almost perpetually apologetic. "But it wasn't certain I'd be coming, and they didn't give me the cases until just before I left."

Kevin watched interestedly. When the lockers were entirely lined with glued-on Velcro hooks, Norsedal carefully began work with the fuzzy Velcro, attaching strips to all his personal gear. Calculator, pencil case, notebook, tape recorder—

"That's a great idea," Kevin said.

"Want some? I brought plenty."

"Thanks, yes." Mostly Kevin was interested in the other man. He didn't seem like anyone Kevin would have thought would go to space. Norsedal was clearly overweight, very visibly so. He sniffed as if suffering from a sinus condition, and one of the objects Kevin had caught for him was a kit containing a hypodermic needle and bottles of what must have been room-temperature insulin. Although it was obvious that Norsedal had thought a lot about life in zero-gravity conditions and tried to make preparations, it was also obvious that he'd never been in space before. He had trouble keeping himself anchored while he worked.

"Who're you with?" Kevin asked. He had to talk much louder than he was used to; the low air pressure didn't carry sound very well. Although there were people in the compartments on either side and the partition was only thin nylon, they couldn't understand the conversations in the next cabins.

"Interplanet." Norsedal continued working with glue and Velcro. The glue smell was strong, but not excessively so. "I hope the air system doesn't have trouble with this," Norsedal said. "I suppose I should have brought water-soluble glue. But I wanted it to dry quickly. Maybe we should ask someone—"

"I wouldn't worry about it," Kevin said. Interplanet, he thought. That was the Zurich-based international consortium that maintained one of the two bases on Ceres. Kevin couldn't picture Jacob Norsedal as a miner or prospector and he certainly wasn't any kind of construction worker. "What will you be doing on Ceres?"

"Computer programming. And experiments with the computer system," Norsedal said. "Storekeeping—I'm supposed to set up an inventory control system for them. And work time-effectiveness studies. Anything that needs doing with computers." He seemed very happy about the idea.

"I—" Kevin hesitated. He didn't want to offend the man. Presumably there would be an opportunity to swap cabinmates once the ship was under way, but in any event there was certainly no sense in getting into an argument with someone you'd have to live with for months. His curiosity got the better of him. "You don't seem like a spaceman."

Norsedal smiled through his beard. "No. That's what the company said when I applied. It took me a long time to convince them. But look at it this way. A ten-year supply of insulin doesn't weigh very much. Nor does it matter if I'm overweight, not in Ceres' gravity, or in none at all. And I had one very good argument: I wanted to go and I can do the work." He began stowing his gear as he glued fuzz onto it. Decks of magnetic-backed cards. Three wargaming books. When he came to those he looked thoughtfully at the reader screen.

"I think I can tie that into my computer," Norsedal said. "We can use it for a display. Are you interested in wargames?"

Kevin had never thought about it. "After a few months in space I expect I'll be interested in anything—"

Norsedal grinned. "That's what I thought. We'll teach this thing to play Star Trek." He reached out to the screen and touched it, petting it like a dog: nice screen. Pat, pat.

They had two days aboard *Wayfarer* before the final boost toward Ceres. Kevin thought it would have been fun if there hadn't been so many people crowded aboard. He learned to eat in free fall, although he still managed to get a lot of the food into the intake grid of the air recirculation system: the only way to spoon food from plastic bags to mouth was in one smooth motion, never stopping. If he halted the spoon on its way, the food kept going to splatter against his face or shoot over his shoulder.

He also learned to do tumbling in zero-gravity. One of the other passengers organized a pool: the winner would be the first passenger to go in a single leap from A deck all the way to the aft bulkhead. No one looked like winning it just yet; four decks was the record. It was Kevin's turn to try when Captain Greiner ordered all the passengers back to their cabins for boost.

Weight felt strange. The ship boosted at about ten percent of Earth's gravity, but Kevin found that quite enough. All over the ship loose objects fell to the decks.

"Last chance." Jacob Norsedal said. "Until halfway there. Anything lost after this boost is done will either go to the air intake grid, or it won't show up at all."

Ninety minutes later the acceleration ended. *Wayfarer* was now in a long elliptical orbit that would cross the orbit of Ceres. Left to itself, the ship would go on past, more than halfway to Jupiter, before the Sun's gravity would finally turn it back to complete the ellipse and return it to its starting point. In order to land on Ceres, the ship would have to boost again when it got out to the orbit of the asteroid.

There would also be minor course-correction maneuvers during the trip, but except for those the ship's nuclear-pile engine wouldn't be started up until they arrived at Ceres's orbit. Then the ship would accelerate to catch up with the asteroid. That wouldn't happen for nine months.

Nine months was a long time, Kevin had thought, but he was surprised at how quickly time passed. With only ten crewmen aboard, the passengers had to take turns working ship maintenance systems. Kevin was assigned to life support, with the job of cleaning out the sewage-processor. It wasn't his favorite work, but he learned a lot about the algae tanks and chemical processors that took human wastes, including exhaled carbon dioxide, and turned them into oxygen and food.

There were also large leafy plants: lettuce, spinach, even watermelons and pumpkins. These vegetables furnished variety in their food, but were not really important to the ship's ecology. It takes a lot of surface area to absorb sunlight enough to convert a hundred people's wastes, and the larger the plants the less surface they had for the mass they took up. Algae are not as pretty as strawberry plants, but they are highly efficient.

The heart of the system was a series of large transparent tanks filled with green water and tropical fish. Once *Wayfarer* was under way the crew erected large mirrors outside the hull. The mirrors collected sunlight and focused it through Plexiglas viewports onto the algae tanks. A ventilation system brought the ship's air into the tanks as a stream of bubbles. Other pumping systems collected sewage and forced it into chemical processors; the output was treated sewage that went to the algae tanks as fertilizer.

Kevin called it the "green slime works" and was always suspicious of the food served aboard *Wayfarer;* harvesting and food processing was somebody else's job, and Kevin didn't want to know the details. He knew that the algae became high-protein flour somewhere along the line—but he also knew what the algae tanks took in. The thought wasn't particularly appetizing.

He got to know most of his fellow passengers. Ellen was roomed with two other women in a slightly larger cabin on L Deck, not far from the stern. Wiley Ralston was one deck above her. So was Bill Dykes, the miner/prospector Kevin had met on the plane to Baja. Kevin met a number of others as well; he had a very popular roommate.

Jacob Norsedal was madly teaching his personal computer to play Star Trek, Galactic Empire, Waterloo, Alexander the Great, Diplomacy, and any other game people wanted to indulge in. He had also invented a three-dimensional interstellar war game with a dozen mutually opposing sides, and that seemed destined to be interminable—the players needed a computer just to tell them their options. Norsedal didn't play games himself, but he loved being referee, and his quarters tended to be a meeting place for those with nothing to do.

Kevin, to his sorrow, wasn't included in that category. On his second day after boost a large man came to the stateroom. "Kevin Senecal?" he demanded.

"Me," Kevin admitted.

"George Lange. Senior Daedalus employee aboard. I guess I'm your boss." Lange held out a stack of cassettes. "You're supposed to study these."

Kevin opened them warily. "That's a lot of reading—"

"It's just a start," Lange said. "I've got a lot more for you. You're expected to *learn* something on this trip." He glared at Norsedal's computer, which was marching armies across the reader screen. "There's *work* waiting out in the Belt."

"And we've got *months*," Wiley Ralston said. He came into the stateroom. With four people inside it was crowded, but not badly: Ralston and Norsedal took places near where the ceiling would have been if there had been a floor and ceiling; with no gravity, there was no up or down and any part of the room was as comfortable as any other.

"There's months' worth of learning to be done." Lange growled. "Look, this ship is *it*. Either we make some profits out of the Belt, or there won't be more ships going. Not even the big companies can keep up this investment without some return. So at least you, Senecal, will get to work learning what you ought to."

Later Kevin found he had tapes on general space operations, mining, prospecting, environmental control systems, composition of asteroids, orbital mechanics—

Norsedal helped him study. He claimed to be interested, but Kevin thought Norsedal had probably learned everything on the tapes and was too polite to admit it. Certainly he was a good coach. Anything that could be done with a computer particularly interested him, and he showed Kevin how to do simple programs to solve most of the problems on the tapes. Slowly Kevin found himself learning what he had to know, even though it left him very little time for social life. His studies tended to keep him busy, so that he conversed mainly with Norsedal.

Three weeks out Kevin finished the first stack of tapes. "I suppose he'll have more," he said.

Norsedal was sitting yoga-fashion on nothing. He looked like a bearded Buddha. "Probably."

"So I don't tell him I'm done," Kevin said. He waved at the stack of tapes. "Gripes, according to that stuff we've licked all the problems, but every time I see Lange he gives me this bit about how desperate everything is, and how much work there is to do—" He stopped because Norsedal wasn't amused and it showed. "Are things that bad? I thought we knew how to live in space—"

"We do," Jacob said. "Technical capabilities exceed requirements by an order of magnitude. But Lange is right all the same. The space colonies aren't self-sufficient, and there aren't many ships. The Luna people want more Earth cargoes, the O'Neill Colony people want the ships, and the big companies can't afford to keep sending ships out to the Belt unless they get something back. I wouldn't be surprised if this were the last ship from Earth until the Ceres refineries prove they can make a profit."

"You mean it's *really* up to us?" Kevin asked.

Norsedal was very serious. "It might be. It's worse than that, really. Earth is so near the edge that if this attempt doesn't make it we may never be able to afford asteroid colonies again."

It was a sobering thought. Kevin looked at the pile of tapes. "I guess I'd better tell Lange I'm ready to get back to work."

Chapter Eight

With 130 people packed into quarters that would have been cramped for half that number it was inevitable that the passengers would get on each other's nerves. Kevin was surprised at just how few fights developed. There were plenty of quarrels and screaming matches, but not many blows. The worst part of it was the almost complete lack of privacy aboard *Wayfarer*.

For the first weeks this was no great problem for Kevin: there was too much to do. He had tapes to study, Norsedal's war-games, extravehicular activity practice under supervision of the crew, maintenance duties and other ship's work that was rotated among the passengers—and just plain getting used to living in zero-gravity.

He spent hours playing with liquids: squirt a dollop of colored water from a syringe, and it immediately became a sphere like a miniature planet. Inject an air bubble into it with a syringe and it assumed a new shape. Blow on it gently to get it rotating and it became a donut of water hanging in space.

There were rivers of stars to see outside any viewport. He had to learn the constellations all over again; there were just too many stars to let him recognize the old familiar patterns as seen from Earth, so many stars that in a darkened room you could almost read by starlight. But during EVA practice, perched above the ship's telescope tower with nothing ahead or above, he felt as if he were suspended motionless in space, a part of the universe. Kevin was always sad when his time was up and another passenger took his place. He eagerly looked forward to his practice sessions outside the ship, and wondered whether, when he reached the Belt and he would be outside for many hours at a time, he would ever get used to the wonder and grandeur of space. He hoped he would not.

As weeks went by, though, he found the lack of privacy becoming more irritating. There were 30 women among the 120 passengers aboard *Wayfarer*. Half of those were married and most of the remainder had formed quasi-permanent attachments. None of this bothered Kevin, since Ellen MacMillan remained at large and seemed to enjoy his company; but he could never be alone with her, and that *was* annoying.

Eventually the problem solved itself: they were assigned to environment systems maintenance during the same shift. Dismantling and cleaning sewer pipes wasn't his idea of a romantic setting, but it did have the advantage that no one else was interested in being in the same compartment while they worked. Felipe Carnel, the ship's Chief Engineer, was happy enough to leave the work to qualified passengers once he'd checked them out; and Ellen was as competent and conscientious as he.

The work was not demanding, merely messy and difficult; they had plenty of time to talk. For some reason Ellen seemed genuinely interested in Kevin and kept drawing him out. She was easy to talk to, and he found himself telling her about his early life, about school, and why he had come to space. Although he was usually somewhat shy with girls it was easy to be friends with Ellen.

"I think I've told you everything there is to know about me," he said finally. "And I don't know anything about you. You never talk about yourself—"

"Nothing to talk about." She squinted up at him and made a face. During the week they'd worked together they'd developed a system of signals. This one meant that she had sweat in her eyes and filth on her hands.

Kevin took a clean tissue and wiped her face. "Thanks." She went back to reaming out the plastic pipe.

"Come on," Kevin said. "You've made me do all the talking."

"There really isn't anything to tell," Ellen said. "I don't have any relatives. I was raised in an orphanage—"

"I didn't think they still had those," Kevin said. "Foster parents and—"

Ellen shuddered. "I was through several of those foster homes. Horrible way to live. Kevin, did you ever hear of the Futurian Foundation?"

"No."

"I guess not too many have. It's an organization that's interested in where—" She laughed. "It sounds silly if you're not a part of it."

"No, please. Tell me."

"Well, we're trying to look at where mankind is going," Ellen said defiantly. "Governments look ahead as far as the next election. The big corporations can look a little farther, sometimes as far as ten years. And nobody worries about what's going to happen after that. Nobody except us. We try to look hundreds, even thousands of years ahead."

"And you're a member of that—"

"Sort of. They raised me. When I was fifteen they bought me from the foster parents I was with.

"Bought you? Sounds like slavery."

She shrugged, a tiny wriggling motion; they had all learned new gestures for use in zero-gravity. She shifted her location, wedging one foot under a pipe clamp so that she could use both hands for the job she was doing.

"In a way it is," she said. "The state pays the foster parents to raise orphans. It's profitable work. They're paid by the number of kids in their home, so the foster parents don't want to let anyone go. The social welfare people don't want to let you go either—if they don't have orphans to take care of, they can't justify their jobs. So the Futurians had to pay off the foster parents, some lawyers, and two social workers. I'm glad they did."

Kevin looked puzzled. Ellen laughed. "Nothing mysterious about it. They have a testing program to catch the right people young and get them thinking about the future instead of themselves. That's all there is to it. I've been brought up to be satisfied with enough to live on, not to want anything more except my work—so I've got everything I want."

"And you think that's not interesting?" Kevin said. "You seem to have found the secret of the ages."

She laughed again. It was a pleasant sound, even muted as it was by the low air pressure. "We don't keep all our recruits, you know. Most of the kids we bring up go off to normal lives. Only a few of us join the Fellowship."

"But you did?" She nodded. "I suppose that's like a priesthood," Kevin said.

His voice had betrayed his thoughts, and she laughed again. "Not really. We're not celibate, you know! Although sometimes you act as if you think I am—"

"Hey, wait a minute, that's not fair," Kevin protested.

She was laughing again. "The way conditions are on this ship we both might as well be monks—either that or adopt the attitude of monkeys in a zoo, and I'm afraid I haven't got to that point yet. There. That's done. You tighten up the connections while I clean up." She looked down at her hands. "Yuk."

Kevin pushed away from the bulkhead and expertly floated over to the pipe assembly. He was proud of his hard-won ability to work in null-gravity conditions. He got one foot wedged into the pipe retainer and braced the other against a wire channel, leaving both hands free, and applied a big wrench to the pipes. The fittings turned hard, and everything took at least twice as long to do in zero-gravity as it would have on Earth. Finally he had it done. "You can turn on the pressure."

The system worked again, with no leaks, and Kevin nodded in satisfaction.

"Now. We're alone, and this is done, and—" He reached for her. She didn't resist.

"I think we'd better stop," she said, after a while.

"Why?"

"Because this isn't a very private place, and I am *not* a monkey in a zoo. The Leones may not mind putting on demonstrations for the other passengers, but I do—"

"Nobody ever comes here."

"Yes they do." She pushed away from him and caught a look at her reflection in one of the big Plexiglas algae tanks. "I'm a mess. Ugly—"

"You're not."

"Thank you. But I am. So are you, for that matter. Our faces are all swollen up, our lips are chapped, *and* we're getting pimples."

"All true but all irrelevant," Kevin said. "We knew that would happen before we signed up for a long trick in zero-gravity."

"But I didn't think I'd look *this* awful."

"You look all right to me." He did a double somersault from his bulkhead and landed just next to her. He grinned and reached for her again.

"Kevin, please . . . " Finally, she pushed away again. "Please. That's enough."

"Not for me—"

"Not for me either, but it's still all we're going to do," she said. "And don't look like a hurt little boy. Kevin, I like you. That's just the trouble. If we—this wouldn't be just a shipboard romance. Kevin, I can't afford emotional involvements. We've both got too much to do when we get to Ceres."

"So we have work to do. There's more to life than work—"

"Sometimes. Kevin, once we get to Ceres we may never see each other again. It's not fair to either of us to—to get too attached to each other."

"I'll take my chances."

"You say that now because I'm the only girl available. You wouldn't if—if you knew what you'd be getting into. I'm not somebody you ought to know, Kevin. I shouldn't have teased you. I'm sorry. I get lonely too, and I forgot that we'll never just be two people—"

"What?" Kevin frowned. There was a strange expression on Ellen's face, a strange look in her eyes, and he didn't understand.

"There's so much you can't know," Ellen said. "Kevin, we're friends. Let's leave it at that." She turned away to stare at pressure and flow gauges. "I think we've got this working again, and I've got some writing to do." She left the compartment hurriedly.

Kevin wanted to follow her, but she moved too quickly, and there were people in the corridors outside. He came back to stare into the algae tanks.

Tropical fish swam through the thick plant growth. They had adjusted to lack of gravity and oriented themselves as if the light source were "up." They no longer seemed confused—but Kevin was, and he didn't like it.

"She said she liked me," he muttered to the fish. "And it's a long way to Ceres." He could comfort himself with that. It was a long way to Ceres . . .

A week later they were both transferred to other ship's duties, not together. Kevin saw her quite often, but never alone.

Kevin's new assignment was on the bridge. His partner was Wiley Ralston, and Kevin found himself telling his friend about his problems with Ellen.

Ralston laughed. "Persistence, old buddy. Persistence and propinquity. Girls aren't any different from guys. They get horny too. Give it time."

"There doesn't seem to be a lot else to do," Kevin said.

"Yeah. Well, you'll have more of 'em to go after when we get to the Belt. Not a lot more, maybe, but more than just one. . . ."

True enough, Kevin thought. But he wasn't sure that was what he wanted. He wasn't sure what love was, or whether he believed in it, but he kept wishing Ellen were around so he could tell her things he'd just thought of, and he made excuses to go find her.

Eventually they were back in the farms and alone; and this time when he kissed her she didn't run away. A long time later, when they could speak again, she said, very seriously, "Kevin, we don't talk about love or the future. We're together while we're on the ship. Nothing permanent; nothing lasts after we reach the Belt."

"Sure," he said; but he didn't believe her.

Kevin and Wiley Ralston had been assigned to the bridge again when the halfway course correction came. Captain Greiner was very casual about it. First he slaved the computer to the high-gain antenna, then took position and velocity readings from both Earth and Ceres. Finally he pointed the main telescope to the bright star Vega.

The ship's computer digested the information for a minute. Then it flashed ready lights.

"And *this* does it," Greiner said. He threw switches giving control of the ship to the computer.

A recorded voice sounded. "Now hear this. Stand by for thirty seconds of very low gravity. Low thrust for thirty seconds, commencing in one minute. Fifty-nine, Fifty-eight . . ."

"Almost as if the ship didn't need me at all," Captain Greiner said. "If it weren't for the maintenance, it wouldn't."

"But you can operate without the computer, while it can't work without you," Kevin said.

Greiner laughed. "Not hardly. Everything's got to be too precise. If we had plenty of fuel, sure, I could navigate by hand calculations; but not the way we're cutting it."

"So even out here the machine replaces man," Wiley Ralston said. "Well, the damned machines can't do everything for us. Some things still need people. Though I wonder just how long—"

Kevin looked at him quizzically. Wiley grinned. "Just so long as they need us a few more years," Ralston said. "Long enough to get rich. Then they can run the whole damned universe by computer."

The countdown ended, and they felt weight again. Not very much weight, about one percent of Earth's gravity; but it felt strange to have a permanent "up" and "down" again. Kevin had found that he could orient himself to think of any direction "above" his head as "up" in zero-gravity; since he was facing forward, he suddenly found himself lying on his back instead of standing. He found later that everyone in the ship had had the same problem.

"Ceres has gravity," Jacob Norsedal said after dinner. "Let's see, about forty centimeters a second—four percent Earth gravity."

"Just enough so you can't jump off," Ellen said.

"A lot more than that." Norsedal said. His voice was apologetic but firm. He was apologetic for disagreeing; but he was never uncertain about his facts. He took his belt calculator, the small one he always carried, and punched in numbers. "You couldn't jump more than about 125 feet straight up," he said. "Of course, you'd take a while coming down." Click-click. "Not so long, thirteen seconds. Half a minute for the round trip, up and back down again. Of course I've left out the mass of your suit and tanks. I could run it with those—"

"Never mind," Ellen laughed. She, like everyone in the ship, had found that if you asked Norsedal a question you often learned more than you wanted to know. "It's going to take getting used to all over again," she said. "Having things fall instead of just drifting around the way they do here. And I've gotten used to sleeping in zero-gravity."

They sat at the entrance to Kevin and Jacob's stateroom. One of the inevitable tumbling contests was going through the central well of the ship. Bill Dykes, the miner Kevin had met on the airplane to Baja, spun past doing somersaults and counting loudly. "Ninety-seven!" he announced with a grin as he went past. He was still centered in the opening, and it looked likely that he'd get all the way to the stern bulkhead. That was no longer unusual; the contest had been won weeks before, and now the passengers were trying to set a record for the number of somersaults before touching walls or decks.

"Damn!" Hal Leone was in Kevin's stateroom playing a stellar war-game with his wife Jeannine. The game used ballistic calculations, and Hal had managed to get his ship into an unrecoverable situation; no matter what he did, it was going to crash into a star. His wife chuckled. What made it embarrassing was that Hal was a mathematician and his wife a physician—but she always won.

Others gathered on F deck. It was almost time for another session of Norsedal's monster twelve-sided game, and the players were assembling. Someone produced a bottle of vodka vacuum-distilled from green slime. Despite its evil source it had no unusual taste at all. The bottle passed around. There was more activity in the well; a twirling contest, men and women pirouetting in midair. Then Bill Dykes came tumbling back toward the bow, followed closely by his cabinmate and partner, Carl Lundgren. They were counting loudly.

"Happy hour," Ellen said.

Suddenly another man leaped across the opening. He collided heavily with Carl Lundgren.

"Look where you're going!" Lundgren shouted.

"Shove it," the other man said. Kevin recognized him: Frank Sales, a loner with a foul temper. Sales was going out to work as a miner. He was a short, almost dwarfish man, who compensated for his small stature with a constant program of exercises. All the passengers were supposed to take their turn with the exercise machines, but Sales was the only one who took extra time on them as a matter of course.

"Goddamit, I was headed for a record," Lundgren said. "What'd you want to do that for?"

Sales grunted and turned away.

"I asked you a question!" Lundgren shouted. "Come back here."

"Hey, buddy," Bill Dykes said, grabbing Lundgren's arm, "Drop it. He ain't worth it."

Lundgren shook Dykes off. "Keep out of this, Bill. That sawed-off little bastard never looks where he's going. Who the hell does he think he is?"

"Are you talking about me?" Sales grasped a stanchion and turned back toward Lundgren. "Are you?"

"Damn right, you little creep."

"Hey—" Dykes protested, but it was too late. Sales dived toward Carl Lundgren and knocked him from his perch against the edge of F Deck. The two men became a tangle of arms and legs tumbling in the central well. Lundgren caught Sales by the hair and pulled; the result was that both tumbled out of control.

Others moved to try to separate them, but only added to the tangle. Someone began to laugh and others joined. Ellen giggled. Then Sales's hand moved to his tool belt.

"Look out, Carl, the little bastard's got a knife!" Dykes shouted.

Lundgren turned frantically toward Sales. One of the others trying to separate them grabbed at Lundgren, missed, and caused him to spin violently again. Three other passengers dove toward the fighting men, and there was another wild tangle of bodies. Then bright blood spurted out to hang in large droplets in the air. It was impossibly red, tiny red planets hanging in space.

Someone screamed, more passengers and a crewman appeared to separate the fighters. When the two were pulled apart they saw that Carl Lundgren spurted blood in rhythmic pulses from a slash across his throat.

"You've killed my partner!" Dykes roared. He started for Sales, but other passengers held him.

"He came for me!" Sales shouted. "You saw it, he ran right into me, I never meant to hurt him."

There was a babble of voices. "Get him to sick bay!" "Hold on to that murdering son of a bitch!" "Jeez, little buddy, you're going to be all right, you gotta be—" "Get a doctor!"

Jeannine Leone came out of Kevin's cabin and dove to the group holding Lundgren. Her hands worked frantically at the wound. "I can't get a grip," she said. "You, hold him against the deck. One of you hold onto my feet. Not like that! Hold me steady, I have to get pressure on this—"

Blood continued to stream into the ship. Bright crimson spheres floated toward the air intake grid. "We need weight," Jeannine shouted. "Send for the Captain—"

"I'm here," Greiner said.

"We need weight. Not much, just enough to let me do steady work. Can you give us acceleration?"

"No," Greiner said. "Can't do it."

"But he'll die—"

"I hope not, but we can't do it!" The Captain's face was grim. "If we accelerate now we won't get to Ceres at all."

Jeannine continued working, but finally she straightened and shook her head. "Too late," she said. "He's dead. I don't know if I could have done anything even if we had gravity." She turned to Bill Dykes. "I'm sorry—"

"Not your fault," the miner said. He looked at his partner's body, then at Frank Sales. "Now we got a murderer to deal with. I say we put him outside now and get it over with."

Chapter Nine

"Trial! We gotta have a trial," someone shouted. The Captain agreed. Eventually it was settled. Of course everyone wanted to watch.

There was no place aboard *Wayfarer* large enough to assemble the entire ship's company. The wardroom deck could hold about half of them, with people perched around the walls and hanging onto the deck above. The rest had to scatter through the central well. Since it wasn't possible to understand what was said from more than ten feet away, Captain Greiner had everyone put on their helmets and tune to a common channel. Eventually everyone was settled, some scattered all through the ship, others on the wardroom deck. It was not an orderly meeting.

"There are few precedents," Captain Greiner said, "but this isn't the first murder in space. I am not sure the previous cases apply, however. In the first space murder the satellite commander tried the case himself, and himself executed the murderer. Although the commander—it was Aeneas MacKenzie, by the way—offered to employ the entire satellite crew as jury, there were complications including threats against the families of crew members, and MacKenzie ended by acting alone.

"However, in that case there was no doubt about the guilt of the murderer, or that the crime was premeditated; the murder was part of a scheme to sabotage the satellite. Few have questioned the justice of Mackenzie's actions."

Kevin felt Ellen shudder.

"What's the matter?" he asked.

"Nothing," she said; but her voice was low and tightly controlled.

"This is farcical," someone shouted. Kevin couldn't tell who it was; the voice came through his headphones. "You can't even establish that there's *been* a murder, and there is no impartial jury. Everyone here is prejudiced."

"Who the hell is that?" Bill Dykes thundered. "Not been a murder? My partner's dead, and this bastard did it, and what's there to talk about? Put him outside and get it over with!"

Someone else shouted, "I got no use for Sales, but we have to let him tell his story—"

"Sure," Dykes said. "We listen to him, *then* we put him outside!"

Everyone began to talk at once. "It was a goddam accident—"

"What the hell, fair fight—"

"Damn murderin' bastard never was any use—"

"Silence," Greiner said. His voice carried authority. "We are holding this meeting to determine what we shall do. It will not become a shouting match."

"There's plenty of precedent from sailing ship days," someone said. "You can do anything you think best for the welfare of the ship."

"I am aware of that," Captain Greiner said. "As most of you know, I am an engineer and aircraft pilot by training. I do not come from a navy tradition and I must say I am reluctant to assume supreme authority—"

"You have to," someone shouted.

"But if that is what is needed, I will do so," Greiner finished.

Someone jumped up through the well to land in front of Captain Greiner. "I'm Martin Pacifico," he said. "I'm a lawyer."

There was a chorus of boos and hisses. "Who needs *him.*" Bill Dykes shouted.

It didn't seem to bother Pacifico. "Captain Greiner, the essence of a fair trial is an impartial jury. Obviously there is no possibility of such here. Even if there had been—and most of the passengers were witnesses to the alleged crime and thus were already not competent as jurors—your insistence on discussing this matter before the entire ship's company has contaminated all possible venire men."

"Oh, shut up!" Dykes yelled. "Captain, get that yo-yo out of here. My partner's dead, and dammit—"

"Enough," Captain Greiner said. "Mr. Pacifico, are you suggesting we wait until we reach Ceres to hold the trial?"

"That won't do either," Pacifico said. "Ceres has no jurisdiction—"

"So we must wait until Sales is returned to Earth?" Greiner asked. "Which could be ten years, or could be never—"

"Shut that goddam lawyer up," Dykes yelled. There were other shouts of agreement.

"May I speak?"

Kevin didn't recognize the newcomer, but Greiner evidently did. "Yes, Mr. Harwitt?" the Captain said.

"Harwitt?" Kevin asked.

"The Westinghouse supervisor," Ellen said. They spoke without using their microphones.

"Captain," Joe Harwitt said. "My company has an interest in this matter. Lundgren had signed up to work for us in the Ceres refinery and we paid for his passage. But now we have no one to do his work. I think that Sales owes us restitution."

"That is a civil matter," Pacifico said. "Not under consideration here. I would be glad to represent you, though—"

"Oh, shut up," Harwitt said. "I don't want money damages ten years from now, I want a refinery worker! It is too late to bring someone else out to take his place, but we can get *some* use out of Sales. He will have to do."

"I say, wait a moment—"

Captain Greiner seemed resigned. "Yes, Dr. Vaagts. I expected to hear from you sooner or later."

"Sales is signed up with Rheinmettal," Vaagts said, "and we will need him. You can't take him for Westinghouse—"

"Does Rheinmettal stand responsible for his actions?" Harwitt demanded. "You brought him here."

"Don't be ridiculous."

"I'm not being ridiculous. *Somebody's* got to compensate Westinghouse for the loss of our worker. I say we have a right to Sales as replacement for Lundgren."

"But he would be of little use to you," Vaagts said. "You admit he is untrained for refinery work. But he has a good record in deep mining operations, and we can use him. Suppose, Joseph, that we keep him working for us, and compensate you for Lundgren's passage with funds withheld from his pay?"

"Rather have a worker than money," Harwitt said. "But I suppose we could make a deal. You'd have to pay interest, of course."

"I think that can be agreed," Vaagts said.

"You are speaking of slavery!" Pacifico shouted.

"Damn it, what about my dead partner?" Dykes demanded. "And his family back on Earth?"

"Ah," Vaagts said. "I suppose restitution to Lundgren's family is in order as well—we will divide Sales's pay between Westinghouse and Lundgren's family—"

"Slavery," Pacifico said again.

"You can't do this to me," Sales shouted.

Everyone began talking at once. "Civil rights—"

"Screw his rights—"

"Put the bastard outside and get it over with," Dykes said again. He didn't sound so positive now. "Only—maybe it's not so bad, making him pay—"

"We still have not established Mr. Sales's legal obligation to *anyone*." Pacifico said.

"Captain, may I respectfully request," Dr. Vaagts said, "that if that extremely unpleasant lawyer person does not keep silent so that interested parties can come to agreement, we put *him* outside—"

"And who'd pay Interplanet compensation for losing Pacifico?" someone asked. "Take up a collection?" another voice added hopefully.

"Let us first determine who are the interested parties," Captain Greiner said. "First, of course, Mr. Sales himself."

"Glad you jokers realize I'm still here," Sales said.

"Shut up," Dykes yelled.

"Second," Captain Greiner continued, "the relatives and friends of Mr. Lundgren. Certainly they must have a voice in any settlement. Third, the two companies: Rheinmettal, which employs Sales and has paid for his passage; and Westinghouse, which has lost the services of Mr. Lundgren. Are there any others?"

"Justice!" Pacifico said loudly.

"If all interested parties are satisfied then justice has probably been served," Greiner said. "Now: Mr. Dykes, what do you propose?"

"Put him out—only I'll say this. If Carol Lundgren and the kids can get something out of this, that'd be better. Won't do them any good if we space this little creep."

"So. And we have heard the proposals of the interested firms," Greiner said. "It now remains to hear from Mr. Sales himself. Sales, you are charged with murder. How do you plead?"

"It was a goddam accident—"

"We can, if you like, call witnesses and determine just what happened." Greiner said. "But I think we already know. There was an argument. You began a fight. You were losing it, and for whatever reason you drew a weapon which you used to menace Mr. Lundgren. Do you disagree so far?"

"Well—I just wanted to make him stop beatin' on me," Sales said. "I didn't intend to hurt him! You all saw it, somebody pushed him, he fell into my knife. I didn't go after him."

"I do not dispute that," Greiner said. "Does anyone?"

There were murmurs, but no one spoke up.

"About the way I saw it," Kevin said. Ellen nodded.

"The fact remains that you drew the weapon and menaced Mr. Lundgren with it, and thus you are the responsible party. You also began the fight."

"He provoked me—"

"But you struck the first blow."

"Fair fight's no murder," someone said.

"Perhaps," Greiner said. "But this was hardly a fair fight, with one party armed and the other not warned. I do not say what I would do if there were a formal duel aboard my ship, but I do say this was not a fair fight as I understand it. Have we established the facts to everyone's satisfaction?"

"This is terrible procedure," Pacifico shouted.

Greiner ignored him. "Then, Mr. Sales, you are certainly guilty of manslaughter. Do you dispute that?"

"He provoked me," Sales insisted.

"And you are accordingly found guilty of that charge," Greiner said. "We have no jail facilities aboard this ship, and it is not my job to provide punishment in any event. I sentence you to forfeiture of all pay and allowances for five years. You will continue to be employed by Rheinmettal, which will take sufficient measures to prevent your injuring anyone else, and your pay will be divided equally between the family of your victim and the company which employed him. So ordered. First Officer, write it into the log and I'll sign it. Dr. Vaagts, I deliver this man into your care. The ship's company is dismissed."

The rest of the trip to Ceres was uneventful—until the last day.

Kevin had once again been assigned to bridge duties, which consisted mostly of keeping the Captain and First Officer company, and making coffee in free fall—not the easiest job Kevin had ever done.

The last phase of the voyage was to be an acceleration lasting nearly three hours. *Wayfarer* was in a long elliptical orbit that crossed that of Ceres; in order to land on the asteroid it would be necessary to both change the ship's direction and to catch up with the tiny planet. The process began hours before the burn, with *Wayfarer's* electronic gear getting a precise position and velocity fix. The ship had to be located precisely with relation to Ceres.

Captain Greiner programmed the radar antenna to seek out the beacon signal from Ceres. "Here goes," he said. He pressed the keys to initiate the position fix, then reached for a squeeze-bottle of hot coffee. He squirted coffee into his mouth, swallowed, and looked back at the control board. Then he frowned. "What the devil?"

"Sir?" First Officer Leslie Seymour floated over to the Captain's station.

"I'm not getting anything," Greiner said. "Nothing at all."

"That's odd," Seymour said. "It's as if the antenna wasn't working. Maybe I'd better have a look—"

"Maybe you had, Mister."

Seymour was already wearing his pressure suit. He reached for his helmet.

"SHUTDOWN. WARNING. COMPUTER SHUT-DOWN," the computer announced.

"The hell you say!" Greiner muttered. He turned to the ship's computer and examined displays. "Damn! Leslie, it says it has a power interrupt!"

"Jeez. Antenna not working and now the computer's going out—"

"Check out the antenna," Greiner ordered. He lifted his intercom microphone. "Chief Engineer! Mister Carnel, get up here on the double. Something's happened to the computer. Leslie, on your way, now."

"Yes, sir," Seymour left the bridge, headed for the main airlock.

"What's happening, Captain?" Kevin asked. "Is there something wrong with the computer?"

"Damned wrong," Greiner said. "And we can't possibly make rendezvous with Ceres without it—there you are, Felipe. Look at this thing!"

Felipe Carnel looked at the shutdown message, then opened a panel and stared at dials. "It says that regulated power's been cut off, Skipper," he said.

"Regulated power? Where the hell's *that* power supply?"

"Back aft," Carnel said. "It's never given any trouble before."

"Better go have a look," Greiner said.

"Rojj." Carnel turned to leave the bridge.

"And have a look at the seals on the cargo hold," Greiner said thoughtfully.

The engineer looked back quickly. There was astonishment and worry in his voice. "Sir, you don't think—"

"Mister, I don't know what to think. Just check things out."

"Aye aye, sir." Carnel left hurriedly.

"Sir?" Kevin asked. "I thought we got power from the reactor."

"We do," Greiner said. "And there's no problem with the main power system. You can see that—the ventilation system's working, the lights are on. Nothing wrong there. But the brain here eats a very precise diet. It wants 400 cycle power, and that doesn't mean 399.9 either. If the brain's not getting what it wants, it shuts down to avoid damage to itself." Greiner frowned. "In fact, I wonder if it's not reporting antenna problems when all that's wrong is the power supply? We'll find out." Greiner didn't seem very worried.

It didn't seem serious, and Kevin went back to making more coffee. After all, they had ten hours before they started the engine. Besides—he could *see* Ceres in the ship's main telescope. He had watched it grow from a point to a recognizable object, no details but definitely a disc. They could aim for it and blast—

First Officer Seymour came back onto the bridge. "The antenna's gone, Skipper."

"Gone?"

"Clean gone. Like it was sawed off, or maybe blasted off with a couple of turns of prima-cord. Gone, anyway."

"Bat puckey. It can't be gone," Greiner said. "Blasted off? Sabotage?"

"Looks like it to me," Seymour said.

"Hmm. Well, we can still navigate with the telescope. If we get the computer running again," Greiner said. "But if—you really think it was sabotage, Leslie?"

"Yes, sir. What else could it be?" They waited in silence. Finally Kevin asked, "If the computer's really out, what happens?"

"We don't get to Ceres," Greiner said. His voice was grim.

"Three years to home," Seymour added. "If we're lucky we can cut some off that, but not a lot. Think this tub will keep us alive for three more years, Skipper?"

"It might. With a lot of work," Greiner said. He looked thoughtful. "Present orbit takes us out to better than three and a half AU before we head back toward Earth. Less than ten percent of the sunlight we get down near Earth. It'd be close for a while. Not much light for the ship's farm."

"But—I can *see* Ceres," Kevin protested.

Greiner laughed without humor. "Sure. But how much do I burn aimed in what direction? Kevin, we've got just enough fuel aboard to set us down on Ceres. Nothing to spare for mistakes. Without the ship's computer we could never do it—"

"Can we get back to Earth without the computer?" Kevin asked.

"No. But that's not the problem. It's only the power supply. If we have to we can build another. We can build another antenna, too—ah." He stopped as Felipe Carnel came back into the bridge compartment. "Well?" Greiner demanded impatiently.

"Cargo seals are all intact," Carnel said. "I put Phelps on watch down there, just in case—"

"Phelps alone?"

"No, I asked three passengers, random selection, to stand watch with him."

"Good," Greiner said. "And the power system?"

"Blown to hell," Carnel said. "Somebody put about fifty grams of plastique into the system. Messed it up good."

"And the spare is gone," Greiner said quietly.

"Might as well be. Been taken apart into little bits."

"How long to rebuild?" Greiner demanded. His tone indicated that he already knew the answer.

"Days," Carnel said. "Three or four days anyway."

"By which time we'll be long past Ceres and headed out to nowhere," Greiner said. "Interesting. Someone put a lot of thought into this. He's sabotaged the exact two systems to keep us from landing on Ceres without actually crippling the ship." Greiner's calm broke at last. "That son of a bitch! He's done it! I can't put the cargo on Ceres—" he shouted.

"And there may never be another ship out here again," Felipe Carnel finished for him. "Somebody's just damned near killed the whole asteroid mining business."

Chapter Ten

"There must be something we can do." First Officer Seymour pounded his fist into his palm. "Raise Earth and have them run off the problem in Zurich—"

"Without the high-gain antenna?" Felipe Carnel laughed. "We can't raise Earth without that antenna."

"Ceres, then," Seymour said. "They've got a big computer—"

"And no programs," Captain Greiner said. "And once again, without the antenna, we can't rely on communications with them. We'll try, but I've no confidence." Greiner looked at the last print-outs from the ship's computer. *Wayfarer's* last known position was one hundred thousand kilometers from Ceres. The ship's orbit crossed that of the asteroid at a sharp angle; *Wayfarer* would have to change direction, then catch up; in practice that meant a smooth curve stretching from *Wayfarer's* present course to the asteroid's orbit, with a slight change of orbit plane as well—and Ceres moves at eighteen kilometers each second.

The problem was not merely to get to Ceres, but to arrive with exactly the same velocity as the asteroid, and going in exactly the same direction. The navigation would be only slightly less complicated than hitting a BB in flight with another BB fired by a gunner who had bad eyesight. An error of a tenth of a kilometer per second would put the ship impossibly far away from its target.

"Leslie, try raising Ceres," Captain Greiner said. "Let's see if they have advice."

First Officer Seymour floated to the communications set and anchored himself to the stool. He lifted the microphone and began calling.

"What I want to know is *who*," Greiner said. "Damned clever chap, whoever it was. This was well planned. We keep our fuel, drift on in our ellipse, and eventually return to Earth. Stops us without committing suicide."

"But why?" Kevin asked.

Greiner shook his head. "Who'd benefit from this? Too many to count. The African mining outfits don't want competition from asteroid mines. Anti-technology people want to stop space exploration altogether—"

"Lunar mining outfits," Felipe Carnel cut in. "Or even the O'Neill colony people—they've been making noises about what a waste Belt operations are—"

"Skipper, I've got them, but they can't understand me," Leslie Seymour said. "OUR COMPUTER IS OUT," he shouted, then looked sheepish. "They just don't read us."

"Maybe when we get closer—" Kevin said.

"By then it will be too late," Greiner said. He stared at Kevin. "You look like a man with an idea. Have you thought of something?"

"Possibly, Captain, I know somebody who can compute the burn for us."

"Who? And how—"

"My cabinmate, Jacob Norsedal."

"Norsedal," Greiner said. "He's been up here a number of times. Very interested in our ship's brain. Yes, I'd say he knows computers, but this isn't a computer problem, Kevin. We cannot rebuild that power supply in the few hours we have left, and we don't need a program, we need a computer—"

"Yes, sir, but he's got his own," Kevin said.

"I've seen it," Greiner said "Kevin, he can't possibly do this calculation with that little belt model he carries—"

"I wouldn't bet on that," Kevin said. "But he doesn't have to. He's got a much bigger one in our cabin. Uses it for war-games. Recreation stuff. And he's been keeping track of *Wayfarer*. He calculated the midcourse correction you made, and said something about it being off, but not much—"

Grenier looked thoughtful. "Felipe, go ask Mr. Norsedal to come to the bridge. And ask him to bring that extra brain with him."

"Right," Carnel said.

"And you needn't tell the passengers about our problem," Greiner added. He waited until the engineer had left the control cabin. "Now. Kevin, how sure are you that Mr. Norsedal isn't the one who bollixed our system to begin with? I wonder who else could have thought of this method?"

"You'd think that was funny if you knew Jacob," Kevin said. "He's a space fanatic. Also a computer fanatic—he likes them more than he likes people. He'd never harm one."

"I point out to you that this one hasn't been harmed," Greiner said. "And I grant you it's not likely, but it's certainly possible that someone who seems to be a space fanatic could be one of the anti-technology people. They do study technological systems, you know."

"Possibly, but Jacob isn't against technology," Kevin insisted.

"I hope you're right."

When Carnel returned with Norsedal, Captain Greiner explained the problem. "Senecal here thinks you can do something," Greiner said.

"How much time do we have?" Norsedal asked.

"The burn was scheduled to take place in four hours." Greiner answered.

"Not much time." Norsedal looked thoughtful.

"No. Well, it was just a possibility. I didn't really believe in—"

"But I think we can do something," Norsedal said. He went over to the chart table and placed an attaché case on it, using the table straps to hold it in place. He anchored himself to the stool at the table, then opened the case and patted the computer inside. "Nice computer. Fortunately, I already have some of the programs we'll need. Now let's see—"

Jacob opened another compartment and took out paper. "Captain, I can program the course, but I can't possibly patch my computer into the ship's drive system—"

"No sweat," Felipe Carnel interjected. "We've got a lot of little special-purpose computers for that. One is slaved to the gyro system and controls the engine thrust. You tell the ship where to go and I'll see that she goes there."

"Good. I thought so," Norsedal said. "If you didn't have a lot of smaller computers dedicated to special purposes, the air system wouldn't work—" He began to work furiously. Pencils and paper floated away from him, to be retrieved by one of the others. He drank coffee constantly.

An hour went by. Then another. Finally Norsedal began punching input buttons.

"Done?" Captain Greiner asked.

"I have the basic program. Now we have to get it checked out and running," Norsedal said. He continued to type inputs. "Now we'll just try—"

He pressed buttons. There was a moment of silence, then the readout screen filled with numbers. "Stopped on an input error," Norsedal muttered. "That's simple enough." He typed for a moment, then looked up. "Captain, have you decided you will fly this course once I have it?"

"I'm still thinking about that," Greiner said. "No point in making decisions unless there's something to decide. Do you think you'll have it?"

"Probably." Norsedal didn't look up from his console. He muttered, sometimes to himself, sometimes to the computer. "Nice computer, tell me what I did wrong this time . . ."

"I don't like this much," Leslie Seymour said.

"Nor I," Greiner said. "But you know what happens if we do not deliver this cargo."

"Yes. I suppose we have to try." Seymour went to the main telescope. "At least we can get decent bearings," he said. "There's Ceres, nice and clear—"

"I hope so," Norsedal said. "I had to compute the course as a function of the position of Ceres relative to Vega. We'll need constant sightings on both."

"We can get them," Seymour said. "Captain, maybe it wouldn't be a bad idea to protect the main telescope. Before that son of a bitch gets to it—"

"Good thinking," Captain Greiner said. "In fact, we ought to locate all the passengers and crew and set them to watching each other before there's more sabotage. I should have thought of that earlier." Greiner was apologetic. "I was never a ship captain, merely an astronaut with the European Space Program. Not the best training for what we're faced with. Leslie, see to it, will you?"

"Right, Skipper. Senecal, come with me, please. I want you to go outside and watch the telescope until we're certain that everyone is accounted for."

"Not alone," Greiner said. "Not that we don't trust you, Kevin—but who can we trust?"

"I understand," Kevin said. "May I use your intercom?"

"What for?"

"To call a friend." He went to the intercom panel and dialed a stateroom number. "Ellen, they've asked me to do an EVA. Will you come with me?"

"Who did you call?" Greiner asked.

"Ellen MacMillan. We've worked together on other jobs in this ship, and I *know* she can take care of herself outside."

"I heard about your difficulty getting to *Wayfarer*" Greiner said. "Yes, I'd think MacMillan would be a good partner. Certainly we could trust her."

"But Skipper," Leslie Seymour protested. "We can't let *her* go outside—"

"Now that she's said she will, have you any way you can think of to stop her?" Greiner demanded.

And what is this all about? Kevin wondered. He had no time to ask.

Seymour sighed. "No. I don't suppose I can," he said. "I guess she'll do nicely. Let's go find her." He opened the companionway door.

There were three people waiting outside in the main corridor. One came in quickly, pushing past Seymour.

"Mr. Pacifico, what the devil are you doing on my bridge?" Captain Greiner demanded.

"I represent the passengers," Pacifico said. His voice, already garbled by the lower atmospheric pressure in the ship, sounded shrill and petulant. "We've been told that the main computer is out, and you're going to chance a landing on Ceres anyway."

"Who told you?" Felipe Carnel demanded.

"It's all over the ship," Pacifico said. He turned to the others who had come in with him. "Isn't it?"

"That happens to be the case," Dr. Vaagts said.

"I hadn't expected *you* to protest," Greiner said.

"Nor am I protesting," Vaagts said. "I merely wanted to know what is happening. Mr. Pacifico certainly doesn't represent me, or Rheinmettal."

"So who do you represent, Pacifico?" Carnel asked.

"Most of the passengers. We demand that we be consulted before you undertake a dangerous maneuver like this. Isn't it true that if you do nothing we'll go back to Earth, but if you try for Ceres and miss we'll have no fuel left? We'll all be dead!"

"True enough," Greiner said.

"And what confidence do you have in—you've got *him* doing it? The wargamer? Captain, you can't do this. You must take a vote—"

"Vote hell. Leslie, you and Senecal were going out to locate all the ship's company."

"Right, Skipper," Seymour said.

"And you, Pacifico, get off my bridge. Now. Or I'll have you thrown off."

"We have rights—"

"Leslie, heave him out."

"With pleasure, Captain." First Officer Seymour launched himself toward the lawyer.

"I'm leaving," Pacifico said. "But you haven't heard the last of this, Greiner. You are not a king, and this isn't the Eighteenth Century—" He went out quickly as Seymour prepared to take hold of him.

Kevin found Ellen in her cabin. He explained what had happened. "Finish getting into your suit," he told her. "We're supposed to go outside and look after the main telescope."

"Sure. You wait out in the corridor."

"Sure you don't need any help?"

"Thank you, no."

When they reached the airlock, Seymour had got most of the passengers together in the central well. A crewman guarded the airlock. Kevin and Ellen checked their air supplies, then went out as Seymour was calling the roll of the ship's company.

Wayfarer had two airlocks. One was right in the bows, a large docking port that allowed smaller space capsules to link up with the ship, and could also be used to link with an airtight corridor connecting the ship with the Ceres spaceport, or even with another ship. The other was a smaller personnel lock on the side of the hull just aft of the bows. Kevin and Ellen went out that way. There was a small ladder leading forward. It wasn't needed as a ladder, but it provided handholds.

With no gravity they had to be careful not to drift away from the ship. It would be easy to jump entirely away from *Wayfarer*. Although they couldn't fall off—they were moving at the same velocity as *Wayfarer*, and would until the ship's engines were started up—if anyone became separated from the ship he would drift away forever, moving slowly out into space.

They climbed carefully to the forward end of the ship and rounded it. Now there was nothing ahead of them at all. *Wayfarer* floated among a river of stars, bright starlight and the black shadows of space, and there was no sense of motion at all. They hung in glory. The sun was behind the ship so that they were both in deep shadow, with just enough starlight so they could see each other. Their flashlights made small pools of light on the ship's dark hull.

"Magnificent," Kevin murmured. "I could stay here for the rest of the trip."

Ellen floated over to him and silently touched his gloved hand. It wasn't a moment for talking. They found places to anchor themselves and waited in silence. The big telescope was a few meters away. It moved slightly as Captain Greiner took sights.

Kevin searched for constellations among the stars. He could make out only a few of the traditional ones; there were too many stars, millions more than the ancient Babylonians who had named the constellations had ever been able to see.

"Now that our eyes are adjusted, we'd best have a look at the telescope," Ellen said.

"Right." They moved across the blunt bow of the spaceship. There were convenient handholds at intervals.

Wayfarer would never enter an atmosphere and had no need for streamlining.

The telescope was large, over a foot in diameter, with flexible seals that let it pass through the ship's hull and into the control bridge. They moved next to it and examined it with their flashlights.

"That doesn't belong there." Ellen sounded very calm and not surprised. Her light indicated something about the size and shape of a coffee can. It was taped to the telescope barrel.

"It may go off anyway. When you move it," Kevin said. "Get away from it—"

"This is my job," she said. "Move back. Farther."

"No. You move—"

"I told you, it's my job. Now move or don't, I'm going to take this thing off."

Kevin felt like an idiot. He was afraid of the bomb, and he was also unwilling to move away to safety while Ellen worked on it.

"Idiot, somebody's got to tell them what happened," Ellen said. "If it goes off. So get away from here—"

"No."

"Stubborn idiot."

"No worse than you are—"

"True. There. I have it." She held up the can. "It didn't explode yet." She crawled toward the side of the ship, then got a firm grip on the handhold with her left hand. With her right she threw the can outward, away from the ship. They watched it dwindle and vanish into space. "Maybe it was old coffee grounds," she said.

"Maybe." Kevin found that he'd been holding his breath. "Ellen—what did you mean, it's your job?"

"I shouldn't have said that. I was scared. Kevin, please—forget that I said that."

"Sure," he said. But he knew he wouldn't.

Chapter Eleven

"Outside party, this is Seymour." The First Officer's voice was loud in Kevin's helmet phones. It seemed a grating irritation in the silent grandeur of space.

"We're here," Ellen answered. "We found a bomb—or something that looked like one—attached to the telescope."

"But when was it put there?" Seymour demanded. "I looked at the telescope when I checked the high gain antenna. I'm sure I would have seen anything—"

"I don't know, but it was there," Kevin said. "Ellen threw it off the ship about two minutes ago. It will be a kilometer away by now."

"More like a couple of hundred meters," Ellen said. "It's difficult to throw anything very hard. But I'm sure it's far enough."

"Good. That's not what I called you about," Seymour said. "There are two passengers missing."

"Who?" Kevin asked.

"George Lange and that Pacifico person."

"George?" Ellen was incredulous. "He couldn't possibly have had anything to do with sabotaging the ship."

"He's my boss," Kevin said. "Always trying to get me to work. Ellen's right, he's not the saboteur. Pacifico—well, he's another matter."

"I think you ought to have a look around," Seymour said. "But don't take long. We start the engines in ten minutes, and you'll have to be inside before that."

"We'll go in just before the burn," Ellen said. "Until then—somebody put that bomb on the telescope. We'll watch."

"Right. Out," Seymour said.

Ellen moved closer to Kevin. "Turn off your radio," she said. When he did, she put her helmet against his. "Do you have any kind of weapon?"

"Only the knife in my tool kit."

"I wish we had a pistol."

"But—there aren't any pistols aboard, no guns at all."

"How do you know?" she demanded. "Kevin, I'm worried."

"About Pacifico? He's a pip-squeak."

"He seems to be. But if Lange is missing, someone killed him. He wouldn't have any reason to hide. He must have caught the saboteurs in the act, and they killed him."

Kevin tried to remember what little he knew about Lange. It wasn't much. He'd brought Kevin the tapes and made him study them, and he'd talked in a general way about the work Deadalus Corporation would be doing on Ceres. Nothing definite. "How can you be so sure it wasn't Lange who planted the bomb?" Kevin demanded.

"I'm sure. Kevin, I think we should separate. You go watch the port side, I'll watch the starboard. Burn is ten minutes from now. We have to keep anyone from getting up here during the next five minutes. Then we'll be safe; and we'll be able to put the cargo down on Ceres—"

She started to move away, but Kevin caught her and pulled her back until he could put his helmet against hers. "Be careful," he said.

"Sure."

And, he wondered as he crawled toward the port side of the ship, what the hell is that cargo? Captain Greiner talked about it. So does Ellen. Everyone seems to know but me . . . there had been one series of launch capsules that had been guarded by company police and Mexican Army tanks. What could be that valuable?

He reached the edge and looked along the ship, past the hydrogen tanks to the big ring at the end of the ship. Nothing moved. He wondered if he should show a light. If someone really wanted to cripple *Wayfarer,* it would only take puncturing a couple of those tanks.

But that would completely cripple the ship. It would be suicide for the saboteur, and so far whoever was doing this had been careful not to really damage *Wayfarer,* just put the ship out of operation for a few hours until it would be too late to get to Ceres.

If he could reach the telescope, though, he could still keep them from landing.

Lange. Could it have been George Lange? How likely that Pacifico could knock out the antenna and computer power supply? Or kill Lange? Pacifico wasn't much larger than Ellen, while Lange was bigger than Kevin. Not that that meant anything—being large was no real advantage in free fall. It just meant long legs to bump into things. But Kevin doubted that Pacifico knew enough about the ship to have been the saboteur—

He glanced at his watch. Five minutes to burn: time to be getting inside. Even as he thought it, Seymour's voice came into his headset. "That ought to do it," the First Officer said. "Best get into the airlock. We're going to start rotating ship for the burn."

"Right, Ellen—"

"Kev, there's somebody out here with us!" Ellen shouted. "I saw him move. Just then. He's down by the tanks."

"Good Lord." Seymour sounded worried. "But we've got to start maneuvers. We can't stop now—the burn must be exactly on time—exactly!"

"I know," Ellen said quietly. "I'm going after him. Kevin, get inside."

"Don't be silly." He clawed his way over the bow of the ship as she vanished around the far side.

"Hang on," Seymour ordered. "In one minute and . . . three seconds we start turning ship. We have to."

"Right," Kevin answered. "Ellen. What's happening?"

There was no answer. He reached the place where he'd last seen her and looked aft down the length of the ship. There was a flash of light from down there somewhere. He went over, pulling himself along the ladder, trying to make sure he was always holding it.

"If you start the engines I'll puncture the tanks!" came a high pitched voice. Pacifico's. He sounded determined. Afraid but determined. "I'll do it!" the lawyer shouted.

"But—why do you want to keep us from getting to Ceres!" Seymour asked.

"I don't care about that," Pacifico said. "I want to go to Ceres. But you won't get us there! You can't navigate this ship with a suitcase computer; you've no right to risk our lives that way!"

"If you puncture the tanks you'll kill all of us including yourself," Kevin said.

"No I won't. We don't need all the fuel to get back to Earth. Stay away from me! I'll do it—"

"We're turning," Seymour said.

The ship moved slightly as attitude jets fired. It rotated slowly. Kevin didn't find it hard to hang on, and then the counter-jets fired to stop the turn. The ship was now heading almost exactly away from Ceres.

Kevin reached the tankage complex. It was dark among the long hydrogen tanks. "Ellen," he called.

"I see you," she said. "I think he's straight ahead of you."

"Get away from me," Pacifico screamed. "I'll do it, I swear I will!"

Kevin moved further into the tankage complex. Pacifico's voice came from nowhere and everywhere; it was weird, hearing him but being unable to locate him by sound. Kevin wondered if the lawyer had seen him. He saw no one. Not Ellen, not Pacifico. "You idiot, all the tanks are connected together," Kevin said. "If you puncture one of them, you'll let all the fuel escape."

"I don't believe that," Pacifico said. "It wouldn't make sense as a design. Meteoroids—"

"I'm afraid what Senecal is telling you is the truth," Seymour's voice interjected. "The tanks don't connect normally, but when we make preparation for using the main engines we have to interconnect them. Otherwise the fuel would be burned out of one tank at a time and we'd get off balance."

That makes sense, Kevin thought. I wonder if it's true? The important thing is to get Pacifico talking and keep him occupied until we find him. And then what? Kevin fingered the knife in his pouch. That seemed drastic—

"Kev! I've got him! Aft of where you are and around clockwise sixty degrees!" Ellen's voice came in panting gasps.

Kevin moved in the direction she'd indicated. He saw Ellen and the lawyer struggling like clumsy wrestlers, their bulky suits preventing either of them from getting a decisive hold.

"One minute to burn," Seymour said. "Can you get into the airlock?"

" 'Fraid not," Ellen said. "Maybe we'll be all right here among the tanks" Her voice rose. "Kevin!" she shouted in terror.

Both of them had moved away from the ship. Somehow they'd both lost their holds on the ship while trying to fight each other, and now they drifted free, a few feet away, unable to get back.

"My God! Help!" Pacifico screamed.

"Burn in forty seconds," Seymour said.

"You can't!" Pacifico screamed. "It's inhuman! You'll kill us!"

"Can't delay," Seymour said.

And he means that, Kevin thought. Not that Ellen would want him to delay. The Belt operation means too much to her. It's up to me, now. He dove forward, through the tankage. His months of practice in somersaulting through the ship let him get through the tanks in a clean arc.

He caught the ladder at the last possible moment, and reached out toward Ellen. "Grab hold!" he called.

She reached for him, missed by inches. He stretched but couldn't catch her.

"Ten seconds," Seymour announced.

"We're drifting free of the ship!" Pacifico screamed. "You can't do this, you can't—"

Kevin grabbed the safety line on his belt and hooked it to the ladder, then, letting the reel run free, leaped out toward Ellen. He grabbed her with both hands, then grunted with relief.

"You damn fool," she said. "You'll kill yourself—"

"Three. Two. One. Ignite," Seymour said.

The ship's engines started. There was no sound and no flame. Hydrogen was pumped from the tanks and into the nuclear pile on its sting at the end of the ship. The nuclear reactor heated the hydrogen and forced it back through nozzles. The ship drove forward at a tenth of a gravity.

Kevin felt Ellen as a sudden dead weight. He threw in the stop on his belt reel, and they dangled from the ladder, with nothing holding them but the thin nylon line. Pacifico, still screaming, vanished behind as the ship drove forward.

As the ship moved, suddenly they and the safety line formed a pendulum. They felt the acceleration as they would a tenth of Earth's gravity as centrifugal force moved them until they swung back and forth in a small arc directly beneath the ladder. Kevin painfully reached up, still holding Ellen's hand with his. She wasn't heavy, only a tenth of what her weight would have been on Earth, but Kevin wasn't used to *any* gravity. He held tightly, irrationally afraid that the thin nylon line wouldn't hold their combined weight of fifty pounds. He couldn't quite reach the ladder.

"Help! You can't leave me here to die in space! Help!" Pacifico screamed in terror. The ship moved inexorably away from him. Within thirty seconds he would be nearly half a kilometer behind, doomed to the loneliest death possible, alone in a river of stars and the emptiness of space.

"Can you let me down a little further?" Ellen asked. "I can almost reach one of the fuel pipes—"

"No hands." Kevin said. "I've—"

"Here. I've got you," Ellen said. "Now let us down a meter or so."

"How can you be so damned calm?" Kevin snarled.

He let go of her with one hand and reached the ratchet control on his belt line. He let the safety line run free for a second, then locked it again. They both fell toward the aft end of the ship, then were brought up short by the line. The thin nylon held easily.

"There. I've got it," Ellen said. "I've got my safety line clipped to the pipe support. Here—let out more of your line, and I'll pull you over."

Kevin did as he was told. Seconds later he had a purchase on one of the fuel pipes. He looked up—the forward end of the ship was *up* now, and that was strange, to have a definite up and down. The pipe supports formed a ladder of sorts. It wouldn't be hard to climb back to the regular ladder.

"I guess we're safe," Kevin said.

"Thank God," Seymour said. "You're sure?"

"Yes," Kevin said.

They could still hear Pacifico's screams. His signal was growing weaker as he fell farther and farther behind.

"Pacifico," Ellen called. "Who hired you to sabotage the ship?"

"I didn't do it," Pacifico's voice said. "You've got to come back for me! It's not too late, I can see you, please, my God. Please, please come back for me, I didn't do it, I only wanted to stop this mad—"

His voice faded in and out now. "Come back. Please come back, you can find me, please . . ."

Kevin felt Ellen shudder beside him. He put his arm across her shoulders and felt her trembling. "It's all right," he said. "We're all right now—"

She didn't answer. After a while she pointed up toward the ladder. They began to climb. It seemed to take forever to reach the airlock. They thought they heard the lawyer's screams, ever fainter, the whole time.

Chapter Twelve

The office was Aeneas MacKenzie's only real luxury. It had a real window of thick quartz that overlooked the barren landscape of the Moon, and beyond that the glory of Earth hung suspended in black velvet. He often sat at his desk and stared out at the fragile Earth, a small blue world wrapped in white wispy clouds. He had lived on the Moon for twenty years and would never return to the world of his birth; but he loved Earth, and he missed her.

So little time, he thought. So little time until—he broke off the thought, because he had a vivid imagination, and it would be all too easy to see the fragile Earth covered with pinpoints of brilliant light, lights that would shine more brightly than the Sun until they faded and the ugly mushroom clouds rose through Earth's clean garments.

It would be easy, too, to imagine that he could see beneath the clouds, watch men and women working their lives out to no purpose but continued misery and starvation. That was life now for all too many; in a few years the globe might be covered with people who had nothing left to hope for. Desperation might tempt them to anything.

There were faint sounds in the office: the whine of the air system, the faint rumblings of his miners digging into the lunar regolith, other sounds of construction and expansion; the sounds of success, and they mocked him. The future of Diana Base, and of Earth, did not depend on lunar miners. It depended on hard-eyed men in dark suits who sat in Zurich boardrooms; it depended on the man in the Oval Office in Washington, and another man in the Kremlin, another in Kiev, and a dozen scattered across the Middle East; but mostly it depended on events more than a hundred million miles away, and over those Aeneas had no control.

His reverie was interrupted by a voice in his head. It made no sound, and if there had been anyone in the room with him, they would not have heard it; the implanted transceiver fed directly into his nervous system, and took its instructions from his thoughts. He had lived with the implant for so long that it was part of him. He would have missed it if it did not work; but he had never liked it.

"THERE IS A MESSAGE FROM CERES," the voice said.

"IS SHE SAFE?" Aeneas thought. It was a ridiculous question; not even the base central computer had been given enough data to know who he meant.

"CANCEL THAT QUESTION. HOW IS THE MESSAGE SIGNED?"

"HOT LIPS."

Thank God, Aeneas thought. He was careful not to think that into the computer. His prayers were not meant for a machine. "I WANT THE FULL TEXT AS A PRINTOUT," he ordered. It would take a little longer, but he would rather read it than hear it. "DECODE AND PRINT. KEEP NO COPY IN MEMORY."

"ACKNOWLEDGED."

"ASK LAURIE JO TO COME TO ME."

—Pause—"DONE."

And now there was nothing to do but wait. He leaned back in the chair, smoothing his shock of white-gray hair with slender fingers. Even in Luna's low gravity he felt his years. He had been forty when he came to the Moon, and even though Lunar gravity did not age men as much as Earth's did, there had been little rest in the last quarter century. Not for Aeneas MacKenzie. Presently he began to doze. Images formed in his mind.

Economists once thought there could never be a period of both inflation and high unemployment. They were wrong. In the last third of the Twentieth Century both were normal conditions. With millions out of work, governments tried to buy their way to prosperity through deficit financing. They printed bonds and certificates and paper money and more paper money, and soon they were all worthless. Wages and prices spiraled. People who had saved all their lives found their savings worth nothing, less than nothing, and simply to live had to turn for aid to governments that had ruined them in the first place. The governments had to find more and more money, and the printing presses were cheap. The results were predictable, but no less disastrous for being so.

The long struggle between the United States and the Soviet Union ended with complete western victory, but the United States, wealthy beyond the dreams of most of humanity, thought itself exhausted. Before 1940 Washington was a sleepy border town, of no great importance. From 1940 to the end of the century Washington expanded, in size and influence, until all roads led there, and all decisions were made there. The result was paralysis just when energy was needed.

All other Earth governments took in money and spent it on what seemed best to government planners; and all over the Earth there was stagnation, regulation, want in the midst of plenty. We all meant well, Aeneas thought. I meant well, and Greg did, at least at first, and everything we did was wrong. We did more harm than good. But we meant well. . . .

All the nations of Earth faced an impossible dilemma. There wasn't enough money to fund both technological research and welfare programs. Technological research was expensive and directly employed comparatively few people. Soon the science and research and space programs were cut back, cut again, cut once more. Meanwhile the anti-technology movements gained recruits. "Only One Earth." "Alternate Technology." "Ecology." Those slogans and a dozen like them became watchwords, and space programs, energy research, electronics research, all began to die.

For a while private industries continued research programs, but soon the governments, desperate for more funds to spend on popular programs, raised taxes so high that there was nothing left for risk investment. The companies cut back as had the governments; especially so as the consumer advocates forced the corporations to accept consumer representatives on their boards of directors, and the consumer representatives were almost universally dedicated against technology and technological "fixes."

Then the United States was rocked by a series of scandals. Watergate began it, but the scars from that had not healed before another scandal emerged, and another after that. The People's Alliance rose to displace the traditional political parties, and swept into Washington as an irresistible reform movement. Its leader, Greg Tolland, and his manager, Aeneas MacKenzie, were the most popular political figures of the century; but then MacKenzie, as Solicitor General of the United States, found the tentacles of the Equity Trust reached even into Greg Tolland's office, and MacKenzie was both implacable and incorruptible. The result was more loss of confidence, more disgust with democracy, more disillusionment among voters who now believed that the citizens could never control their government.

While the United States was paralyzed by scandals, and what had been the Soviet Union was rocked by nationalistic movements and civil wars within the former empire, a few international corporations banded together to create the first industrial satellites and the first laser-launching system. The heiress Laurie Jo Hansen built the *Heimdall* industrial satellite, and that proved so profitable that other companies first joined with Hansen Enterprises, then set up competing space industries. Based in Zurich and Singapore and Hong Kong and other places of refuge from taxation, the international corporations moved into space even as governments found themselves unable to do so.

Governments looked with envy on the high profits and great potential of space industries. Tolland's lieutenant, Aeneas MacKenzie, led the fight for U.S. takeover of the Hansen empire, ensnarling Hansen Enterprises in a web of legal problems, taxes, regulations, complexities; he might have ended with Hansen nationalized by the United States had not he found corruption in Tolland's staff, and been forced from his office by the President he had created. MacKenzie had to flee for his life, and he had no place to go but to his enemies. From Tolland's Washington MacKenzie went to Laurie Jo Hansen; and because he had known Laurie Jo many years before, and because she with the whole world knew that Aeneas MacKenzie's pledged word was worth more than his life, he became first her consort, then her prime minister, finally her partner.

Yet Tolland and the People's Alliance never forgot who had ruined Tolland's dreams of a country remade by whatever means he thought were needed; his agents had been relentless in pursuit, until Laurie Jo sold out most of her empire to found Diana Station, and took her minister-consort to the Moon. Not even the President of the United States could follow them there.

And by now no one is interested in killing us, Aeneas thought. Except Greg, and he has no real power. The People's Alliance protected him from the scandals, but the real leadership doesn't trust him. Not anymore.

The office door opened without warning and he swiveled quickly. After more than twenty years he loved the sight of her. He suspected the red hair was dyed now, but he had never asked and never would; and despite all the temptations of low gravity, she had kept her figure. Her smile lit the office.

"She's safe," Laurie Jo said.

"For a while."

"Can't you ever simply be happy without worrying about the future?" She did not wait for an answer. Instead she crossed the office quickly and sat in his lap. They kissed with the affection that comes only from long friendship and love. Then Aeneas opened a desk drawer, took out papers from the computer printer concealed there and began to read.

Although she desperately wanted to know what the message said, she did not read over his shoulder, but waited until he had finished the first sheet. He handed it to her without looking up and read the next. There were only two. Then he waited until she had finished.

"They're on Ceres," Laurie Jo said. "With the cargo safe."

"And someone tried to kill her. At least twice. Someone knows," Aeneas said. He cursed, softly. "I'm a fool. I underestimated the danger."

"She knew the risks," Laurie Jo said. "And who else could we trust with something this important?"

"It was a stupid plan. I should never have let her go."

Laurie Jo laughed. "Could you have stopped her?" she demanded. "No one could control *us* at her age, and she believes in this. You could not have stopped me when I was her age."

"God knows I couldn't."

It had been so long ago. She'd been Laurie Jo Preston then, an orphan girl living alone under the guardianship of bankers and supported by trust funds. They'd met at UCLA when Aeneas was political manager for Greg Tolland. No one had ever heard of Greg Tolland then. The young Congressman, just beginning his meteoric career, was one of the founders of the tiny movement that would one day be the People's Alliance, but then it was nothing more than a dream shared by Tolland and Aeneas.

Aeneas and Laurie Jo Preston had two years. They lived together and hitchhiked across the nation, through Mexico and Baja. They sang and drank and made love and were happy with their dreams until her bankers came to tell her that her name was Hansen, not Preston, and that she had inherited one of the largest fortunes on Earth; then everything changed. "I couldn't control you, and I almost lost you forever," Aeneas said.

"Hush." She put a finger gently on his lips, then bent to kiss him again.

"I miss her," Aeneas said.

"I have missed her terribly from the day she decided to go to Earth," Laurie Jo said. "But I'm proud of her."

"And so am I. Laurie Jo, I feel so helpless! Someone knows. If they tried to kill her once, they'll try again. Before she even left Earth! And she didn't tell us."

"Because we would have stopped her."

"It doesn't make sense," Aeneas said. "They tried to kill her before she ever got to the ship. And they tried to stop the ship from landing on Ceres. That makes no sense at all! We hadn't expected trouble before she got to Ceres. They need that cargo as much as we do—"

"My darling husband," Laurie Jo said. "Use your brains. You're letting this be too personal—"

"How could it be otherwise?"

"—and you're making mistakes because of that. Someone wants to stop the ship from landing. They tried. Perhaps it was Pacifico—have you asked for his dossier?"

"Presently. Not yet."

"More likely someone else," Laurie Jo said. "But who-ever it was didn't want *Wayfarer* to land at all. We hadn't expected that."

"No." Aeneas leaned back in his high-backed chair and pressed the tips of his fingers together. His eyes half closed, and his hands pressed gently together, drew apart, pressed together again.

Laurie Jo smiled as she watched him. This was more to her liking. This was the man who had brought down a President.

"So there's another group working in the Belt," Aeneas said.

"You don't sound surprised."

"With billions at stake, I would not be surprised if everyone in the Belt were corrupt," Aeneas said. "How many can resist that kind of temptation? When it is quite feasible to offer bribes in the millions and still make fabulous profits? I expect this was done by the Africans. They don't fancy competition from asteroid mines."

"I don't much blame them," Laurie Jo said. There was sadness in her voice. "They don't have anything to sell except their minerals, and we're driving the price down and down."

Aeneas nodded. They'd discussed all this before. Ruin for the African bloc meant prosperity for the rest of the world; cheap iron and steel and copper and aluminum, the basic stuff of industrial civilization, would let billions live well who now had no hope at all. Eventually it would mean prosperity for the Africans themselves, but not soon, and not for those who now controlled the African bloc.

"So we are facing two sets of enemies," Laurie Jo said.

"Probably more. At least two. One group wishes to stop the shipments altogether. I doubt they have finished. They'll keep trying, but they won't have many allies in the Belt. It's the others I worry about—and George Lange is dead. She won't have his help." Aeneas leaned back again, his hands moving slowly and gently.

Laurie Jo waited. "VALKYRIE STATUS REPORT." The words formed in her head with no accent, but she always knew when she heard Aeneas speak to the computer, although she could not have told how that was different from hearing the computer report to her.

"READY FOR DEPARTURE IN FIVE HUNDRED HOURS," the computer told them.

"EARLIEST POSSIBLE ARRIVAL TIME ON CERES?"

"ONE HUNDRED AND TWENTY DAYS FROM PRESENT TIME."

"With Lange dead, we'll have to send someone else," Aeneas said.

"Who? There's no one we can trust with something this important. And neither of us can go. Nothing has changed, Aeneas. We're needed here. If we lose control now, there's no point to any of this. We'll lose everything we've worked hard for."

"I know. We can only trust ourselves. Or the boy. Or we could give it all up."

"Neither of us will."

"No. Neither of us will."

She didn't care for the tone he had used, and she looked at him sternly. He was leaning back again, his fingers moving in the familiar pattern that she knew meant he was lost in thought; and she was frightened even before he spoke again.

"There's a better way," he said. "The boy's more valuable here."

"*No.*" Her voice rose. "I lost you for sixteen years once! And then almost lost you again, when we'd just found each other. I will not be separated from you again. I will not."

"Laurie Jo." His voice was very calm now. "You can manage the finances. You're better at it than I am, and you *must* stay here; but I've outgrown my usefulness."

"That's not true, you're the base commander—"

"A function that Kit Penrose can fill as well as I can," Aeneas said. "And Kit can train young Aeneas, who will be far more useful here than floundering around out in the Belt. He's not ready for this, Laurie Jo. I don't think our daughter was ready either, but I know our son isn't. He can help you, yes. He understands boardroom tactics, and he's becoming a better engineer than Kit, but he does not know intrigue and corruption. Not yet."

"Nor do you!" she shouted.

"Now really, Laurie Jo—"

"Aeneas, it has been twenty years since you were Solicitor General—"

"Laurie Jo." His voice was quiet and his tone calm.

"And I won't lose you again—"

"I am still a very careful man," Aeneas said. "There is not much risk to me—and I am less valuable than our son. We cannot risk both heirs. If it is a choice between myself and young Aeneas, there is no choice at all, nor would I be—" He stopped, because her face had changed.

She had lost her anger. Now her expression held only sadness.

"You know I'm right," he said. He was not insisting; he merely stated a fact they both understood. She nodded; then buried her face against his shoulder.

"I love you," she said. Then she tried once more, but only because she had to: "Couldn't Kit go? Or—"

"He couldn't, and there is no one else. Not for this. Is there?"

"No. You or our son."

"And thus me." He kissed her gently. "We have twenty days. And when I return, we'll have many more. I'll come back, Laurie Jo. I always have."

"Yes," she said, and she turned away from him quickly so that he would not see the glistening tears in her blue eyes.

Chapter Thirteen

Henri Stoire was a satisfied man, and what's more, he was certain he had every right to be pleased with himself. Since he'd come to Ceres as Interplanet's resident general manager, the output of the mines and refineries had tripled. The enormous Mylar plastic mirror, over two kilometers in diameter, hung in synchronous orbit 760 kilometers above the asteroid, providing heat and light for the colony twenty-four hours a day (he still thought of days as having twenty-four hours even though Ceres rotates once each nine hours, five minutes). More miners arrived each month, the capacity of the refineries continued to expand, and a prospecting party had found a large vein of nearly pure water-ice deep under the surface, thus insuring both drinking water and reaction fuel for the nuclear ships like *Wayfarer*.

Henri Stoire was satisfied, but his superiors were not. His production goals were set in Zurich by men who knew nothing of the conditions on Ceres, but who knew a lot about international competition, manipulation of commodity futures, and always about banking and money; the goals they set were high. Of course, Henri thought when he tried to be fair, the costs of the Ceres operation were very high as well. It took eleven new francs to get one kilogram from Earth's surface to Earth orbit, a hundred more to get it to Ceres, and Ceres required thousands of metric tons of supplies, food, equipment, and men, always more men. The return had to be high or the investment couldn't be justified.

Henri met their ever-increasing production goals, but his costs were always higher than estimated. No incentive bonuses for Stoire, not this year. Perhaps when a full cargo from the Belt reached Earth orbit . . . even iron ore delivered to Earth orbit would be highly valuable for more orbital factory construction. Iron in orbit would sell for almost Fr. 12,000 a metric ton, and Henri had ten thousand tons to ship, along with one thousand tons of tin (Fr. 6,720,000), fifteen hundred tons of nearly pure silver (Fr. 315,000,000) and a few hundred million francs' worth of assorted other metals. The total value of the cargo he would shortly send down would be considerably more than half a billion francs; a respectable sum indeed. Now he had only to get the shipment to Earth. The incentive bonuses would follow.

Actually, Interplanet's bonuses interested Henri far less than his employers—or at least most of them—knew. True, Henri had enormous debts, the result of unwise speculations: had he known as much about the international commodity market as the men who set his production goals did, Henri would never have come to Ceres in the first place. His debts were further increased by Henri's unfortunate addiction to chemin de fer and roulette, and his even less fortunate tendency to borrow money from any source available. He had been born a rich man, of a great and wealthy family, and he had lost everything. He needed money.

Although Zurich's bonuses were not small by normal standards, Henri needed far more money than could be acquired by ordinary means. Had his employers known just how much money Henri owed, they would never have sent him to Ceres, or anywhere else; but his creditors were careful men who never advertised the names of those who borrowed from them; and they had many suggestions for Henri. There was no way, bonuses or not, that Henri could earn what he owed; but with any luck he would leave Ceres with his debts paid and more money than he had ever had in his life. If all that was merely a small part of the profits his creditors would make from his work, Henri was not an avaricious man. He truly believed that he asked for no more than he was entitled to and certainly he had high abilities.

Henri was a small man, very neat in appearance. Even on Ceres he looked neat, and that was often very difficult. His small size was no handicap in space. In many ways it was a decided advantage. In low gravity, long legs were mostly good for running into hard objects and otherwise getting in the way.

Though small, Henri was no weakling. He exercised daily and he was always willing to give the men a hand with a tough job. Henri could do the job of nearly any man in his employ; he took great pride in that, and it was certainly a useful ability. Some of his latest activities, those in favor of his creditors and unknown to his employers in Zurich, could not have been accomplished if Henri had not understood every detail of the automated refinery operation, known how to construct conveyor systems, dig out chambers in rock with explosives. . . .

Those skills, though needed, were not the key to his plan for resuming his place among the idle rich in Monte Carlo. More important than any of them was the study he had made of computer operations. That was the key to it all, and it had gone so smoothly that had Henri been a superstitious man, he might have been frightened.

Sometimes he was appalled by what he was doing. He felt no guilt about betraying the Directors of the Interplanet combine; if they paid him what he was worth, he would not have to resort to embezzlement. (Henri preferred to think of it as misallocation of company resources, or even as a legitimate perquisite to his office.) He felt no guilt, but he was sometimes disturbed by the sheer magnitude of the operation. Not only was something like one hundred million francs involved—and that was a large enough sum to impress even Henri Stoire—but also the follow-up implications would be even larger. Mankind had never succeeded in getting nuclear fusion to work on a commercial scale. Fission worked fine and had since the 1950s, but the far more valuable and efficient fusion process continued to be too expensive, too difficult; and the result was a continuing energy crisis that affected nearly every nation on Earth. Fertilizer prices depended on energy prices, which meant that energy prices controlled how much the poor would eat. Cheap fusion would bring cheap food—and Henri was turning fusion over to a gang of international criminals.

Still, he felt no guilt. If food was dear, it was because people were cheap. If the fools wished their children to eat well, let them either work to earn enough money or have fewer children. It was no concern of Henri's what happened to children in India, Bangla-Desh, Africa, South America. . . .

Nor was he worried about being caught. As manager for Interplanet he controlled the only police force on Ceres. The company guards worked for him and took his orders. The accountants reported to him and could only gain access to the computer through him. They could ask Interplanet's computer questions as long as they liked; even if they knew the real questions they should ask, it would not tell them without his authorization, and they didn't know anyway. Besides, in a few weeks it would all be over, and there would be no record of what Henri had done.

Henri Stoire sat at his desk, the only real desk on Ceres and a mark of his importance, and despite his satisfaction with himself and his work, he frowned as he read the report brought to him by Captain Greiner.

Wayfarer had arrived with cargo intact; excellent. But someone had tried to prevent the ship from coming to Ceres, and that was not. *Wayfarer's* cargo was the key to everything. Without it they would never get all that iron and copper and tin and silver to Earth. Who had done this?

It took him only moments to dismiss Pacifico. The lawyer had been sent by Zurich, and was rumored to be a clever accountant as well. He would have been a nuisance, and it was as well that he was dead; but he had almost certainly not been responsible for nearly crippling *Wayfarer.* No. It was very likely that Pacifico's part was exactly what he had said it was, a frightened man trying to keep Captain Greiner from taking high risks with the ship.

Nor was it likely that the missing George Lange had been the saboteur. The Daedalus Corporation had far too much at stake, and they hired carefully. Daedalus was responsible for getting Henri's cargo safely back to Earth; the loss of one of their senior engineers would be inconvenient, possibly worse than that. All true. But Daedalus had a deeper role in this game. Henri's creditors had warned him that Daedalus, supposedly owned by other Zurich bankers and itself one of the stockholders in the consortium that created Interplanet, had its nose in far too many places. His creditors suspected that Daedalus worked for very powerful interests indeed—possibly even for MacKenzie and Hansen; that Daedalus engineers were often spies reporting to Interplanet stockholders, and whenever they were around, Henri should be careful. The warning was appreciated but not needed; Henri was always careful. But it made it unlikely that Lange had tried to sabotage *Wayfarer*. Far more probably Lange had been snooping around and had caught the saboteur, and was put outside the ship for his trouble.

So who might it be? Henri scanned the passenger and crew lists. Anyone might be an African sympathizer—Henri had already concluded the African bloc was the most likely sponsor of the sabotage—and that would not necessarily show in the kind of resumes sent out with passengers. Or the saboteur could be working for money. He lifted a microphone.

"READY," the computer said.

"I WANT COMPLETE DOSSIERS ON ALL PAS-SENGERS AND CREW ARRIVING ABOARD *WAY-FARER*. HIGHEST PRIORITY REQUEST TO ZURICH HEADQUARTERS. JUSTIFICATION: NECESSITY TO IDENTIFY SABOTEUR."

"ACKNOWLEDGED."

He returned to his scrutiny of the passenger list. He read names and specialties, paying no particular attention to what he saw, until he came to "Norsedal, Jacob. Computer Specialist. To be supervisor of computer operations, Interplanet."

He read it again, then cursed. Zurich had not told him of this! True, he had requested a new programmer, but he was satisfied with his computer staff and its acting head. He had certainly not sent for any experts to take control; under his present arrangement Henri himself was the real supervisor of computer operations, and he liked it that way.

This could be bothersome, especially now. Did Zurich suspect something? He would have to be very careful with this Norsedal. Was Norsedal curious? An agent of Zurich? He must be watched closely. Henri continued to scan the list.

MacMillan, Ellen. Engineer, no employer. Henri smiled at that. Every ship brought two or three unemployed single women, and most claimed to be some kind of engineer. They might very well have their degrees, but generally they made a great deal more money in a far older occupation. He wondered where the MacMillan girl would go. To one of the established houses, or would she prey on the miners and prospectors and refinery workers from her own quarters? From curiosity he lifted the microphone again, "I WANT A PHOTOGRAPH OF

ELLEN MACMILLAN, PASSENGER ON WAY-
FARER."

"ACKNOWLEDGED."

A few seconds later the facsimile emerged from a slot
at the side of his desk. He looked it over, smiling at the
blonde hair and blue eyes, pug nose; a pretty girl, young,
one who would command a high price, for a while. Then
the smile faded. Was there something familiar about the
face? Where might he have seen it before?

No. He was certain he had never seen the girl. But
she reminded him of someone. He did not know who,
but it was disturbing. She reminded him of someone he
feared. He laughed to himself, because he feared no one;
but he kept the photograph and put a tick mark against
her name on the list to remind him to take some care
with her dossier when it arrived.

Henri Stoire was a careful man indeed.

Chapter Fourteen

Kevin wandered through rock corridors, not quite lost but not entirely sure of where he was. He was somewhere inside the Ceres complex and as long as he did not go through an airtight door, he couldn't be very far from the central area; but he was looking for Ellen and he didn't have any idea of where to find her.

When *Wayfarer* landed, the passengers had to help unload the ship and transfer cargo—most of the cargo, Kevin reminded himself. One compartment remained sealed. When Kevin's share of the work was over, many of the passengers had already gone inside. Kevin followed through the airlock doors, relieved to be off the harsh and barren surface of the asteroid. No one would say that Ceres was a pretty place, although the stars were spectacular; but Kevin had had enough stars to last him a long time.

Why had Ellen left without telling him where she was going? he wondered. He would have to report in for work soon, and they might not have much time together until he could find out where he would be stationed. Then they could arrange something more permanent.

The corridors shone. They had been painted with plastic to seal in air leaks, so that it was possible to move around inside the Ceres Station without a helmet. There were lights at intervals. Kevin hoped to see someone to ask directions from, but before he did, he came to a signpost.

It showed DAEDALUS CORPORATE OFFICES just one corridor down. Kevin went there eagerly. They could tell him where he would be staying.

There was an elderly man in the Daedalus Corporation offices. The offices themselves were merely two rooms cut in raw rock off the corridor. They were obviously little used; there was almost no furniture, and an automatic message-recording system was the only piece of large office equipment.

The man was well over fifty, with a network of red lines around his mouth and chin that betrayed long exposure to face masks. He had wrinkles at the corners of his eyes, and much gray in his hair. He frowned at Kevin. "You'll be Senecal."

"Yes."

"I'm John Eliot. Senior man for Daedalus out here. You got our other people with you?"

"No—"

"You should have. You're an engineer. It's your responsibility to look after non-professional employees.

Now we'll have to go find them. We don't have much time. Time, Senecal, is the most valuable commodity in the Belt just now."

"Yes, sir. Look, Mr. Eliot—"

"Call me Johnny. We'll either be friends or you'll hate me before long, but either way, it works better if we use first names."

"Johnny. Yes, sir. I am Kevin."

"Yeah. I know. You were saying something?"

"Mr.—Johnny, this is my first job. I'm no professional. I'm just an engineering student, and the idea of my looking after people twice my age is funny. They wouldn't take orders from me."

"We'll see. Did they get on all right with Lange?"

"Yes, sir."

"Too bad about him," Eliot said. "What happened, anyway?"

Kevin explained all he knew. "George just vanished," he finished. "Never did find him, no trace of him. Nothing."

"His stuff missing?"

"No," Kevin said. "Captain Greiner has it. He didn't know what to do with it."

"We'll collect it before we go up. May as well see to that, and to finding our workmen. You can leave that gear here."

"All right." Kevin set down the travel cases he carried and started to go out into the corridor.

"Nope," Eliot said. "Get your hat. Didn't they teach you that? First rule, never go *anywhere* without your helmet. We don't often have blow-outs on Ceres, but it only takes one to kill you if you don't have your hat with you. Remember that."

"Yes, sir." Kevin retrieved his helmet, then thoughtfully put on his tool belt as well.

"Good," Eliot said. "Now let's go." He led the way through the bare rock corridor. "They'll probably be at Fat Jack's," Eliot said. "Most head there when they get off work or off a ship. Surprised you didn't get there first."

"I was hoping someone would tell me where I will be staying," Kevin said. "I didn't see any hotels—"

Eliot laughed. "Hell, you won't be staying on Ceres."

"Sir? Johnny? If we won't be staying on Ceres, where will we be?"

"Didn't Lange tell you anything?" Eliot demanded. "Don't you even know what you'll be working on?"

"No, sir. I asked once, and he said I'd find out in due time. But I never did."

Eliot laughed. "Well, that was the company's orders all right, but it's damn foolishness. Everybody on Ceres knows our big secret, not that it's anything to be secret about anyway. Daedalus is responsible for the delivery system to get cargo to Earth. We're building it. I expect Lange kept everything about that a big secret too?"

"Yes—"

"Okay. Up there about a thousand kilometers above Ceres there's a rock a couple of hundred meters in diameter. It's mostly nickel-iron, good stuff. We're busily mining out corridors and putting in life-support systems. When we're done, we'll pack it with all the refined minerals Interplanet has collected and take it home."

"Take a two-hundred-meter rock home? How?" Kevin demanded. "It must weigh five million tones—"

"Thirty million," Eliot said. "Hell, it's simple. We put hydrogen bombs at just the right place—have to calculate the center of gravity pretty carefully—and light 'em off. Do that a few times and we'll have that rock in just the right transfer orbit. Off she goes to Earth. Down there they do it again to stop it. No sweat." Eliot chuckled. He was obviously enjoying the look on Kevin's face. "Lange really didn't tell you, eh? Well, that's what we're up to. You brought the bombs with you, on *Wayfarer*. That's why everybody got so excited down here when we heard you were in trouble. Needed the H-bombs. Without 'em, we'd really have troubles. No other way to get all that stuff home."

"And somebody's going to ride this thing to Earth?" Kevin said.

"Sure. Safest place around. There'll be a couple of hundred meters of nickel-iron and rock between the crew and the bombs—what could happen?"

That made sense, but Kevin still didn't like the idea much. "Are we supposed to be the crew?"

"Naw. Interplanet provides the crew. They wouldn't trust a half-billion francs' worth of cargo to anybody but their own people. Understand the manager, Mr. Stoire himself, is going. Guess I can't blame them much."

They moved on through the rock corridor. In Ceres's low gravity they couldn't walk, nor could they simply glide from place to place as they would in no gravity at all. Instead they moved in a series of bounds, like oversized kangaroos.

They came to a cross corridor, and Eliot turned down it. There were bright lights at the end, their glare contrasting with the dim light in the corridor. They heard sounds: shouting and singing. Happy sounds.

"That's Fat Jack's place," Eliot said. "Best bar on Ceres. Mainly because it's the only bar here. Pretty good place, though. You can get nearly anything you want. Not that you'll be here all that often."

Kevin had already thought of that. "Don't we get to come—down to Ceres?"

"Sure, the company provides recreation trips when we're caught up on the work. Don't cost that much to run the scooters."

It looked as if everyone who had come in *Wayfarer*, and half the permanent crew of Ceres, were packed into Fat Jack's. The proprietor was a burly man with no legs. When one of the newcomers asked why he hadn't gone back to Earth, the owner laughed.

"Sure, they'll pay my way back and give me a goddam pension, but I don't want it. What the hell use is a cripple on Earth? Out here I don't need legs." He waved to indicate the crowd in his saloon. "I make my own beer and whiskey and I get good prices. I've got a thousand friends. What do I want with Earth?"

The saloon consisted of a large chamber carved from rock, a few tables and booths, and one long bar running across the back of the room.

All the drinks were served in covered containers with straws, although most of the customers had learned the art of popping open the top, sucking out a drink, and closing it before their beer or whiskey drifted away.

Kevin pointed out the Daedalus employees, and Eliot went to round them up. While Kevin was waiting, Ellen came in. Bill Dykes was with her.

"Hi," Kevin shouted. He went over to them. "Glad I found you. They want me to go up to one of Ceres's moons—"

"C-4," Dykes said. "The one they're fitting up as a spaceship."

"Right. How did you know?" Kevin asked.

Dykes shrugged. "No secret what Daedalus does. Everybody on Ceres knows about the H-bombs. Wonder why they were so damn close-mouthed aboard *Way-farer.*"

"Well, they *are* hydrogen bombs," Kevin said.

"Sure. And bombs can kill people. Lots of other ways to get killed out here. I need a drink. You, Ellie?"

"Yes, thank you."

Dykes went to fight his way to the bar.

"I get some recreation visits," Kevin said. "I won't see you often at first, only when I'm down. Where will you be staying?"

"I—I'll be staying with Bill," Ellen said.

It took Kevin a moment to understand what she had said. "In his—"

"Yes, I'll be living with him."

"But—damn it, he's old enough to be your father!" Kevin shouted. He wanted to say more: That at first she had put him off because she didn't want lasting attachments, and now they were lovers, and what was this? Bitterness made him say more: "I get it. He can pay you more than I can."

"It's none of your damned business," she said. She spoke loudly, so that many of the people in the bar could hear her. "You don't own me and you have no right to make judgments."

"No. I don't suppose I do," Kevin said. "Except—except that I thought we were friends."

"If you're my friend, you don't act much like it," Ellen said.

"Trouble, Ellie?" Dykes was back, without the drinks he'd gone after.

"Not really," she said.

"Kevin. Are you about ready to leave?" John Eliot called.

"Yes. I'll wait for you outside," Kevin said. He turned and left without looking at Ellen.

"Hell, this place is getting to be a drag," Bill Dykes said. His voice carried through the room and out to where Kevin stood. "Let's split and throw our own party."

"All right," Ellen giggled. It was obvious what kind of party Dykes had in mind. She followed the miner out. They came past Kevin, and as they did, Ellen said, very quietly, "Kevin. Please. I know you don't understand, but please trust me. And for God's sake, don't let anyone know I've said anything to you. Make people believe you hate me." With that she went on without looking back, and when Dykes made a loud ribald comment about Kevin, she laughed.

Ceres has five moons, if you can call small rocks a few hundred meters in diameter "moons." Three of them had been extensively mined, but two had been temporarily abandoned when better grades of ore were found on Ceres itself. The other one, C-4, was Kevin's home for the next few weeks.

There was plenty of work and not enough people to do it. First, the asteroid had to be surveyed to find the exact center of gravity. Once that was located, a pit was to be dug for the hydrogen bombs that would be used to turn the tiny moon into an enormous rocket ship. On the opposite side the Daedalus crew would carve out chambers for the crew to live in, more compartments for the gold and silver and copper and other refined metals produced on Ceres. Meanwhile, another crew would set up huge mirrors on C-4 and use those to concentrate sunlight so they could boil and refine the ores extracted from the planetoid. "No point in wasting anything," Eliot had said.

When they were finished, C-4 would carry a cargo worth nearly a billion francs. In addition, the asteroid itself would be valuable—nearly ten million metric tons of nickel-iron, which would end up in Earth orbit. Refineries there would extract the iron to use in space construction. Even the twenty million tons of rock would be useful in orbit. The asteroid could be used as a platform.

Kevin's job was installation of the life-support equipment for the flight crew. With the help of miners and a lot of mining machinery, he hollowed out the crew chambers, then sprayed them with a thick coating of plastic; when the plastic dried, the chambers were airtight. Airlock doors were machined from chunks of the moonlet itself, and set on hinges. Sometimes the whole structure reminded Kevin more of a series of bank vaults than a spaceship; everything was massive, and rather crudely made.

There were no work shifts, there was simply a job that had to be done. Eliot explained what was needed and was available for consultation. Otherwise he left Kevin alone. When one task was completed Eliot would check it out, then assign another.

Kevin found the job exacting, but it was important work, and everyone was enthusiastic about it. They were taking part in something that might change man's future.

"Think about it," Eliot said. "If we can get all of Earth's metals out here, they won't have to strip-mine on Earth. No pollution down there. You know, in fifty years Earth can be one big park, with all the industries out in space."

Kevin became lost in a maze of calculations: food, oxygen, and water consumption for a crew of two (with standby provision for three) on a trip four hundred days long; g stresses which the equipment would endure when the one-megaton H-bombs went off; finding stress seams in the nickel-iron moonlet so they could be reinforced. Slowly the "ship" began to look like something that could support human life, with fuel cells for electric power, caves of ice for water and cooling, telescopes and radar for finding the exact position; navigation computer, galley, bunk rooms—with a separate stateroom for each of the crew, there being no space limits at all.

Finally Eliot relented and took the work crew down to Ceres. They went in a scooter much like the one used to get from the Earth satellite to *Wayfarer*: an open framework with seats for the passengers, a baggage compartment, and a large kerosene-oxygen rocket engine. The scooters also had a navigation computer; C-4 moved around Ceres at more than a third of a kilometer each second, and the total velocity change needed to get from the "moon" to Ceres was more than eight hundred miles an hour. The transfer orbit was tricky.

Kevin talked with the scooter pilot in Fat Jack's after they arrived on Ceres.

"Yeah, sure, I could eyeball it," Hal Donnelly said. "But it'd be tough. Not like flying an airplane." Donnelly had once been a test pilot, and would be one of the crew accompanying C-4 on the long trip to Earth. "Airplanes have air to work with. You can turn a corner, or slow down. Scooter doesn't work that way."

Kevin wasn't really listening to the pilot. He was thinking about Ellen. There had been so much work on C-4 that he hadn't had much time to brood about her before—except when he was ready to go to sleep at night—but he had felt a quick excitement when Eliot announced they were going down to Cerès, and he hoped to see her. He didn't know what to say to her, but there had to be some way—

He didn't know how to ask about her. He was afraid of what he would hear. His fellow workers on C-4 had talked about the various prostitutes on Ceres, and although none of them had mentioned Ellen by name, they all assumed that any single woman who came out not under contract to one of the companies could have only one purpose in mind.

Why the hell was she living with Bill Dykes? She'd hardly spoken to Dykes on the ship. She certainly hadn't known him very well, yet she moved in with him her first day on Ceres. It didn't make sense.

Of course it makes sense, Kevin thought. She likes the guy and I just didn't know it. She's got every right to move in with anybody she wants to and you've got no call to be jealous about it. She said everything would be over when they got to Ceres. It was just a shipboard thing. He could tell himself that, but it didn't help.

"You haven't heard a damned thing I said," Hal Donnelly said. "You drink my liquor but you don't listen to me." The pilot was grinning slightly.

"Oh—uh, sorry," Kevin said.

"No sweat. I know what you need. I'm about to go looking for a little poon myself. I know a good house. Want to come along?"

The idea was not attractive. Kevin still hoped to meet Ellen. He knew that wasn't very reasonable, and that she was likely to be with someone else, but there was always a chance—"Thanks, Hal. Not just yet. I'll have a couple more."

The pilot shrugged. "Suit yourself. We lift out of here in thirty-four hours. Meet you here."

"Right. And thanks for the drink."

" 'S okay. You'll get me one next time. Right now I've got a more urgent urge. . . ." Hal grinned again and left the bar.

And just what the hell am I doing here? Kevin wondered. I don't know anybody in this place. He ordered another drink. The vacuum-distilled whiskey was rough and strong and cost too much. Kevin sipped at it disconsolately.

He didn't want to leave because Fat Jack's was the place where everyone came to find people. The recreation schedule for the C-4 crew was known and posted in Fat Jack's. If Ellen wanted to see him, she'd know where to find him.

Jacob Norsedal came into the bar. "Hello," he said. He took a place across from Kevin. There was no real need to sit in Ceres' low gravity, but the habit dies hard; and it is convenient to anchor yourself in one place. "I've been computing the trajectory your moonlet will take back to Earth."

"I'm still not sure this will work," Kevin said.

Norsedal looked surprised. "Of course it will. Think of it as a fusion spacedrive. Plenty of energy in a megaton. One million tons of TNT, ten-to-the-twenty-second ergs . . ."

"I wasn't thinking about the energy," Kevin said. "It's the navigation. We can't really locate the center of gravity all that well—too much guesswork."

"Run it off," Norsedal said. He offered his belt computer. "Takes a lot of energy to get that much iron to rotate. So they're off a little—you've got little tamped-implosion kiloton bombs to correct that, and the rocket motors for fine adjustment."

"Yeah, I've seen the numbers," Kevin said. "It looks silly as hell, mounting big rocket engines on the ground. Big things." The four Saturn-sized rocket engines were mounted in a cruciform pattern, pointing away from the center of the cross. They would be used to turn C-4 in the right direction. "But it's still using *bombs*," Kevin said.

Norsedal shrugged. It was obvious that to him bombs were just another device to channel energy; it was doubtful that he thought of them as bombs at all, or even imagined the real devices. They were more input numbers into his equations, data to be fed into the computer. "Have you seen much of Ceres?" Jacob asked.

"No. I was only here a few hours after *Wayfarer* landed, and this is my first trip down since."

"Well, I know a good place to eat," Norsedal said. "The food in the Interplanet commissary is all right, but it's nothing to rave about. I can find some real steaks—"

"Steaks? Terrific. We've been eating reconstituted stew. And textured vegetable proteins. And—"

"Spare me those horrors," Norsedal said. He patted his ample belly. "If I had to eat that way, I'd waste to nothing. Come on, let's get a good dinner." He hustled Kevin out of the bar and off to one of the rock corridors.

Ceres was honeycombed with passages. Some were still used as working mines. Others were abandoned mine shafts, now used as part of the living quarters. There were airlocks at intervals along the corridors.

Jacob led the way through a maze of passages, and soon they were a long way from the inhabited parts of Ceres Station.

"Where the hell are we going?" Kevin demanded.

"Shortcut." Norsedal continued to scurry along. As he'd predicted when Kevin first met him, his weight and ungainly appearance were no handicaps in low gravity. They turned another corner and went upward. There was an airlock there.

Jacob came very close to Kevin and spoke softly, almost a whisper. "We're going outside now. Please, just follow me, and don't use your suit radio whatever you do."

"But—why?" Kevin kept his voice low to match Norsedal's.

"Will you trust me? It's important."

Kevin nodded. He'd known Norsedal through the whole trip out; whatever Jacob was doing, it wasn't dishonest. He put on his helmet.

Norsedal opened the airlock and they went through the double doors. It was night outside on Ceres, but the overhead synchronous satellite mirror left the surface bathed in light. Down in the crevasse where the airlock opened they could see only by starlight, and Norsedal did not use a flash. He led the way, Kevin following closely.

Then he turned into a cavern so deep that there was no light at all. He went on, downward, and turned a corner before he switched on a flash. Then he gestured, finger to lips, and went around another turn.

There was an inflatable shelter there with its own airlock. The outer door stood open. Jacob gestured toward it, then followed Kevin in. There was the hiss of pumps and the airlock chamber pressurized, then the inner door opened.

Ellen MacMillan was inside.

Chapter Fifteen

"I don't think anyone noticed us leaving," Norsedal said. "But I'll have to get back quickly. I have to go on duty in the computer center."

Kevin hardly heard him. He was staring at Ellen. He thought she was lovely. "But—"

"We'll explain," she said. "I wanted to keep you out of this, Kevin, but I can't. I need help. Will you help me?"

"I'll try. But—"

"Yes. It's such a long story, I don't know where to begin," she said. "Kevin, I didn't come here to work as an engineer. Or to be a prostitute, either."

"I never thought that," Kevin said quickly.

"That's sweet of you. But I hope everybody else does," she said. "I'm really not very good at the secret-agent business. Kevin, I—I work for some of the owners of

Interplanet. For Hansen Enterprises. They have a contract for all the Arthurium mined in the Belt."

Arthurium. One of the super-heavy elements. In the first quarter of the Twentieth Century scientists thought there were only ninety-two elements. Then the nuclear engineers discovered they could make plutonium, and californium, and a host of other elements heavier than uranium-92, but all the new elements were unstable. Finally a stable natural element, atomic number of 124, was discovered. In the years that followed, other super-heavy elements were found, but only in trace amounts. The super-heavies were in the cores of the planets, and planetary cores are hard to get to: thousands of miles underground.

Ceres was only a couple of hundred miles in radius, but had once been the core of a much larger planet: there were super-heavy elements in abundance. Abundance is a relative term, of course: the supers are still very rare, found only in fractions-of-a-percent concentration; but they were available, and the most valuable of all was Arthurium, a member of the Tin-Niobium family, with the property of being superconductive at temperatures far higher than any other known superconductors.

"And somebody is stealing the Arthurium," Jacob Norsedal said. "I'm sure of it."

"That's what I came out to look into," Ellen said. "When the manager here reported only a few kilograms of Arthurium had been extracted, we wondered. Understand, it might have been true. Arthurium is very rare. But from the original assay figures, we thought there should be hundreds of kilograms of Arthurium, and we—Hansen Enterprises—need it. Hansen scientists think they can solve the fusion problem if they have enough!"

Kevin found a place to sit. The shelter wasn't well furnished; in fact it wasn't furnished at all; but there were several boxes of gear stacked at one end next to the pumps and air supply, and Kevin found a perch on them. He tried to digest the information he'd been given. Fusion power would be priceless. And Arthurium, the little that was known to exist, sold for over a hundred thousand francs per kilogram. Hundreds of millions of francs, perhaps billions, were at stake here.

"What do you want with me?" he asked. His voice was harsh.

"Why are you angry?" Ellen asked.

He didn't say anything.

"Dykes," Jacob Norsedal prompted.

"Oh." Ellen smiled. "Kevin, Bill Dykes has known my father for—since long before I was born. He worked for Hansen Enterprises on the Moon. When I needed a place to stay, I had to ask him, because I was afraid someone here might suspect me, and I didn't want anyone else to get hurt. They killed George Lange, don't forget. I have no right to ask your help, but I don't know where else to go."

"You mean—" Kevin's grin was broad and sheepish. "And I almost drove myself crazy thinking about you and—"

"I'm sorry."

"I have to get back," Norsedal said. "If anyone asks, I'll say you didn't want steak after all and went to find a cat house. I doubt that anyone is interested in you, Kevin, but they might be and it's best to have a story."

"I must be stupid," Kevin said. "I don't know where you fit into this, Jacob."

"He's an honest man," Ellen said.

"I was hired by the Zurich office," Norsedal said. "And I'm supposed to report directly to them if I find anything wrong. Not that Zurich is suspicious of the management here, but with all that money at stake, they wanted an independent check—to make certain."

"Just as we did," Ellen said. "Only we were suspicious."

"And you found something?" Kevin asked.

"Yes." Norsedal nodded vigorously. "There are whole memory areas in the computer banks that I can't access. And the programs run too long. That means the computer is following instructions that don't appear in the flow diagrams. I haven't found out what's going on yet, but I think I will. I managed to get a print-out of the computer's core, all the instructions. They're in binary of course, so it takes time to analyze what I have, but I'm sure there are operations going on that don't appear in the log. Mining operations, for example."

"And in the refinery," Ellen said. "It wouldn't take much to cover up a few hundred kilograms missing among all the thousands of tons of rock they process, tons of gold they've extracted—"

"And the refinery is nearly automatic," Norsedal added. "I can use the computer to find out just who might be involved by analyzing the work schedules, but I've been afraid to do that until I know just who's been using it and for what. It might be programmed to tell whenever people ask that kind of question." Norsedal went to the airlock and squeezed through the narrow inner door. "Good luck." He closed the lock and started the pumps.

"How does he—why are you two working together?" Kevin asked. "Are you sure you can trust him?"

"Yes. Henri Stoire, the manager, sent for dossiers on all the passengers aboard *Wayfarer*. They came twenty hours ago, and Jacob had to pass them along—but he figured out who I am from my resume sheets."

"If he could, so can Stoire—"

"I know," Ellen said. She sounded worried. "That's why I'm here. I don't know what to do. Ever since Stoire got the dossiers, there's been no communication from Ceres to Earth. The equipment has malfunctioned, Stoire says—but Jacob says it hasn't."

"And who are you?" Kevin demanded.

"Do you really want to know—no. Please, Kevin. I don't want to tell you."

"All right." He went to her and held out his arms. After a moment she crossed the tiny distance that remained and kissed him.

"Not very passionate in these pressure suits," Ellen laughed.

"We could—" She looked at him sharply. "Oh, hell," he said. "You wanted my help. I won't complicate things by—Ellen, I think I've been in love with you for a long time. Damn it, I know I am. Why else would it have bothered me so much when I thought you were living with Bill Dykes, maybe being—"

She cut him off with another kiss. "We can talk about this later. And we will. We really will. But now—"

"What is it you need?"

"I have to set up communications to reach off Ceres," she said. "Everything happened so fast. I was here for weeks, and I didn't really learn anything. Bill Dykes thought there was something strange happening at the refinery, but he couldn't be sure. They're very careful who they let work there. I didn't really have anything to report, nothing solid to be suspicious about, until Jacob came to tell me about discrepancies he found in the computer log. Now I've got to get a message to the Moon."

"How?" Kevin demanded.

"Bill and Jacob got this equipment," she said. "Bill knew about this shelter, and Jacob was able to cover the communications gear by listing it as lost in the computer inventory. So we have enough electronics and power supply to set up a high-gain antenna and get off our message, only there's too much for me to do by myself. Jacob isn't very good at outside work and he'd be missed if he didn't show up. And Bill thinks they've been watching him ever since he began asking questions. A few hours ago they gave him a special overtime assignment; that's not unusual, and if he didn't take it, they'd know something was wrong—so I couldn't think of anyone to help, and Jacob knew the scooter would be down from C-4 and he went to find you and I hoped you would help me—"

"Shhh. Of course I'll help you." At that moment Kevin would have done anything for her, including digging a hole all the way through to the other side of Ceres. He decided that he liked being in love.

The gear was heavy. Weight is not a very meaningful concept in gravity as low as Ceres's, but even in low gravity things have mass; large things are hard to start moving, and just as hard to stop. The surface of Ceres is rugged: the asteroid has been battered by collisions with other rocks for billions of years, and there is no atmosphere to smooth out the craters and crags the constant bombardment creates. Carrying several hundred pounds of equipment—even when it only "weighs" thirty pounds or so—is not easy.

Ellen had gotten from Bill Dykes a map of the area around Ceres Station itself, and Dykes had selected a plateau three kilometers away as the best location for the transmitter. It was cut off from the Station by high peaks, but had a good visibility to space. They struggled across the crags and craters with their enormous loads, using their flashlights sparingly, and not talking at all.

Despite the hard work, Kevin felt exuberant, filled with joy and love—and hatred for whomever was trying to thwart the development of fusion power. Kevin remembered the energy shortages in his childhood, and although he knew that what he had called poverty would have been fabulous wealth to much of the world, he could remember the hard times he had grown up in. Fusion could change much of that for the whole world, and it was in danger from selfish people who only wanted money.

They reached the plateau. Kevin came close to Ellen and put his helmet to hers. "We can't get this done without communication," he said.

"Yes. I guess we'll just have to risk using our suit radios at lowest power. I don't think anyone is looking for us. Why would they be?"

"No reason," Kevin said, but he worried anyway. They opened the cases and took out a collapsible antenna. The elements bolted together to form a large parabolic dish which could be pointed toward Earth.

The work was maddening. Each nut and bolt seemed a live thing, ready to slip from their heavy gloves and fall to vanish in the deep shadows. Connectors and parts that would have been simple to work with inside with plenty of light became complex puzzles, shapes not recognizable from the instruction diagrams.

"Putting together Christmas toys," Ellen said as she searched for a large part that had somehow simply vanished in shadow although it couldn't be more than a meter away.

Eventually they got it done, and began to set up the telescope and quadrant they would use to point the antenna toward Earth's Moon.

"Earth's still below the horizon," Kevin said as they leveled the telescope platform. "I think we're going to make it. Ellen, tell me something."

"Yes?"

"You didn't grow up in any orphanage. They don't assemble Christmas toys in foster homes and orphanages."

"Yes they—"

"And you said the first day I met you that your father—'Daddy' you called him—made you study gymnastics."

"Oh. I'd forgotten I told you that," she said. "We—I was distracted at the time." She laughed softly.

"So who are you?" Kevin asked.

"Oh come now, Mr. Senecal." The voice was a man's, cultured, and entirely strange to Kevin. Kevin jumped in a startled reaction and almost upset the telescope. "Haven't you guessed that yet? Allow me to introduce you to Miss Glenda Hansen-MacKenzie."

There were two men on the plateau with them. One held a small rifle, the other a pistol. "Please keep your hands where I can see them," the smaller intruder said. "Sorry to interrupt you, but I really don't want you sending messages to Earth. I'm glad we found you in time."

"Who the hell are you?" Kevin demanded.

"It's Henri Stoire," Ellen said.

"Good morning," Stoire said calmly. "Hal, get their tool belts, please."

"Yes sir."

"Hal Donnelly?" Kevin said.

"Sad but true," the scooter pilot said. "Too bad you had to get mixed up in this, Kevin. And you owe me a drink, too." Donnelly moved expertly, his pistol held well out of reach, and took their tool belts.

"What are you going to do with us?" Ellen demanded.

"Well, now, that is a problem," Stoire said. "There is a great deal of money at stake here. A very great deal. I can hardly allow you to get in my way."

It's happening again, Kevin thought. It was exactly like the time in the alley when the muggers had taken his wallet. He felt violated, humiliated, helpless—and Ellen—no her name is Glenda, he thought irrelevantly —they'll kill her. He tensed, ready to jump at Donnelly. Maybe Glenda could get away if he tried—

"On the other hand, you are worth a great deal of money," Stoire said. "What would your mother and father pay to have you back safe? Our scheme is almost perfect, but we all know there are no perfect plans. Right, Hal?"

"I don't know, sir—"

"There is the sabotage group," Stoire said. "True, I believe I have identified their agent, but suppose I have not? If he were to stop C-4 from going on schedule, we would be left with nothing. It would do no great harm to have Miss Hansen-MacKenzie hidden away, ready to produce when needed. I expect Aeneas MacKenzie would not even be above getting all of us off scot free in exchange for his daughter. It never hurts to have insurance."

"Well, yes sir," Donnelly said. "If you put it that way. But where can we keep them?"

"I believe I have an idea," Stoire said. He moved closer to Donnelly and they spoke helmet to helmet for a moment.

"Right. Come on, let's go," Donnelly said. "That way." He pointed with his flash. "And don't try anything, all right? I got nothing against either one of you. But I'll sure as hell shoot if I have to. There's just too much riding on this."

"How did you—how did you find us?" Glenda demanded.

Stoire's voice was maddeningly calm in their headsets. "When I first looked at your photograph, you reminded me of someone," he said. "I could not think who, although I have an excellent memory for faces. It concerned me sufficiently that I made a careful study of your dossier. An intriguing document. Carefully done. Really good work. But a few minor discrepancies. Your medical profile shows excellent physical condition, perfect teeth. Is that usual for foundlings? I do not think so. And the education you claim in your dossier does not match the abilities you showed aboard *Wayfarer*. A few other such things, all minor in themselves, but enough to make me think again. Where had I seen a blonde woman who frightened me? And then I remembered. I met your mother many years ago, at least thirty years. She was blonde then and was not so shy of having her photograph taken. A remarkably lovely woman, your mother. And you very much resembled the way she looked in the days before she married your father."

"Down there," Hal said. "Take that trail. And go slow."

"But how did you find us?" Glenda demanded.

"Ah. Once I knew who you were, it was obvious that I would have to question your, ah, lover. Mr. Dykes was most uncooperative, but he is not security minded. There was a copy of a map, marked, in his quarters. It took no great ability to go on from there."

They reached a wide ravine and started down into it.

"I don't suppose you would like to tell me how much you have found out," Stoire said.

"Go to hell," Kevin told him.

"Be polite." Stoire's voice had a hard edge. "So far I have been as gentle as possible under the circumstances. You can be made to talk, Senecal, and you are expendable. I point out that we have more air in our tanks than you have in yours. We need only wait. For that matter, I expect you would tell us anything to spare the young lady the ordeal of our questioning—"

"Kevin, don't say anything!" Glenda shouted.

"But you see, it doesn't really matter what you know," Stoire said. "I have Dykes, and we have drugs. It will not be necessary to question you two, which is as well for you."

They reached the bottom of the ravine. There was a scooter there. "Get on," Hal said. He took wire from his tool kit and bound Kevin and Glenda to the scooter seats. "All right, sir, I can handle them," the pilot said.

"Undoubtedly," Stoire said. "But—I think I will accompany you. Miss Hansen-MacKenzie is not above offering bribes—"

"I know better," the pilot insisted.

"Of course you do. Still, I think we will both be happier if we know we can trust each other—and the ride should be entertaining." Stoire climbed onto the scooter seat. "Let's go."

Chapter Sixteen

The pilot came around and turned off their transmitters. He left the receivers on. "Okay, kids," he said. "Hang on." He climbed into the saddle and ignited the rocket motor. The scooter rose swiftly from Ceres. The pilot studied the plot in his navigation screen, then made careful course corrections. They moved rapidly away from Ceres, out into the black depths of space.

Kevin leaned toward Glenda. Their helmets touched. "It looks like he's taking us up to C-4," Kevin said. "That doesn't make sense."

"Kevin, we've got to get loose—"

"Sure. How?" He strained against the wire that held him. Nothing gave. "I can't do anything. And Stoire's watching—"

"I don't know what to do either."

"I love you."

"Kevin, I'm—do you really think they meant it? Where could he be taking us? I think they're going to dump us in space."

"They want you as a hostage," Kevin said. He tried to sound more confident than he felt.

And yet, he thought, it made sense. If there was a place Stoire could keep her, it could be important to have Glenda Hansen-MacKenzie on tap. MacKenzie's reputation was known all over the world. If he made a promise—or a threat—he'd keep it. What might he do to get his daughter back? But it didn't make sense to keep Kevin Senecal alive. . . .

There was a stony rock a hundred meters in diameter just ahead. It was smaller than C-4. There were signs of mining on it, but no lights or people. It looked deserted.

Donnelly carefully maneuvered the scooter toward the rock, and finally set it down. "Well, here you are," he said. "Your new home."

"Where are we?" Kevin asked.

"C-2," Stoire said. "Abandoned three thousand hours ago. There was enough equipment left here to keep you alive. Food, oxygen, fuel cells. We will take your suits and radios—"

"Do you really want to do that, sir?" Donnelly asked. "May as well kill them and be done with it. Their radios won't reach Ceres, and they will probably have to make outside repairs. If you want them alive, you'd better leave them their suits."

"All right," Stoire said.

"Of course, there aren't any scooters here," Donnelly said. He came around with a pair of wire cutters. He clipped the wires holding Kevin's left hand to the scooter, then pulled Kevin's hands together and took a turn of wire around them. Then he did the same to Glenda before he cut them free from the scooter.

"There," he said. "I'll leave your tool kits, too. You'll get loose with a little work. The airlock's right over there. Now, off you go. Go on, jump. Move. Get going."

They jumped off the scooter.

"Careful how you wiggle around," Donnelly said. "You can jump right off this rock. Won't do you any good except to kill you, of course, but you can do it. 'Bye." He started the scooter engine.

"*Au revoir*," Henri Stoire said. "Actually, I expect that's a misstatement. I do not think we will meet again." The scooter moved rapidly away.

Kevin found the wire cutters in his tool kit and helped Glenda free her hands. Then she cut him loose and they went to the airlock.

"Gauges show pressure," Glenda said. "I guess we really can live here."

"Sure." Kevin cycled the lock and they went inside. "We can stay alive, but—there's just no way we're going to get off this rock. We could be here for years."

They explored their prison. There wasn't much to see. A few hundred meters of tunnels sprayed with plastic to hold air, some chambers carved out as quarters, and gear left when the mining operation was suspended.

"There's a lot of valuable stuff here," Kevin said. "Surely someone will come back for it."

"When Henri Stoire orders it done," Glenda said bitterly. "It all belongs to Interplanet."

"Yeah." Kevin continued to check the equipment available. "There's mining stuff."

"So we mine the rocks, refine steel, and build a scooter," Glenda said. "Somehow I don't think that's going to work."

"No. I guess not." Kevin continued to wander. A small kitchen. Bathroom. "Hot showers," Kevin said bitterly. "All the comforts. And they weren't lying about food. Enough to keep us going for months. Not much variety, I'm afraid. TVPs. Dehydrated stew. Well, we won't starve."

They wouldn't run out of power either. There were tanks of hydrogen and oxygen, and a dozen fuel cells to produce electricity from them.

There was even a thick window set in the outer room of the mine. It looked down on Ceres. The tiny rock was locked in rotation with Ceres so that it always faced the asteroid below.

"So near and so far," Kevin said. "It might as well be a million instead of three hundred kilometers." He watched as they moved over Ceres. It would be simple enough to jump off their moonlet prison, but it would do no good: they would still be in orbit around Ceres.

Kevin took out his pocket computer. "C-2. We are 284 kilometers above the surface and we're moving at not quite three-tenths of a kilometer a second relative to Ceres. That's just about a thousand kilometers an hour."

"Which might as well be a million," Glenda said. "Could we send a message? There are energy sources here, we can make a spark-gap transmitter. Send an SOS."

"And who'd hear it first?" Kevin asked. "The probability is pretty good that Stoire would get it. He controls all the communications. And the computer. And I doubt that he'd like it. Donnelly would be the logical one to send up to 'rescue' us, and then—"

"Damn. I have made a rather thorough mess of things, haven't I?"

"I'm worried about Jacob."

She nodded. "So am I. I haven't even dared think about him. Do—can they make Bill Dykes tell them that Jacob was helping us?"

"Given enough time, or the right drugs, anybody can be made to tell anything."

"And then they'll kill Bill and Jacob both." Glenda's voice was bitter and full of self-accusation. "It's my fault. I wanted to be certain. I wanted to find out where they had hidden the Arthurium. Catch all the conspirators. Give the whole package to Aeneas, all wrapped up."

"You tried to get a message off. What more could you have done?" Kevin demanded.

"I don't know. I could have tried to get help. I think Dr. Vaagts would have believed me. Or Joe Harwitt. Westinghouse has a lot to lose—"

"Not if they're buying the Arthurium. And you can't know, Glenda. With this much at stake, anybody could be involved. Anybody at all."

"I know. That's what my father warned me about before I left. He didn't want me to come—"

"I don't blame him much."

"But I had to be so damned smart! And I've gotten my friends killed, and there's nothing I can do. I couldn't even get a message off!"

Kevin shrugged. "We did the best we could—"

"Did we? I didn't try everything. I could have sent something through the main computer."

Kevin frowned. "I suppose Jacob could have done that. It would have been dangerous. What we tried was better. A few more hours and we'd have done it. Or if Dykes hadn't left that marked map. . . ."

"Jacob had another plan," Glenda said. "He was working on the instructions Stoire gave the computer. Jacob thinks he can take control of the main computer away from Stoire. With just a little more work. Then we'd have been in control of the whole station."

"Yeah, but it has to work the first time," Kevin said. "All they need to do is keep Norsedal away from the control console."

"They couldn't keep me away," Glenda said. "If I knew the key commands, I could make the computer obey me. I should have waited, but no, I had to do things my way. Damn, I'm an idiot."

"Don't be so hard on yourself. How could you order their computer around?"

"Implant. I have a transceiver implant, and an acceptor was put into the Ceres main computer when it was built on Earth. It was supposed to be my secret weapon, but I never got a chance to use it."

"Implant." Kevin fell silent for a moment. "I'm told those cost half a million francs."

She didn't say anything.

"I keep forgetting. You have half a million francs. A lot more. What—how does it feel to grow up rich?" he asked.

"Confined. Filled with obligations if your father is Aeneas MacKenzie."

"Yeah, I guess it would be like that."

"I ran away from it," Glenda said. "Oh, not really. But I grew up on the Moon, and I was the little princess, and it was stifling. When I was fifteen, I convinced myself I couldn't stand it any longer. I went to Earth for an education." She shuddered. "It was terrible at first. Getting used to high gravity, to rain, and dust and storms and cars and freeways—terrible and magnificent too. Sailing. I learned to sail a boat. You can fly on the Moon, but you can't sail.

"So I went to school on Earth and I had this phony identity, and I kidded myself I was independent, but of course I wasn't. I was still taking mother's money. And I was always afraid any boys I met would find out who I was and then they'd pretend to like me because I was the little princess—I was a mess, Kevin.

"I realized that finally, that I was worse off than ever because I was taking the benefits of being a Hansen-MacKenzie and I was shucking the responsibilities. So when I went back for a visit and heard about the Ceres operation and heard mother worrying about the small yields of Arthurium, I decided it was time to try to earn my keep."

"So it was all made up, about you and the foster homes, and the Futurians?"

"Most of it. Not the Futurians. They're real, and I am a junior member of their Fellowship. I thought Aeneas would be upset about it, but he wasn't. He supports them, and they've helped us. They're one reason you're here, Kevin."

"How's that?"

"Dr. Farrington is one of the Fellowship. One of the leaders. After—when we were on the ship, I was curious about you, so I sent for more information. One of the messages I got back was from him. He thinks highly of you."

"But—why did you want to know more about me?"

"Do I have to tell you?" She moved closer to him. "Kevin, I'm afraid I've made a thorough mess of everything. I don't feel much like Miss Supercompetent Independence just now."

"And I'm one poor excuse for a hero," Kevin said. "But I do love you—"

"And you said so before you knew who I was. That's important," she said. And then they didn't talk at all for a long time.

The scooter came back thirty hours later. It didn't land. Instead it closed to a few dozen meters from their moonlet and a suited figure leaped off. As the scooter drove away again, the newcomer landed with a suit reaction pistol and came to the airlock.

"Jacob!" They let him in eagerly. "What happened?" Kevin demanded.

"They caught me," Norsedal sighed. "And it's worse than that. They killed your friend Dykes—"

"Oh no." Tears formed in Glenda's eyes.

"And Wiley Ralston," Norsedal said.

"Wiley? How was he mixed up in this?" Kevin asked.

"He was an agent for the African bloc," Norsedal said. "Stoire had him arrested and held a trial. Accused him of murdering you two, and George Lange. He was probably guilty of killing Lange, and he confessed to trying to kill the two of you when you were leaving Earth—"

"He was the saboteur on *Wayfarer*?" Kevin asked. "Wiley?"

"It looks that way," Jacob said. "He was executed for it."

"Damn," Kevin muttered. "There goes that chance. I was trying to see how Stoire intended to get away with it. I mean, the Hansen-MacKenzie heir can't just vanish! Aeneas MacKenzie would be out here with a shipload of Hansen security agents and blood in his eye—"

"And now he's got a scapegoat," Glenda said. "Dad will be suspicious, but—is there any evidence left?"

"There is now," Jacob said. "The computer still has a record of what happened. But Stoire will have done something about that before Mr. MacKenzie arrives. He is coming, by the way. There was a report that *Valkyrie* left Luna Station seven hundred hours ago. I wouldn't be surprised if he were bringing company police. But you've been reported dead and your murderer has been caught and executed."

"Looks pretty hopeless," Kevin said. "Unless you brought along a pocket scooter."

"Alas, no," Norsedal said. "They even took my computer."

"I don't understand why you're alive," Kevin said.

Jacob grinned slightly. "They're having some problems with the main computer just now. If they ever get them fixed, I'll be expendable, but they thought it might be best to have me around just in case they don't find the bugs."

"Will that stop them?" Glenda asked.

"Alas, no. Mr. Stoire is very clever. He'll figure out what I did, just as I finally figured out what he did."

"You know, then?" Kevin asked.

"Yes. Could I have some water?"

"Sure. There's plenty. Plenty of everything. We could be here for years," Kevin said.

"Not me." Norsedal's voice didn't change. "You see, they didn't leave me any insulin."

"How—how long?" Glenda asked after a while.

"If I'm careful about what I eat, three or four hundred hours," Jacob said. "Perhaps longer."

"We've got to get out of here," Glenda said.

"I agree, but I confess I don't know how," Norsedal said. "I was telling you what Stoire did. It was very clever, really. First he programmed the computer to report a much lower percentage of Arthurium in the ore. Understand, the computer knew better, and the refinery operated just the same as it always did, but the reported recovery was low. They told the computer to forget about one storage area, and routed ninety percent of the Arthurium there. Simple, clean, and really very pretty. And once Stoire erases the real log, there'll be no record of it at all."

They had explored every tunnel in the prison a dozen times, but found nothing. A hundred hours passed.

There was nothing they could do. No laser equipment to send signals with. No electronics. Nothing but some mining gear and the basic materials for staying alive. Even that took a lot of work. The algae in the tank farms had died, and their own power source was fuel cells. There were tanks of hydrogen and oxygen for those, but the carbon dioxide scrubbers needed constant recharging. They had less time than Kevin had thought.

"I would say two people have a thousand hours more oxygen," Norsedal said. "I could—" He hesitated. "I can add a couple of hundred hours to that, and it won't really matter."

"I'll be damned if you will," Kevin said. "Something will turn up."

"I doubt it," Jacob said. "C-4 is scheduled to go in about nine hundred hours. Daedalus is putting in the final equipment right now."

"And then Stoire and Donnelly are gone," Kevin said. "But how does he get away with it?"

Jacob shrugged. "It would be no great trick to put the Arthurium aboard C-4. As gold, for example. The bombs go off, C-4 heads for Earth. Somewhere between here and there a ship—it wouldn't have to be a very large one—meets them and when C-4 arrives in Earth orbit, the Arthurium is gone, with nothing left aboard that's not supposed to be there."

"And it was stupid to leave us alive," Kevin said. "Once he's ready to leave, he'll come back with Donnelly and finish us. No evidence, no embarrassing bodies—"

"More likely he will take Glenda on C-4," Jacob said. "Donnelly is part of his crew."

"I'm going to go have another look around," Kevin said. "There's got to be *something* we can do."

"I hope you think of it," Glenda said. "I can't."

"Alas, nor I," Jacob added.

Kevin prowled through the corridors of their prison. There has to be some way, he told himself. Ceres mocked him from below, less than three hundred kilometers down. It hung huge in the night sky.

Three hundred kilometers down, and we're moving about half a kilometer a second relative to Ceres, Kevin thought. That's not very much velocity. Under a thousand miles an hour. It doesn't take much energy to get to that speed. How much gasoline does it take to accelerate a car on Earth up to a hundred miles an hour—a gallon or so? We only need ten times that, not even that much.

There's plenty of hydrogen and oxygen. Marvelous rocket fuels if we only had a rocket. More than enough to get us down, except that the temperature of hydrogen burning in oxygen is a lot hotter than anything we have to contain in it—

No. That's not right. The fuel cells do it. But they do it by slowing down the reaction, and they can't be turned into rocket engines.

He remembered the early German Rocket Society experiments described by Willy Ley. The Berliners had blown up more rockets than they flew, and they were only using gasoline, not hydrogen. Liquid-fuel rockets need big hairy pumps, and Kevin didn't have any pumps.

What did he have? Fuel cells, plenty of them, and so what? An electric-powered rocket was theoretically possible, but Kevin didn't have the faintest idea of how to build one, even if there was enough equipment around to do it with. He wasn't sure anyone had ever built one—certainly he couldn't.

Back to first principles, he thought. The only way to change velocity in space is with a rocket. What is a rocket? A machine for throwing mass overboard. The faster the mass thrown away goes in one direction, the faster the rocket will go in the other, and the less you have to throw. All rockets are no more than a means of spewing out mass in a narrow direction. A rocket could consist of a man sitting in a bucket and throwing rocks backward.

That might get a few feet per second velocity change, but so what? There simply wasn't enough power in human muscles—even if he did have a lot of rocks. Was there any other way to throw them? Not fast; and unless the thrown-away mass had a high velocity, the rocket wouldn't be any use. He went on through the tunnels, looking at each piece of equipment he found, trying to think of how it might be used.

You can throw *anything* overboard to make a rocket. Hydrogen, for example. That's all *Wayfarer*'s engines did, heat up hydrogen and let it go out through the rocket nozzle. We have hydrogen under pressure—

Not enough. Nowhere near enough hydrogen and nowhere near enough pressure, not to get velocity changes of hundreds of miles an hour. Ditto for oxygen. Gas under compression just can't furnish enough energy. What would? Chemical energy; burning hydrogen in oxygen would do it, but it gave off too much; there was nothing to contain that reaction except the fuel cells and they did it by slowing the reaction way down and—

And I'm back where I started, Kevin thought. Plenty of energy in the fuel cells if I could find a way to use it. Could I heat a gas with electricity? Certainly, only how—

His eye fell on the hot-water tank in the crew quarters. An electric hot-water tank. There was a pressure gauge: forty pounds per square inch. Forty p.s.i.—He looked at the tank as if seeing it for the first time, then went running back to the others.

"Glenda, Jacob, I've got it."

Chapter Seventeen

Jacob Norsedal bent over Kevin's pocket calculator. "I have worked it by three different methods and I get nearly the same answer each way," he said. "I believe it will work."

"Sure it works." Kevin grinned. "Steam at forty p.s.i. will come out *fast*. About a kilometer a second."

"I believe you," Glenda said. "But it sounds silly. *Steam* rockets?"

Kevin shrugged. "It is silly. There are a lot more efficient systems. But this will work—"

"In a low g field," Jacob said. "You will not have much thrust. Of course you won't need much."

"I'm sure it works," Kevin said. "Now all we have to do is build it." He made himself sound confident; he knew how much room for error there was in his figures.

"Look, it takes nine hundred and eighty calories to turn a gram of water into steam. We heat that steam up another thirty or forty degrees and let it out. The energy is moving molecules. We know the molecular weight of water, so we can figure the number of molecules in a gram and—"

"I worked it too," Glenda reminded him. "And I get the same answer you do, but it doesn't mean I trust it."

"What else can we do?" Kevin asked.

"Nothing. You're right. Let's get to work."

They disconnected the hot-water tank and drilled holes in it. Several turns of heating wire went through the holes, then they sealed them in epoxy. At one end of the tank they drilled a large hole and threaded a pipe into it, threaded a large valve onto the pipe, and welded a makeshift rocket nozzle beyond that.

When it was done they tethered the tank and filled it with water, then connected a fuel cell to the heating leads. "Here goes," Kevin said. He threw the switch to start the heaters.

Slowly the water inside heated, then began to boil. The pressure shown on the gauge began to rise. In half an hour they had forty-five pounds of pressure. "All right, let's try it," Kevin said.

Glenda turned the valve to let out steam. A jet of steam and water shot out across the surface of the moonlet. Ice crystals formed in space and slowly settled to the rocket surface. The jet reached far away from them, well off the moonlet itself. The tank pulled against its tether lines, stretching the rope.

"It works!" Kevin shouted. "Damn it, we're going to make it!" He shut off the electricity. "Let's get her finished."

It didn't look like a spaceship. It didn't even resemble a scooter, crude as those were. It looked like a hot-water tank with fuel cells bolted onto it. For controls it had vanes set crosswise in the exhaust stream, spring-loaded to center, with two tillers, one for each vane; a valve to control steam flow; and switches to connect the fuel cells to the heaters. Nothing else.

The tank itself was fuzzy: They'd sprayed it with Styrofoam, building it up in layers until they had nearly a foot of insulation. There were straps on opposite sides of the tank to hold two passengers on.

The tank held nearly a hundred gallons of water. Kevin calculated that they had more than enough energy to boil it all in their two fuel cells, and they would only need sixty gallons to get to Ceres. The number was so small that he ran it four times, but it was correct.

The strangest part was the stability system: a pair of wheels taken from a mining cart and set up in front of the water tank. Electric motors rotated the wheels in opposite directions.

"Damndest gyros in the history of space research," Kevin said when they got the ship completed. "In fact, it's the damndest rocket ever."

"It ought to have a name," Glenda said. "Something heroic, fitting a knight rescuing us from durance vile—"

"How about Fudgesicle?" Kevin suggested.

"You'll hurt its feelings," Glenda said.

"The Gump?" Norsedal asked apologetically.

"Stop that! *Galahad.* That will do nicely, I think."

"You're crazy," Kevin said.

Norsedal laughed. Glenda's own laugh was strained. "I'm about to get aboard that thing, and you say I'm crazy? And you built it? Kevin, are we ready?"

"I guess so. I've been putting off the awful moment, but—"

"Right. Come on, Jacob—"

Norsedal sighed. "I have been over the calculations. That Gump *cannot* carry three people. You will be lucky to get down alive with two. Therefore I am not coming."

"You have to!" Glenda insisted. "If you don't get down, it does us no good—"

"Not true," Norsedal said. "I've given you the key words. And you do not know where you will land. Now it's true that I get around better in low gravity than I ever did on Earth, but it is also true that I am not athletic. I doubt that I can make my way over hundreds of kilometers of ravines—not in my present condition."

"You're feeling the lack of insulin?" Kevin demanded.

"Yes," Norsedal sighed.

"One of us should stay with you—" Glenda said. She sounded doubtful.

"Nonsense. You must go, because Kevin could do nothing alone once he gets there. Kevin should go because it is more likely I will be rescued if you two get down safely, and two are more likely to succeed than one. Now, are you ready?"

"I guess so," Kevin said.

"Then let's do it before we lose our nerve," Glenda said.

"Right." The total mass of *Galahad* with full water tank was just under 550 kilograms. In C-2's tiny gravity it was no problem at all to carry it outside.

They stood on the rocky surface of the moonlet to let their eyes adjust to starlight. Ceres filled a full sixty degrees below them, a third of space, so close they could not even see all of it. It loomed huge and darkly forbidding, its surface lit by sunlight to a brightness much less than Earth's moon, but it was enormously larger than any full moon.

"We won't have any trouble finding it," Kevin said.

"No," Norsedal said. "But finding it is not your main problem."

"Don't I know it."

Glenda said nothing. All three of them had tried to work the problem of a landing orbit, and they couldn't do it with a pocket calculator. The equations for low-thrust trajectories were too complex, and they had too little data about *Galahad's* probable performance. They would simply have to navigate by eye and hope to cancel out all their velocities.

They carried the hot-water tank to a low peak on the moonlet and pointed it so that the rocket nozzle was aimed as close to the direction they moved across Ceres's face as they could manage.

"Time," Kevin said.

"I'm scared—"

"I'm terrified," Kevin said. "But what choices have we? You know damned well Stoire and Donnelly will be back—"

"Yes. Let's do it."

It took only a gentle effort to push the steam rocket away from the moonlet, but the cartwheel-gyros resisted any effort to turn it. Finally they got it oriented properly in space. Then they climbed aboard.

"Full head of steam," Kevin said. "Almost fifty pounds. Ready?"

"Ready—"

He twisted the steam valve. At first both steam and water were expelled from the tank, but as they began to accelerate, the water settled and the exhaust valve let out only steam. C-2 dropped away. They missed it. It was a prison, but a safe one; now they had only their makeshift steam rocket.

Galahad showed a tendency to tumble, but with the gyros resisting, they were able to control it with the steering vanes. A plume of steam shot from the tank, rapidly crystallizing into ice fog that engulfed them.

"Damn. That's going to make it hard to see," Kevin said. "Nothing we can do about it." He peered down toward Ceres. It didn't seem any closer. Jacob's farewell faded in their headsets.

Norsedal's calculations had shown that twenty minutes' thrust should be enough to cancel all their orbital velocity. It would use up just about half their fuel. Once *Galahad* was stopped dead in orbit above Ceres, they would fall toward the asteroid, and they would have half their steam left to counteract that.

The trouble was that Jacob couldn't calculate how high above Ceres they would be when the twenty minutes were finished. As they lost velocity, they would lose altitude, and their orbit would no longer be a smooth circle, but an ellipse intersecting Ceres—somewhere. At the end of twenty minutes Kevin cut the power off. He was pleased that they still had thirty pounds of steam pressure.

He waited for a half hour that seemed to take forever. They watched as Ceres grew larger. "Closer. But we're still a long way off. I think we should wait—"

"Time sure goes by fast when you're having fun," Glenda said.

Kevin grinned. "Yeah. OK, I can't stand it. Let's start up the steam again. There. Now we come right a bit—"

"Too far!"

He adjusted the vanes and overshot in the other direction.

"We don't have any steam to waste—"

"I knew that."

"A little more—Kevin, I think you've got it! We don't seem to be moving so fast—"

They were falling now, with much less horizontal motion. "Time to wait some more."

As they came closer, they could see details on the craggy surface below. Rugged canyons, high peaks, deep valleys, and rocks everywhere. Kevin had a protractor which he used to measure the angle Ceres filled in the space below them. Then he used that to calculate their altitude. It was crude and certainly not accurate to better than ten percent, but it was all they had.

"I read a hundred degrees," Kevin said. "That puts us just about a hundred kilometers above Ceres. If I've figured everything right, and if I'm reading the angles right—"

"You have to be right, don't you?" Glenda said. "There's nothing else we can do."

She was right. They couldn't get back to C-2 now, and they wouldn't be able to find the tiny moonlet even if they had the reaction mass.

"Time for another turn," Kevin said. "I think."

"We're still moving—"

"Yes, but that's what the numbers say."

"All right."

And a year ago I was working equations in school, Kevin thought. Numbers to crunch and write down for examinations. Now they're something to stake your life on. He twisted the tiller slightly. The tank rotated, and he pointed the tiller the other way to stop it. It took several more adjustments before he thought he had it right. Now the steam jet pointed almost directly toward Ceres, counteracting the asteroid's pull.

He was tempted to change the steam flow, but he didn't dare. That was the part he couldn't calculate at all. The mass of their tank changed constantly as steam spewed out, and as the mass fell, the thrust increased. If they turned the steam valve up too high, it would more than counteract Ceres's gravity, and they would move away from it; and when they ran out of steam, they would fall again, this time with no stopping, impacting at seven or eight hundred miles an hour.

"I feel like singing," Kevin shouted. "I am I, Don Quixote, the Lord of La Mancha, my destiny calls and I go—"

"Which makes me Dulcinea, the scullery maid?" Glenda demanded.

"You would rather be Sancho Panza?—No, that's Jacob. And *Galahad* is our charger. Now I need a broken lance and a bent sword—"

"I think we're getting closer."

"So do I." Kevin took out his protractor and eyeballed the size of Ceres below. They could no longer see much of the asteroid; they were low enough that there was a definite horizon less than 150 kilometers to each side. "When we get closer, we have to kill our velocity relative to the ground. Otherwise the landing impact will kill us."

"Where will we hit . . . I mean land?"

"I don't know. Fifty, seventy-five kilometers from the station, I hope. We brought plenty of spare air tanks."

For a long time they had seemed to be falling very slowly. Now, as they got closer, they seemed to be moving faster. Much too fast. Kevin couldn't estimate their speed, but it was many meters per second. He used the tillers to turn *Galahad* directly toward Ceres, opened the steam valve wider.

Not too wide, he told himself. Not too wide, or we'll use up steam too fast and—

The temptation to blast as hard as they could was almost irresistible. The craggy ground came up toward them at frightening speed. They were definitely coming down too fast, and they were too close. Desperately he opened the steam valve all the way, and switched full power to the heaters—

A minute went by. Another. Now they were very low—and they didn't seem to have much approach velocity, but they were moving across the surface much too quickly. Painfully they rotated the tank until the exhaust pointed in the direction they moved over the ground, then tilted it again toward Ceres. Kevin opened the steam valve again.

"We've still got pressure," he said. "But I have no idea how much water is left in the tank—"

"Don't talk about it," Glenda said grimly. "We're so close—"

"Sure." Now they were less than a kilometer high, still moving too fast. Again Kevin rotated toward Ceres, ignoring their lateral velocity to kill their falling speed. "Keep a lookout for large objects in our path—"

"I'd say we're moving fifty miles an hour," Glenda said. "Enough to kill you—" But slowly the rocket lost velocity toward the ground, and they were able to turn again. "Pick a landing site," Kevin said. "Something under our ground track."

"Over there. Ahead of us." He looked quickly toward the plateau she had selected. It was rocky but as good as anything else in sight. He rotated the rocket again; they were moving slantwise toward the ground, and Kevin kept the exhaust pointing straight in their direction of travel.

The steam pressure was falling. They were running out of water, or else they were using steam faster than the fuel cells could boil the water; it didn't matter. A few more seconds and they'd be down, one way or another—

The plateau came up toward them, but not so fast now. The steam valve was wide open. Nothing else they could do.

They were over the plateau and falling directly toward it, a hundred meters high and falling-plummeting straight down.

"Cut loose from the straps," Kevin shouted. "Be ready to jump clear just before we hit."

He worked frantically at the buckles, but he couldn't unfasten them and keep control of the tillers. The rocket showed a definite tendency to tumble now as Glenda moved in her perch, but there wasn't time for more talk, for more of anything—

Fifty meters. Twenty-five. Slowing all the time. Maybe they'd make it after all—

Then the ground came up and swatted them. They hit tail first. The rocket nozzle collapsed beneath, and steam spewed out, forming an ice fog that condensed on the rocks and on his face plate. He worked at the buckles and got them loose—

And realized he was lying on the surface. He couldn't see, but he heard Glenda's voice in his helmet. "Kevin! Are you all right?"

She didn't sound hurt. Gingerly he worked each limb. Nothing seemed broken. "We're down," he said.

Kevin estimated their landing velocity at about ten miles an hour. The crumpled rocket nozzle had absorbed much of the energy of the crash, and neither of them had been more than shaken up. "Any landing you walk away from is a good one. A pilot told me that once," Kevin muttered.

"What?"

"Nothing. Something Donnelly told me once. When we were still friends. Glenda, I haven't the faintest idea of where we are."

"Sure you do. Why do you think we have visibility even though we're on the night side?" She pointed up at the bright disc above them. "The station is just under the synchronous mirror."

"Yeah. I'm not thinking too well—"

"You're doing all right." She pointed to the remains of their steam rocket. "Splendidly, I'd say."

They loaded up all the full oxygen tanks and set out toward the satellite mirror. Kevin stopped to take an observation with his protractor, then punched numbers into his calculator. "I make it ninety to a hundred kilometers," he said.

"Not too bad. A few hours of following yonder star. We've got enough air."

"If we don't use it up talking." Kevin started bounding across the surface of the asteroid. Glenda followed.

They moved in long leaps. It was much easier than walking, almost like ice skating or skipping down hill; as long as they could keep going in a straight line, it took very little effort. Turning or stopping was much harder.

They could leap crevasses up to forty meters wide, and it was easy enough to go around bigger ones. If they had to climb, they could jump thirty meters upward, or jump down steep slopes.

It was like a combination of flying and skating, leaping across the surface of Ceres, and Kevin shouted with the sheer joy of being alive. They *were* alive, and for a while they were safe.

In seven hours they were within sight of Ceres Station. They paused on a hilltop looking down on the leveled plain which served as the spaceport.

"We could try to steal one of the scooters," Kevin said. "I think we can trust John Eliot and the Daedalus people."

"Except that the scooters are guarded, and our best chance is the plan we already worked out. *Everyone* on Ceres can't be corrupt. Most of the people here believe in the future of the Belt—"

"All right," Kevin said. "Let's go."

They went directly to the main entrance to the station. There was no one in the airlock, and once inside, they went into Fat Jack's bar.

The bar was crowded with people singing and shouting. One by one they fell silent as they stared at Kevin and Glenda.

"You're dead," Joe Harwitt said. "Damn it, Bill Dykes said you were dead! He said you'd been killed by Ralston!"

"Did he say it to you?" Glenda asked. "Did you hear him say it? Or did Henri Stoire and Hal Donnelly tell you that's what he said?"

There was a short silence. Then one of the miners said, "Hell, Stoire and Donnelly were the only ones with Bill when he died. You saying they lied to us?"

"Damn right," Kevin said. "They're the ones who marooned us on C-2."

"On C-2?" Joe Harwitt seemed to have difficulty comprehending that. "C-2?"

"Yes. Jacob is still up there."

"He's supposed to be dead, too," one of the miners said. "Supposed to have had some kind of fight with you, Senecal. What the hell's going on here?"

"Henri Stoire is stealing Interplanet blind," Kevin said.

"We'll find out about that," another miner said. "He's coming now."

Stoire came in with four armed company police. "What is happening—Miss MacMillan! We were told you were dead."

"Good act, Stoire, but it won't work," Kevin said.

"Have you gone mad?" Stoire asked. "What are you talking about?"

"He claims you've been doing some embezzling," Joe Harwitt said.

"And what have I been stealing?" Stoire asked.

"Arthurium," Kevin said.

"Nonsense. All the Arthurium is accounted for. Six thousand, seven hundred and nine grams. No great amount, but more than has ever been seen on Earth—"

"It won't work," Glenda said. "I know precisely how much Arthurium was mined. Almost four hundred kilograms. And I know where it is."

"Ridiculous," Stoire said. "Young lady, I am trying to be patient with you and your impetuous friend, but it is obvious that you must be restrained for your own good." He turned to the others. "I don't know what she wants, but I do not have to listen to accusations from a common prostitute. Lieutenant, arrest those two."

"Yes, sir." The company police stepped forward.

"I'm no prostitute," Glenda said. "You know who I am, Mr. Stoire."

"Who?" Joe Harwitt demanded.

"I think I'll let someone else tell you," Glenda said. She looked at Stoire. "Does this mean anything to you? Balaclava, 17 September, 1976."

Stoire suddenly looked worried.

Glenda smiled faintly. "That's the code phrase he used in his secret transactions with the company's computer. Without it the computer won't deliver the full records. Jacob Norsedal figured it out from the machine language. And now—" She was quiet for a moment, a look of concentration on her face.

"HER NAME IS GLENDA HANSEN-MACKEN-ZIE," the overhead speaker said.

"What the hell is that?" a miner shouted.

"She's making the computer say that," Stoire said.

"And how the hell is she controlling your computer, Mr. Stoire?" the miner asked.

"Implant," Joe Harwitt said. "A rich young lady indeed. Only I never knew the computer could accept instructions from implants."

"Done in Zurich," Kevin said.

"Where is the missing Arthurium?" Glenda said aloud.

"I DO NOT HAVE THAT INFORMATION."

Stoire looked smug.

"How much was refined?" Glenda asked.

"THREE HUNDRED AND NINETY-TWO THOU-SAND SIX HUNDRED AND NINETEEN GRAMS."

"Four hundred kilos!" Joe Harwitt whistled. "Is there that much money in the whole solar system?"

"Enough that each one here can have one million francs," Henri Stoire said. "One million for each of you, if you help me."

"Jeez, that's a lot of money," someone said.

"Where will you spend it?" Glenda asked. "I have already had the base computer send a message to Hansen headquarters on Luna. You shouldn't have 'fixed' the high-gain antenna, Stoire."

"Wait a minute." Harwitt looked from Glenda to Stoire. "I don't know what to make of this. You're saying that you are Laurie Jo Hansen's kid—"

"Hell, she is," Fat Jack said. The bar owner launched himself in a smooth curve that took him next to Glenda. He looked at her intently.

"Yep. I worked for Hansen Enterprises, twenty, twenty-five years ago now. She looks like the big boss did back then. Same eyes. Yeah, I think she is. Look at her!"

"Where is the Arthurium?" she demanded.

Stoire shrugged. "It appears that you know something I do not. I never knew there was any more."

"You're a liar," Kevin said.

Stoire shrugged. He turned to Glenda. "I really suggest that we go somewhere and talk quietly."

"Out here." She led the way to the corridor. Kevin and the others followed. The company police looked to someone, anyone, for orders.

Glenda and Stoire moved away from the crowd. Kevin was just close enough to hear.

"It really is simple," Stoire said. "If no excess Arthurium is ever found, there is no real evidence of any crime—"

"Kidnapping—"

He shrugged again. "Possibly. But the question is, do you want your superconductors? Because if any harm comes to me, you'll never see that Arthurium again."

"It's on C-4; we'll find it." Kevin said.

"Of course," Stoire said. "With a hydrogen bomb next to it. I doubt your superconductor would be much use after it is vaporized by a one-megaton bomb."

"You're bluffing," Kevin said.

Stoire smiled thinly. "You have reason to know I believe in insurance. This is another form. Now—shall we negotiate?"

Chapter Eighteen

The H-bomb went off in silence. A bright flower of intolerable blue-white, dying to a dull red glow.

"Just off center," Jacob Norsedal said. He looked at the computer read-out. "They'll have no trouble correcting the slight tumble. The next detonation will go off on schedule."

Aeneas MacKenzie nodded. "So C-4 is on its way. I'm surprised you didn't go with them, Jacob."

Norsedal laughed. "Three's a crowd. Newlyweds don't need company, and they can certainly manage the navigation."

"Yes. I suppose they can," MacKenzie said. He glanced at the wreckage of *Galahad*. It hadn't been easy to find, but he'd offered ten thousand francs to the miner who could locate it. He told himself that Laurie Jo would want to see it. "I still can't believe that thing worked. Ingenious young man, my son-in-law," MacKenzie said.

"Sure is. I've got good reason to know it," Norsedal said. "What will happen to Stoire?"

MacKenzie shook his head. "We'll pay his debts and send him home."

"Rich."

"Yes, but I doubt he'll stay away from the gaming tables long."

"It seems a shame that he gets off so easily," Norsedal said.

MacKenzie's voice was gruff. "Bill Dykes was a good friend. I don't like it much that Stoire gets off, but I don't doubt the price for vengeance was damned high. Higher than I could pay, and I doubt Bill would have wanted us to waste that much revenge."

"Yes," Norsedal said. "He had the entire cargo ready to blow. Arthurium, gold, all the refined metals—"

"And not even Laurie Jo could have put more money into space without some return," MacKenzie finished. "Glenda made the only deal possible. The human race advances, but sometimes we pay in strange coin, Jacob."

"Time," Norsedal said. The viewscreen flared again, a point of brilliant white fading rapidly. Norsedal studied the radar returns. "Well done," he said. He watched the computer read-out a moment longer, then looked up. "Will you be staying long?"

"No. I'm taking the Arthurium back to Luna in *Valkyrie*. We can be back months before C-4 arrives, and our fusion people are anxious to get to work. They think they may have a demonstration reactor by the time the kids arrive."

"If Kevin doesn't come up with a better design," Noresdal said. "He's got a good computer and lots of time to work." Norsedal typed inputs. The viewscreen blurred, then showed a map of the solar system and C-4's orbit from Ceres to Earth. "THREE HUNDRED AND FOUR DAYS," it announced.

"A long trip," Aeneas said.

"I doubt they'll notice." Norsedal's grin was wide.

Aeneas MacKenzie looked wistfully at the viewscreen. "Laurie Jo and I once had sixty days to ourselves. Sixty days with nothing to do but get to know each other. I think you're right, Jacob. They'll find this a short trip."

Norsedal grinned slightly and typed again.

"PROGNOSIS CONFIRMED," the computer announced.

• the end •

Emerald Sea
(pb) 1-4165-0920-8 • $7.99

Against the Tide
(pb) 1-4165-2057-0 • $7.99

East of the Sun, West of the Moon
(pb) 1-4165-5518-87 • $7.99

Master of Real SF
Von Neumann's War with Travis S. Taylor
(hc) 1-4165-2075-9 • $25.00

The Looking Glass Series
Into the Looking Glass
(pb) 1-4165-2105-4 • $7.99

Vorpal Blade with Travis S. Taylor
(hc) 1-4165-2129-1 • $25.00
(pb) 1-4165-5586-2 • $7.99

Manxome Foe with Travis S. Taylor
(hc) 1-4165-5521-8 • $25.00
(pb) 1-4165-9165-6 • $7.99

Claws That Catch with Travis S. Taylor
(hc) 1-4165-5587-0 • $25.00

Master of Hard-Core Thrillers
The Last Centurion
(hc) 1-4165-5553-6 • $25.00

The Kildar Saga
Ghost
(pb) 1-4165-2087-2 • $7.99

Kildar
(pb) 1-4165-2133-X • $7.99

Choosers of the Slain
(hc) 1-4165-2070-8 • $25.00

Flag in Exile 0-7434-3575-3 • $7.99

"Packs enough punch to smash a starship to smithereens."—*Publishers Weekly*

Honor Among Enemies 0-671-87723-2 • $21.00
0-671-87783-6 • $7.99

"Star Wars as it might have been written by C.S. Forester...fast-paced entertainment."–*Booklist*

In Enemy Hands 0-671-87793-3 • $22.00
0-671-57770-0 • $7.99

After being ambushed, Honor finds herself aboard an enemy cruiser, bound for her scheduled execution. But one lesson Honor has never learned is how to give up!

Echoes of Honor 0-671-87892-1 • $24.00
0-671-57833-2 • $7.99

"Brilliant! Brilliant! Brilliant!"—Anne McCaffrey

Ashes of Victory 0-671-57854-5 • $25.00
0-671-31977-9 • $7.99

Honor has escaped from the prison planet called Hell and returned to the Manticoran Alliance, to the heart of a furnace of new weapons, new strategies, new tactics, spies, diplomacy, and assassination.

War of Honor 0-7434-3545-1 • $26.00
0-7434-7167-9 • $7.99

No one wanted another war. Neither the Republic of Haven, nor Manticore—and certainly not Honor Harrington. Unfortunately, what they wanted didn't matter.

At All Costs 1-4165-0911-9 • $26.00
1-4165-4414-3 • $7.99

The war with the Republic of Haven has resumed...disastrously for the Star Kingdom of Manticore. The alternative to victory is total defeat, yet this time the cost of victory will be agonizingly high.

1633 with Eric Flint
hc • 0-7434-3542-7 • $26.00
pb • 0-7434-7155-5 • $7.99

1634: *The Baltic War* with Eric Flint   pb • 1-4165-5588-9 • $7.99

American freedom and justice versus the tyrannies of the 17th century. Set in Flint's *1632* universe.

THE STARFIRE SERIES
WITH STEVE WHITE:

The Stars at War I   0-7434-8841-5 • $25.00

Rewritten *Insurrection* and *In Death Ground* in one massive volume.

The Stars at War II   0-7434-9912-3 • $27.00

The Shiva Option and *Crusade* in one massive volume.

PRINCE ROGER NOVELS
WITH JOHN RINGO:

March Upcountry   0-7434-3538-9 • $7.99

March to the Sea   0-7434-3580-X • $7.99

March to the Stars   0-7434-8818-0 • $7.99

We Few   1-4165-2084-8 • $7.99

"This is as good as military sf gets." —*Booklist*